The Emerald Storm

The Emerald Storm

An Ethan Gage Adventure

William Dietrich

HARPER

An Imprint of HarperCollins*Publishers*
www.harpercollins.com

HarperCollins books may be purchased for educational, business, or sales promotional use. For information, please write: Special Markets Department, HarperCollins Publishers, 10 East 53rd Street, New York, NY 10022.

FIRST EDITION

Library of Congress Cataloging-in-Publication Data has been applied for.

ISBN: 978-0-06-198920-9

12 13 14 15 16   OV/RRD   10 9 8 7 6 5 4 3 2 1

FOR NOAH, A BUDDING ADVENTURER

I was born a slave, but nature gave me the soul of a free man.

—Toussaint L'Ouverture

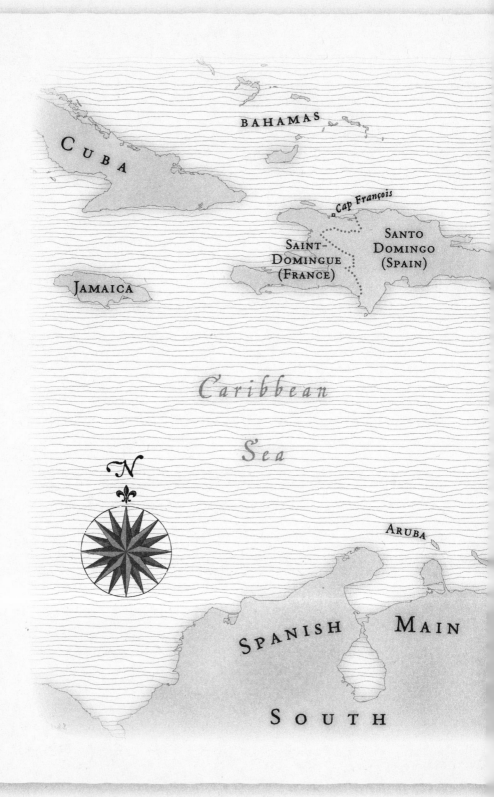

Atlantic Ocean

TORTOLA

PUERTO RICO   ANGUILLA
                     ST. MARTIN

                          BARBUDA

ST. CHRISTOPHER   ANTIGUA
        NEVIS
    MONTSERRAT   GUADELOUPE

                     DOMINICA

Caribbean   MARTINIQUE

         Diamond Rock

                     ST. LUCIA

Sea   ST. VINCENT   BARBADOS

                     GRENADA

                     TOBAGO

                     TRINIDAD

AMERICA

Part One

CHAPTER I

My intention was to retire.

After learning in 1802 that I had fathered a family, then rescuing mother and son from a tyrant in Tripoli, and finally escaping in a submarine invented by crackpot American inventor Robert Fulton, I was more than ready to trade heroism for domesticity. My preference is lover, not fighter. No one tries harder to escape adventure than me, Ethan Gage.

So why, in April of 1803, was I clinging to the side of a frozen fortress in France's Jura Mountains, sleet in my eyes, a bomb on my back, and hemp rope heavy as a hangman's noose slung round my neck?

Despite my best efforts to settle down, my new family was in peril again, and scaling Napoleon Bonaparte's impregnable prison had become a necessary step toward domestic bliss.

I was grumpy at this predicament. As one matures (a slow process in my case) the unpredictability of life becomes less exciting and more annoying. French police and British spies claimed the fault was mine, for trying to pawn a stolen emerald, but I felt the jewel was small compensation for my battles with the Barbary pirates. Now there was a far bigger treasure at stake, strange aerial conspiracies, brewing war between France and England, and the need to retrieve my own nearly three-year-old son, whom I kept losing like a button. So here I was on the French frontier, boots scrabbling on an icy wall.

The promise that motivated me: If I could break a Negro hero to freedom, I, my bride Astiza, and little Horus, or Harry, might finally be able to live somewhere in peace.

"And you'll further the cause of liberty and equality as well, Ethan Gage!" my old compatriot Sir Sidney Smith had written me.

I'm skeptical of such causes. The idealists who dream them up send employees to carry them out, and said employees have the habit of dying early. If everything in this latest mission went well, the best I could hope for was flinging myself into space aboard the untested flying contraption of an eccentric Englishman, of which that nation has a surfeit. And that experiment was *after* my new bride pretended to be the Creole mistress of the world's most notorious Negro, locked in Napoleon's gloomiest prison.

In short, my quest for retirement had gotten me in a mess of political causes well above my station, and once more I was supposed to straighten the world's difficulties out. I seem forever a pawn of both British and French, and both countries wanted my expertise applied to flying machines and lost Aztec treasure in hopes it could decide the war between them. Damnation! Slave revolts, naval mastery of the Caribbean, and staving off invasion of England were exactly the kind of weighty issues I'd pledged to get away from.

It's even more exhausting to be necessary, given my flaws. My human habits of greed, lust, impatience, vanity, sloth, and foolishness tend to hobble my idealism.

To explain my fate as reluctant hero: While my mentor Benjamin Franklin did his best to instill character in me before he died, my instinctive aversion to honest work, thrift, and loyalty had provided a pleasant if aimless life in Paris as the eighteenth century drew to a close. Then circumstances threw me in with a young rascal named Napoleon and no end of adventures involving books of ancient wisdom, Norse gods, Greek superweapons, and a tormenting seductress or two. I've found that heroism doesn't pay very well, and is frequently a cold, filthy, and painful occupation as well.

I originally went adventuring because I was poor and a fugitive from an unjust murder charge. Now, if I could profit from the emerald I stole from the Barbary pirates, I would emulate the rich and never do anything interesting again. The entire point of being wealthy, as I understand it, is to escape life in all its miseries, and to avoid work, discomfort, unfamiliarity, and challenge of any kind. The rich I've met don't have to live but merely exist, like pampered plants, and after battles, tortures, broken hearts, and nightmare terrors, it had become my goal to become as dull and self-satisfied as the highborn. I would think about horse breeds and ledger books, offer predictable opinions to acceptable acquaintances, and spend four hours eating dinner.

It would be a pleasant change.

Accordingly, Astiza, Harry, and I had traveled from Tripoli to France to sell the gem I'd snatched. The very best jewelers, paying the very best prices, are in Paris. My plan was to make myself wealthy, cross the Atlantic, buy a quiet home in America, pass my wisdom to young Harry, and sire more little Ethans in the off-hours with my voluptuous temptation of a bride. Perhaps I'd toy with something mildly ambitious like taking up astronomy and looking for new planets like Herschel, the telescope builder who'd first spied Uranus. His sister Caroline was good at finding comets, so maybe Astiza would take peeks at the sky as well, and we'd reinforce our renown as a couple of clever savants.

But things had gone awry. First I had to scale Fort de Joux

and break free from prison one Toussaint L'Ouverture, liberator of Saint-Domingue, the tormented western half of the island of Hispaniola that the natives call Haiti.

The black general L'Ouverture, an adopted name meaning "the opening," had reconquered his country for France, been tricked into arrest because he succeeded, and been rewarded for loyalty by imprisonment. The slaves in the Caribbean had risen against their French overseers, you see, and the Spaniards and the British had seen an opportunity to invade a French possession. The French had rather cleverly recruited rebel armies back to their side by promising freedom, and then arrested Toussaint just when he was on the brink of achieving it. Now Napoleon was trying to reverse time by reinstating slavery, and Saint-Domingue was a hellhole of fire, massacre, torture, and oppression.

The question I was blackmailed into seeking an answer for was: Did L'Ouverture, locked in icy Fort de Joux, know a fantastic secret of an ancient treasure that held the secret of flight, and thus mastery of the world?

The French border fortress of the medieval Joux family had started as a wooden stockade on a rocky outcrop in 1034, my British advisers had informed me. Over the nearly eight centuries since (I was climbing in the predawn hours of April 7, 1803), it had become a barnacle-like accretion of tower, wall, parapet, and gate. By now it had three moats, five concentric walls, and a view of La Cluse Pass that was literally breathtaking, given that the altitude and climate of the place were enough to bring on apoplexy. Even in April the sheer wall I was ascending was coated with a particularly nasty veneer of frost. What a ruthless place to imprison a Black Spartacus from the tropics, leader of the first successful Negro slave revolt in history! There's dampness to Fortress de Joux more penetrating than the actual temperature, and the mountains around are brown, bleak, and spotted with snow. Napoleon hoped the cold would squeeze out the black general's revelations, and the British wanted him before it did.

The English-paid, French-born agent who recruited me for this insanity, Charles Frotté, tried to make my assignment sound reasonable.

"The fortress is quite picturesque, and delightfully quiet when armies aren't marching its way," said Frotté, a spy with more allegiances than a courtesan in the Kingdom of Naples. He was a Vatican hireling who'd tried unsuccessfully to rescue poor King Louis before the guillotine dropped, and was still a royalist who'd been signed up by Sidney Smith (my old ally, now appointed to Parliament) with English gold. There were rumors the Austrians, Dutch, and Spanish were paying Frotté as well. I owed the man a favor for saving me in Paris, but assaulting a medieval monstrosity single-handedly seemed extreme payback. Unfortunately, I had little choice. I needed help in getting back my son, who'd been kidnapped, and getting free my wife, who had talked her way into L'Ouverture's cell.

"Quiet?" I responded. "Then won't they notice whatever noise I make?"

"The guards hate the gloomy weather as much as you do, and stay indoors. Wretched place to play sentry. That's to your advantage when you go up their blind side. A quick ramble across the rooftops to L'Ouverture's chamber, a clever application of English science, a history-making escape, and off you'll be to cozy London, toasted for pluck and genius. It's splendid how things work out."

"That's exactly what Sidney Smith said. They don't work out at all."

"Just try not to jostle the cylinder on your back, Ethan. I'd hate to see you explode."

The cylinder contained some witches' brew invented by an English chemist named Priestly. I was also carrying two hundred feet of fine-stranded climbing rope, a grappling hook, a five-pound sledge, a cold chisel, two naval pistols, a frontier hunting knife, coat and boots for the man I was rescuing, and winter dress for myself. I'd had to sign a receipt for all of it, and buy my own leather gloves besides.

Yes, it was a ridiculous assignment, but I kept my mind on my goal. Get my jewel and family back, learn of Aztec treasure, and leave these lunatics behind.

"What if they don't let my wife out?"

"That's exactly why your scheme must succeed. When a medieval knight returned from the Crusades to this fort and suspected his seventeen-year-old bride Berthe of infidelity, he locked her in a three-by-four-foot cavity for ten years. She couldn't stand or stretch, and her only view was of the skeletal corpse of her alleged lover, hanging from a cliff opposite. All the evidence attested to her innocence, but the old warlord wouldn't listen."

"This is supposed to reassure me?"

"Inspire you. Astiza is only pretending to be a mistress, and we don't lock adulterers in cages anymore. Modern times! Still, it's reason not to tarry on your way up the cliff. When you jump back off, remember to take her with you."

I recalled this conversation as I picked a route away from the village of La Cluse-et-Mijoux, following a concealing line of pine up a steep slope on which the madman George Cayley, my other English confederate, lugged his contraption. That put me at the foot of a limestone cliff, which I ascended to the base of a limestone wall. The top of *that* wall was the highest tower of the castle. In other words, to stay out of sight I'd chosen the very hardest place to climb.

"You're sure your glider will work?" I again asked Cayley, who had nagged the entire way, reminding me not to tear fabric or fray a wire. The English like nothing better than a disagreeable journey with scant chance of success. Their occasional luck accomplishing the impossible only encourages them.

"Perfectly," he replied. "In theory."

I am neither monkey nor fly, but I did have factors in my favor. The fortress wall was not absolutely sheer, instead having a slight inward tilt to add stability. It was also so inaccessible that it was in modest disrepair. Frost heave or tremors had opened cracks and twisted stones, giving me handholds that would have been absent in a newer wall. If only I could stop the shake of my limbs! I clawed my way up while not daring to look down, until I could jam my left elbow in a yawning crack, plant each boot on a canted stone, and swing my climbing rope up with my free right arm. I'd used a bowline to tie on the grapple, and now I swung line and hook until it began to rotate in great circles, whistling as it cut through the night.

Finally I leaned out as far as I dared to give myself the best angle and let the line fly. The hook sailed upward, snagged the stone gutter of a conical tower roof, and yanked taut. The other end of the rope dropped to where Cayley was waiting. He began tying on his machine.

I began hauling myself up, eyes blinking against sleet, the extra coat for L'Ouverture flapping like a loose sail. I came near the top, a parapet to my right, and crab-walked across the face of the tower, my boot toes teetering as the angle of the rope steepened.

Almost there!

Unfortunately, I had angled my way in front of a grilled tower window. A candle was burning low inside, almost guttering. A figure rose from bed. Had I made a shadow or sound? Tousling her long hair, a woman peered out.

My face was like a full moon outside the slit of her window.

She was young, pretty, and her nightdress hung temptingly on her form. Lovely breasts and belly, as near as I could discern, and the face of an angel. I paused for a moment, instinctively enchanted.

Then she opened her mouth to scream.

CHAPTER 2

Astiza and I had been married less than a year, joined in wedlock the summer of 1802 by Lieutenant Andrew Sterett on board the American navy schooner *Enterprise*. That dashing officer had plucked us out of the sea near Tripoli after we escaped the Barbary pirates.

I suppose our shipboard union wasn't exactly a woman's ceremony, given that there could be no flowers, bunting, or bridesmaid. But we did have three redoubtable savants as witnesses (my companions Robert Fulton, zoologist Georges Cuvier, and geologist William Smith) plus my little friend Pierre Radisson to warn my lover that she was crazy to marry a man as senseless as me. Fortunately, I'd met Astiza during Napoleon's campaign in Egypt, and she'd had ample opportunity to judge my merits and shortcomings. Cupid had seen fit to reunite us.

The crew did make the ceremony festive by stringing signal flags from the rigging, crafting a temporary bridal train from a scrap of old sail, and organizing an orchestra consisting of fife, drum, bell, and horn that managed barely recognizable versions of "Yankee Doodle" and "Heart of Oak." A wedding march was beyond their repertoire. After Sterett pronounced us man and wife, I kissed the girl with gusto, danced a jig with little Harry, fondled the emerald I'd stolen from the pasha of Tripoli, and looked forward to a life of ease.

Pierre also gave us a locket he'd lifted in our headlong flight from Tripoli, set with diamonds and worth a gentleman's yearly income.

"For your honeymoon, donkey," he told me.

"But you need a reward, too!"

"There's nothing to buy where a Canadian voyageur goes. Spend this gift on your wife and son."

Certainly our marriage began as an idyll. Sterett put my family ashore in Naples, and we visited the newly excavated pits at Pompeii dug by antiquarian William Hamilton, who seemed to have permanently lent his wife, Emma, to my old acquaintance Admiral Horatio Nelson. Ruins fascinate Astiza, and even I was intrigued, given that I'd seen Pompeii artifacts in the mansion of Malmaison outside Paris, bought by Napoleon's wife, Joséphine. We congratulated Hamilton on his industry and saw gratitude that we were interested in something other than his straying wife. I judged him happier without the tart, who was too young for him anyway and a parvenu as shameless as me.

From Naples, Astiza, Harry, and I made our way to Rome and its overgrown Forum, and so northward, enjoying the European peace between Britain and France. We had a sunny Christmas on the island of Elba and then, after New Year, 1803, made the quick crossing to France, which was visibly prospering since Napoleon had seized power. We drifted toward Paris, busy learning to be husband and wife.

Astiza was the kind of bright, independent woman whom some men would run from, but who fascinated me. She was seductive as a siren, poised as a goddess, and as commonsensical as a midwife. What she saw in me I can't say, unless I represented a challenging remodeling project. I simply knew I was lucky to have her, and hauled in my winnings.

I first met her after she helped her Alexandrian master take potshots at Napoleon, and she's proved a scrapper ever since. She'd been a brilliant slave—highly educated, with a scholar's curiosity about ancient mystery and a wizard's determination to make sense out of existence. We'd fallen in love on the Nile, just like Antony and Cleopatra, except with a lot less money.

Despite my infatuation, I daresay there's more work to a marriage than poets let on. Negotiations are worthy of a Talleyrand. What time to bed and which side do you sleep on? (Left, for me.) Who tracks the money (her) and suggests ways to spend it? (Me.) What rules govern our child (hers) and who works off the boy's energy with romping play? (Me.) Do we sup in candlelit cellars with hearty portions of ale (my preference) or sunlit terraces with vegetables, fruit, and wine? (Hers.) Who decides on a route, deals with innkeepers, sees to the laundry, drags along souvenirs, initiates lovemaking, rises first, reads late, sets the pace of travel, decides appropriate attire, sketches out an ideal home, lingers in a library, contemplates ancient temples, pays extra for a bath, burns incense, rolls dice, or takes coach seats facing backward or forward?

More seriously, I was set on finding us a home in America, while my wife longed for the sunlit mysteries of Egypt. Trees enclosed her soul while sheltering mine, and I was drawn to mountains while Astiza preferred the shore. She loved me, but I was a sacrifice. I loved her, but she pulled me in directions to which I was reluctant to return. When unmarried, the future was vague and full of endless possibility. With marriage, we began to make choices.

Wedded bliss is certainly more complicated than the rapture of falling in love, but once you share out the victories and defeats and come to compromise, there's more contentment than I'd ever enjoyed. The growth of little Harry is a marvel, and the warmth of a nightly lover is a relief. We became comfortable with our intimacy, leading me to wonder why I hadn't seriously considered marriage before.

"You're actually a quite suitable father, Ethan," Astiza remarked with mild surprise one day, watching me build a dam on a little rivulet near Nîmes with Harry, who would turn three in June.

"It helps to retain the mind of a twelve-year-old," I said. "Most men do."

"Do you ever miss your independence?" Women forget nothing, and worry forever.

"You mean the bullets? The hardship? The scheming temptresses? Not in the least." I pointed out some more dam-building rocks to Harry, who was working like a beaver. "I've had more than enough adventure for any fellow. This is the life for me, my love. Dull, but comfortable."

"So I'm dull, now?" Women pick at words like a barrister.

"You're radiant. I just meant my new life is pleasantly placid, without the bullets and hardship."

"And the temptresses?" See what I mean about women forgetting nothing?

"How can a man be tempted, when he has Isis and Venus, Helen and Roxanne?" Yes, I was becoming quite the husband. "Here's some more stackable stones, Harry—let's build a castle on the shoreline!"

"And blow it up!" he cried. I was teaching him to be a boy, even though my wife sometimes frowned at our games.

So my family came to Paris. My plan was this: A precious gem is more portable, and easily hidden, than a sack of money. Accordingly, we'd wait to sell the emerald where I judged I'd get the best price. Only then would we set off for some safe and sleepy place in America, my homeland.

I'm afraid there was vanity in this schedule. I had, after all, recently found and destroyed the mirror of Archimedes, rescuing Harry and Astiza from pirates in the process. I couldn't resist the possibility of hobnobbing with the first consul again in hopes of being told how brilliantly I'd performed. There was also the lingering question of the vast Louisiana Territory that France had acquired and which I now considered myself expert on, having been dragged there by a Norwegian lunatic. I'd already advised Jefferson to buy and Napoleon to sell, but the negotiations had stalled while the president sent a new diplomat named James Monroe to Paris. I was just the man, I thought, to hurry things along before I retired as a gentleman.

That's the trouble with success. It makes you feel indispensable, which is a delusion. Pride exacts more trouble than love.

Accordingly, when my family arrived in Paris in mid-January of 1803, I was asked by American envoy Robert Livingston to lobby Napoleon about the fate of the wasteland west of the Mississippi River. Since Livingston offered to put us up in a hotel and was working with my friend Fulton on a new contraption called a steamboat, I persuaded Astiza we should enjoy Paris while I sought another audience with Bonaparte. The city was buzzing with talk of renewed conflict with England, which is always entertaining: war is perennially exciting to society people with little chance of having to actually fight it. Astiza was curious to explore the city's famed libraries for texts on mystery religions.

So we lingered like gentry. I was proud that while we'd once been imprisoned in Paris, now we were invited to its salons.

What we both wouldn't dare admit is that we were still treasure hunters at heart.

Which set the stage for disaster.

CHAPTER 3

I couldn't resist auditioning for history when I finally obtained an audience with Napoleon. France's first consul, who had replaced the incompetent Directory with his own dictatorship, had spent a million francs rehabilitating the dilapidated palace of Saint-Cloud outside Paris to serve as his latest home. It was a headquarters six miles from the stinking heart of the city, prudently distant from democratic mobs, and far bigger than Joséphine's Malmaison. This new pile had the room to house the first consul's growing retinue of aides, servants, supplicants, and schemers. It could also properly impress visiting ministers of state with wasteful opulence, the standard by which the powerful rank one another.

Having first met Bonaparte on the uncomfortably crowded warship *L'Orient* in 1798, I reflected how much grander and more beautiful his homes were each time I saw him. In the brief period since he'd ascended to power, he'd collected more palaces than I had shoes. I still had no house at all, and the contrast in our careers couldn't have been plainer when I crossed the Pont de Saint-Cloud across the Seine and turned up the walled gravel avenue that led to the Court of Honor. The U-shaped palace is an imposing five floors tall and enclosed a graveled yard where messengers dismounted, diplomatic coaches reined up, ministers loitered, footmen smoked, dogs barked, tradesmen delivered, and servants scurried, the entire arena dotted with horse droppings and overlooked by Joséphine's grand apartments. The gossip was that Napoleon's long hours had prompted the couple to keep separate bedrooms, and that the new quarters were so confusing that when the first consul wanted to sleep with his wife, he'd change into his nightshirt and cap, ring for his secretary, and be led down the dark corridors by a single candle to her bed.

I, of course, arrived in daylight, and was ushered by his new valet Constant Wairy, an unctuous functionary with well-fed face and muttonchop whiskers who sniffed at my clothes as if I were a private standing for inspection. I congratulated him with a goad, "What a grand place to be a lackey."

"If anyone has experience with that," he gave right back, "I understand it to be you, Monsieur Gage."

Our mutual snobbery established, we ascended a grand staircase and strode down a paneled hallway, entering a library the size of a barn.

Napoleon was wolfing down the déjeuner being served in this study, since there was no designated room in his palace (or any other palace, for that matter) for regular meals. He occupied a settee covered with green taffeta, eating his lunch from a portable campaign table. He'd already bathed—despite the skepticism of his doctors, Napoleon had embraced the modern French fashion of scrubbing every day, now that he had servants to heat the water—and was dressed in a simple blue military coat with red collar, white breeches, and silk stockings. I thought he might offer coffee and a roll, not to mention some soup or chicken, but he ignored my hunger and gestured me to an upholstered chair.

I looked about. There was a large writing table Napoleon had designed in the shape of a kidney or viol so he could squeeze into its middle and have incoming and outgoing correspondence flank him. It was heaped with papers and had legs carved like griffins.

A smaller table was assigned to his new secretary, Claude-François de Méneval, who had abruptly replaced Bourienne when the latter became embroiled in speculation over military supplies. Young and handsome, Méneval glanced at me now, reminding me that we'd met at Mortefontaine when celebrating the American treaty. I nodded, though I had no memory of him.

Behind this scribe, clifflike bookcases covered the walls from floor to ceiling, helping insulate the cavernous office from winter's chill. Bronze busts of the ancient antagonists Hannibal and Scipio eyed each other on the mantel as if wishing for more war elephants. The last time I'd discussed Hannibal with Napoleon I found myself guiding his army over the Alps, so this time I vowed to stay entirely away from military history.

"Gage," Bonaparte greeted me matter-of-factly, as if we'd just conferred yesterday instead of nearly a year ago, "I thought the pirates might have finally extinguished you, but here you are again, like a misfire you can't pry loose from a muzzle. The naturalist Cuvier tells me you actually succeeded in accomplishing something."

"Not just destroying a dangerous ancient weapon, First Consul, but finding a wife and son."

"Remarkable that someone would have you." He took a drink of his favorite Chambertin, a pinot wine with a rich, fruity flavor. It reminded me I was thirsty, too. There was, alas, only one goblet.

"But then I spied merit in you as well," he said with his usual bluntness. "The secret to rule is to find the natural talent of each man and woman. Yours, it seems, is to perform odd errands in peculiar places."

"But now I'm retiring," I said, lest he get the wrong idea. "I had some luck in Tripoli and plan to settle down with my bride Astiza, whom you'll remember from the Egyptian campaign."

"Yes, the one helping shoot at me."

He had a memory as long as a woman's.

"She's more agreeable now," I said.

"Be wary of wives, Gage, and I say that as a man mad about the one I have. There's no greater misfortune for a man than to be governed by his wife. In such a case he is a perfect nonentity."

Napoleon's disdain for women beyond their sexual charms was well known. "We're partners," I said, a concept I wasn't sure he could comprehend.

"Bah. Be careful how much you love her." He took another bite. "The guilt of many men can be traced to overaffection for their wives."

"Are you guilty because of your affection for Joséphine?"

"She's as guilty as me, as you know from Paris's tiresome gossip. But all that trouble is in the past. As rulers, we're models of rectitude now."

I knew better than to express my doubt of that claim.

"Our difference is that I regulate my emotions, Gage. You cannot. I'm a man of reason, you of impulse. I like you, but let's not pretend we're equal."

That was obvious enough. "Each time I see you, First Consul, you seem to have done better for yourself."

"Yes, it surprises even me." He glanced about. "My ambition doesn't hurry, it simply keeps pace with circumstances. I feel as if I'm being driven to an unknown goal. All life is a stage set, playing out as the seers promised."

He'd told me of his visions in the Great Pyramid and prophecy from a legendary gnome called the Little Red Man. "You still believe in destiny?"

"How else to explain where I am? I was laughed at for my Corsican accent in military school. Now we're putting the finishing touches on the Code Napoleon, which will remake the laws of

France. I started too penniless to buy my own uniform, and now I accumulate palaces. And how but destiny to explain an American like you, with more lives than a cat? The policeman Fouché was right not to trust you, because your survival is so inexplicable. And I was right not to trust Fouché. Police invent more lies than they ever discover truth."

I'd heard that the minister of police who'd arrested me the year before had since been dismissed and become a mere senator, just as Sir Sidney Smith had gone from Near East warlord to the relative obscurity of the British Parliament. I was relieved at both events; lawmakers do great mischief, but seldom do they personally throw you in jail. "Do you wish to get my impressions of the Mediterranean?" I offered.

Bonaparte poured himself a coffee and picked up a pastry, still offering me nothing. "Forget the Mediterranean. Your young nation is keeping the Tripoli pirates occupied with its little war, and I'm drifting toward a big war with the perfidious British. They've refused to depart Malta as they promised in the Treaty of Amiens."

"France hasn't upheld its obligations, either."

He ignored this. "The British, Gage, are evil. No man is more peace loving than me, a general who has seen the horror of war. Yet the Lobsters have sent threescore assassins to stalk me, stirred Europe with spies paid by English gold, and scheme to take back all of North America. Our two nations, America and France, must unite against them. I received you in order to talk about Louisiana."

My impression of that huge territory had been of black flies and bad weather, but I knew Thomas Jefferson was eager to get hold of a property several times bigger than France. American negotiators had hoped to buy New Orleans to assure trading access to the Gulf of Mexico. I'd suggested a bigger bargain. "I hope our two countries can come to agreement on that wilderness," I agreed. "But I thought you were sending an army to create an empire there."

"I *had* an army, until yellow fever took it in Saint-Domingue. As well as my brother-in-law General Charles Leclerc, leaving my poor sister Pauline a widow." He eyed me as he chewed his pastry. I'm pretty sure he knew I'd tupped his sister when helping with another treaty at Mortefontaine. The tryst had really been the girl's idea, and it was a romp I paid dearly for, since it forced me into temporary exile on the American frontier. But brothers view such flings through a particular prism; my history with Bonaparte was complicated, and Pauline was one of the complications. I tried not to show my relief that her husband was safely dead.

"What a tragedy," I said.

"My imbecile sister cut her beautiful hair to show her grief. She hardly liked the man, and certainly wasn't faithful to him, but appearances are all." He sighed and picked up a letter. "She also took the first boat back to France. She has the hardheaded practicality of a Bonaparte."

"Beauty, too."

"This is a communication from Leclerc last October, just weeks before he died." He read: "*'Here is my opinion on this country. We must destroy all the negroes in the mountains, men and women, and keep only children under twelve years old, destroy half of those on the plain, and not leave in the colony a single man of color who has worn an epaulette. Otherwise, the colony will never be quiet. If you wish to be the master of Saint-Domingue, you must send me twelve thousand men without wasting a single day.'*" He put the letter down. "What does that sound like to you, Gage?"

"Futility."

He grimly nodded. "I keep you in my service for your honesty, don't I? Saint-Domingue is tormented by longing for freedom in a place where freedom can never work. In trying to make all men equal, the blacks have succeeded only in making them equally miserable, and I'm left to put things back as they were. I've captured the leading rebel L'Ouverture and locked him up in the mountains, but the Negroes don't know when to quit. The war is eating whole regiments. I have no twelve thousand troops for Haiti, let alone men to send to Louisiana."

"Sorry to hear of your difficulty," I said, even though I wasn't sorry at all. It wasn't like the first consul deserved another million square miles. He'd bullied Spain into giving Louisiana back to France a couple years before, but the Spanish flag still flew in New Orleans because Napoleon hadn't bothered to put anyone there to take possession. He was busy trying to hang on to France's richest colony, the sugar isle of Saint-Domingue, by reinstating slavery to make its sugar competitive on the world market. As a result, that onetime paradise had become a charnel house. His policy was a complete betrayal of the ideals of the French Revolution, and stupid as well. It baffles me why people believe they can force on others what they'd never tolerate themselves.

Meanwhile, Tom Jefferson was the only one in the world crazy enough to actually *want* Louisiana. Having not seen the hell that is the American West, he believed it heaven, and mused about sending his secretary Meriwether Lewis to explore it. Promising to persuade Bonaparte to sell the place had won me a good bottle of wine with the president. Jefferson, like Franklin, was genius enough that he'd spent his diplomatic days in France learning to properly eat and drink. He later bought so much wine on credit that he'd assembled the best cellar, and worst debt, in America. The Virginian is also a far better conversationalist than the brusque Bonaparte, and by the time we got to the bottom of our bottle, I'd decided to vote him another term, if I lived to get the chance.

Napoleon had less patience for life's pleasantries. He waved, and servants materialized to take his silver serving dishes away. Whether it was palace cuisine or infantry biscuits, he ate at lightning speed.

"So your nation, Gage, can benefit from European folly. I need you to go to the American negotiators and convince them that buying all of Louisiana is their idea. It will set the United States as a counterweight to Britain in Canada, and give me money to fight the English in the coming war. If I can't control Saint-Domingue, Britain shall not control the Mississippi Valley. The United States will block English ambitions for France like a prodigal son."

That's not how my nation thought of itself, but I did see a deal could be to everyone's benefit, including mine. I'd played a small role in ending an undeclared naval war between America and France back in 1800, and now I was go-between again. Napoleon wanted to unload an expanse he'd acquired with a stroke of a pen, before England's navy took it from him. It appeared I could make everyone happy, except Britain.

"I'll make my countrymen think in grand terms," I promised. "Why purchase a mere city, New Orleans, when you could buy an empire?" My stomach growled from hunger. "What do you want for the dustbin, anyway?"

"Fifty million francs. Suggest double that, and they can take pleasure in bargaining me down. When I conquer London and put an end to the British navy, your country and mine will become the greatest trading partners in the world. Louisiana is a first step. This is an opportunity as significant as our revolutionary victory at Yorktown. I'll fire every American dollar I receive at the English from the mouth of my cannons, and all of us can enjoy the spectacle."

"Agreed. But after this service I'm determined to retire."

"On what pension?"

"I acquired something of value in Tripoli I intend to sell."

He eyed me with shrewd curiosity. "What is it?"

"No concern of the French government. A trifle, but enough to set my family for life."

"That's a remarkable trifle."

"I've finally had remarkable luck."

"You've been quite valuable at times, Gage, if annoying at others." Napoleon had almost had me shot two or three times.

"Realize that one doesn't resign from destiny at will. Yes, you're American, but when your interests coincide with France's, then you become French. Do you understand?"

"I understand that's exactly what I wish to retire from. I'm working very hard at being useless. Except for Louisiana, of course."

"It's important we complete this sale, Gage. You must stay in Paris until it's concluded."

"I understand. But given that I haven't actually sold my trifle yet, I wonder if an appointment could come from all my hard work? Especially if you're about to gain fifty million francs." It's always smart to look for crumbs from the diplomatic table. "A salary will convince American negotiators I truly represent your thinking."

"Ha! If you wish to pretend partnership with me, you should adopt the habit of my most trusted agents."

"Which is?"

"A discreet tattoo, signifying their loyalty."

"A tattoo of what?"

"The initial N, surrounded by a laurel wreath."

"You must be joking."

"Life is filled with enemies. There has to be some way to tell friends."

"Not by wearing another man's brand."

"It's a secret legion." He was annoyed that I wasn't flattered. "Or you can have a more temporary badge, but you must give it back should you ever displease me."

"What's that?"

He opened a drawer in his desk and drew out a small medal on a chain. It was the same design as the tattoo but in gold, an ornament to wear around the neck. "Only a handful of agents are so favored."

It would give me credibility, I supposed. I took it in my palm. Small, light, unobtrusive, and removable. "Not very much metal."

"There are a million men who would pledge their lives for such favor."

"I appreciate the honor." I didn't, but wanted to avoid insult.

"And your discoveries, when on missions for me, belong to France."

"A last mission on Louisiana, in Paris, and then home. Something to buy bread would help in the meantime," I persisted.

When it came to money, he could be evasive as a loan officer. "Get Louisiana for your president, Gage, and they'll make you a congressman."

CHAPTER 4

So I worked to double the size of my homeland, arranging a meeting with Livingston to plant the idea of buying every savage-infested acre. We actually had something in common. Robert Livingston had been the grand master of Freemasonry's Grand Lodge in New York before traveling to France. I was a Mason as well, although I didn't tell him it was of the most casual and disreputable kind.

"It was Benjamin Franklin himself who introduced me to the precepts of your fraternity," I said to ingratiate myself. "I've striven to live up to them ever since." Striven, but not succeeded. "If my government could afford a modest salary, I might be able to linger in Paris to see the bargaining through. I'm a confidant of Napoleon, you know." I showed him the pendant.

It helped that Livingston had struck up a friendship with my American colleague Robert Fulton after meeting the inventor at one of his "panoramas," or huge circular paintings on such lurid themes as "city conflagrations." Fulton charged admission to earn a living while designing unnecessary machines. We'd lost the tinkerer's submarine *Nautilus* when rescuing Astiza and Harry from Tripoli, but now Fulton had a grander scheme for a contraption called a steamboat. It was to be two and a half times as long as his submersible, and painted bright as a carnival. It would be captained by a man called a mechanician and would go three miles an hour against the current, cutting the time for freight to go from Nantes to Paris from four months to two weeks.

Such speed seemed unlikely, but Livingston (a steam engine enthusiast who'd written to the inventor of that device, James Watt, in London) had joined Fulton's project. The eccentrics were as happy as boys with a play fort, so to keep their favor, I quit pointing out that machines are expensive, heavy, and deafening. Like all men, the pair liked things that made noise, be it a lusty wench at full gallop, the crack of a cannon, or the headache-inducing thump of boiler and crank.

"I guess we could spare you a small stipend," Livingston said.

Bonaparte also gave me a letter of introduction to his minister François Barbé-Marbois, the French negotiator. I got on famously with him as well, because we were both victims of the unpredictability of fortune. François had actually served as intendant of Saint-Domingue in 1785 before the slave revolt began, and was well aware the colony was swallowing Napoleon's army. After the revolution, his moderation made him suspect by royalist and revolutionary alike, since reasonable men like us are always threatening to the ambitious and fanatic. For a while he was imprisoned in hellish French Guiana. Now that Bonaparte was firmly in power, his common sense was deemed useful again.

I confided that I'd had my own ups and downs. "I've had a pharaoh's hoard and a book of magic slip through my fingers, and until I got married I had the devil's own time with women. But I remain ambitious. I'll try to get the Americans to raise their sights. If you could advance me a French salary for my expenses, I can afford to wait to bend the ear of James Monroe."

"You really think your countrymen will pay to take this waste-land off our hands?" Barbé-Marbois could scarcely believe we Americans were so gullible.

"I had companions who thought Louisiana was the Garden of Eden. One killed, the other wounded, but they were optimists."

So my chance to draw pay from both America and France, and to encourage the greatest real estate deal in history, caused us to linger in Paris into the spring of 1803.

It was a pleasant interlude. We strolled the Tivoli Gardens, where fireworks and acrobats delighted my son. There was a teth-ered elephant, two rather bored and ratty-looking lions in iron cages, and an ostrich that Napoleon's troops had brought back from Egypt. It displayed considerably more ferocity than the cats.

At the competing Frascati amusement park (only a franc a day per person) there was a miniature village of mills and bridges that absorbed my boy like a Gulliver. "Look, a real castle!" he'd cry at fortifications three feet high.

The balloon ascents we watched at the Tuileries brought pow-erful emotions to Astiza and me, given our history in Egypt. The exotic costumes of street performers brought to mind perilous times in the Holy Land.

I found married life altogether different from our frequently in-terrupted courtship. We were no longer allied by danger and didn't have the flush that comes from novelty and infatuation. Instead, there was deepening affection and security. Like many great men, my mentor Benjamin Franklin had been a poor husband who hadn't hesitated to expound on what makes a good one. Marriage was an investment in time, commitment, and compromise, he told me, a work for which the profit was contentment and even, "at times," bright happiness. "The most natural state of man," he'd counseled.

"If natural, then why are our heads always swiveling toward the next woman like a dog spying a rabbit?"

"Because we don't catch the rabbit, Ethan, or, if we do, we scarcely know what to do with it."

"On the contrary."

"Marriage saves us from confusion and heartbreak."

"Yet *your* wife is five thousand miles away, in Philadelphia."

"And I take comfort knowing she is there, waiting."

I counted myself astoundingly lucky, then. I'd snatched an emerald, yes, but what was the real jewel from Tripoli? My wife beside me. We walked arm in arm under rose arbors, ate sugared ices, swayed to accordion bands playing on brilliantly lit stages, and watched up to three hundred people at a time wheeling to the new German waltz. The crowd thinned when the more complicated quadrille and mazurka were danced, but gaiety had returned to Paris.

There was also quiet anxiety, because the newspapers were full of tension with England. Rumor contended that Napoleon had ordered work on an invasion fleet of barges to cross the Channel. Once the boats were ready, war would return, predictions went.

"Ethan, if we tarry much longer, we may be trapped in Paris," Astiza warned as we crossed the new pedestrian Bridge of the Arts at the Louvre, an iron novelty that was one of several bridges Napoleon had ordered to unite both banks of the city. "Britain will blockade, and France may arrest any aliens."

She was not just beautiful (the antiquity-inspired fashion of high waist, puffed sleeves, and a vale of décolletage enhanced her Greek Egyptian sultriness to a bewitching degree) but practical as well. She thought ahead, a novel quality, and despite Napoleon's prejudices, was probably closer to his habits than I was.

She also gave me a wifely elbow when my eye lingered too long on other consular beauties, some of them with breasts in mere gauze. Unfortunately, that happy fashion was being discouraged by a more conservative, militarist ethic that began with Bonaparte himself. The Corsican was proving stern, announcing that the primary purpose of women was not to display their charms but make future soldiers. Given male instincts, I thought the two went hand in hand, but I think he wanted sex, like everything else, bent to efficient purpose.

For myself, I saw fashion as one of life's pleasures and necessities, its display as articulate as bright conversation. Astiza and I made quite the dashing couple, given that I'd copied the *incroyable* dandies with the long boot, tight coat, carefully wrinkled shirt, and stylish top hat, a precisely calculated mix of elegance and disorder to mirror the turmoil of our times. We were a couple at the height of fashion, and I enjoyed being glanced at. It was mostly bought on credit, but once I sold the emerald my debts would be erased.

"The British are already leaving the city," Astiza went on as we strolled. Harry would run ahead and then come back to announce he was exhausted, and then run ahead again. "There are rumors Napoleon wants to invade England."

"Since he's ordered the building of boats, it's more than a rumor." I paused to watch the traffic on the Seine. Paris was a pleasing spectacle on a sunny March day. The polluted river glittered, its banks skirted with bright arcades and singsonging merchants. Palaces and church towers punctuated bright blue sky like exclamation points. Napoleon's rule had brought stability and reinvestment. "But I'm supposed to wait for Monroe and finish the purchase of Louisiana. Even if war breaks out, we're neutral as Americans." I knew she didn't think of herself as American yet, but I intended she become one.

"Two dueling navies, and Ethan Gage, the hero of Acre and Mortefontaine?" she responded. "You've managed to make enemies on all sides. We've a son to think about. Let's take ship for New York or Philadelphia, settle before Nelson or Napoleon strikes, and you can seek an appointment from Jefferson. You've got a family now, Ethan."

Indeed I did, a revelation no matter how many times I remembered it. "But we still have to sell the emerald. We'll get a far better price here than in the United States, but I don't want to have to worry about coin until negotiations are concluded. Let's wait until the proper moment."

"The proper moment is now. The first consul is not content without a war."

This was true. People repeat what they're successful at, and Napoleon had made himself with generalship. For all his trumpeting of peace, he was forever listening for the roll of the drums. I suspected this next war would dwarf all that had come before.

So I looked at her fondly and decided to indulge. Worry made her look vulnerable, uncommon for Astiza, with a beauty that stirred my heart. "Very well. I've lent the negotiators what wisdom I can. Let's sell the stone and retire to the everlasting peace we both deserve."

CHAPTER 5

Joséphine Bonaparte's favorite jeweler was Marie-Etienne Nitot, a man who had apprenticed to the great Auber, jeweler to Marie Antoinette. His success demonstrates anew that revolution disrupts everything but the desire for luxury. Nitot coupled his mentor's artistry with a salesman's flair, and after the queen lost her head he'd quickly built a clientele among the new elite of France. Gossip said the jeweler met Bonaparte when grasping the bridle of Napoleon's skittish horse on an avenue of Paris, preventing a fall, and that he'd cultivated the relationship ever since. The handsome craftsman opened a smart shop called Chaumet at 12 Place Vendôme, near the clockmaker Bréguet, and both did a bustling business. The plunder of Napoleon's early victories had fueled a mania for bright baubles displaying France's new pride and power.

The necklaces and rings on display were clustered near Chaumet's bright windows. For an appraisal of my emerald, Nitot took us to the rear of his establishment, locking the workshop door for privacy and carefully washing his hands in a basin, a delicacy few surgeons would bother with.

Gray light filtered from a skylight gridded with iron bars to discourage thieves. Lamps lent a honeyed glow. There were banks of drawers that no doubt held treasures, and a workbench with vises, clamps, and jeweler tools, bright bits of silver and gold glittering like fairy dust. Thick ledger books held records of trades and treasures from all over the world.

I could almost smell my coming coin.

"Monsieur Gage, I'm so honored to have your business," Nitot began. "A man of dash and daring, and rumored to have recently returned from a secret mission against the pirates for Bonaparte." I couldn't help puffing. "And your beautiful wife, so exotic, so regal! I beg you, madame, to allow us to grace your lovely neck."

"We're here to sell a jewel, not buy one, Monsieur Nitot," she replied. "I have a young son we had to leave in the care of a nursemaid in our apartment, and I'm eager to have our business concluded and get back to my boy." She had a mother's instinct to stay close to her young.

"Yes, but how wonderful to sell *and* buy, no?" Nitot went on. "It's merely a suggestion inspired by your radiance. Just as a great picture deserves an inspiring frame, so does jewelry demand exquisite complexion. And yours, of amber and olive, alabaster and silk! Your neck, your ears, your wrists, your ankles! You are your husband's ornament, and the world begs to decorate you!"

I'd had quite enough of this, since the compliments seemed a little forward, and potentially expensive to boot. No wonder this rascal was doing so well; he had the persuasive instincts of the devil. But I was no mere brigadier looking for a way to hang martial plunder on a consort. I was a savant of sorts, an electrician and a Franklin man, determined to finance a contemplative life with a rock stolen from a pasha. So I kept my emotions in check. "We need an appraisal, not a commentary on my wife."

"Of course, of course. I'm just so vulnerable to beauty! I lay at its mercy, a poor artisan, helpless at my desire to bring splendor to the world. My apologies, monsieur, at being at all presumptive. I am here only to assist."

I was partially annoyed because Astiza had actually suggested she stay home to watch little Harry, and now I wished I'd let her.

"Why do you need me to sell a jewel?" she'd asked in our hotel.

Because this was the first time in my life I could anticipate real wealth, and I wanted to show off by letting my bride watch me impress a jaded jeweler. Now I was foolishly jealous that Nitot's attention was on her, and not on my cleverness for getting the stone in the first place.

"I'm just a man who's prompt about business," I told him. I was nervous, because the simple job of hawking my trophy was tinged with foreboding. I hadn't, after all, really earned the stone. Though I attribute my gambling success to my wits, this time I was selling plunder.

"*Oui, oui,*" he said. His eyes assessed me, guessing my discomfort and fearing he might miss a bargain. "Your stone, please."

I kept it in a felt purse on a metal chain hung round my neck to discourage any thief or pickpocket. Now I fished out an emerald the size of a robin's egg.

Nitot gasped, which was gratifying. Even in this light the jewel glowed with green fire, heavy, slick, and imposing. It was decoration fit for a king, and my hope was that the jeweler would know a royal in Russia or Rome eager to pay dearly.

"Where did you get this?" He seemed almost in shock.

"From an Ottoman who got too close to my wife."

"It is truly incredible."

"And worth quite a bit of money, I'm betting."

He set the stone on his workbench and went to a shelf with old, leather-bound volumes. He pulled one down called *Lost Treasures of the Pagans*, and for some minutes studied it, occasionally glancing at the emerald.

"And where did the Ottoman get it?" he finally asked.

"Stole it, I imagine. The man was a pirate who wounded his mother and killed his brother, and wasn't very polite to me. He kept that jewel in a cage with a leopard grumpier than a tax auditor. Astiza was in the thick of a catfight." It was quite a tussle, but I said no more because I doubted the jeweler would believe me.

"I see," Nitot said, even though he didn't see at all. "Well, there are stories about this stone. This may have been the legendary Green Apple of the Sun, Monsieur Gage. If so, it was stolen while en route to the pope as a present from his Catholic majesty Philip II of Spain, emperor of the Holy Roman Empire in the sixteenth century. That has always been conjecture, however, because both the jewel's existence, and the greater treasure it came from, have been a matter of historical mystery."

"I love a good mystery. So the stone is worth what, exactly?" When dealing with an expert, you have to work to keep them on track, like putting blinders on a horse.

"As a precious gem, it has one price tag. But as a piece of tragic history, its value is almost incalculable. You may have stumbled on one of the most astonishing artifacts in history."

I swelled again. "I'd like to think it was more than just a stumble."

"Monsieur, have you ever heard of *La Noche Triste*?"

"Is that another jewel?"

"It means 'The Sad Night,' Ethan," Astiza said. "In Spanish." Did I mention one reason I loved the girl was because she was bright as a penny?

"I've had a few of those, I'm afraid."

"*La Noche Triste*, Monsieur Gage, was when the Aztecs managed to briefly drive the Spanish out of their capital in Tenochtitlán. They rose in a fury, overcoming the volleys of conquistador muskets with fearless numbers. Jade club against Spanish steel! Hernán Cortés lost hundreds of men and most of his artillery, but also something even more significant. As he retreated on the causeways that led across a lake from the spectacular city, his men lost the captured treasure of Montezuma. They died with it in the waters of Lake Texcoco."

"You think this stone is part of a larger treasure?" He had my attention.

"Look in the book here. Legend describes that one of the Aztec emperor's treasures was a spectacular emerald from the jungles of South America, the size and cut of this gem. It was a small but distinct part of riches that would dwarf those of our own kings: a bounty of gold, jewels, and silver such as Europe had never seen. There were great golden and silver wheels said to predict the future of the universe. Gold collars that could bend a proud warrior with their weight. A metal alligator, with gems for eyes and crystals for teeth. Silver birds; golden idols. If this is really part of the Aztec emperor's hoard, it means at least part of the treasure was not just lost, but at some point found. And then lost again."

"What do you mean?"

"When the Spaniards reconquered Mexico City, no mention was made of the wealth the retreating soldiers had desperately hurled into the lake. And ever since, there has been speculation. One story is that the Indians recovered the precious goods and took them on a perilous journey to forgotten mountains to the far north of Mexico. If so, no one knows where the burial place is."

"One story?"

"Another is that the Spaniards forced the Indians to dive and salvage the treasure for shipment to Spain, putting to death the native slaves so that no word would leak to other European powers. A galleon with the recovered hoard set out in secret for the Spanish homeland, but disappeared in a hurricane. This single gem was kept by the only survivor, a cabin boy."

"So the rest of the lot is at the bottom of the ocean?"

"There were rumors that escaped slaves, called Maroons, eventually salvaged what was lost by diving in the shallows of the reef where the galleon was dashed. Some of the loot was melted, lost, or stolen, but much was reportedly hidden. Just why is not clear. And that's the last anyone heard of the hoard until an announcement was made that this emerald was on its way to the pope. But it never arrived, making some wonder if Montezuma's treasure existed at all. Some say the entire story is a myth."

"Until now."

"Exactly. Does this mean the wreck was salvaged? And if it was, what became of its contents? Have blacks passed down its secret whereabouts, each generation to another, waiting until they rise as a nation and can reclaim it? Now here is famous Ethan Gage, hero of the pyramids, explorer of the American wilderness, appearing with a token in his hands. Is this but a precursor of more astonishment to come? Do you have a ship's hold of Aztec treasure in your apartment?"

"If I did, I'd have more than an apartment, wouldn't I?"

He smiled. "Even this single gem will buy you more than an apartment, Ethan Gage."

"I certainly hope so." He still hadn't given an appraisal.

"And if it's from the lost treasure of Montezuma," Nitot went on, "it may buy us both a palace, you as source and me as dealer. It becomes not just adornment, but historic majesty imbued in stone. So I must ask your permission to leave the emerald here while I consult more texts concerning its provenance. If we can establish its identity, its value goes up astronomically. The question becomes whether you are merely wealthy, or *fabulously* wealthy."

This was just the kind of talk I wanted to hear. No wonder this Nitot sold to dukes and duchesses; he certainly knew the trigger to pull for a mercenary like me. Aztec treasure! My, I'd never even been to Mexico.

But leave the stone? We were skeptical. "How can we trust you with its safekeeping?" Astiza asked.

"Madame, this is not a stone one pawns without notice. To steal it, I'd have to flee the lucrative life I've built for myself and try to sell a jewel that would instantly mark me as a thief. Don't worry, there's more profit in being honest. Let me make some inquiry so we know its true value."

"We are, as I said, in a hurry," I reminded.

"Then come back in one week. Soon, *all* of us may be famous."

I *knew* I was onto something when I spied that green egg on Karamanli's turban. After all my years of fruitless treasure hunting, at last I was to be compensated, and more generously than I'd guessed! Yes, we were brilliant, and about to be richer than I dreamed.

I turned to my new bride. "This is better luck than I ever hoped."

CHAPTER 6

Luck is fickle.

I've come near to drowning more times than I care to remember, and I've decided it's the "near" part that makes the experience so unpleasant. If one truly drowned, consciousness would be mercifully lost, and the victim would pass to other worlds. But I have the habit of never quite succumbing, and thus revisit the experience in all its horror. Which was precisely the intention of a renegade secret policeman named Leon Martel. One week after my first visit to Nitot's shop, he had my ankles roped, I was suspended upside down from a butcher's hook, and an iron collar was locked to my neck. He was methodically lowering me into a trough of cold water.

"I regret the necessity, Monsieur Gage," he told me as I sputtered. "My ambition is to become a gentleman, but you are notoriously uncooperative."

"No, I'm not! I'm just confused!"

And down I'd go again.

I'd hold my breath as long as I could, suspended so my hair just grazed the bottom of the tin. Finally I'd writhe in growing terror, explode a gush of bubbles that sucked water into my lungs with searing pain, and then be lifted, coughing and gasping. The idiot leaned close with garlic breath and asked, "Where is the lost treasure of the Aztecs?"

"I'd never heard of it until last week!"

Down I'd submerge once more.

There were at least two reasons I should have suspected something like this was about to take place.

First, my luck always falls short of true fortune, so why did I expect to neatly sell my fabulous emerald the way an ordinary man might? Treasures have been elusive every time I've touched them.

Second, Nitot's jewelry shop was uncharacteristically quiet when we returned as scheduled to learn the history of our stone and receive payment. Its front was closed to customers, and it was only by tapping on the window that a clerk let us in. Astiza was once more impatient, nervous about leaving Harry to play with his toys. She'd argued that people kept looking at us in odd ways, and that she'd seen the same scrutinizer three different times. I suggested that they were looking at *her*. "You're too modest," I reassured. "You've no idea how lovely you truly are."

"Let's beg off sick and go some other time. The portents aren't aligned." She was superstitious as a sailor.

"And leave a king's fortune with Nitot? Now *there* is something to worry about. You're the one who's in a hurry. If you're so concerned about impending war, the best thing is to conclude our bargain and be off to America."

Merchants are usually affectionate when money changes hands, but the clerk avoided my eye when he allowed us into the shop, scurrying to his bench.

"Where's Nitot?"

"In the back, monsieur." His eye was pressed to a loupe to watch a diamond as if it might get away. Of course I'd already spent my new fortune in my imagination several times over, and was oblivious to the odd atmosphere. My naive assumption was that our sale was so monumental that the jeweler wanted privacy to let me scoop up my gold.

I *had* purchased a small magnifying glass hung on a cord around my neck as I'd hung the jewel. I'd prudently studied my stone before surrendering it for appraisal, and would examine it again. I didn't want Nitot switching emeralds and then backing out of a sale. So I *was* being clever and cautious, in my own modest way. Just not clever and cautious enough.

To Astiza I'd given Napoleon's *N* pendant to advertise our importance and discourage any sales nonsense about "decorating my ornament." It actually looked good on her, and except for the fact it came from a megalomaniac, I rather liked the piece.

Now she put her hand on my arm. "I should have stayed with Horus," she whispered. "Paris always smells wicked to me."

"That's just the fish market and the plumbing. Let's finish our business." Our boy had also been playing quite happily with thimbles and spools, rolling the latter into the former while his nursemaid watched. I doubted he missed us a whit.

So we returned to the back room. "Marie-Etienne?" I called. I thought he could have set out little cakes or a decanter of brandy to celebrate, but the room was gloomy. The clerk, oddly, moved behind us.

"Are you here?" I repeated.

The door slammed shut and shadows became animated. Half a dozen ruffians in tricorn hats and heavy black cloaks, dark as morticians, materialized from the gloom. The workshop was suddenly as crowded as a privy at the opera when the singing has gone on too long.

"Damnation. Robbery?" I was so surprised that I was momentarily stupid. Then I realized we didn't have the jewel to rob and felt momentarily cheered. "I'm afraid we have nothing of value, gentlemen."

"Not robbery, Monsieur Gage," said their leader. "Arrest."

"Arrest?" I groaned with annoyance. Even though I try to do the right thing, people are constantly trying to incarcerate me. I make a poor prisoner, having a knack for escape. "For what this time?"

"Withholding information from the French State."

"Information?" My confusion was growing. "About what?"

"A significant archaeological discovery, the Green Apple of the Sun."

Were they greedy gendarmes or impatient historians? "It's exactly such information that I'm seeking, not that I have. And arrest on whose authority?"

"Minister Fouché."

"But he is no longer minister of police. Don't you read the papers?"

"He should be."

When Joseph Fouché had arrested me the year before, he was one of the most powerful men in France, his ministry the stronghold of Napoleon's military dictatorship . . . but by his very success Fouché had become dangerously powerful, and Bonaparte had temporarily dismissed him. Napoleon liked to keep his acolytes off-balance. However, the ambitious policeman had left behind a police organization more efficient and insidious than the world had ever seen, and the reassignment of their superior to the legislature had apparently not dampened his investigators' conspiratorial instincts. This bunch had decided to act as if their boss had never changed.

"And you are?"

"Inspector Leon Martel," the ringleader said, his heavy cavalry pistol pointed at my midsection. His colleagues also had guns out. Their piggish gaze lingered a little too long on Astiza's figure for my taste, and for policemen these seemed a loutish bunch. I tensed for the worst. "You must share with us what you know."

While Fouché had the sly, thin-lipped look of a lizard, Martel had the bright concentration of a cat, hazel eyes giving him a look of feline cunning. "You came into possession of a valuable jewel, and we require answers on its history."

"I know nothing. And where *is* my valuable? Where's Nitot?"

"It's been confiscated, and the jeweler has been sent home."

"Confiscated? You mean stolen?"

"It is you who stole it first, monsieur, from the pasha of Tripoli."

"Help! Thieves!" I cried.

"No one can hear you. The real employees have been ordered to leave the shop for the day. You've no allies or hope of rescue."

"On the contrary, the first consul is my friend and patron," I warned. "Look at my wife's neck. She wears his pendant."

He shook his head. "He's no patron when you hide secrets critical to the future of France. Present your wrists for manacles, please."

I've learned that hesitation with unpleasant people only encourages them; it's best to establish immediately where the relationship stands. I was also heartily tired of people pointing firearms at the lover who was now my wife, and mother of my child. So I *did* present my wrists, but only to lock my fists together like a hammer and launch them fiercely up under Martel's annoying pistol, knocking its muzzle toward the ceiling. The gun went off, flew like a juggler's pin, and I kept swinging, ramming my fists into the bastard's nose. Martel howled, quite satisfyingly, with pain. Astiza, as quick-witted as me, fanned her cloak like a batwing in front of the scoundrel's henchmen, packed too tight in our closet of a room. I leaped after the cape, plowing into the lot while more pistols went off, gun smoke roiling. The renegade gendarmes and I crashed together into the bank of jewel drawers, toppling them and spilling baubles everywhere.

By some miracle no one was hit, though a quite-expensive cloak was ruined with half a dozen bullet holes. But the nice thing about muzzle-loaders is that everybody's weapon was now empty.

"Run for Harry!" I shouted as we thrashed and cursed on the floor, the jeweler's workbench turning over. And then, as I clawed for one of their pistols in hopes of using it as a club, hands grabbing my throat and ankles, something struck my head, and everything went black.

CHAPTER 7

I awoke in a vaulted cellar of smoky stone, suspended upside down like an unhappy possum
and annoyed that the police, if that's who they were, wanted *me*,
since I knew not a whit.

As I woozily came to, I got an upside-down look at my assail-
ants, including Martel, recognizable because he had a bandaged
nose and foul expression. Corruption had hardened him. His jaw
was shovel-shaped, as if in the habit of digging into others' affairs, and his skin was cribbaged from some kind of pox. I theo-
rized this cruelty of fate made flirtation difficult and kept him
in bad humor; people who don't have frequent congress are sour
and mean. Martel's Gallic skin was dark from sun and weather,
and his thick, unruly hair was barely controlled by a cord on his
queue. Dark brows met over his now-broken nose, heavy lips
tended toward a sneer, and his face had the overall grimness that
comes from a desperate childhood, too much drink and disappointment, or both. He was the sort of man who either guards

a prison or inhabits it. Not a cat, I decided, but a feral rodent. While useful to superiors, he can never be one of them because his edges are too rough. I could tell Martel knew that, and it gnawed at him. He could rise only so high.

"Where did the emerald originate, Gage?" His breath was like that of a diseased Neapolitan whore who subsists on cheap wine and suspect foods like tomato and eggplant. Italians, I'd learned, would eat anything.

Not that I necessarily know anything about diseased Italian whores.

"Where's Astiza?" I countered.

It seemed a reasonable question, but one of his henchmen hit me with a carriage whip for asking it. I yelped. Martel stuck his bandaged nose in my face again. The man needed a good tooth-brush, and a pick, too. "What do you know of the flying ma-chines?"

"The what?" It occurred to me that I'd been captured by lu-natics, which is always more dangerous than the merely covetous. "Say, did my wife get away?"

The switch struck again, which I took to be an answer in the affirmative. They were angry at how things had gone, which was encouraging. But they also plunged me into cold, filthy water, which was not.

I didn't even have time to take a breath that first time, and be-gan choking immediately. They hauled me back up as I wheezed and coughed, shaking my head like a dog so I could spray their breeches. It was all the defiance I could muster.

"Who the devil are you?" I gasped. "You're not just thieves. You're worse."

"We're the police, I told you. Inspector Leon Martel. Remem-ber that name, because in time I'll make you pay for my nose with your own, unless you tell me what I want to hear. The fact we've lost our patron in the ministry doesn't erase our loyalty to France. We act on our own for the good of the state."

A criminal with a badge is the very worst kind. "Your superiors have no idea what you're up to here?"

"They'll thank us for it."

It's never good when evil thinks it's doing the right thing.

"I do know one secret," I tried. "I have friends trying to build a steamboat, which is a vessel powered by one of Watt's clamorous engines. It's going to be demonstrated for Napoleon on the Seine this summer. I wouldn't care to fetch the boiler wood myself, but it may prove a brilliant investment opportunity, though personally I can't see the logic, yet men like you wagering on the idea at this opportune stage—"

I was plunged down into the water again.

Their questions hammered at me. How had I learned about the jewel? Where was the treasure of the Aztecs? What did I know about flying machines? Oh, they were balmy, all right, and not a little happy to keep me so rattled that it gave them an excuse to dunk me again and again. They were having a jolly good time of it, whereas I experienced the shock of cold water, the dark and helplessness, the agonizing holding of breath, the terrible sensation of drowning, excruciating resurrection back to the light . . . how precious is the air we so take for granted! Searing pain of lung, raw throat, leaking nostrils, the dread of extinction . . .

I've had better conversations.

"I took it from a heathen pasha!" I sputtered. "It's only proper recompense for serving the first consul. He's a friend, I warn you!" And down they sank me again.

Each time was longer, but instead of loosening my lips, the torture was turning me insensible. They began to realize this, as Martel started pacing.

"Maybe he's really as stupid as he says," one of his henchmen suggested.

"The great Ethan Gage? Hero, explorer, and negotiator? He makes fools of men by playing the fool. The one man in the world to find this emerald just happens to be the one who has roamed from the Holy Land to Canada? Who befriends savants and politicians? Who served the foul Englishman Sir Sydney Smith? No, Gage knows far more than he's telling us. Look at him hang there, playing the idiot."

"But I am an idiot," I tried. And down I plummeted again.

Living a significant life is terribly overrated.

"I believe the treasure is in the Great Pyramid of Egypt," I tried the next time, making up nonsense just to get them to stop. "The Aztecs and Egyptians were one happy bunch, you see, with nearly the same kind of architecture. Of course I've no idea how to get back inside, but with enough gunpowder—"

They lashed me again, grunting each time they swung the switch. Flogging never works, but we live in an age when it's the first solution to everything. Lord, it hurt! But at least they didn't dunk me, since I truly was on the brink of drowning.

"What do we do now, Martel?" the accomplice said. "Fouché can't protect us anymore, and Bonaparte will be impatient. I warned you that no man brings his wife on a treasure hunt, or dawdles in Paris while riches await."

"Silence!" He glared at me. "He *must* know more than he's telling."

Why do people assume this? Men never want my advice when I have any, and whip me for it when I don't.

"To hell with him," Martel went on. "Let's drown Gage and throw the body into the Seine."

"His wife had Bonaparte's ornament."

"And Gage his iron collar. By the time anyone finds him he'll be rotted to cheese."

An unpleasant picture. "Why don't you just keep the emerald?" I countered. "I promise not to tell, and if I hear of any more riches, I'll be sure to let you know. . . ."

Then there was a shot, loud and shocking in the close cellar, and a bullet hit the rope I was suspended by, twanging it like a harpsichord string. It frayed, I twirled, it broke, and then I dropped like an anchor toward the tub of water, hitting the bottom with a great splash. Even submerged, I heard a blaze of other shots ring out. And then I truly began to drown.

I should have sold the thing in Naples.

CHAPTER 8

At first, being shot down into water deep enough to drown seemed worse than being deliberately dunked, since there was no block and tackle to haul me out and the iron collar kept my head hard against the bottom. I wiggled in my ropes like a worm, but I'd awkwardly jammed.

Thinking further, I remembered the gunfire and considered whether staying under for a spell might not be the safest strategy after all. Instead of thrashing, I tried to be inconspicuous while hard things pounded the tub's sides.

Soon I neared the limit of how long I could hold my breath. There was an unholy clamor through tin and water, and I wondered what the devil was going on.

Should I surface?

The decision was made for me when my nose emerged of its own accord. Bullets had pierced the tub, missing me, and the receptacle was rapidly draining.

Strong hands grasped and hauled me upright.

"I know nothing!" I sputtered again. Which was close enough to the truth.

"Good God, Gage," someone said in English, "you're just as much trouble as Sidney Smith said you'd be."

Sidney Smith? My old savior (or was it nemesis) from the Holy Land? I'd fought for him against Napoleon until fate cast me again on the French side, and he seemed to have retained a fondness despite my confusion of alliances. I *am* profoundly likable. "You're English?" I asked the men, more baffled than ever.

"A French Anglophile. Charles Frotté, sir, at your service, with compliments of Sir Sidney." He began sawing at my bonds with a knife large enough to make me hope his energy was matched by precision. Two bodies of renegade gendarmes were sprawled on the floor, and the others had fled. Frotté's companions were reloading their guns. "I'm afraid Martel has gotten away and is no doubt mustering help. We must hurry."

My veins stung as circulation began to return. "I'm afraid I'm not up for running."

"We have a coach."

Frotté had that intensity common to small, wiry men that can be wearying except in an emergency, which was now. My bonds fell away, and one of his confederates worked the latch on the iron collar at the back of my neck. It toppled with a clang, narrowly missing a toe. My boots had disappeared. The magnifying glass had dropped from my neck to the bottom of the tub, and I instinctively snatched it up again, in case I somehow got my gem back. When your income is as uncertain as mine, you don't forget anything that might help preserve your fortune.

Frotté's men half carried me from the cellar. Dark and caped, they looked exactly like the ruffians I'd just escaped from. There's uniformity to the spy trade; its practitioners have far more in common with one another than whichever nation they serve.

A black coach waited in an alley, its hubs almost touching each wall. Two heavily muscled black horses were in harness, snorting and steel-shod, with a restlessness conjured out of a nightmare. Vapor huffed from the animals' nostrils, and a coachman hooded like death hunched on the driver's seat. I looked about. Unfortunately, there was no frilly cabriolet.

"We have to save my wife, too," I finally managed as my wits returned.

"Your wife, Monsieur Gage, has saved *you*. We're off to confer with her." Frotté shoved me into the coach with him, a shotgun and musket leaning against its seats. Two companions hung off the back, and with a crack of the coachman's whip we were off.

"Who the devil—" I began.

"They're running to block us, sir!" the coachman shouted from above.

"Excuse me," said Frotté politely. He picked up the shotgun, leaned out the carriage door, and fired ahead.

There were howls, answering shots, a pop as a bullet hole dilated our coach cabin a foot from my head, and then we bumped over something prone and yelling on the muddy street. I heard a crack of bone. The horses galloped, mud spraying. One of our saviors grunted in pain and fell off the rear of our vehicle with a thud. Our wheels skidded, then held.

There are proposals to pave Paris's streets, but it's a faddish and wayward idea. A dirt lane can be repaired by anyone with a shovel, and swallows its own manure and refuse. Stone cobbles, in contrast, keep horse droppings on display, like one of Nitot's jewels. Dirt isn't clattery like cobbles, and horses can get up a good grip. Paving sounds very smart, but it's as questionable a strategy as steamboats and submarines. Dandies complain of the mud, but that's what boots and planks are for.

I'm nothing if not opinionated, and right more often than I'm listened to.

Another ball punched a hole in our coach, the hole as round as a trollop's lips, its appearance jerking me out of my civic reverie.

The other confederate hanging on our stern fired a pistol in reply. We were being chased.

"Gage, I'm told you're something of a shot?"

"With an American long rifle. Mine, alas, was lost to a dragon in Tripoli."

Frotté raised his eyebrows but decided not to pursue this history. He thrust the musket into my hands. "Can you slow them while I reload the shotgun?"

I don't think I'm so much an expert marksman as a sensible one, so I picked up the piece, leaned out my window, looked back, and considered the situation. At least three men were atop a coach chasing us: the driver and two renegade policemen struggling to reload their own guns. I figured my first shot was critical, since I might not get another. Yet muskets are notoriously inaccurate, and even more so from a bouncing platform.

I could aim for the coachman.

Or, his propulsion.

"Take a corner!" I shouted.

I felt our speed dangerously slacken to make a turn into another twisting lane, our pursuers whooping as they closed the distance. Then we scraped the side of a house, hub squealing, sparks flashing, and with a cry and crack of whip we accelerated again. I leaned farther out. Our foes were making the same turn, their driver swearing. At the moment their horses and harness had made the corner, but the coach had yet to follow, I fired at my biggest target, a lead animal. The horse fell in its harness, dragging its companion sideways, and by doing so the coach crashed where we'd scraped. The frame exploded, and occupants flew. A mess of horse, harness, wheels, and men tumbled into the street.

Frotté pounded my shoulder. "Perfect shot, Gage!"

"It *was* perfect, because it was easiest," I said modestly. I peered back. The coach's disintegration was particularly satisfying after my torture, and no one else seemed to be following. So I flopped against the seat back and watched Frotté finish loading his own gun, the ramrod chattering as our vehicle rattled and he tamped down buckshot.

"Who are those rogues?"

"Renegades, Jacobins, freebooters, and pirates."

That seemed to cover most mischief I could think of. "And now, what of my wife, son, and emerald?"

"We're going to meet her in a house outside the city and set you on a course to retrieve not just the stone, but more treasure than you've ever imagined."

"More treasure?" Was this bunch lunatic, too? "But I've retired."

"Not anymore. You're working for England now."

"*What?*"

"We're your newest friends. Gage, your proper alliance is with Britain. Surely Bonaparte has taught that by now."

"And the cost of this alliance?"

"Breaking the King of Saint-Domingue out of Napoleon's grimmest prison, and solving a mystery that has baffled men for almost three hundred years."

CHAPTER 9

Any man is flattered by a job offer, not stopping to think he's probably being asked to do something the employer prefers not to do himself. So I'd felt for a moment that maybe I was lucky after all, until Frotté made clear he'd saved me for what sounded like certain suicide. We pulled our coach into a barn at a farm outside Paris, hiding it from pursuing police, and came into a stone house with plank floors, hand-hewn beams, and a blaze in a fireplace big enough to roast a goat. Astiza was impatiently waiting, anxious and angry, and our son was nowhere to be seen.

"Where's Harry?"

The trouble with love is that it exaggerates other emotions as well, from lust to disgust. Now she looked at me with an expression of agonized loss and frustrated regret that cut to the quick. Happiness had turned to horror in an instant. I was taken aback, and felt guilt without thinking myself entirely guilty. Imagine a painting of paradise that you could magically step into so that a viewer identifies you with all things sweet and serene. This magic happens to lovers, in lovely places, all the time. Now imagine a painting of hell. It was as if Astiza were studying damnation, and I'd wandered into her view.

It was unfair, and yet why did I, the father, have to ask her where my own son was? I felt the shame that comes from miscalculation, and the emptiness that drops the bottom out of your chest when you lose a child. Yet I wouldn't express my fear, lest I make it true. "Is he still at our hotel?"

Her eyes had the same blaze as the fire. "The renegade gendarmes kidnapped him," she said. "When I ran to our inn, the maid was tied and gagged, and Harry was gone. The girl said men seized him shortly after we set out for Nitot's shop."

My God. I'd lost my son once before to the Barbary pirates, and now this? I mislaid my boy as easily as a bookmark. Being dipped upside down in a tub is nothing compared to the monstrosity of making a child a pawn in a game of nations. I silently cursed Leon Martel. He'd regret not killing me.

Nor could Astiza keep a mother's accusatory tone out of her voice. She'd urged me to be prompt, and I'd procrastinated. She'd had a hunch to stay with Horus, and I'd insisted she come along so I could show how clever I was. She'd wanted to retire to her studies, and I'd wanted to play a hand in the disposition of Louisiana.

The Greeks, I believe, called it hubris.

"And you?" My voice was a little strangled.

"I ran from one band of spies into the hands of another: these men." She was impatient. "Instead of pursuing the French bandits, they've held me here while finding you. Ethan, what if Harry is dead?"

"Not dead, madame," Frotté tried to reassure. "A hostage, surely."

"How can you know that?"

"Because while alive, he can be used to manipulate you. For us to rush a rescue without planning is the one error that would assure he dies. You don't want your boy in a gun battle."

This new spy confirmed to me that Astiza had been rescued by English scoundrels, trading one band of hooligans for another. The worst people pursue me, as persistent as gulls after a fishing smack. I felt sick. I'd lost my son for a piece of green glass.

A stone that would have fed my family forever.

"This is the worst luck," I managed. "The French took our only child?"

"To control you, not to do harm," Frotté reassured.

"And you saved my wife?"

"To manipulate you, again."

At least he was candid. Spies understand spies, and Frotté was confident his foe's motive mirrored his own. Agents depend on one another to be nefarious masters of calculation and the double-cross, lest they all become unemployed. "How?"

"We British need your desperate daring to rescue Toussaint L'Ouverture, the Black Spartacus of Saint-Domingue, from an icy French prison. We believe L'Ouverture may know the truth about the fabled treasure of Montezuma, and that we can use his secrets to find it ourselves. At that point, we can negotiate with Martel for your son and the emerald, ransoming both while keeping a truly important secret out of French hands. You've unwittingly become necessary again, Ethan Gage—the key to France and England."

What bitter honor. "But I was practicing being unnecessary. I should tie strings to my arms. Ethan Gage the puppet! And now you want me to rescue a condemned Negro? How?"

"The plan is to make an escape with a flying machine, a bird-like contraption called a glider."

Ridiculous. "I've flown once before, in a French balloon. It was more terrifying than a ministerial meeting on tax reform, and more disastrous than a mistress wanting to discuss a relationship's future. Astiza fell into the Nile, and I crashed into the sea. I can assure you, men don't have wings for good reason. God's intention is that we stay on the ground."

"We don't have gills, either, but you've journeyed under the sea," Frotté argued. "Yes, yes, we know all about your adventures in Tripoli with Robert Fulton's plunging boat. Come, Gage, we've entered the modern nineteenth century. You're a man of science—no one should be more excited about the future than you."

"My future is a dignified retirement, financed by a gem I went to no small trouble to steal but that has now sundered my family to pieces."

"Martel has restolen your gem as well, which means your retirement is on hold until you can get it back. He's kidnapped your only son and tried to seize your wife. Your only hope is to have something to bargain with, meaning that your chance is alliance with England. Sir Sidney Smith says you're the most expert treasure hunter in the world. Get L'Ouverture, and you can put your life back together again."

He was earnest as an undertaker, but his compliment was nonsense, since despite my best efforts of grubbing in tunnels and tombs I continued to come up penniless. But I *am* susceptible to flattery. I'm also accustomed to fate being frustrating. Nonetheless, I stubbornly shook my head. "You realize that, as usual, I haven't the slightest idea what is really going on."

"At stake is the thwarting of a Bonaparte invasion of England and mastery of the world, which means we're fighting for nothing less than civilization itself. You, I'm afraid, are key."

I had a headache. "I'm a neutral American trying to help negotiate a land purchase with the first consul."

"You're Harry's only chance, my love."

"Astiza, you know I'm as heartbroken as you."

"I'm the mother, Ethan." It was a trump I couldn't match. "Horus is why fate brought us together again, and Horus is all I care about now. We have to do whatever it takes to save him."

"I just wanted to give you peace and security for your studies," I said wearily. "My plan was precisely to avoid dilemmas like this."

She took a breath, summoning back her familiar courage.

"Destiny has other plans for us. This Martel has pointed the way toward a challenge greater than we wanted, and then the gods sent these English spies to give us a slender opportunity. We're being punished for trying to relax, I think, but also given a chance for redemption. The only way we'll get Harry back is to ransom him with what everybody seeks."

Astiza believed in fate, you see, which gave her an equanimity most people lack. It's relaxing not having to blame everything on yourself, though that didn't stop her from silently blaming a good part of this fiasco on me. If I were an ordinary fellow, none of this would have happened, but then again, she'd married me because I wasn't ordinary. For which she probably blamed herself.

Emotions are entirely too complicated.

I turned back to Frotté. "The lost treasure of the Aztecs," I said resignedly.

"Which contains information that must never fall into French hands," he added.

A countryman between two lawyers is like a fish between two cats, Benjamin Franklin once said. The same is true, I think, of an American between two great European powers. For me, it was like choosing between two difficult lovers. The British invented liberty, bequeathed it to the American imagination, and stood for order and predictability. The French hailed the rights of man, had helped win our Revolution, and had better cooking, but had made the devil's bargain called Napoleon for that same order. The two nations hated each other because their idealism was too alike, and Yankee Doodle—me—was caught in the middle.

Ben also said, *The first mistake in public business is the going into it*, but he was no better at following his advice than I am. He played the statesman in Paris, and flirted shamelessly while lecturing me on marriage.

"So where is this treasure, exactly?"

"That is what you must find out. It seemed lost to history until the slave revolt in Saint-Domingue and the reappearance of your emerald. Rumor for years is that black generals have heard legends of its whereabouts and hope to finance their new nation with its rediscovery. Accordingly, Leclerc tricked the Negro Spartacus, L'Ouverture, into capture. He's been locked in the Jura Mountains in hopes he'll disclose the treasure's location in return for his freedom. But he's tight as an oyster, and dying from cold. No one took the legend entirely seriously until you showed up with an actual stone. Now both sides fear the secret will die with him."

"So this Martel thinks that because I had an emerald rumored to come from this treasure, I know the hiding place of the rest as well?"

"Yes. Sidney Smith, in contrast, merely believes you could learn it. L'Ouverture may trust you if you tell him about the emerald and your boy."

"But why did Martel ask me about flying machines?"

"One of the stories is that the Aztecs, or their ancestors, knew how to fly. This treasure reportedly contains representations of their fabulous machines."

"That's nonsense. Why didn't they beat the conquistadors, then?"

"Maybe the secret had been lost, and they only retained fragments. In any event, it doesn't matter if the story is true, it only matters that Martel believes it true. If he could come to Napoleon with flying machines from a fantastic treasure, he would be not only rich, but powerful."

And if Leon Martel had the sense of ordinary men, he'd settle down and enjoy life for what it was, not what it could be. Alas, that's not the way of the ambitious, is it?

"But I'm perfectly useless. I've known nothing of this until now."

"As a neutral American and slightly famous hero, you're the one man who might convince Toussaint L'Ouverture that his best hope is England. Tell him that he can help Haiti secure its freedom from the French by letting us secure the treasure's secrets.

Britain's victory is L'Ouverture's victory, and Britain's defeat is the reenslavement of the oppressed blacks of Saint-Domingue. You have the motivation to break him free from his cage, get him to safety, and learn what he knows."

"*What* motivation?"

"Well, ten percent of any treasure, to start."

"Ten percent! Why not all of it?"

"You'll need British expertise and pluck to pull this off, Gage. The lion's share goes to the Crown and the black rebels, plus expenses. You'll still be a very rich man."

I frowned. "I'm to risk my life for ten percent? A week ago I had an entire emerald and not a care in the world."

"That was a week ago."

"Ethan, don't you see?" Astiza said. "We need to rescue L'Ouverture to get the treasure to trade the secret of flight to return our son."

"Certainly there can be no thought of 'we,' " I grumbled. "I've already dragged you into a dangerous trap." There was no false gallantry here; I was merely afraid I'd misplace her, too.

"This spy's plan is that I slip ahead to L'Ouverture's cell by pretending to the French guards to be his whore who can solicit secrets from him," she said matter-of-factly. "He's notorious for concubines of every color. The French will think I am working for them, and the British for them, while we're really working for Horus."

"You have the mind of a spy, madame," Frotté said admiringly.

"If we don't succeed," I protested, "you'll already be locked in their prison!"

"So you must win, Ethan, in order that Martel is forced to bargain with us and we can get our son back."

Frotté nodded. "And then kill Martel, on ground of your choosing."

CHAPTER 10

So after the robbery of my emerald and the kidnapping of my son, I found myself scaling a prison wall in wretched spring weather at the edge of the Alps. When the woman at the window of the Fortress de Joux opened her mouth to scream, I put my finger to my lips and raised my brows suggestively. It's difficult to appear suave when dangling from a grappling hook above a precipitous drop, laden with equipment and spattered with snow, but I do have practiced charm.

Accordingly, I wasn't surprised when she hesitated in her alarm. An encouraging smile from me, and she bent forward to peer into the blackness at my peculiar situation. Motioning for the damsel to wait, I finished crab-walking to a crenellation and hauled myself over the lip of the wall, muscles shaking. I looked back down. I couldn't see aeronaut George Cayley or his contraption, but I tied off the rope to the stonework and jerked the line as a signal. It jerked back, like a fish on the end of the line.

Well, first things first. Glancing about for sentries (they were huddled inside as promised, the idlers), I danced lightly to the parapet door of the tower I'd just scaled and rapped. The beauty opened it a crack and looked out cautiously. "Monsieur, why were you hanging like a spider outside my window?" She was ripe, rumpled, and Rubenesque. Lord, it's hard to be married.

"Not a spider but a butterfly, my wings opened by the fires of love," I cheerfully lied, a necessity with strange women. I gave her a quick kiss on the cheek, which gave her a start but also a blush of excitement. And yes, I was mindful that my wife was in theory somewhere in the castle below, pretending to be L'Ouverture's long-lost mistress. What can I say? Ours is a unique marriage, and the fate of nations was at stake, not to mention the rescue of brave little Harry. "Prepare yourself, my love, while I haul up a surprise."

"Monsieur," she said, confused but intrigued, "do I know you?"

"If you know longing, if you ache for beauty as I do, if you dream desire, then you know my heart. Please, patience for just minutes more! I will confess all, soon!" And I gently pushed her backward and shut the door. With any luck she was a romantic nitwit who would sleepily confuse me with some other swain who'd given her the eye.

Then I hurried back to the fortress edge and hauled on the rope. Cayley's flying machine, a twenty-foot-long cylinder of sticks and twine wrapped in canvas, as delicate as a veined leaf, came lurching up toward me. I heaved it over to lie on the parapet and cast the rope back down for the inventor to pull himself up. The plan was he'd assemble his flying machine while I rescued the Negro. Assuming either of us was still alive by then, we'd trust our lives to something that was little more than lattice and oiled cotton.

Well, it would be quicker than waiting for the guillotine.

For days, Cayley had tried to assure me he knew what he was doing. "The wings of Daedalus and Icarus need not be mere myth,

Mr. Gage," he told me as we prepared for our mission. "Not only is man destined to fly, he already has."

I had peered upward skeptically. "Not that I've seen."

"The Berber Ibn Firnas launched himself from a mountain near Cordoba with artificial wings in about 875. The monk Eilmer flew from a tower at Malmesbury Abbey just before the Norman Conquest. Leonardo da Vinci sketched flying machines, and the Spaniard Diego Aquilera flew from the highest part of the castle of Coruña del Conde just ten years ago."

"What happened to them all?"

"Oh, they crashed. None died, however. A few broken bones for the early ones and just bruises for Aguilera."

"I suppose that's progress."

"I've studied bird wings and learned from my predecessors' failures, which included the lack of a tail. I believe we can launch from Fort de Joux and glide for miles, far outdistancing any pursuit. All it takes is courage."

"There's a fine line between heroism and idiocy." I'm an expert.

"My test models suggest curved wings provide more lift, just like a bird, and the knack is adjusting the weight. The real problem is stopping. I've yet to duplicate the legs and talons of a raptor."

"So you're proposing a controlled fall down the side of a mountain and a crash at high speed? Just to be clear what we're planning."

"No, I'm proposing that we aim for a lake for our landing."

"Landing where there is no land? End of winter? Freezing water?"

"Frozen water, perhaps. It will take the French entirely by surprise, won't it? Ingenuity against élan, Ethan, that's the English secret. This is just a first step. Someday ordinary men will fly everywhere in luxurious comfort, in enormous padded chairs in floating cabins, attended by beautiful servant girls feeding them courses worthy of a Sunday dinner."

Obviously the man should be packed off to an asylum, but what stopped me from laughing is that while we had a plan to get into L'Ouverture's prison, we didn't have one to get back out. Or, if we did, we could expect the entire angry garrison to hunt us down. The French would spare no effort to recapture the Black Spartacus, and Cayley was the only person with a scheme to give us a head start.

When every other option means imprisonment or execution, lunacy becomes attractive. So I'd signed us on.

Cayley called his artificial bird a glider. "Unfortunately, it can only descend, not ascend," he said.

"I can do that already, by myself."

"But not with the gentleness of a feather, right?"

"Frankly, I don't like falling at all."

"It will be like sliding down a banister."

Our strategy was threefold. The glider for escape, I to crack open our prisoner's cell, and Astiza laying the groundwork with womanly charm. L'Ouverture had a reputation as a prodigious womanizer that left me, frankly, a little envious. He'd had black, white, and brown wives and concubines, and Astiza had approached the French commandant by posing as one of these. She suggested to the French that she might solicit treasure secrets with warmth where cold wouldn't do, seducing L'Ouverture for his secrets in return for a share of any treasure. She'd fled the war-torn tropic colony and was trying to make her way in cruel France, she explained.

I wasn't entirely happy at her calm confidence in being able to pull this charade off. The less innocent a man is, the more innocent he hopes his wife will be. But I knew better than anyone just how irresistible Astiza could be when she put her mind to it. I was sending her into the lion's den and hoping she could persuade L'Ouverture to join our lunatic escape without too many objections. Worse, I knew she'd likely achieve the coup. She'd be seductive and ruthless, persuasive but distant, winsome but steely, with hardly an extra breath. Women are by natural law inferior, Napoleon insists, except that every time I meet one I'm forced to doubt the truth of his maxim.

We had two reasons for this seduction. One was that Astiza as pretend mistress could demand that the viewing port into Toussaint's cell be closed for conjugal privacy, giving me time to break out L'Ouverture from the roof. The other was to alert the imprisoned general that he was about to be rescued and to prepare him for being hoisted through a hole and catapulted into space. There'd be no time for debate. We'd flee across the castle battlements and use Cayley and his flying machine to meet Frotté and his mix of spies where they waited in a snowy meadow. Then we'd flee to the Swiss border and onward down the Rhine to the North Sea and Britain.

Or such was the plan.

"How many can this flying machine carry?" I'd asked Cayley.

"By my calculations, three," the inventor had replied.

"I count four." Gambling gives one familiarity with arithmetic.

"One of you will surely be dead by the time you launch," Frotté pointed out. "And we don't have time to invent a bigger flying machine."

He had a point. The only thing worse than our scheme was doing nothing at all.

The first problem I must overcome was that the only way out of our prisoner's cell was an overhead skylight, bare of glass but grilled with stout iron bars.

"It will take me until Easter to saw through them," I'd objected. That holiday was four days after our planned assault.

"English science has the answer, Ethan," Frotté assured. Why a French-born spy was so enamored of English ingenuity was unclear, though I suspected it had something to do with the payments he received from Sir Sidney Smith. Or perhaps it was my own reputation. I am, after all, a savant of sorts, an electrician, antiquarian, marksman, and expert in plunging boats.

But first I had to keep the girl in the window quiet. We hadn't predicted that I'd encounter a sentry of such beauty, a woman as fair and encapsulated as Rapunzel, anxiously awaiting rendezvous with me, a married man. I was entirely too civilized to simply bludgeon the girl insensible, and even if I'd wanted to be unfaithful, I didn't have the time. What to do? While Cayley climbed, I tapped on the maiden's door again.

Astiza, I was fairly certain, was meanwhile waiting impatiently in L'Ouverture's cell below.

The lovely answered, wrapped in a cloak artfully opened just enough to suggest there was nothing underneath. Since I had turned my back, she'd built up a little fire in her chamber hearth and pinched her cheeks to give them color. She grasped and pulled on me. "Come inside before you wither."

No chance of that. "I'm glad you keep a careful watch."

"It's Papa who watches *me*. You're so clever to come up the wall."

Was she the commandant's daughter? And did her lack of astonishment mean suitors were reliably persistent? Well, to look at her I could see why. She enjoyed the attention, too, the minx.

"It's Papa I worry about," I whispered. "I saw a shadow on a distant parapet and worry it might be a soldier gone to alert your father."

Her eyes grew wide with alarm.

"The safest thing to do is pretend you're fast asleep while I wait and watch. It's imperative that you don't stir an inch, no matter what noises you hear. Now, when all is quiet—if no alarm is sounded—I will come to you later. Let's give it an hour, to be safe. Will you wait for me, my pretty?"

She nodded, excited at the promise of sexual skullduggery. Thank God this wasn't my daughter, and thank God I so far had no daughters to police, since girls sound like a positive plague to raise and govern. I wouldn't let a man like me within five hundred yards of a daughter. "Wait for me in bed. Not a sound, now!"

"How gallant you are!" The cloak slipped from one shoulder as she closed her tower door. I peeked as far as I could, glimpsing a swell of a breast, and then congratulated myself on my own rectitude for not following instinct and wrecking our mission. As a husband, I am a model of restraint.

Yes. Onward to Astiza and L'Ouverture, waiting in his cell.

CHAPTER II

We live in an age of science, modernity, change, and odd invention. It's hard even to keep up. I was assaulting a castle because French and British lunatics thought it might be possible to flap around like birds, upending military strategy and everyday experience. Dangerous missions are often inspired by impossible ideas instead of sensible ones, and the revolutionary fervor that gave rise to notions such as equality have also uncorked the dreams of every tinkerer in Europe and America. Britain leads the world in discovery and experimentation, and I was told the English had come up with scientific sorcery that would make quick work of the iron grill above L'Ouverture's cell.

"It's carbon dioxide squeezed at 870 pounds per square inch," Frotté explained as we prepared for the mission to break the prisoner out.

"Carbon what?"

"It's a component of air," said Cayley, the thirty-year-old

lunatic who dreamed of flying. He looked the part of inventor, with high forehead, long nose, lip pursed in contemplation, and inquisitive eyes. He seemed as puzzled by my presence as I was by his. "The chemist Priestley published a paper before we were born on how dripping oil of vitriol on chalk can produce the gas in pure form."

"I think I missed that one."

"If you condense the resulting carbon dioxide tight enough, it liquefies. Expose it to air again and the liquid flashes into gas. Evaporation turns the carbon dioxide into a snow with a temperature more than a hundred degrees below zero."

"I can scarcely conceive of more useless information." Who cares what air is made of?

"We're going to give you a canister of it to release on the bars," Frotté explained. "The iron will go brittle from the cold, and a sharp blow with a chisel should snap it like an icicle. You'll punch through to L'Ouverture in seconds."

"See what science is for?" Cayley added.

"I'm something of an expert on electricity myself. I've used it to fry my enemies, find ancient hiding places, and make the nipples of ladies hard during private demonstrations."

They ignored this. "The only drawback is that you'll be carrying a carbon dioxide bomb of such extreme pressure that it could explode, ripping apart your torso and instantly freezing your guts," cautioned Frotté. "The result would be startling and painful."

"Not to mention fatal."

"Which means it's best to be careful," added Cayley unnecessarily.

"Why doesn't one of *you* carry it?"

"Because you've the incentive to rescue your wife, while George here will be busy with his flying machine," said Frotté. "There's no room for me, so I'll organize the horses. Thanks to your emerald, fate has provided us with the hero of Acre and Tripoli for a most truly dangerous part." He hoped flattery would give me spine.

"It *was* my emerald. Now that damned French policeman has it."

"Once you know all of L'Ouverture's secrets, imagine what you can bargain for!"

With those words in my ear, I scuttled across the castle roof. There was a flat parapet following the walls, towers poking up here and there. The center of the castle was a series of barrel-arched stone vaults over the cells. I'd been briefed on the location of L'Ouverture, and faint light emanated from a hole in the center of his vault. Across the hole were iron bars, and down it, I hoped, were the people I was to break from prison.

"Astiza!" I hissed.

"Here, Ethan."

"Thank goodness. He hasn't molested you, has he?"

"He's so old and sick he can barely stand. Please hurry!"

"Was it hard to have them let you in?"

"The French are bored," she said impatiently. "They found the idea of seducing him for secrets quite amusing. They're probably listening for sounds of love."

I pulled out the canister. "Is L'Ouverture ready?"

"Not really. He thinks us quite mad."

"Well, he hasn't lost his judgment, then."

"The guards are suspicious. Stop talking and act."

"Moan to buy us time." Women are good at noises.

The bars formed a cross, meaning I had to break the rods in four places to get my wife and the black general out of their hole. I held the cylinder, used my gloved hands to loosen a screw cap the English had devised, and readied the spout over one of the bars. "Stand back while I release this," I warned.

A lever freed a cork the final way and something—I suppose it was liquefied carbon dioxide—gushed out, flashing into white snow as promised. I dunked what Frotté had called "dried ice" on the point where an iron rod jutted from the masonry. Snow and steam swirled upward. Then I took my chisel and hammer and struck a blow where I'd frozen the iron. The bar snapped with a ring, surprising me with its glasslike fragility. Maybe this would truly work.

It's clever being a savant, but noisy, too. I glanced about. No sentry yet.

I repeated the operation on the next bar, and the next.

A prison guard, alerted by the noise, pounded on the cell door below. "Mademoiselle?"

"Please, we are busy!" Astiza protested, feigning breathlessness.

"On the fourth blow, the grill will fall inward. Try to catch it," I reminded. I froze the final bar and got ready to swing, but what I hadn't counted on was that the fourth rod snapped all on its own from the weight of the grill, and dropped before I could even tap it.

It bonged like a bell on the floor below and I winced.

"What is going on?" the guard demanded.

"Games," Astiza called, as if impatient at his interruption. "Do you know nothing of love?"

I poked my head down into L'Ouverture's prison. It was a rather generous thirty by twelve feet, with a fireplace on one wall, a door at one end, and a narrow bed with rude blankets. A coal-dark face looked up from the bed in amazement, the bright white of his eyes the most arresting feature in the gloom. L'Ouverture looked thin, ill, and rather homely, with graying hair, thick lips, sunken cheeks, and thin limbs. This was a notorious womanizer? The fatalism of his gaze was disconcerting. He looked up at my head, framed in the skylight, as if I were some kind of angel, but not of mercy. Rather, the angel of long-wished-for death.

More guards pounded on the cell door. "Mademoiselle? Is he abusing you?"

"How can I finish my interview with all this knocking, you

idiots," my wife snapped. "Go away and give us privacy! We're playing a game."

I dropped a rope into the cell. "Astiza, use the bed to block the door. Toussaint, tie this under your arms."

"Ethan, he's too sick to move."

"Then *you* move him."

"No man goes before a lady," the black general said, his voice deep but raw. He coughed, horribly. Damnation, he *was* feeble! He stood as if arthritic, grabbed his bed, and manfully dragged it to the wooden cell door to barricade it. "Your wife—whom I have not touched, monsieur—goes first."

L'Ouverture was the first gentleman I'd encountered in some time.

And no time to argue! She expertly tied a noose (we'd practiced), slipped it under her arms, and I leaned back against the bricks of the barrel roof and heaved her up. Being much lighter than a man, in seconds she was up and beside me, giving me a quick kiss and glancing about as warily as a sparrow. Her eyes were bright, her smile crooked. She was enjoying this, I realized.

No wonder we'd married.

"I'm glad I didn't have to hear you talk your way in."

"You simply let men imagine more than they will ever get."

Women practice that, keeping us constantly befuddled. Now some of those frustrated men were again banging on the door, shouting questions. L'Ouverture limped over to stand beneath the hole. "I am already dying," he called up. "You are rescuing a corpse."

"Not before you help freedom with your secrets. For liberty!" I dropped the rope again. With agonizing slowness he stepped into the noose and lifted it to his chest. I yanked to make it tight. The peephole in the cell door opened. Angry cries now, recriminations from an officer, and the squeal of keys. The French guards were unlocking the barricaded door.

Astiza seized the rope, too. "Pull!"

We hoisted. L'Ouverture spun like a top, ascending to heaven, limp with a curious resignation. Did he somehow foresee his end? Then there was a crash, the door butted in, the bed smashed into splinters, and then a volley of gunshots flashed in the gloom. The Haitian hero's body jerked as it was riddled. Astiza and I looked at each other, horrified.

We dropped the rope in surprise. There was a thud as L'Ouverture's body hit the floor. Had my hopes of rescuing my son died with him? The smoky room filled with soldiers, some of them glancing up at the hole in the roof. The two of us leaned back so as not to be seen. Their muskets were, for the moment, empty.

"Where's his mistress?" one asked.

"On the roof somehow. She has an accomplice. Raise the alarm!" A bell began to clang. "Upstairs, you morons!"

"Time to flee." I grabbed my wife and we sprinted back for the wall where we'd climbed. Cayley had made it up to the parapet there as planned, and had unfolded and assembled his invention behind its crenellation. The glider looked to me a kind of wooden bed frame from which canvas wings jutted, like flaps on the skeleton of a goose. No sturdier than a stack of jackstraws.

He greeted our arrival with relief. "Thank goodness we can go." He glanced past. "Where's the general?"

"Shot trying to escape." I couldn't keep the despair from my voice.

"Then all this was for nothing?"

"Not entirely," Astiza murmured.

I didn't have time to ask her what she meant, because the door opened to the tower room I'd climbed past. My would-be female companion, her hourglass charms on display in a linen shift, stood backlit by revealing candlelight. "Monsieur, what is that bell? Is it time for our rendezvous?"

"No! I told you to wait."

"Ethan?" My wife's tone was understandably suspicious.

"I had to tell her *something* to keep her from crying out."

"Tell her what? That you were going to cheat on your wife?"

"Wife?" the girl asked, realizing another woman was beside me.

"It's not what it seems," I said to both of them.

And now the damsel did scream, screeching for Papa like a fury. Damnation, women are difficult.

Another door from another tower banged open, and more soldiers appeared, their primed muskets tipped with glinting bayonets.

"Time to fly!" Cayley cried. He picked up Astiza, heaved her onto the flimsy frame without apology, and tugged at me. "Lift on the other wing!" We hoisted and climbed up the low crenellated wall at the brink of the castle.

The guards were raising their guns. "They're after the colonel's daughter!" one cried.

I held the glider with one arm, pulled a pistol, and fired, my fist bucking, to throw off their aim. One of them actually went down. I threw the empty gun, making them instinctively duck, and then pulled and fired my other pistol.

"Now, now!" Cayley cried.

There was a volley of muskets, bullets tearing toward us.

Or rather, tearing toward where we'd been.

We'd launched into the abyss.

CHAPTER 12

We hurtled into a black void. There was the sickening sensation of falling, stomach left behind, and then a gust of wind swooped us sideways. Cayley shouted something unintelligible, I clung to the frame, and Astiza was squashed and half smothered between us. Our "goose" felt pregnant with our weight. More shots, the hiss of musket balls, and then we began to glide just above the tips of a downward-sloping comb of mountain pine, jutting like stakes to impale us. I could smell the forest in the wind.

"It works!" Cayley cried.

I waited for his invention to make my son an orphan.

I hate modern times.

Our machine was nothing like the angel wings of an Icarus. Its spine was a pole twenty feet long with a cruciform tail of little wings, like two kites melded at right angles to each other. This appendage, the inventor explained, was to give us balance and direction. The two main canvas wings were more reminiscent of a bat than a bird, thin canvas fabric stretched over a wooden framework like dried skin. Thin cables led from tail and wings to a rectangular framework suspended below the pole. The Englishman had lit a small lamp that hung from the central strut. It would allow our allies (and the French, I thought gloomily) to follow our progress.

Or find our bodies.

The swooping glide was like a sled run; I'd never traveled so fast. Cayley had one cable in his teeth and another in a hand. "Pull your line to the left!" he commanded.

I did so, and the machine leaned, almost spilling us out. Astiza shrieked, sensibly.

Or was that me?

"Not that much!"

I slacked off, groaning. But then he shouted, "Enough!" and we flattened and steadied. We were still descending, but on a long, gentler trajectory. Patches of snow went by beneath us like blurred clouds. The experiment actually worked.

We heard the rip of a cannonball cutting through the air, sounding like tearing fabric, and then the boom of its cannon echoing from the fort. I was impressed they'd gotten even one shot off. We were flying what seemed like fifty times faster than any horse, Fort de Joux's mountain far behind, and a rent in the clouds lit up a palette of grays that showed fields, woodlots, and the lines of road.

Ahead was a lighter gray, the blob of a pond.

No, a lake. It was rapidly growing as we neared it. By Creation, that was more than enough to die in. I tensed all over again.

"George, the ice will be like pavement if it's thick, and we'll drown if it's thin."

"I'm going to aim for the water near shore. The ice will bend like a cushion. Frotté will follow, with dry clothing." His voice was tight, his concentration enormous. The wings of the glider rocked as we flew, gusts bucking us up and then dropping us down. Wind sang in our rigging. I heard gasps and hugged Astiza. Or was that me doing the snuffling?

"It will be like a bird crashing into a window."

"Thin glass, in April." English scientists are unrelentingly optimistic. "However the landing, we've made history, my friends."

I gritted my teeth. "I'm sure they'll put a stone up."

Now we were skimming over ice, the lake growing ever larger and more menacing. A tracery of snow had been blown into patterns, some of it puffed up as we raced just above. Instinctively, we all cried out and braced. Then before I could take breath we slammed onto the surface of the lake, breaking through crust as fragile as frosting and plowing into freezing water. The glider disintegrated into kindling. Canvas wings caught ice floes and floated off. Meanwhile, we heavy humans plunged into black depths. I clutched Astiza, determined to die with her in my arms. The cold was paralyzing.

All was dark. We kicked, looking for the surface. Our heavy winter clothes were like weights, and she pushed away from me to sensibly shed hers.

Then my feet touched something.

A rocky bottom!

I staggered upright, surging through shards of ice and snow to freezing air, throwing off water like a frenzied dog. I could stand, and haul up my wife, and so I did so. "Astiza! Are you all right?"

"Alive." Her eyes mirrored my own shock. "It's so cold it hurts!"

I held her close. "It's shallow," I gasped. "You can walk."

We half waded, half swam, up the pebbled shore.

"Where's George?"

"I think I can salvage it!" he cried from behind us. He was still chest-deep, hauling in pieces of his shattered flying machine.

"Leave it, Cayley! Maybe they'll think we drowned!"

Even an eccentric can discern logic at times. He nodded reluctantly and let the pieces of his prize float away, struggling toward shore himself. The three of us staggered out of the bitter water and up onto a frosty, snow-glazed meadow. The clouds had closed up again, and there were no lights to be seen. We were soaked, the wind was numbing, and we'd survived glider flight only to die of exposure.

"Of all the bollocks-backward schemes I've been involved in, this was the worst," I wheezed, using the anger to warm myself.

"Actually, I'm amazed it worked at all," Cayley confessed. "Too bad it will have to remain a secret, given the necessities of espionage. I think my aerial machine could also benefit from improvement."

"The object of our rescue shot dead, your invention ruined, the three of us on the brink of freezing, and no closer to dealing with Leon Martel for my son than before," I recited, just to make clearer the actual situation. "Astiza, why didn't L'Ouverture climb faster?"

"He was already dying," she said. "Chilled to his marrow and thin as a stalk. You could see death in his eyes. Betrayal and imprisonment had broken his spirit. He didn't look at me as if I were a rescuer, Ethan. He looked at me as a messenger of doom."

"And now our modern Spartacus has been crucified for nothing."

"Not for nothing. For science," Cayley said.

"Yes. How fast can we freeze in place?"

The inventor ignored my skepticism and staggered up a snowy slope. We heard hoofbeats on frozen ground. Cayley waved. "It's Frotté! He's coming with horses and clothes!"

So we might live after all, if the spy brought brandy to light our core. My heart was racing like a hummingbird's wings, trying to keep warm, and I was furious at risking the life of my wife to rescue a man already almost a corpse. "All for nothing," I growled.

"But it wasn't for nothing, Ethan," she whispered while she shuddered.

"What do you mean?"

"I'd time to explain the emerald and the treasure to L'Ouverture, and I could see he understood what I was talking about. His eyes gleamed with hope. Just before you lifted me, he gave a clue."

I saw the spray of snow from the rescuers who would spirit us toward Switzerland. The French, I guessed, were mustering their own cavalry to pursue. "What clue?" I chattered, shaking with cold.

Astiza looked as miserable as I'd ever seen her, but her eyes were bright. "To look for the emeralds in the diamond."

CHAPTER 13

The heat of the Caribbean in June, the beginning of the sultry hurricane season, was like a heavy shroud of sweaty muslin. As the British frigate *Hecate* ghosted into English Harbor on the island of Antigua, sails limp, pitch on deck seams bubbling, tarred rigging hot as a throbbing vein, my wife and I studied what officers called the Graveyard of the Englishman. The sugar isles were colorful hell, they said, a muggy mystery of thick green scrub, iridescent turquoise water, truculent black slaves, and poisonous vapors. A soldier or sailor assigned there was far more likely to die of disease than from a French or Spanish bullet. Europeans went to the sugar isles for one reason and one reason only: to get rich. Then they rushed home before fevers took them, vermin bit, their own Negro maids poisoned them, or a rebel Maroon—an escaped slave—slit their throats.

"The rain comes down like an overturned bucket," Captain Nathaniel Butler warned us, turning the serene harbor into an enclosing net of menace. "The air is alive with insects, and the ground with ants. The groundwater is bad, so you must doctor it with spirits, but in order to drink enough the planters are intoxicated from breakfast to bedtime, and drunkards all. Every English item costs three times what it does in London, and a tropical tempest can knock down a decade's hard labor. Yet just one of these islands produces more wealth than all of Canada. An ambitious man can carve a plantation out of jungle and double his money every year. Sugar, Gage, is white gold. And men die for gold."

"I daresay this is a good hurricane hole," I ventured. English Harbor was surrounded by steep, verdant hills, and the serpentine bay wound back into the island like a rabbit's burrow. A hundred black cannon poked out from various batteries to deter attack. This was the most closely defended graveyard I'd ever seen. "Perhaps a dip in the sea would make it bearable."

"Most unwise," said the ship's surgeon, Thomas Janey, whose bloodletting had hurried two seamen to the burial shroud in our brief passage, a record that kept three more sailors sick at their posts lest Janey get his hands on them. "I know eccentrics like Nelson bathe in buckets of seawater, but all physicians know that too much washing is a sure invitation to consumption, or worse."

"Bonaparte bathes every day."

"Then he is a dead man. I will tell the secret of health in the tropics, Mr. Gage. Keep bathing to a minimum. Wear stout shoes against insect bites. Do not open your windows to poisonous night airs. Fortify your constitution with strong spirits and, if feeling ill, have a physician bleed you profusely. It's little more than common sense. Our race is healthier in England than here, so it stands to reason that to the degree possible, we must dress, eat, and treat our sicknesses like Englishmen."

"But dark-skinned people seem to go around half-naked and feel better for it." My clothes itched. I was sweating so much that Astiza kept her distance. All the Englishmen aboard were equally rank.

"Sin and savagery, sir. Sin and savagery."

It's hard to argue with an expert, but I was reminded of what Napoleon once told me: *Doctors will have more lives to answer for in the next world than even we generals.* Physicians are clever only in that they take credit for any cure and blame any death on the Almighty. Such odds making impresses a gambler like me.

"At least it's beautiful," murmured Astiza, surveying the bay.

"Beautiful? Madam, it is bright, I'll grant you that, but remember it was the Garden that hid the serpent. What you see is the beauty of corruption. No sane white man comes here by choice, except to make his fortune. It is an isle of necessity, as hideous as Jamaica or Martinique."

"Orange flowers." She pointed to trees that spotted the hillside with blossoms. "A sign that I'm getting closer to my son."

O ur transition from a frozen lakeside in the French Alps to the sultry airs of Antigua had been dizzying. Our calamitous but pioneering flight suggested that Leon Martel's babbling about flying machines was not complete nonsense, and aeronaut Cayley was anxious to get back to his English workshop to perfect his designs. We galloped as planned with the spy Frotté to the Swiss cantons of the Helvetic Republic, the spy having purchased our border crossing in advance with English gold. It was odd how slow our escape seemed after flying. How convenient it would be if these dreams really worked, and you could cross the ocean above the pitching sea!

Then north to the German states and the Rhine. Our escape was helped by political preoccupation with the *Reichsdeputationshauptschluss*, or Napoleon's ambitious reorganization of hundreds of Germanic duchies and kingdoms that bordered France. Some three hundred German states were reduced to thirty, disenfranchised petty princes compensated by having their private fortunes enhanced by lands seized from the Church. The compression was instigated by Bonaparte's foreign minister Talleyrand and forced on the reluctant Austrian emperor Francis II as tribute for recent French military victories. It cemented French dominance of the continent and began to draw to a close the thousand-year history of the Holy Roman Empire.

The pope grumbled, but Napoleon had more cannon.

The winners in this reshuffling in theory passed into the French sphere of influence, securing his frontier with new allies. Yet I wondered if the political unification of the industrious Germans was the wisest course for France or Europe. As princelings they were robber barons charging tariffs for passage on the Rhine; as French satellites they were mercenary generals muttering about German nationhood. Princes who are elevated become ambitious, inevitably resenting the master who did the elevating because he didn't promote enough. I wondered if these states would someday turn on Napoleon.

That was in the future. For the present, we fugitives fled down the river from Basel without undue interference because customs and tolling stations were in chaos from political change. We slid along the broad current under sail, sweeps, and rudder, admiring old castles that clung to gorge walls in picturesque ruin. At the Batavian Republic we took ship with the Dutch across the Channel and arrived in London in early May, just two weeks before the Peace of Amiens ended and war resumed between Britain and France.

London was a city of a million people, larger than Paris and even muddier and more chaotic. Here England's naval power was apparent. The masts on the Thames formed a forest thick as Sherwood. Lighters crawled between larger vessels like water bugs, casks rolled on quays with constant thunder, and press gangs swept up sailors for His Majesty's navy with the brutal efficiency of slavers. The crush of street traffic made it impossible to get anywhere, banks were grander than churches, and the extremes of wealth and poverty were more grotesque than in revolutionary France. Winding alleys were jammed with beggars, thieves, whores, and drunkards. My instinct was to hunt for a card game and brothel, but then remembered I was married and long since reformed.

London was also glorious, its steeples and domes catching the spring sun now that wind had blown away the worst of the winter's coal and wood smoke. If the rims of carriage wheels were brown with shit and splatter, the hubs shone under the constant polishing of legions of footmen. If gutters were full of trash, windows gleamed like diamonds after polishing by indentured Irish girls. If the piers stank of tide, fish, and sewage, theaters and hotels were scented with perfume, flowers, and tobacco. The counting houses were a babble of languages, and there was money from the markets of empire, colonies counted like chips in a game. Britain could wage war forever.

Napoleon, I thought, should have kept the peace.

We met Sir Sidney Smith at Somerset House, the new government ministry built on the shore of the Thames. Its grandeur was a symbolic choice, a union between water and land, and the building was so intimate with the tide that arches gave entry to boats beneath its stone promenade. You could walk to its chambers or row to them; we walked from the rooming house we'd taken after being rowed ashore from our Dutch ship.

The edifice reflected the growth of the British bureaucracy under the pressure of war and empire, both in ambition and its half finish. Recent combat had robbed the taxes needed to complete this architectural elephant. Smith, however, had secured for our meeting a recently finished room overlooking the Thames, still smelling of paint and lacquer, warmed by a low coal fire, and lit by spring sunlight that played peekaboo through clouds to the south. Cradled in one corner was a globe a meter in diameter to keep track of world domination. There were crossed claymore swords, tea sets from China, otter pelts from the Northwest Coast, and wooden war clubs from Pacific isles. We entered exhausted from escape and travel and at the same time impatient to set out after our son.

"Ethan Gage! At last we are allies again!" The newly appointed lord had the smile of a Cairo rug salesman. "And the lovely Astiza is your bride? Who said endings can't be happy? You look radiant, my dear."

Well, that was friendlier than Napoleon. Smith and I had been doughty comrades in arms at the siege of Acre, and he remembered my wife's courage.

"I'm flushed with worry over the fate of my son," she coolly replied. "My husband attracts the worst kind of people." It was clear from her tone that she wasn't exempting Smith from this assessment. Frankly, our lives had been at a boil since meeting him in Palestine, and while we needed British help, she feared Sir Sidney would only add to the heat.

"And if we were truly at a happy end I'd be a retired country gentleman in America," I added grumpily. "I've had quite enough adventuring and planned to settle down, Sir Sidney, but it never seems to happen."

"But that's because of Napoleon and Leon Martel, no?" Smith was never one to be rattled by discontent. "I'm trying to save you from them." He was still fit and handsome, the kind of swashbuckling adventurer who'd built the British empire. Books about his exploits have made women swoon and men jealous, and now he could call himself a lord. I can't say I envied his having to sit through debates in Parliament, but I did think, my emerald gone, that too many of the men I meet seem to do better than me. In a better mood I might have asked for friendly advice, but instead I wanted to puncture his good cheer.

"Fort de Joux was a fiasco," I said.

"I'd say your escape was a credit to British pluck and engineering, thanks to the genius of George Cayley and Joseph Priestly. And you never give yourself enough credit for your own success,

Ethan. It's not every father who would leap off a castle for his son." The man chugged ahead like a machine. "That scoundrel Martel is a skunk of a schemer, but you're with the right side now. And you *were* saved, by my own Charles Frotté. It should be in the papers, but for the moment we need secrecy."

"Saved to play a role in English intrigue and skullduggery?"

"Skullduggery!" He laughed. "Ethan, I am in Parliament! We statesmen are not even supposed to have knowledge of that word. No, no, not skullduggery. Alliance against the worst Bonapartist tyranny and intimidation. The man has not kept a single precept of the Treaty of Amiens."

"Nor has England." Thanks to my role as go-between, I got to hear the same complaints from both sides. Being a statesman can be as tiresome as refereeing quarreling children.

"Napoleon has betrayed every revolutionary ideal, set himself up as military dictator, aspires to dominate Germany and Italy, and plots invasion against your own nation's Mother Country. He's attempting to reinstitute slavery in Saint-Domingue against every precept of his own nation's declaration of rights, and steal an ancient treasure he has no rights to that could leave us defenseless. No one should see through his hypocrisy better than you. Ours is a noble league, you and I. A league against brutal Caesar, just as at Acre! We're a bulwark against tyranny."

I first met Smith when he helped defend the Ottoman city of Acre against Napoleon in 1799. The English captain was handsome, dashing, energetic, brave, ambitious, vain, and more intelligent than almost any officer he encountered, which meant he was thoroughly detested by most of his naval peers. His knighthood had come from service to the king of Sweden, and his escape from a Parisian prison, with the aid of women he'd wooed, had all the elements to make him celebrated. Bonaparte had railed at his success. The English, meanwhile, were never quite certain if he was a genius or merely odd, and so stuck him in Parliament, where he'd be at home in either event.

THE EMERALD STORM · 87

"I've taken up with Napoleon in a way," I confessed. "As an American I'm not really sure which side I'm supposed to be on."

"Expediency, Ethan, expediency. Yes, I've heard of your work on negotiations over Louisiana. You're clever as a fox, but then so is Frotté here, who somehow draws payments from half a dozen governments at once. You're both rascals but useful rascals, and now your interests are aligned with mine. Is that not so, Astiza?"

"Only because the French have kidnapped my young son," she said. Women have a formidable single-mindedness when it comes to children.

"And the English are going to help you get him back." Smith beamed.

She was skeptical, but I was of the mind we needed whatever help we could get. "See here, Sir Sidney, I agree that ours is an alliance of convenience," I said. "I was simply trying to sell a jewel when a renegade secret policeman stole it, kidnapped my son, Horus, and demanded secrets I don't have. We've no idea where Martel is, or what to tell him if we find him. Nor am I entirely clear what he really wants."

"He wants to conquer England. Have some tea, please, and I'll tell you more of what I know."

We sat around a side table as the service was set, oil paintings of stern-looking dead Englishmen looking down on us as if in judgment from a secular Sistine Chapel. Life for the upper class is constantly trying to live up to the standards of ancestors who never seemed to have had a good time. Out the windows, the Thames through the wavy glass was a parade of watery commerce, sails slipping by like bird wings.

"First of all, Leon Martel is a scoundrel," Smith began. "He was an underworld boss of some sort—the rumor is he turned country girls to prostitution and orphan boys to pickpockets—when he decided to join Bonaparte's new secret police rather than risk being caught by them. His allegiance is to himself, and he reportedly had hopes he could succeed Fouché someday as police minister, either through promotion or betrayal. Instead, he's now found himself out of the police and suspect to his fellow criminals as turncoat and informer, so he's extorting people like you and shopkeepers like the jeweler Nitot. He's made a close study of torture and uses it on people who cross him. He's also a coward; he was drafted into the early French Revolutionary armies and deserted."

"A man who makes anyone else look good," I summarized, glancing at my wife. Those of us with flaws are encouraged by such comparisons.

"As the two of you know as well as anyone," Smith went on, "England is a nation with a powerful navy. By the end of this year we'll have seventy-five ships of the line and hundreds of frigates, while France has but forty-seven battleships. We hear nineteen are being built, and we must always fear alliance between Bonaparte and Spain. Still, our confidence in our navy is high."

Indeed. The English seemed to win almost every sea fight they picked.

"However, we have a relatively weak army. We believe our soldiers are the finest in the world, but they are relatively few and spread over a large empire. If Bonaparte can get a hundred and fifty thousand men across the Channel, which our spies tell us he intends, London will fall. There will be an eternal reign of terror."

I was of a mind that London cuisine could benefit from a French invasion, and that a glass of wine in late afternoon was preferable to a pot of tea, but I kept such subversion to myself. The English would die like lions to defend boiled mutton and dark beer.

"That means the English Channel is key," Smith went on. "If Napoleon can control it, even for a fortnight, he could land an army and conquer our kingdom. He might achieve passage with a decisive naval victory, but we believe that unlikely. He might lure our ships away, but I hope Nelson is too clever for that. Then there's the chance of strange new machines of war—yes, I've heard of Fulton and his plunging boat, or submarine—but it takes time to perfect new inventions. Or Bonaparte could take to the air."

"Ethan and I have been in a balloon," Astiza said.

"You never quite got all the way *in* the balloon," I amended. I still had nightmares of her fall.

"I remember," Smith said. His ship had rescued me when I crashed in the Mediterranean. "But balloons can be shot down, and are slow and victim to the vagaries of the wind. Cayley's glider only descends. What if such a craft could go up as well as down, and travel exactly where you pointed it? What if men could fly like hawks, wheeling and plunging and sending down bombs from heaven?"

"A ghastly idea," I said. "Unfair, to boot. Thank God no one's close to doing it. I tried Cayley's contraption, and I can assure you, Sir Sidney, if you can get Napoleon into something like *that*, your war is all but won. He'll plunge like a shotgunned sparrow." And yet Mexico's Aztecs had apparently made a golden replica of just such a device, putting me in this predicament. There's something to be said for conservatism, where nothing ever changes.

"George Cayley is just at the beginning of his experiments," Smith said mildly. "There is, however, an earlier civilization rumored to have mastered the art of flight, or at least to have produced models that look like flying machines. The speculation is that they not only enjoyed a controlled descent, but an ascent as well."

"You mean the Aztecs. But how? What could make that web of sticks go upward?"

"We've no idea. A steam engine, perhaps? You yourself, Gage, are reputed to be somewhat of an electrician, a master of lightning. Perhaps that mysterious force can somehow drive an aerial craft. Mechanicians like Fulton and Watt are coming up with all kinds of peculiar ideas. In any event, the ancients were clever and might have had far better understanding of flight than we do. If the French could learn from an earlier civilization, they might swoop ahead of us and descend on our fleet like vultures."

"Earlier civilization?"

"So the stories go. The recent notion that those in the future might know more than those in the past, or that the present age is the equal or better than our origins, is very new. For most of history, people believed the ancients knew more than us. The Aztec empire, Mr. Gage, believed it learned the arts of civilization from its gods, and is rumored to have immortalized the designs of their god's flying machines in the gold and jewels of lost treasures. If the treasure of Montezuma could be found, and provides a model for flight, such a discovery might turn the tide of the war. The Channel could be leaped. That is what Leon Martel has heard, and that is what he's after in the hoard."

"But from Indians?"

"You understand better than anyone that the world has lost secrets in deep places. The pyramids? Mythic Norse artifacts on the American frontier? Greek superweapons?"

I had to give him the point. Our planet is a lot stranger than most people are willing to admit. I'd found a number of clever oddities in my time and had nearly died trying to harness them. Clever races or supermen seemed to be mucking about long before our own culture got started, and it wouldn't surprise me if they flew, as well.

"We know the Caribbean is littered with the wrecks of Spanish treasure ships," Smith continued, breaking into my thoughts. "In the century after 1550, as many as six hundred such vessels sank, each bearing an average of four to eight million pesos. It says something of the wealth of Mexico and Peru that even with such losses, enough survived that Spain became the richest kingdom in Christendom. Does Montezuma's treasure exist? Was it lost, recovered, and finally rehidden? Who knows? But even if Martel's theory is improbable, the barest possibility makes it imperative he is stopped. Empires are at stake. A true flying machine could tip the balance of power in an instant. Imagine a regiment of French cavalry mounted on the equivalent of flying carpets, swooping down the Thames like Valkyries."

As I've said, Smith was barking mad, not to mention having the habit of mixing metaphors. "You enlisted me because you seriously fear Valkyries?"

"We enlisted you, Ethan, in hopes you could get L'Ouverture to tell us where the treasure is, so we can lay claim to them."

"The French, alas, filled him full of holes." The death of the Black Spartacus had been reported in the newspapers, but the French blamed L'Ouverture's end on disease, not a failed escape attempt. "He was dying anyway, but they shot him as we hoisted him."

"Barbarians. So . . . did he give you any clue?"

I hesitated. Did we want to share what little bargaining we had with the greedy British? Astiza, a mother, didn't hesitate.

"He said the emeralds are in the diamond, but we don't know what that means," she spoke up. "Please, share that with Leon Martel and get our son back, Sir Sidney. We don't care about this treasure of Montezuma. You can follow Martel when he goes looking for it and take it away from him then. We just want to get our boy and go home."

And where did she imagine home was? I wondered. Would she follow me to a new one in America, after I'd helped lose our son?

Smith shook his head, sympathetic but stern. "Absolutely not. We don't share secrets with the enemy, Mrs. Gage, and have no doubt, Leon Martel is your enemy. Moreover, he's not easily contacted. In anticipation of war, he's already crossed the ocean with Horus before he could be stopped by the British navy."

"Crossed the ocean!"

"And not with Napoleon's consent, I suspect. Martel's a renegade, operating on his own, so far as we know. He rowed out to a ship bound for Saint-Domingue during a brewing storm, on the pretense of visiting a friend. When the gale came, the captain was forced to weigh anchor and sail to gain sea room, taking Martel and your son with him. Presumably, the villain has arrived in the embattled colony. We're also informed that he has relations on the French sugar colony of Martinique. That's the childhood home,

I'm sure you know, of Bonaparte's wife, Joséphine. Martel thinks the treasure is somewhere in the Caribbean, and he's no doubt sending evil minions out to find it, in order to ingratiate himself with the first consul and his family."

I wondered if the French would call me an evil minion if I signed on again with the British. Astiza had given me back Napoleon's little pendant, and I'd secreted it in case we needed to sneak about French possessions. If hung around my neck, it would make a splendid target for a firing squad from either nation.

But what choice did we have but to join Smith? We really knew nothing, and if we were to get my son and emerald back, we either needed a clue to bargain with or the British navy to back up our demands. "What do you want us to do?" I asked resignedly.

"I want you to go to the West Indies, find the treasure before Martel does, and lure him into a trap. At the end you'll get your son, the emerald, ten percent of anything you find, and everlasting fame." He nodded, already victorious in his head.

The West Indies! For many men they were a death sentence. I already knew Napoleon's army was being destroyed by yellow fever and revengeful slaves. "But how?" I asked.

"L'Ouverture is dead, but his successor, General Jean-Jacques Dessalines, fights on in Saint-Domingue. I need you to go to the slave war, Ethan, and find out if the Negroes are hiding the most important golden models in human history. You have an enormous advantage: The French government has no idea it was you and your wife racing across the rooftops of Fortress de Joux. For all Napoleon knows, you're still his go-between with the American negotiators, correct?"

"I told his ministers in Paris that I was taking leave to draw a map of my explorations for Monroe," I conceded. "Then we sneaked off to rescue L'Ouverture."

"That means you can go yourself to the French garrison in Saint-Domingue as an American agent and pretend to be their friend."

Smith was even more devious than me, which is saying something. "But what good will that do?"

"You need to learn their military secrets and then trade them to Dessalines for the secret of the treasure." He said this as if it were simple.

"But won't the French hang us both as spies long before that happens?" Astiza asked. She has impeccable logic.

"Not if you pose as negotiators for Louisiana," Smith said, "and explain you need to inspect the state of the war in Saint-Domingue to report to both the American and French agents whether a sale makes sense. Can France hold the colony, and, if not, is it best that Napoleon get money for New Orleans? All this is true enough. You can pretend you're important, even though you're not."

Astiza thought out loud. "While Ethan poses as a diplomat in Saint-Domingue, I can look for Harry and Martel."

"Exactly. You're double agents, pretending to work for France and America while you really work for England and the slave army. You will pretend to Dessalines that you have been sent by L'Ouverture to find the treasure to finance their new nation. After lying to everyone, you escape and deliver the secret to us, the British." He smiled with the satisfaction of a burrowed fox watching baying hounds thunder past, tongues out and saliva flying.

For Smith, of course, the question was simple. My loyalties were more complicated. I liked France, and the French, if not their henchmen. It had been France that had helped my own country win independence, bankrupting itself in the process, and the French Revolution that bankruptcy precipitated was closer to American ideals than England was. If I could just persuade Bonaparte to return to its precepts, I might be more at home in Paris than London. Yet it was England I needed now, thanks to treacherous Martel. So I must go back to the French in their tropic headquarters in the midst of pestilence? I tried to weigh the odds.

"If I find Harry and the emerald in Saint-Domingue, why would I share anything with you?" I am honest to a fault.

"Because our navy will help you retrieve what must be a remote treasure, since no one's found it. With your ten percent, you'll be the richest man in the United States. Play the spy just once more, Gage, and you'll have the retirement you desire."

Chapter 14

Our safe arrival at the English island colony of Antigua in the Caribbean was something of a miracle, given the tumult that ensued once Britain and France renewed their struggle. I've often pondered the popularity of war, the peculiar eagerness of nations for fleeting glory and insane butchery. Ten thousand deaths, and borders barely change. But the truth is that many people make money off conflict, and nowhere can fortune be made or lost so quickly as at sea. Ships become pawns, and we were captured and then recaptured in the first two weeks of combat. We started our journey on a merchant tub, transferred to a French privateer, and ended on a British frigate.

From London, Astiza and I took the express coach to Portsmouth to sail for the West Indies on the merchant brig *Queen Charlotte* in hopes of getting ahead of trouble. The ship was a regular transatlantic trader that was carrying a cargo of china, furniture, and fabric it would exchange for sugar, molasses, and rum. The Portsmouth Express, however, proved to be a waste, given that we hurried to the city only to wait a week in harbor for favorable winds and, it turned out, the onset of war. Astiza remained in a fever of anxiety about the fate of our son, and easily irritated since we both felt my procrastination in Paris had led to this mess. Like too many married couples, we didn't talk out our resentments, and they festered. I was solicitous, but she remained cool. She was polite, but I was stubborn about admitting blame.

I had to get our boy back. I paced the port, trying to will the wind. Maybe steam engines aren't such a ridiculous idea after all. I still wore my magnifying glass around my neck to confirm the identity of my emerald: no one can say I'm not, in my own way, an optimist. I also still carried that medallion of confidence from Napoleon. Yet I was on no one's side but my own. Switching sides and trusting no one is a wearying place to be. Not only does every man seem a potential enemy, you also get confused about what you stand for. Another thing I plan upon retirement is becoming an unblinking American patriot and giving allegiance to my country's policies, no matter how daft, so I can mix with neighbors who think that I think the thoughts they think I should have, even while I don't have to think very much at all.

We finally set sail on May 18 and began working south to catch the trades off Africa, not knowing that our departure was the first day of renewed conflict. Accordingly, we were captured one week out by the French privateer *Gracieuse*, a brigantine of a dozen guns. A privateer is a pirate made legal with a license, to bring profit to the government that allows its piracy. This particular privateer fired shots off our bow, our captain discharged a single cannon from our stern for honor's sake (taking careful aim at a swell, so as not to annoy the Frenchmen), and our vessel struck its colors without bloodshed. With a French supervisory crew and the English captain comfortably locked in his cabin, our little convoy of two vessels set sail for Brest. I had nightmares of Astiza and me returning to Fortress de Joux not as liberators, but prisoners.

Accordingly, I'd tried to talk our English master out of his hasty surrender. "Can't we make a run for it?" I asked before our capitulation. Our captain was a rheumy-eyed drinker named Greenly, with failing eyesight and a limp he said came from being gnawed by a shark. The mate told me it had actually been caused by dropping a block and tackle on his toes while trying to load cargo in the rain after a night's carousing.

"I judge her faster, Mr. Gage," Greenly opined when I tried to arouse his martial spirit. He squinted at the trim of the French sails. "Better captained, too."

"I'm really not eager to be captured by the French in what may be a frightfully long war," I said. "My wife and I are in a hurry to get our boy back and positively must get to the Caribbean. How about we mount a well-aimed volley as they try to board, and then a sudden turn to knock off their bowsprit and bring down their foremast?" I don't usually feel particularly brave, but the threat of imprisonment stiffens me. I suggested naval tactics I'd learned from a lurid adventure novel. "A predator will back off if stung."

"Will it now? And if you're wrong, and my head is taken off by a cannonball in defense of a cargo I don't own?"

"Surely your employers would compliment your steadfastness. Perhaps with a pension for your widow, if there should be one."

"I admire your ferocity, Gage, but we ain't all of us heroes of Musselmen wars and battles with Red Indians. Surrender is more prudent, since the likelihood is that I'll be swapped for a French captain within a month. Fortunes of war, I'm afraid."

"But who will *we* be swapped for?"

"I've no idea. I can't imagine you'll be seen as useful by either side."

"Ethan, they've got a dozen cannon," Astiza prudently pointed out. "Maybe we can get the *French* to send us to Martel and Saint-Domingue." As I've said, she's practical and clever. "After all, they may think you're still working for them. You have the pendant."

"Working for them from an English ship? And if the daughter of Fort de Joux or her father gets another look at me, might I not be hanging outside her window permanently?" My pessimism about capture, and women, is justified. No man is friendlier than me, or accumulates more enemies.

"You can tell the French sailors humorous stories about Napoleon, and pretend you're an American diplomat eager to go to Saint-Domingue," she coaxed.

"I *am* an American diplomat eager to go to Saint-Domingue. Bonaparte, however, is not particularly amusing."

"I'll flirt with the captain and persuade him we were saved by his privateer. He will be our liberator, not our captor, and will be flattered to send us on our way."

I was dubious, fearing that if we persuaded the French we were significant, they'd be even likelier to hold us in case we could be sold to one side or the other.

Fortunately, we didn't have to test Astiza's plan, because our captivity was brief. The beginning of war had unleashed a flurry of prize-hungry captains on both sides, and two days later, the British frigate *Hecate* intercepted and recaptured the *Queen Charlotte* and took *Gracieuse* as well. Fortunes of war, indeed, and now our captain's pusillanimity seemed prudent. Maybe Greenly wasn't an idiot after all.

The French privateer was sailed with a prize crew for England while our merchant brig and navy frigate set off again for the West Indies. I talked our way onto the faster warship by promising to tell tales of my own adventures. That offer didn't seem to excite anyone, but the British officers gazed at my wife as a miracle of femininity. Adventurers never plan it, but it's actually quite useful having a woman along. A damsel can distract an enemy, disarm a tyrant, and disable the angry. The British were entranced by Astiza's stories about the gods of the pyramids, though the truth is she could have talked about insurance premiums and still held these female-starved officers in thrall.

She was useful for another reason. I retained Napoleon's gold N and circlet of laurel wreath, but didn't think the British navy would be amused by this favor. A ship is close quarters, and my trinket might be discovered. So I gave it back to Astiza to hold on her own body, reasoning correctly she'd be given privacy as a woman that I wouldn't have.

"Is it risky to keep it at all?" she whispered.

"We keep volleying from side to side. You never know."

So she slipped it in her undergarments, and we sailed south-west.

By boarding a warship we traded comfort for speed. The frigate was jammed with men needed primarily for the rare battle; discipline was harsh and cruelty routine. We were mustered to see three floggings in six weeks—for thieving food, talking back to a midshipman of thirteen, and sleeping on watch—and that was considered a relatively mild exercise of discipline. The beatings broke the men instead of reforming them, but the ship's company couldn't imagine a society not based on physical fear. There was also the camaraderie of shared misery and daily salvation in the form of rum. It was pointless to be critical; grimness ruled the world.

There was also gloomy foreboding. Astiza was in the habit of meditating, and while a frigate has little room, space for what she called a prayer chamber was found on the deep orlop deck, private because it was adjacent to the spirit room and guarded by marines to keep sailors away. There was no natural light in her cubby, but her lamp was deemed sufficiently far from the powder magazine so as not to pose a danger. (That room was covered in felt to prevent any stray sparks, and no lamp or candle was ever allowed inside. The dim lamp that sailors saw by shone through a thick glass window built into the magazine wall, lest some idiot blow the entire warship to hell.)

Astiza got her chamber by insisting she must study away from prying male eyes, a desire the officers were sympathetic to. Sailors tracked her movements like dogs entranced by a squirrel.

So, once out of sight, she quietly set up a secret temple to a democratic pantheon of gods that might have gotten us burned in a different century. I didn't want my wife accused of being a heathen, so I stood watch while she lit incense, pulled out little bone and stone idols from Egypt that she carried in a velvet bag, and prayed for the future. Good thing, too, because we were admittedly peculiar. Astiza consulted the Christian pantheon but was considerably more ecumenical about religion than the narrowminded norm. Sailors are a superstitious lot, and I didn't want us pitched overboard. Her allotted chamber was hardly bigger than a confessional, and it was thick with that ship smell the brain remembers for weeks after disembarking: a musty reek of rope, bilgewater, wet wood, hundreds of inadequately washed men, kitchen coal fire, rancid cheese, moldy bread, and, until it ran out in the first month, beer. An Egyptian tomb would have been a cheerier spot, but Astiza needed solitary contemplation the way I need flirtatious conversation.

I explained to any officer who asked that her meditation tended to bring good luck, and that our own rescue by the British was proof. Just to be safe I threw out some additional nonsense about female modesty, piety, contemplation, and Egyptian eccentricity, and the crew generally swallowed it.

I hoped she'd emerge encouraged, but the idyll made her moody and uncommunicative. She looked at me sadly when coming up for air, and I feared she'd fantasized some supernatural message about the loss of our son.

I left her alone as long as I could stand it, but when she stood by the windward rail that night—by now the climate had warmed, and the sky was thick with stars—I finally approached to talk things through, which I should have done long before.

"Is Harry all right?" I asked.

She was a kind of witch, but a good one, and I'd come to trust in her witchcraft. I believed she could see distant places, and the future, too.

She didn't answer for a long time, so I touched her elbow, as tentative as a stranger. She twitched.

Finally she turned.

"What if it was a mistake to marry?" Her tone was hollow.

No oath or insult could be more devastating. I recoiled, as if from a blow. "Surely you can't mean that." Astiza was all I wanted or needed, and to suggest fate didn't want us together was like a stab to the heart.

"Not for you, Ethan," she said sadly. "Not even for us. But for our son."

"What did you see? Is he sick?"

"No. No . . ." She sighed. "Is the future fixed?"

"Certainly not! Certainly fixable!" I said so even though I secretly shared her dread about fate. "My God, what is it?"

She shook her head. "Nothing specific. Just a feeling of a severe test ahead, a test that might separate us instead of unite us. Danger when we're together, as if we draw trouble."

"But that's not true. We escape it. You know we have, a dozen times. We must run down this French thief Martel. Once we do, then we have the rest of our lives for quiet happiness. That's what I took the emerald for. Us."

"I know that, Ethan. Fate is strange." She looked over the waves. "I'm so far from home."

I took her in my arms. "We're *going* home. You'll see."

CHAPTER 15

And so we came to the isle of white gold and black labor, air thick with flower scent and rot. The Caribbean was hell, the British promised, but hell with a seductress's allure. Silken air, dazzling color, and a sweaty leisure supported by slaves in decadence that would do Romans proud, overlain by ominous pestilence.

Coming ashore at English Harbor was our first introduction to what seemed, after a century and a half of slavery, an African isle. There were whites aplenty, looking half suffocated in heavy red military uniforms. They shouted orders amid the clamor of squealing blocks and rasping saws as the base hurried toward war. But fully three-quarters of the men we saw plaiting rope, mending sail, forging iron, coopering barrels, and standing sentry were black. Some were slaves, and others skilled freemen who gleamed in the heat and worked with a cheerful energy the enervated Europeans lacked. They were at home in this climate, and we were not.

The officer who had been sent to conduct Astiza and me to a

meeting with the island's governor was pink of skin and red of coat, a cheerfully talkative army captain named Henry Dinsdale. The potentate we were to meet was Lord Lovington (a planter born Ralph Payne) who would instruct us further in West Indies strategy and politics. Dinsdale, meanwhile, served as the governor's secretary, liaison with the island's military, and escort to visitors. He was tall, thin, sardonic, and eager to inform, clearly jolted out of boredom by the chance to be a guide to my lovely wife. He bowed to the gracious architecture of her figure with the reverence of a Muslim to Mecca.

"Lovington resides mostly at the new Government House in Saint-John's on the other side of the island," Dinsdale said. "But at the moment he's checking on his plantation at Carlisle. You'll dine with him tomorrow there, and learn something of the islands. Smith's introductory letter got his attention."

Sir Sidney Smith had given us a letter we could show to any British authority who asked for passage to Saint-Domingue, where our son might be, and to help with forged documents to fool the French.

"There are more dark faces here than Tripoli," I remarked. "More than in my nation's new capital between Maryland and Virginia. Even your garrison seems to be made up largely of Negroes."

"You are perceptive," Dinsdale said. "There are only three thousand whites on Antigua, and the slaves outnumber us more than ten to one. Most of the trades are occupied by black and mulatto freemen, and even the bulk of our infantry is black. Our fortunes here rest on sugar, but no white man can survive the fieldwork required to cultivate it. So the island is a Congo."

"You don't fear revolt?"

"We've had half a dozen of them in our history." He glanced at my wife, hoping, I suppose, to thrill her with shock. "We impale, burn, castrate, pour hot wax on lash wounds, and chop off feet." He wiped some perspiration with a handkerchief scented with perfume. "We hang, shoot, manacle, and chase escapees with dogs. It's mercy, because it prevents worse trouble. If you'll pardon my candor, Mrs. Gage."

She looked more composed than us, having been raised in hot Egypt with its own castes. "The world could use more candor, Captain, if it is ever to reform. The first step to correcting the worst is to acknowledge it exists."

He cocked his head, regarding her intelligence as an unexpected and rather alarming curiosity. "No reform is needed. It's no different than mastering a herd of farm animals. Slave and master have come to a rough understanding of each other. Conveniently, the black regiments keep the peace and defend the island; they're the only units that withstand yellow fever. Obedient, too. I'd rather lead a black regiment than a white one. Here, I mean." He fanned himself. "Not in England."

"So you appreciate their sacrifice?" Astiza asked.

He frowned. "There's a natural order in the West Indies, Mrs. Gage. Without the whites, there is no market. Without the blacks, there is no product. The French toyed with upsetting this power structure on Saint-Domingue with wild talk of revolutionary freedoms, and the result has been a massacre of planters and a decade of devastating war. Here, all know their place, which is precisely why Britain is fighting the frogs. The goal is to preserve order. We Antiguans represent, I think, the front line of civilization."

"With whip and chain," Astiza said. My wife is blunt, and I love her for it.

"With class and station. Black freedom, Mrs. Gage? Go see how it works in Africa. It's a hard life the slaves lead, but a safe one if they allow it. No cannibalism. No tribal war. And don't think they don't enslave one another; they came to our slave ships already in chains, led by their own people or the Arabs. Their plantation life is hard, ma'am, but a blessing for them as well. They have a chance to save their own souls from eternal damnation. The pregnant ones are even exempt from flogging. You'll see."

We spent the night in the officer's quarters at English Harbor, shutters flung wide to catch some breeze despite the doctor's warning, and our bed tented by mosquito netting. The plank floors and brick walls were no different than a good hotel in England, except the ceilings were higher and the prints of ships and royalty had more mildew. Tree frogs set up a roar like surf after the sun went down.

The long shady porches were a concession to the climate, however, and before retiring we sat to contemplate a landscape as vivid as an opium dream. Life bent to the sun as it did in Egypt. If this were hell, it was a rather languid and nurturing one, and we sipped punch and watched boats on the water with release mixed with impatience. Somewhere little Harry was waiting, we hoped, and we hoped he was near. There was relief at having successfully crossed the ocean, disquiet that we must journey farther to find our son, restlessness that it took so much time to track him, and apprehension that such a journey would take us to Saint-Domingue, a hellhole of war and torture. Yellow fever had killed the French general; would it kill Astiza, Harry, and me?

Given the climate, we set out for Carlisle before dawn, at the coolest time of day. A black domestic in waistcoat and bloused shirt drove our carriage. Dinsdale sat beside with two pistols and cutlass in his belt and a musket lashed upright beside him like a lamppole. Astiza and I were behind, clutching the broad straw hats we'd been issued as protection against the sky.

The first quarter mile into the forest was like entering ink until the day began to lighten, and even then the jungle made a dark tunnel as we worked our way up a hill to overlook the harbor. Once away from the water the sea breeze completely vanished so that even the dawn air seemed oppressive. But then we cleared the ridge crest, the trees disappeared, and the wind resumed. The morning suddenly felt fresh. Behind us, the crowded bay looked idyllic with its anchored ships. Ahead was a rolling landscape of seemingly endless sugarcane, each hill crowned with a stone windmill, their great sails majestically wheeling. For a while we were quite comfortable, and maybe Antigua wasn't entirely the hell the English claimed.

"The Spanish quite naturally skipped over these small islands and headed for larger Cuba, Hispaniola, Mexico, and Peru," Dinsdale narrated as we clopped along. "The Carib Indians who lived in the Windwards and Leewards were fierce, and their little knobs of green seemingly useless. But then English, French, and Dutch colonists began to pick up these Spanish leftovers and tried everything they could think to survive. First the Caribs and wild pigs were hunted down and exterminated, creating space for farming. When ordinary crops didn't take hold, we attempted tobacco, coffee, cocoa, indigo, ginger, and cotton. And when all of those products failed to compete with Virginia and Brazil, we tried sugar. A ton from every acre!"

"Which made these islands wealthy?" I asked politely.

"So it promised, but wage earners quit the work, and indentured servants fled. The cane fields are hot, dusty, and endless. We finally copied the Portuguese and brought in slaves from Africa. They endured the heat that killed the white man, subsisting on the corn, plantain, beans, and yams that white workers threw away. The blacks consume loblolly, a cornmeal mush, and even maize right from the cob, eating the kernels like animals. The planters are not ungenerous. They give their slaves a tot of rum on Sundays and even meat, if a cow or sheep takes sick. Breadfruit, too, the plant that Bligh was after in Tahiti. And the blacks are rather clever in their own way; they make alcohol called mobby from sweet potatoes, and perino from cassava. They're even allowed to have their own thunderous dances that put our revelry to shame. Yes, we're tolerant here in Antigua. And the Negro is everything the European laborer is not: sociable, adaptable, enduring, kind, domesticated, and disciplined. A white man wants treasure. A black wants a hut."

"You seem quite the student."

"We learn our slaves the way an Englishman learns horses: The Whydahs and the Pawpaws are the most tractable, the Senegalese the brightest, and the Mandingos the gentlest, but they are prone to worry. The Coromantees are courageous and faithful, but they are also stubborn. The Eboes are despondent; they don't last. The Congos and Angolans are good in groups, but stupid individually. All these characteristics are reflected in their pricing. The Negroes are marvelous in their own way. They hardly need clothes or tools. The planters give them a hoe, an ax, and a curved cane knife called a bill, and get ten hours good labor, even with a two-hour break at the hottest time of day."

"And what are the planters doing?"

"Seeing to accounts and organizing amusements, like all rich men."

We were quiet a moment. "Every fortune is built on a crime," Astiza finally said.

Dinsdale wouldn't take offense, which is perhaps why he had the job of squiring visitors around. "And what is yours, sitting high with me in this carriage?" he asked rhetorically. "Bargaining with Bonaparte, from what I hear." Seeing me startled, he continued, "Yes, I've heard of the reports to the governor; little is secret on Antigua." He shrugged. "I'm the son of a landlord in the Midlands, and our vicar there takes heavy rents from the poor to live like a comfortable squire. Not exactly what Jesus preached. Our ships are ruled by the lash and noose, as you've just seen. Our infantry is mostly forbidden to marry, and beaten bloody at the least excuse. France tried to abolish such distinctions and had chaos. Now Napoleon is setting things to right. For the life of me, I don't see why we're fighting him. He's trying to reestablish slavery in Saint-Domingue, which is exactly what needs to be done."

Dinsdale clearly thought himself a realist, but a realist who did not have the imagination for an alternate reality. It's a pessimistic view, but I understand the fear of conservatives. The more I see of the world, the more I believe civilization is a thin varnish on a hulking cabinet of human passions, fears, and cruelties: a dark armoire that hides the truth of our natures, ominously thumping to get out. Our natural barbarism is barely held in check by priests, hangman, and potential humiliation.

"You are not a liberal, Captain," I said mildly.

"I am practical. I study the Gospels, but I live in Antigua."

"Can blacks ever be free?"

"If they are, the economy of sugar is at an end. No freeman can afford to grow it. The former slaves will live in emancipated poverty, on islands dreaded as incubators of disease. No man will ever come to Antigua for pleasure. Only for profit."

"There's no voice for abolition here?" The subject was becoming a heated one in England, I knew. Taking ideas from France, men were agitating for the end of the slave trade, or even the end of slavery entirely. All the revolutionary tumult in the world has brought remarkable notions.

"There are Quakers, who are politely ignored. Parliament, however, is full of dangerously utopian ideas that attack free market values, fostered by comfortable liberals with no sense of reality. West Indies society is one of necessity, Mr. Gage. Send a white regiment here, and as many as nine-tenths are dead in a year of yellow fever. But the blacks are bred to it. Necessity, Mr. Gage, necessity. And don't forget that a tenth of them have managed to win their freedom, thanks to the mercy of their masters. They are the carters, the carpenters, the shepherds, and the fishermen. You're an American, believing in freedom? It's freedom, is it not, for we Antiguans to have the right to develop our own society, in our own way? Freedom to make an honest living, even if it does involve the purchase and nurturing of slaves?"

Dinsdale, clearly, was impervious to irony.

So we bounced along without comment for a while. Astiza and I both sipped some punch of water, lemon, and Madeira. We often had to drink in the humidity, giving our journey a drugged drowsiness even in early morning.

"The windmills make it look like Holland," my wife finally observed. Their great sails were all pointed exactly into the wind, a trick I didn't understand yet, turning with tireless efficiency in the trades. Even at great distance, you could hear the squeal of their gears and rollers.

"There's no waterpower here, and in fact, drought is our biggest enemy. The only way to crush the cane is with the power of the sea breeze."

The sugarcane was like an eight-foot wall on either side of our red dirt road. The sun rose above the stalks and we put on our hats. Then we heard a horn, and another, and another.

"Conch shells," said Dinsdale. "The slaves are being called to work."

Insects began to rise with the sun. We waved and slapped.

"The gnats and mosquitoes are the most constant," Dinsdale said. "At the beaches and in the mangroves you see the land crabs—white, sickly, and hideous. Always wear shoes and stockings against chiggers, which can be agonizing. We also boast woodlice, bedbugs, lizards, and cockroaches that look hatched from lobsters. In the plantation houses the servants keep them at bay, but you'll see field slaves with faces furrowed by cockroach scars. The creatures come at them at night when they sleep on the dirt of their huts. Ants, too, of course, billions of them. Termites. Wasps. Snakes."

"Are you trying to frighten my wife, sir?"

"Certainly not, and I mean no offense. It's simply that England paints a lyrical picture of the planter's existence as a life of leisure, when, in fact, it is one of constant struggle. The spoonful of sugar in a cup of London tea has an epic story behind it. No European understands the real cost of cake."

"You have fire as well, it seems." Astiza was gazing beneath the brow of her wide planter's hat as columns of smoke began to rise from distant fields.

"We burn the fields after harvest. It's the only way to keep down the snakes and rats. We lose a third of our crop to vermin. At Carlisle, they put a bounty on rats—a cob or a crust for each one—and slaves caught thirty-nine thousand of them. Can you imagine? We joked they were breeding the pests. Sugarcane takes fourteen to eighteen months to ripen, and everything is done by hand, not the plow, so we have to keep animal invaders in check. Losing a slave to snakebite is more expensive than losing a horse. We burn the fields to make them safe."

We passed some blacks planting new cane in a harvested field. Their skin glistened in the hot sun, hoes swinging up and down in ceaseless rhythm. Black overseers watched from horseback in the shade of a giant tree left standing for lunchtime shade. Clay jars lined the furrows, but whether the water was for the plants or the planters I didn't know. The men were in loincloths, dust turning them red. The women were naked to the waist, some stooping with babies tied to their backs.

"A white man is lucky to live five years in this climate," Dinsdale said. "But if he does, he can increase his fortune fivefold."

We entered jungle again, a steamy corridor of plants snarled and voluptuous. Flowers erupted like dots of light. The mosquitoes became even more incessant, and we sweated in quiet misery.

"Apply vinegar for the bites," the captain offered.

Then we began passing into lawns, a grand clearing in the forest. At its center was a stately house like a mansion in heaven. The plantation home was wrapped in a cool two-level porch, each window bordered with shutters, the clapboards painted a gay yellow and wicker chairs and hammocks beckoning us to rest. Huge tropical trees surrounded it with shade. A flower garden was a quilt of color, and a stream flowed into an artificial pool. It was an oasis.

"Carlisle mansion," Dinsdale said. "Now you can discuss your real business with the governor."

CHAPTER 16

A chief occupation of the planters of Antigua is dinner, a ceremony occupying three to five hours at the height of the day's heat. Lord and Lady Lovington, corpulent yet dapper in their fine London clothes, greeted us enthusiastically on their shady veranda. Like all colonists, they were eager to hear the latest gossip from London and Paris. Fashion comes to the West Indies six months late, meaning winter costumes arrive just as the tropical summer deepens, but no planter can resist wearing them, everyone sweating without embarrassment.

Our hosts were as amiably tipsy as we from the water purified by wine and rum, imbibed from dawn to dusk to hydrate perspiring bodies. The governor and his wife were in their sixties, successful but not entirely secure; they were political survivors who had reluctantly sided with Prime Minister William Pitt in order to win appointment to a governorship that provided salary and brought them back to island landholdings burdened by debt. The truth was, for every planter who got rich, another went bankrupt, and Lovington returned to Antigua to prevent his plantation from declining into ruin. The jungle, storms, war, and the gyrations of markets were always threatening to destroy what had been built; and dreams of retiring to London were thwarted by the difficulty of managing holdings from thousands of miles away. The constant financial risk of the planter's life gives island gaiety a sharp edge. I knew the demeanor from the swells I'd encountered at gambling tables. They are cocky, but desperate.

To go from the dazzle of the sunlit yard to the dining room was like entering a cave until our eyes adjusted, but once inside we saw a reasonable replica of England. There was a massive mahogany table and sideboards, fine china, heavy cutlery, prints of hunts and battleships, and silk wallpaper spotted with mold. The table legs rested in pans of water.

"Keeps the ants off the meat," Lord Livingston explained, settling into his chair at the head of the table with as much weighty deliberation as starting a day of work. "I daresay if the Garden of Eden had so many bugs, Eve would have spent her time scratching instead of eating apples."

"Governor, what a silly thing to say," his wife scolded.

"I've no doubt Mr. and Mrs. Gage have made that observation on their own, eh? This island grows all things crawling, hopping, creeping, biting, and stinging, and grows them bigger, and faster, than any place civilized man is born." He waved his arm and flies orbited our table. "You boys there, fan faster, will you?" Two young black domestics put a minute of brief energy into waving large palm fronds before going back to their usual desultory pace.

"The island certainly has lush beauty," Astiza offered. "The forest is completely opposite my native Egypt."

"Egypt!" Lord Lovington exclaimed. "Now that's a place I'd like to see. Dry as toast, I hear."

"Even hotter than Antigua," I said.

"Hardly possible, what?" He laughed. "But we have our own

advantages, too. No frosts. No coal fires. Rains in buckets, but stops like turning off a tap. Some good horse racing; maybe you'll have time to see it."

"I think our mission will force us to hurry on," I said.

"Our three-year-old son is in the hands of a renegade French policeman on Saint-Domingue," Astiza explained.

"What? Frogs have your boy?"

"They want to exchange him for a secret," I said. "Trouble is, we don't know what the secret is, and we need to find out."

"That's the most damnable thing I've ever heard. The French! Do you know we held Martinique for a time and were pounding English sense into it when we gave it back in the last peace? Foolish thing to do. Go back and bombard it, I should think."

"What we really need is information and passage," I said.

"Yes, yes. Well, let's have a bite, and then I'll show you the sugar factories, Gage. Plotting strategy, I think, works better after digestion."

Like the room, our feast was a partial replica of England, a ridiculous cornucopia of rich food in limpid heat. There was lamb stew, hot and cold cuts of beef, hot and cold fish, turtle soup, pickles, white bread, ginger sweetmeats, roasted plover and doves, a ham, and slices of pineapple. There were sweet jellies, a bread pudding, cream, coffee, tea, and half a dozen wines and liquors. One servant was dressed like an English butler, his face beaded with perspiration, but other male and female blacks shuttled in and out dressed in secondhand calico and with bare feet. The huge palm fronds continued to fan the flies, while the open windows and doors allowed in not just island breezes but cats, dogs, skittering lizards, and a chicken that pecked at crumbs on the floor and was ignored by all involved.

"This new war is our chance to chase the French out of these islands once and for all," Livingston went on. "The fevers are destroying their troops in Saint-Domingue. Their defeat is God's will, I believe. Punishment for the reign of terror."

"They hope to sell Louisiana to the United States," I said.

"Do they now! To America? And whatever will *you* do with it?"

"President Jefferson estimates it will take a thousand years to settle."

"Let England take it, is my advice. You Americans are having trouble enough governing what you have. Vicious elections, I'm told. Lies, pamphleteering, and demonstrations by the rabble. You'll want the Crown back someday, mark my word."

"We have some loyalists here on the island waiting for that happy day," Lady Lovington added.

"Our independence was confirmed twenty years ago by treaty."

"I'm still correcting mistakes I made forty years ago!" Our host guffawed.

It was five, the shadows lengthening, by the time the governor took us on a tour of his plantation. His wife had offered to entertain Astiza at the house, but she'd demurred, preferring to come with me. I knew why. She found domestic chitchat boring. And after the botched sale of the emerald in Paris, she didn't trust me on my own.

I'd merely picked at my food but still felt bloated in the heat. I was not alone. Three-quarters of the food was sent back untouched, presumably consumed by slaves happy to benefit from European attempts to maintain home customs.

We mounted horses to tour the fields, the epic blue of the sky hazed by field smoke and dust.

"Sugar, Mr. Gage, is the one thing that turns a profit here," the governor said as we rode sedately toward a mill. "Up to eighteen months to grow, excruciatingly difficult to extract, and expensive to ship. What makes it possible is slavery, and the British abolitionists seeking to end the trade are seeking, sir, to end the prosperity of the empire's richest colonies."

"Captain Dinsdale said the same thing."

"It's why the revolt in Saint-Domingue is so worrisome."

"How many slaves do you own?" We were three pale, sweating inspectors white as frosting, touring a dark chocolate of earth and skin.

"Two hundred, and they represent most of my capital. More than my herds, more than my horses, more than my sugar mills, and more than my houses. Even L'Ouverture insisted the freed blacks of Saint-Domingue continue to labor on the plantations. He knew there was no alternative. He needed money to buy arms and powder from America, and the only source of money was sugar. To strip the blacks away would be like dismantling the masts, sails, rigging, cannon, and ballast of a ship. It cannot be done, sir. It cannot be done, for their sake and ours."

We came to the bare crown of a hill. The windmill rose there, its sloping stone walls fifty feet high. Opposite the blades of the mill was a huge timber as long as a mainmast. It led from the axle of the great windmill sails at the top of the tower down to a track in the ground. Now I saw how every tower's blades had been aligned so neatly to the prevailing wind. The timber worked like a great tiller, pushed along the ground so that it turned the mill's top to face the breeze's direction. From within the structure came the great grinding, as cane was fed into the mill's presses to be squeezed of brown juice.

We dismounted and went into the dimness. It was even hotter there, the trade winds not penetrating. Donkeys were led laden into the gloom with the last of the season's harvest, their backs carrying a small mountain of harvested cane weighing more than two hundred pounds. A release of the hemp ropes that secured it, and their burden cascaded onto the mill's floor. Then the cane was fed by the slaves into the gears of the windmill, the juice squirting to be caught in a tin trench below.

It's my habit to be friendly, and I thought I might say something to these sweating laborers, but they ignored us as completely as working ants, their eyes only for their ominous, enormous black overseer in one corner who held a curled whip. The laborers' movements were choreographed by gears and rollers. I couldn't understand what they were saying to each other; their jargon was a broken mix of English and African, with bits of French and Spanish littering as well, all thickly accented.

It nagged at me to try to communicate, to somehow bridge our gulf of humanity, but what could I say? I was observing a brutal workshop from which no hope of deliverance was possible. The quips of we masters—and by the color of my skin I was one of those—were as irrelevant to these slaves as Marie Antoinette's blabbering about baked goods. The French had succeeded in crushing a revolt in Guadalupe inspired by the language of the French and American revolutions, but only by roasting the ring-leaders over open-pit fires like spitted pigs. Liberty was restricted to one color only.

My own country's Constitution says much the same thing: no black man or woman can vote. So I felt inadequate to the heat, stench, and cruelty, a participant in a system I'd no say in inventing. Morality suggested I talk like an abolitionist, but practicality sug-gested I keep my mouth shut. I needed Lovington's cooperation—meaning passage on a ship to the slave revolt in Saint-Domingue—to rescue my son. I cast about for something to say.

I was surprised to see a bright, well-sharpened cutlass hanging near the mill rollers. "You risk giving your workers a weapon?" I finally asked the governor, pointing to the sword.

"It's for the overseer to chop off their arms," he said matter-of-factly. "If they reach too far forward, the rollers catch their fingers and the pressure inexorably draws them all the way in, their heads crushed like melons. I lose valuable property, and a trough of juice is ruined by blood. A one-armed slave, on the other hand, can still be trained to do light chores. I keep the sword burnished to remind them of the danger. Stupid, some of them. Or careless. I let them know there'll be whippings if there is any blood sugar."

"Surely you could invent a safer mechanism," Astiza said.

He was annoyed. "I am not a mechanic, madam."

"Hot work," I said more diplomatically, attempting to change the topic. I felt I was on a tour of Dante's Inferno.

"Bearable for Africans. They're lazy, actually, caring nothing about my profit, no matter how much I exhort them. They don't really want to work at all." He seemed perplexed by this, flicking his riding crop against his own thigh. "Come, I'll show you where it really gets warm."

We walked next door to the boiling house, a rectangular stone building shaped like a barracks. The air above it quivered from the heat within. Inside was a long, shadowy, luridly lit gallery. "Here's the truly hot work, Mr. Gage. Israel there is my most valuable possession, because the boiler man makes or breaks the quality of the sugar."

Five huge copper kettles hung over a trench of glowing charcoal. This Israel, stripped to a loincloth, moved between the steaming pots, ladling the cane juice into the first and biggest, skimming out the impurities that boiled to its top, and then ladling the purified remainder to each smaller pot in turn until the sugar juice began to turn thick and ropy.

"From a gallon of juice we can get a pound of muscovado sugar," Lovington said. "The syrup is tempered with lime to become granular. Just before it crystallizes the boiler must judge the moment and ladle it into a cooling cistern. This work is more dangerous than the mill, because the hot syrup can stick like tar and burn its way down to your bones. Israel there moves like a minuet, does he not? In fact, I orchestrate at Carlisle a great dance. The cane must be crushed within hours of cutting lest the sugar deteriorate, and then the juice has only hours to be fed to the boilers before it ferments. We've been operating here day and night for three months now."

"What happens when you're not harvesting?"

"We plant, burn, weed, manure, and repair."

"Do the slaves have religion?" Astiza asked. It seemed a digression, but she had great interest in that subject.

"African witchcraft, mostly, with scraps of Gospel they've absorbed. We try to discourage it, but they do their own ceremonies in the woods. It was after one of those woodland Sabbaths that the revolt broke out in Saint-Domingue, you know."

"Do you believe slaves have souls?"

He squinted at my wife, clearly not accustomed to a woman asking such questions, or having a woman along at all. "I am a planter, not a preacher, Mrs. Gage. We do try to introduce them to their Savior."

"So there are slaves in heaven."

The governor decided to ignore her and turned back to me. "Now. We mostly ship muscovado, or brown sugar, which is further refined in England, but if we seal the cooling pot with a moistened clay cap with holes in the bottom for the molasses to run out, we can make clayed sugar of the purest white. It's a four-month process, however, and only Barbados has abundant clay. On Antigua we mostly just drain off the molasses from the brown sugar and use it to make rum. I run both farm and factory, herds to feed us all, and supervise coopers, carpenters, coppersmiths, blacksmiths, and domestics. Free blacks are going to sustain this on their own? I think not. The white man guides, and the black labors. The African, Ethan, is happiest in servitude. Each race to its place."

"Yet when given the choice, they seem to prefer not to do the work of animals," I observed. "They become tradesmen. Or soldiers. And by all accounts, in Saint-Domingue they are beating the finest troops that France can send against them."

"Disease and climate are beating the French. We English beat superstition and savagery out of the Negro. It's God's work, what we do."

I've noticed that whenever men want to justify what they desire, they attribute their choice to God. The meaner the ambition, the more they swear it is the Almighty's desire, and it is the very greediest who insist most vigorously that their covetous hoarding is the Creator's will. Judging by what's claimed, God blesses the armies of both sides, kings indiscriminately, and the poor not at all. Ben Franklin and Tom Jefferson were both skeptical of this truck, but even they seemed to hope there was some divinity or destiny to make sense of life. Some slaves, I knew, had converted to Christianity, but their new god didn't seem to have improved their lot, and I wondered what they thought about fate. What was life like, laboring like an animal, with no hope of change? "It certainly must be complicated to organize," I said, needing Lovington as an ally.

"Only condemn us when you're willing to stop eating sugar," the lord replied. "Your Southern Americans understand what I mean. Ask your Virginians. Ask your President Jefferson. The French are oscillating between anarchy and tyranny, Gage, and must not win. You and I will not let them."

"Which brings us to Saint-Domingue." I had not just the fate of races but a missing son to worry about, and every minute of factory tour slowed my search for Harry.

He nodded. "Let's ride where we can't be overheard by the blacks."

"I can't understand them. They can understand us?"

"More than you know."

We took a lane through the cane fields to a rocky outcrop with a view over a forested valley. Beyond was the deep blue of the Caribbean, its shallows the color of angel eyes, its beaches seemingly poured from the produced sugar. What might such an island be like with a less ruthless economy? Even in the wind I continued to sweat in my coat and vest, a necessary uniform when visiting with a governor. I kept sipping from my flask.

"I'm told by Sidney Smith that you're the last man to see L'Ouverture alive," Lovington said. "Is this true?"

"Yes. Except for the guards who killed him, I suppose."

"In his introductory letter, Smith said you found part of an ancient treasure the French believe could hold strategic secrets."

"A cad named Leon Martel apparently has a strong imagination, but yes."

"Do you know where the rest of the hoard is?"

"No." I thought it best not to mention L'Ouverture's enigmatic clue; let that be a card that Astiza and I kept until we learned more. "But if the Black Spartacus knew, probably other blacks in Saint-Domingue know, too. That's why you must send us there."

"I hear they want to call it Haiti. Imagine that, choosing their own name." He was pensive, a man who suspected that his way of life was slipping away as we marched into the modern nineteenth century. Everyone gets old, and all of us are eventually defeated by change.

"I need passage to the island so I can contact their generals," I said. "I understand a man named Dessalines has taken charge."

"A black butcher. Worse than Toussaint L'Ouverture."

"But a winner, too. The French are falling back."

"Yes." Lovington bit his lip.

"I'll learn what I can from the French, trade it to Dessalines for their own secrets, and discover whether this treasure exists and how to get it."

"And then what?"

"Get your garrison's help to fetch it." It was a lie, but a necessary one. I'd no idea who would prevail if the blacks, French, and English battled over treasure, but I didn't see any of them deserving it more than me. I hoped to use the secret of its whereabouts to get back Harry and the emerald long before the rest of them had at it, and then take all I could carry. I'd also give payback to Martel, killing the villain once I had my boy.

"How will you persuade Dessalines?" the governor asked.

"First, I'm American, and the blacks have relied on trade with my country the entire decade of their revolt. They will listen. Second, I tried to save L'Ouverture, and they'll be curious about his fate. Third, I'm going to spy on the French and offer my military expertise to their Negro strategists."

"You're going to help the blacks win?" The thought made him uneasy.

"To help Britain conquer the French. It's a game of enemy and ally. You know that."

He nodded reluctantly. "You're white. Dessalines may just impale you on a stake as he has many others."

"But affable." Actually, I was fearful of going to Saint-Domingue, but what choice did I have? "Once we betray the French positions, everyone may want to hang us. A pox on all of them. They shouldn't have taken my son."

Astiza smiled at this, a reassertion our host noticed.

"Your wife should stay here. Lady Lovington would enjoy the company."

"You're very kind," I said, as a way of sparing Astiza from having to answer.

"You'll find Carlisle very comfortable," the governor told her. "And safe."

"I care more about my son's safety than my own."

"Yes." I was surprised he wasn't more insistent at her keeping to a woman's place, but he was shrewd in his own way, and maybe not all that eager to have my spouse give his wife odd ideas. "And there is one advantage to going with your husband."

"What's that?"

"The French commander, Rochambeau, has a weakness for ladies."

"Your meaning?" I asked, even though I knew perfectly well his meaning.

"He's the son of the general who helped your nation win independence at Yorktown, but he doesn't have his father's intelligence or character. His strategy is terror, which has united the whole island against him. His distraction from disaster is women."

"You want me to prostitute my wife?"

"I think he's suggesting I play a role again," Astiza said.

"Exactly. Rochambeau is the French weakness, not their

strength. Instead of leading an attack on Dessalines, he holds balls and carnivals. If you want to learn the French strategic positions, I believe Mrs. Gage may discover more with flirtation than you will with a sketchbook and telescope."

Well, she'd already posed as L'Ouverture's concubine. And we needed *something* to take to Dessalines. "Flirt, nothing more."

"Of course."

"I know where to draw the line, Ethan."

"Rochambeau is ruled by his emotions," Lovington said. "Such a man is vulnerable."

This was a terrible idea, except it wasn't. Astiza would cutlass her own arm off before being stuck for weeks or months with an aristocratic twit like Lady Lovington. She was hot to hunt for Harry and would castrate Leon Martel herself if she got the chance. Her sorceress reverie in the ship's hold had warned her of things, and she wanted to manipulate fate by doing the unexpected. And I would be along to defend her honor. "Surely this French general is too cautious to woo the wife of an American diplomat," I said.

"On the contrary, I think making men cuckolds gives him as much pleasure as the sex itself. He beds with impunity, protected by his soldiers."

"That's not reassuring."

"Ethan, it will never go that far; I'm pretending only."

I sighed. "Yes. What could ever go wrong?"

Astiza turned to the governor. "You must deliver us to Saint-Domingue."

Lovington nodded. "Your wife has a decisive frame of mind."

"That's one way of putting it."

"We've captured a French privateer. We'll take you to Cap-François in that, still posing as a frog vessel. You'll both row ashore as Yankee diplomats."

"Then it's settled," she said.

"I don't get a husband's vote?"

"What *is* your vote, Ethan?" She was erect as a knight.

Well, it was clear enough what my answer was supposed to be. I reluctantly saluted her. "That you use your charms to find our son so I can shoot Martel once and for all. Maybe this Rochambeau, too. I'll aim low."

"And once more you get to play the hero, Mr. Gage," Lovington said. "A spy in the French camp and an adventurer in the jungle, conspiring with savage black rebels on an island set afire." He beamed. "The ultimate object of which is, let's be clear, to keep Carlisle here safe."

Part Two

CHAPTER 17

Yellow fever starts with sharp pain. Not just in stomach and loins but, oddly, in the feet and eye sockets. Eyeballs feel as if they might explode, the afflicted told me in Saint-Domingue. Then they become glazed and gush with tears.

Each case follows the same progression. Faces flush. Fever rages. The sick find it hard to breathe and fear suffocation, puffing in terror. A thick, white-yellow fluid coats the tongue and teeth, vomit yellow, feces red. The mouth blackens with a crust. Patients cannot drink. Wounds open spontaneously, inflamed and eerily deep. It's as if the body is dissolving from within, and the inflicted's weight drops by half.

A ghastlier disease can scarcely be imagined.

Cruelly, the patient recovers, or seems to. Usually this rally only signals the end. A few hours respite, and then there are agonizing cramps, nosebleeds, and a flagging pulse. Liquids gush from all orifices. The body is "already a corpse," in the words of one doctor. Physicians can think of little to do but drain pints of blood in a vain attempt to balance the body's humors. In the French hospitals, every bed was accompanied by a bowl of blood.

The bleeding never works. The only thing that can be said for this cure is that it hastens the end. Soldiers viewed confinement in a hospital as a death sentence. Of ten who contracted the disease, nine died.

Doctors were defeated. Then they died, too.

Such was the horror that had annihilated Napoleon's Caribbean legions. Bonaparte recruited two regiments of Polish mercenaries, and half were dead within ten days of landing. A Swedish ship arrived with military munitions; every crew member expired but a cabin boy. Newly arrived French officers succumbed so quickly that those already on the island avoided befriending them, lest the new companion be in a shroud a week later. What the French called *mal de Siam*, named after similar fevers seen in the kingdoms of Asia, retreated in the cooler winter months. But it doomed every campaign and made a mockery of every march. The white race seemed cursed.

The remnants of French power had retreated to Cap-François on the north Haitian coast, a ring of fortifications keeping their former slaves at bay. Here they held, and withered. The grand avenue of trees that led into the city from the plantations was denuded, its palms chopped down to make breastworks. Between the stumps were crosses and the freshly heaped red dirt of graves, both filled and waiting. The few slaves who'd not escaped the city were made to dig dozens of new holes each day in anticipation that they would soon be filled by their masters.

The disease was worse in humid summer, and medical belief held that miasmas of air that rose from the swamps caused the malady. But as food grew scarcer and the siege continued, what the British called yellow jack persisted into the cooler months of October and November. Anxious celebrations were held by the

French aristocracy to stave off despair. As wine cellars emptied, courage became more and more dependent on rum.

Here in this sunny death house we'd seek our son, Harry, and his kidnapper, Leon Martel. It was early November. We'd celebrated his third birthday of June 6 in his absence, and prayed he was well enough to see a fourth. Nothing was more commonplace in 1803 than the death of young children. For Astiza, separation had been agony. For me, it meant guilt and anger. I condemned myself for not better safeguarding our boy and chafed under my unaccustomed saddle, responsibility. I was a father, but so far mostly in name only.

From the sea, Cap-François still had the pleasing prospect of many a tropic town. A broad bay on Saint-Domingue's north coast was fronted by a palm-lined boulevard at the water's edge called the Quay Louis, a name left from royalist days. The city behind was like a stage set, its narrow flat platter of buildable land a porch in front of steep green mountains. It shimmered in the sun as if lit for effect.

Next to the quay was a row of sturdy brick and stone warehouses with red-tile roofs, such as one might find in a European port. In happier times this harbor area was thronged with wagons of rum and sugar, swank carriages, auctions of slaves, and quick commerce: island planters averaged higher annual incomes than French royalists had once boasted at home, and the nouveau-riche colonists spent their money as fast as it came in. Luxury furnishings would be hoisted from ferrying longboats. Trunks of dresses arrived from Paris shops, and tea and dinnerware came packed from China after transit in Europe. Trains of chained African captives would shuffle to be inspected, just as I had shuffled in chains in Tripoli. They were stripped naked and prodded like pieces of fruit.

But now the warehouses and factories were shuttered after a decade of war. The promenade looked tired and dirty, dotted with broken carts no one bothered to repair. There were drifts of refuse. Homeless blacks camped there in thatch shelters, their owners dead from massacre or fever. These Negroes didn't flee because they feared being drafted by Dessalines and his rebels outside the fortifications. They weren't claimed by anyone else because there was nothing for them to do, and no food left to feed them. They foraged, stole, and waited for the city to fall.

Beyond the quay were Catholic steeples and a grid of streets as neat as a Roman camp, leading to government houses, barracks, parks, and a parade ground. Backing all were tropical mountains so precipitous that they formed a natural wall, the height exaggerated by towers of cloud poised like opera curtains and colored by rainbows. The tangle of jungle and slippery mud was so steep that it made trying to attack from that direction a strategic impossibility for a large army. In a rain, muddy torrents ran down from the hills and through the city.

To the east, however, a river debouched from the Haitian plain that had once been a rich network of plantations. Between this river and the protective mountains, Cap-François was nearly flat and open toward the dawn. There the old sugar fields seemed to run forever, and there the rebel army prowled. French ramparts and redoubts built of piled dirt, logs, and stones snaked across from river to mountains to protect this last French capital, tricolor flags marking the position of cannon batteries. Beyond were columns of smoke and, Astiza and I assumed, the notoriously cruel general we had to seek if we were to learn more about the treasure of Montezuma. If Toussaint L'Ouverture had been the Black Spartacus, Jean-Jacques Dessalines was portrayed by his followers as the Black Caesar, and by his enemies as the Black Attila.

We were ferried ashore from the captured privateer that Lord Lovington had provided, an English crew flying the French flag from the ship until they could creep back out of the harbor.

We told authorities at the quay steps that the brig, the *Toulon*, was en route from Charleston to Martinique and had dropped my wife and me on a diplomatic mission. With Bonaparte's permission, I was to judge if the French attempt to hold Saint-Domingue could ever succeed and, if not, make recommendations to the American and French governments on the disposition of Louisiana.

It was plausible enough. Yet sentries stared at us as if we were lost.

Why had we been put ashore in Hades?

What a wonder the Paris of the Antilles must once have been! Clear, warm water lapped at mossy stone steps that led from the boat landing to a stone plaza between town and sea. The bay was blue sapphire, the shallow sands golden. A stone balustrade worthy of Versailles marked the perimeter of the breakwater, but after years of war it was marred, chips knocked away by cannon and musket shot. Decorative pillars held up what once must have been a welcoming monument, but that statuary, too, had been blasted away like the nose of the Sphinx. Other royal statues in the parks were headless, a reminder of revolution a dozen years before.

To our right, or west, was a stone fort. Leclerc's army had stormed it to recapture Cap-François from the rebels nearly two years before, and it showed fresh repairs from bombardment. Black cannon jutted from embrasures, but soldiers were invisible, artillerymen staying out of the sun. I was struck by the somnolent quiet of the place, a city waiting for the end.

A French lieutenant named Levine was summoned from the fort to study the forged documents I brought. Lord Lovington's Antiguan office had helped make French and American papers testifying to my diplomatic status.

"Your mission is out of date, monsieur," he said. He spoke to me but looked at my wife, his eyes a mix of appreciation and speculation. Maybe he expected me to expire of yellow fever within days, removing the annoyance of a husband. I wished the same plague upon him. "We're told Louisiana was sold to America late this spring."

News travels slowly, so my surprise was genuine. "If a sale of

Louisiana has already been concluded, I couldn't be happier," I said grandly. "I had a hand in the early negotiations, and now can take some credit for success."

"It's not just that, monsieur. With renewal of war between England and France, our position here is even more precarious. A British blockade could force our defeat. I must counsel that you put your wife in grave jeopardy by bringing her here."

I turned to scan the sea. "My wife has a mind of her own, and I see no British ships." This was my little joke, since I was looking directly at the masquerading *Toulon*. "But I would like to bring the freshest assessment possible back to my American government. Is it possible to obtain an interview with the commanding general, Donatien-Marie-Joseph de Vimeur, Vicomte de Rochambeau?"

Levine glanced at Astiza again, as if thinking that was not the best of ideas. "I am sure something can be arranged," he nonetheless said. "Do you require lodging?"

"If you could suggest a still-functioning guesthouse."

"It functions. Just."

The lieutenant called a carriage. Our wardrobe was modest, but we'd borrowed a large empty trunk from Lovington so we'd look the part of baggage-heavy diplomats. Our black hire gave us a quizzical look when he lifted the container into the vehicle. We should have stuffed it with extra blankets, but too late now. Then a crack of the whip and Astiza and I rode into town.

While the main boulevards were cobbled, most of the side streets were dirt or, when it rained (which was almost daily), mud. Some buildings were masonry as firmly rooted as a German burgher's, but the majority were wooden island colonials, elevated on posts a few feet off the ground. Palm fronds, litter, and lumber hid underneath.

"The stilts let the breeze and water through," our black teamster told us, in thickly accented French. "Hurricane, too."

The buildings were mostly two stories high, with a continuous arcade along the bottom floor that ran above the ground like a floating sidewalk. From the bedrooms above jutted narrow French balconies with iron railings, just large enough for an occupant to step from a bedroom to survey the world, hang laundry, or empty a chamber pot. Flowers spilled from planting boxes—ragged looking in the stress of the siege—and paint flaked in the humidity.

Despite the humid decay and stress of war, the whites (some of them French born and some locally born Creoles, like Napoleon's own wife, Joséphine) dressed smartly, if illogically. Even in the heat there were plenty of splendid blue uniforms, tailed coats, and dresses that closed all the way to the throat, reflecting new fashion. At least the civilian hats were broad-brimmed, and often white or straw.

More eye-catching were the coloreds. Even besieged, the city was at least a third black and mulatto from house servants, field slaves, and freemen who hadn't joined the rebellion. The worst were in rags, but the mixed-race population formed a secondary aristocracy at Cap-François that was more finely attired. There was a complicated gradation of color with the lightest skin conveying the highest status. Quadroons were the offspring of a mulatto and white, mustees of a quadroon and white, and mustefinos, the finest of all coloreds, were from white and mustee—seven-eighths European but still "colored" by custom and law. Relations between this palette of skin had once been as precisely regulated as court ritual, and now habits were breaking down. Even the loveliest tan had been caught up in an enormously complicated war.

When the revolt began in 1791, Lovington had explained, there were approximately thirty thousand whites, forty thousand mulattos, and more than half a million black slaves in Saint-Domingue. In the last dozen years all three racial groups had at times both allied or been at odds with each other, while forming temporary partnerships with invading Spanish, English, and French. Slaughter had been met with counter-slaughter, and victories with betrayal. Many of the rich had already fled, and I'd seen some of the refugees disembarking two years before in New York City.

Yet what glories of the human skin still mingled in this city! People moved slowly here, but with a floating, flowing gait enchanting in its gracefulness, the sway of the women accentuating hips and bust. Their smoothness made the white troops seem clumsy by comparison, and their beauty was striking with colors from cream through nut, cocoa, coffee, chocolate, and ebony. Teeth were bright, necks high, muscles smooth, carriages erect, and some colored men and women wore fabulous hats topped with plumage as bright as parrots. In gayer times, this would have been paradise.

Cap-François, however, showed the wear and tear of war. Paint was unobtainable. Gunfire pocked bricks from when the city was taken by blacks in 1793 and then back by the French in 1802, with numerous battles between. Several blocks were blackened shells. Even in sections still inhabited, broken windows were boarded rather than repaired, because there was little glazing and fewer glaziers. Garbage lay in heaps because it was too dangerous to cart it to the countryside, and the slaves who'd performed this job had fled. The entire town had a pungent odor of rot, sewage, and smoke, with the redeeming whiff of the sea.

"This place has the smell of disease," Astiza murmured. "I fear for Horus if that monster brought him here. Martel is no nurse."

"And Harry is a handful. I'm hoping he's vexed his captor. Maybe by now the devil wants to give him back." It was a poor attempt at humor, but we needed to lift our spirits.

My secret worry, however, was that my three-year-old had adapted to captivity and kidnapper quite well, and scarcely remembered his father at all.

Cap-François also had the scent of a farmyard. Some of the burned-out lots now held penned animals, presumably brought into town for food. There were cows, donkeys, sheep, and chickens. Goats and pigs wandered freely. Flies buzzed off deposits of manure.

The city's squares were still geometrically planted with palms that shaded shaggy lawns and sculpted shrubbery. But instead of statuary there were gibbets from which rebels hung. We passed three decomposing black bodies while journeying from the port to guesthouse, the corpses turning in the breeze like weather-cocks. No one but us gave them even a passing glance.

We took quarters on the Rue Espagnole, not far distant from Government House, where we'd find Rochambeau. The British had provided a little money for expenses since we were otherwise destitute; how I missed my emerald! It was just as well there was little to buy in this besieged city since our allowance was so mod-est: I've always felt pinched doing government work, better to stick with trade and gaming.

"Everyone seems to be waiting," Astiza said as she sat on the bed.

The guesthouse was shabby from neglect, shutters broken and small green lizards clinging to its walls. The maids were sullen, the floors grimy. My dreams of joining the wealthy were once more in abeyance, while Aztec riches beyond imagination beck-oned somewhere in the Caribbean.

It was time to spy.

I looked toward Rochambeau's headquarters. A hundred yards from its door was a guillotine, blade bright in the sun.

CHAPTER 18

While we waited for an audience with the French general, Astiza and I mapped a plan to explore Cap-François, hoping to sight our son. Given her interest in religion, she'd start at a church and ask about orphans, runaways, or odd parishioners. I didn't think Leon Martel was likely to turn up in pew or confessional, but it was possible a wayward child or a newly arrived adult of poor character might come to the attention of nuns.

Given Martel's past, I thought a hunt of brothels would be likelier to find him than a hunt of cathedrals, but I'd been married long enough now to know not to propose that as a beginning. I decided instead to master the military geography of the city in hopes I'd find something useful to take to Dessalines. How we'd cross French lines to this Negro Hannibal I'd no idea, but my experience is that if you poke into a bear den you might find a bear, which had happened during my sojourn with the Dakota Sioux. I don't believe things always work out, as Sidney Smith claims, but I do believe trouble will find you easily enough, should you go looking.

So I began to stroll, trying to make a crude estimate of the garrison while keeping an eye out for Harry. I'd try to flush Martel out with my mere presence. It didn't occur that far from hiding, Martel had made himself part of the French government and likely knew of our arrival as soon as we climbed the steps of the quay.

So did others. Survival had become precarious in Saint-Domingue, and the key for all sides was using eyes and ears to prevent surprise.

At first my foot patrol seemed fruitless. The town was desultory, traffic listless, weather sultry, and clouds mounded on the peaks and then clawed overhead like a drawn tarp. There was a growl of thunder to echo the occasional boom of siege guns. Then afternoon downpour turned the streets of Cap-François into temporary rivers. Raindrops as heavy as musket balls rattled while I stood on a boardwalk under a porch roof, watching a slurry of silt and garbage flow toward the sea.

How was I to cross this deluge to continue my scouting?

Someone dark and gigantic came striding out of the murk from the middle of the street, as impervious to the pounding water as a bull in a paddock. "Can I offer you a ferry, monsieur?" A strapping black looked up at me on my boardwalk with a smile that glowed, each tooth dice bright and his gums pink like an orchid.

I peered into the curtain of rain. "Where is your carriage?"

"My shoulders, adventurer."

I glanced down the street. Another white was boarding the shoulders of another Negro like a toddler climbing aboard his father, the human foot ferry keeping his cargo's feet clear of the mud. And another, and another. It was clearly the odd custom of this place. The first passenger was carried to the boardwalk on the opposite side of the avenue and deposited like a delivery of mail. A coin changed hands.

"There's an entire company of carriers," my entrepreneur explained. "Even in a revolution the black man has to make a living, yes?" I saw another duo go by, the human mule singing African songs with the gusto of a Venetian gondolier while the white hunched with hat streaming. It seemed a parody of oppression. But when in Rome . . .

"What's your name, broad shoulders?"

"Jubal, monsieur."

I've always found it convenient to have big friends, or quick little ones. This fellow was an extraordinary specimen, six and a half feet tall, with polished skin the color of coal, muscles like a dray horse, and broad smile as brilliant as a snowdrift. He wore a tattered and patched infantry coat that was wet as a washcloth, his pantaloons cut off at the knee so that he could wade barefoot in our tideland of a street. A red kerchief gave his neck a jaunty air, and his belt was wide as a pirate's. There was poise to his posture completely different from the hunch of the wary slave, and his eyes sized me up with the calibration of an engineer. I was impressed but not surprised. While my race has no shortage of philosophers arguing our God-given superiority, such arrogance has been contradicted by the sheer capability of brown Arab, red Indian, and black African I've met in my travels. The races aren't very different at all, but Europeans seldom believe me. It's easier to sort people out by pigment.

"Come, monsieur, we will make the voyage to the Left Bank together! I am the Mercury of mire, a Columbus of navigation! Climb on my shoulder and Jubal will take you where you need to go."

"You seem a very erudite porter."

"I can read, and even think. Imagine that, from a Negro."

"And why would an educated freeman work as a mule?"

"Why do you assume I'm a freeman?"

"By your bearing and industry."

"Maybe I'm just cocky. Climb aboard and find out."

"And how much for this favor?"

"A franc. But Jubal is the best carrier, so you may wish to give me two."

It was like mounting a sturdy horse, and off we went into the rain. I'd kept my planter's straw hat from Antigua, and looked out at the world through a veil of water dripping from its brim. My shoulders were instantly soaked, but the downpour was warm and the ride enjoyable. I felt ridiculous, but at least I wasn't calf-deep in mud.

Jubal set his own course. Rather than wade straight across to the other side, he splashed to the middle of the avenue and trudged parallel, making us drift toward the harbor.

"No, no, I want to go there!" I pointed. He might not even get his franc.

"You will get there. But perhaps you wish to talk to Jubal first. Out here in the street, in the rain, where no Frenchman can hear us."

I was immediately alert. "About what?"

"Yes, talk to mighty Jubal, who knows both mountains and sea. Jubal, who has heard of an American diplomat arrived at the harbor with his striking wife, seeking information on the liberation of Haiti. Jubal has heard about this electrician who walks into the lion's mouth, to ask about the lion."

My heart beat faster. "How did you learn that?"

"The black man knows all in Cap-François. Who rows first to a ship, hoists a trunk, or drives a carriage? The black man. Who mops out a meeting room, serves at a banquet, or digs new entrenchments? The black man. But should an American ambassador talk only to the French side? Or should he seek information from the African legions as well, the ones who will soon rule this country?"

I looked down on his woolly head, glistening in the wet. "You mean Dessalines, who trades with the United States for weapons."

"The Washington of our revolution. Yes, Jubal knows."

"You're a soldier for the other side?" The last men I would consider for that role were human camels.

"It's the rare black man in Cap-François who doesn't serve two, three, or more masters. It's necessary for survival, yes? The *mambo* Cecile Fatiman foresaw that a white man is coming who knows our hero Toussaint L'Ouverture. Is this true?"

"Yes. But who is Cecile Fatiman?"

"The wise witch who preached our revolt a dozen years ago in the Bois Caïman, the Alligator Wood. That's where it all started."

"You mean the war?"

"She danced with the rebel Boukman and slit the black pig for blood. I saw the slave frenzy with my own eyes, because I'd already slain my master and become a Maroon who hid in the jungle. Cecile is led by the voodoo spirit Ezili Danto, the seductress who knows all. Our *mambo* prophesized that an American would come, and here you are."

I was still trying to get straight the complex history. "What happened to Boukman?"

"His head was put on a pike. His revolt, though, goes on."

Here was opportunity with broad shoulders. I was in an odd position for negotiation, but also felt a glimmer of hope. "I *was* the last to see Toussaint L'Ouverture alive."

"And he told you something, no? This is what Cecile sees."

"He told my wife. She's a bit of a priestess herself."

"The dead Toussaint now waits for us in Africa with all our loved ones and ancestors. If we fall in battle, we go to L'Ouverture. Dessalines promises that."

"I envy such conviction."

"We rely on it, which is why we will win. Did you know that our soldiers are so inspired that they put their arms into the muzzles of the French cannon? What do you think of that?"

"That it's as risky as it is bold." When it comes to faith, I'm wary to a fault.

"When the cannon fire, their souls fly to our homeland. Then the comrades who are left hack the cannoneers to pieces."

"I admire such courage. Although I'm cautious about self-sacrifice, unless there's a real need. Not cowardly, exactly, but prudent. It just seems practical to preserve oneself for another day." My self-assessment fell short of being ennobling, I suppose.

"No one knows if the next day will come. You are an instrument of Fa, monsieur, our spirit of fate, but you are also in grave danger. Men have heard these prophecies and might be jealous or fearful. So you need Jubal. Bad men will send Death against you, the dark *loa* we call Baron Samedi. Or seek to make you a zombi."

"What's a zombi?" We'd now circuited a block, as if I couldn't decide where to go. I was wet as a sponge, but I must say the conversation was more interesting than dinner at a planter's house.

Jubal ignored my question. "Dessalines will meet you, Monsieur Gage, if you can bring him something worth knowing."

"I hope to inspect the French lines."

"We blacks have *built* the French lines. You must do better than that. You are to speak to the French? Then keep your ears open, and perhaps we will keep our eyes open for you."

For an escaped slave, this fellow was quicker than a clerk. I wondered at his background. "It's true I saw L'Ouverture, and it's also true I may help the rebel cause. But my wife and I are looking for our kidnapped son, a three-year-old named Horus."

"I could keep an eye out for him."

"His mother would be grateful."

"For her, I would look even harder."

"How about a swarthy man named Leon Martel. Heavy-jawed, with the look of a weasel?"

"I haven't seen him. The French do not invite me to their parties."

"Martel is a renegade policeman. Cruel, like Rochambeau."

"But I may have *heard* of him, because the black man hear everything."

"You have?" I bounced on his shoulders.

"I will ask," he said enigmatically. Now he changed direction to finish crossing the street.

By a gunner's ramrod, what else did this creature know? "And I want to learn island legends that might help you and me."

That stopped him. "What legends?"

"About treasure recovered by escaped Maroons that was hidden, lost, and awaits rediscovery by the right cause."

"If I knew about treasure, would I carry you?" He laughed. "No, Jubal knows no legends. Maybe Cecile does. Listen, we need the key to Cap-François, not old stories. Bring that, and I will take you to Dessalines and Cecile Fatiman. Then we will help find your son." He finally set me on the opposite boardwalk, dripping as if I'd fallen into a river, my boots still clean. "These are cruel commanders you've come to, Ethan Gage. After a dozen years of war there is no mercy. Take care to recognize who is your friend, and who is your enemy."

"How do I do that?"

"By how they treat your wife."

"They'll treat her correctly or pay with their lives."

"You must treat her correctly, too, because you never know when she might be taken from you."

"What does that mean?"

"To take care. Good-bye, now."

"Wait! How will I find you again?"

"I talk with Dessalines. Then *I* will find *you*."

I turned to go, both enlightened and mystified.

"Monsieur?" he said.

"Yes?"

"A franc, if you please."

I gave him three.

CHAPTER 19

Rochambeau was a famous name in the United States. As Lovington had recalled, the elder count led the French forces that helped Washington defeat Cornwallis at Yorktown, finally winning the American Revolution. His son had the good luck to inherit his father's renown and the bad luck to inherit Leclerc's sickened army, after that general succumbed to yellow fever. So far the second Rochambeau had shown more cruelty than initiative. He'd retreated to Cap-François and fortified his morale with women and drink.

I wasn't surprised, then, that the invitation to call upon his headquarters was issued to both Mr. and Mrs. Gage. Word of Astiza's exotic beauty had spread quickly around the city, and the notorious Rochambeau was likely contemplating a different kind of conquest to make up for his lack of victories on the battlefield. We had to let him think such corruption was possible, while not allowing it.

Certainly I recognized the danger. Plain women are more

devoted, older ones more appreciative, but I, too, have an eye for beauty—it's a fault of mine—and knew I had to defend the woman I'd married.

The French Government House was a two-story, white stone building flanked north and south by orderly landscaping meant to emphasize power. Now the complex betrayed physical and moral decay. Window sashes were peeling, flower beds had gone to weed, litter curled in corners, and four small cannon were aimed on the lawns as if this governor was as threatened by his own population as the rebel army. The building's court and foyer were thick with French officers and military bustle, but their assembly was untidy in the way of men who are losing hope and discipline. Maps and papers were in heaps, swords and muskets leaned in disorderly tangles, and unwashed bottles and plates drew flies. Hats were off, coats thrown across furniture, and muddy tracks crisscrossed the floors.

Astiza and I had our papers inspected and then were escorted to the general's office upstairs, the mahogany door opening to the scent of tobacco and cologne.

Rochambeau didn't make a good first impression. He was a squat man with a round, soft, rather sullen face, reminding me of a stocky schoolhouse bully. His head was sunk between his shoulders, and a brown birthmark surrounded one eye so he looked punched. He received us in a hussar's hot uniform, blue breeches and cavalry shirt with red collar and silk sash, the finery making him sweat. His plump torso was buttoned tight with rows of horizontal silver frogging that, to an American rifleman, would function mostly as tempting target. His shoulder epaulettes were sturdy enough to balance beer mugs on. The dress was gaudy, but I knew some women have a weakness for peacock display. He stood from his desk to inspect us, we wearing clothes similar to what we'd paraded on the Louvre iron bridge.

I glanced about; I have the habit of orienting myself because it's useful to have an escape route when life becomes too exciting.

Rochambeau's office windows looked down across the gardens toward the port and its forest of ships, as if to remind where escape lay. A balcony extended next door to his private quarters. Heavy French curtains hung damp, too heavy to move in the breeze.

The general greeted me by name but came out around his desk to Astiza, bowing, kissing her hand, and simpering a compliment like a clumsy Casanova. His eyes were small and, I decided in predetermined distaste, piglike. Many women apparently considered him oddly handsome, given the allure that high birth and money brings, but I didn't see it. Leclerc's death, I suspected, had been disastrous for France in more ways that one. It had left their army to a man void of imagination for anything but reprisal and infidelity.

Of course, I was traveling under false pretenses myself, and Rochambeau could justifiably have me shot as a spy, should he learn my real mission. Here again, Astiza was useful. She'd donned the little pendant Bonaparte had given me at Saint-Cloud, a fine chain letting it fall to the swell of her breasts.

"I admire your jewelry, madame."

"A gift from the first consul." She blushed modestly.

Rochambeau's brows rose. "And this is for?"

"Persons he favors. It actually is in honor of my husband. Ethan is such an able diplomat."

"Well." The general sat back down, regarding us with new respect and, I sensed, suspicion. "I hope you appreciate the significance of that bauble." Anyone close to Bonaparte had as many enemies as friends, I knew.

"I view it as protection," she said calmly.

The general nodded uncertainly, beckoning us to sit. Then he tapped the forged papers I'd brought with the pretend signatures of American delegates Livingston and Monroe. "I appreciate your wish to understand our strategic position in the Americas, Gage, but unless I get reinforcements, anything you report will be obsolete. Louisiana has been sold, and the English are attacking everywhere. They've already taken Castries in Saint-Lucia and then Tobago, and are scooping up Dutch islands like walnuts in a barrel. Where is my navy? Hiding in French ports, as near as I can tell. If the British blockade, our position will be precarious indeed. The colony may become entirely black, which means, of course, entirely savage. Yet the remedy seems beyond our grasp."

"Remedy?" I glanced about. His office had the usual masculine decoration of flags, standards, swords, firearms, and old halberds and pikes, as if they'd cleaned out the Bastille's attic before tearing the prison down. There was also a purple velvet settee strewn with yellow silk pillows, and a sideboard with wines, brandies, and liqueurs with a set of fine crystal.

"The ultimate solution is to exterminate Saint-Domingue of its present Negro population, which has been infected with radical ideas, and bring in an entirely new and docile population from Africa. The novice slaves must be kept from reading or hearing anything, prohibited from meeting, and taught that disobedience results in indescribable pain. It's no different than training a dog or breaking a horse." He examined his rounded fingernails. "But to do that, I need a huge army, and our army has melted away with fever like frost before a sun. It's as if God is against us, which I do not understand. Does he want the rule of pagan voodoo? Churches made of trees and swamps? Peasants growing yams instead of plantations growing sugar? We've had a *Code Noir*, the Black Code, which spelled out the rights of master and slave alike. The result was paradise. Now the Negro has chosen anarchy."

"Maybe it wasn't paradise for them."

"It prohibited beating or execution at whim. And we've done them a favor by rescuing them from Africa. Under the *Code Noir*, all men had their place. The king himself helped draft it, when we had a king. But that was long ago, wasn't it? Now Bonaparte is trying to restore calm by reinstating slavery, which is the only economy that ever made sense. But the blacks have become fanatics. So I've been left to fall back on my imagination to keep barbarism at bay. I'm a creative man in my own way, but I am

misunderstood and little appreciated, even by my own officers."
He sighed, the very picture of self-sacrifice.

"Great men are not always recognized in their own time." I
figured flattery might prove more useful than truth.

"My primary concern is the protection of innocents such as
your wife," he continued, aiming a smile at Astiza. "I also work to
fortify our morale with entertainments. There's a ball tomorrow
night; you both must come. Our worst defeat would be to give
up civilization. So I work tirelessly to sustain normalcy, just as I
work tirelessly to keep us safe from Dessalines, who has hanged
and tortured more good Frenchmen that one can count." He gave
her a nod and a wink, the bastard. "We must not let him at our
women."

"I appreciate your gallantry," my wife said, with such astonishing pretend sincerity that I appreciated again the ability of females
to negotiate relationships with the skill of actresses. "I *do* hope
you can keep us protected during our sojourn in Saint-Domingue,
my dear vicomte."

"You can be sure of it." He picked up a pistol to fondle absently, and I could only hope it was unloaded. "The secret to dealing with the Negro is ruthlessness. Leclerc did his best to be stern,
tying some of his captive to heavy flour sacks and throwing them
into the harbor to drown, but that's a waste of good bread. There
was a point beyond which he would not go. I have no such scru-
ples. I have hanged, I have shot, I have burned, and I have boiled.
Have you ever watched men being boiled alive, Mrs. Gage?"

"Never." She gave a little shudder. If anyone could wring secrets out of Rochambeau, I supposed, it would be Astiza. But I
was damned if she'd do it near his bedroom. "How soldierly to
carry it through," she continued, as I shifted uncomfortably.

"It takes a certain hardness," he boasted. "Many officers quail
when the victims begin screaming. And yet the result on the rest
of the blacks is salutary. If I could only torture and execute ten
thousand, I could bring order to a million."

"So it's a kind of mercy," Astiza said.

"Exactly!" His eyes kept falling to the swell of her breasts, as if some physical problem prevented his gaze from staying level with hers. Not that I blame him, I've had the same problem. "I locked a hundred of them in the hold of a ship and suffocated them with sulfur, and then made a hundred more hurl the bodies into the sea. Word of that got around the island, I daresay."

"I should imagine."

"My latest innovation has been man-eating dogs. I've used my own money to import them from the Spanish in Cuba. Now, no black army can stand against a French regiment in the open field, you can be sure. But every time we pursue the rebels into the jungle, an ambush ensues. It's maddening, and my men are becoming timid. The dogs, however, smell and ravage the rebels and give my forces fair warning. I haven't been in the engagements myself, but I'm told the beasts are truly terrifying in how they rip their victims to pieces."

My God, he was madman and sadist. I was about to blurt honest revulsion when my wife responded first. "Horrifying," Astiza said. "And clever."

"It's only for the protection of beauties such as yourself. Every monstrosity I invent is but a necessity to save France's children."

"Your valor is known in Paris, I can assure you, Vicomte. And if it's not, we will celebrate it when we return."

He nodded, expecting as much.

Why do butchers feel compelled to boast? The truth was that Rochambeau and Dessalines would each slit a million throats if it furthered their personal ambitions, and both would destroy the whole island before letting their own demise occur. Nor would they ever muster the courage to duel in an arena by themselves, preferring to sacrifice thousands of others to settle their hash. The man kept eyeing my wife, and I sourly decided he had the soft look of too many pastries and not enough marching.

"So you believe there's a chance of victory?" I interjected, after clearing my throat.

"There's always a chance, Monsieur Gage, and an obligation to make a valiant stand if there is not. Remember the Spartans at Thermopylae! I'm hoping God will still see the justice of our cause, and bless us against the forces of darkness."

"I understand the blacks believe they have supernatural protection, too."

"From African witchcraft. Their courage is quite baffling." He glanced out his window again at the harbor, and the ships that could carry him away. "Well. I must plan my ball, and I'm eager that you grace it with your presence. You'll promise me at least one dance, Madame Gage?"

"I would be flattered, General." I swear she batted her eyes. Was she enjoying this charade? But no, I knew Astiza: her mind hadn't strayed off her quest for little Harry for one second. "I *do* want to meet all your brave officers. And my husband is eager to study your strategic dispositions. He was involved in the siege of Acre in 1799, and has been a student of fortification ever since."

This was complete nonsense, since that bit of epic bloodletting had taught me to stay away from sieges as much as possible. Yet she was playing her part to the hilt.

"Is he really?" The general looked at me speculatively.

"Perhaps he can lend your officers advice."

"I'm an amateur savant," I said modestly, "an electrician and explorer, but I flatter myself to have slight military expertise." Yes, I can lie, too. "I was actually wondering if I could learn from your engineering. It's to your credit that you've held off the rebels this long."

He nodded cautiously. "I appreciate your curiosity. But, monsieur, you are a foreigner talking of military strategy. Secrets, if you will."

"As Lafayette was a foreigner to Washington."

"My husband is ever so good at keeping secrets." Astiza leaned forward, giving him an eyeful. "And he might share some of his."

"I don't know if I have an escort to spare . . ."

"I, however, am not fond of riding around in the sun," she added.

I saw where she was going. "And I'm uncomfortable leaving you alone in a new city, rife with tension," I told her.

Rochambeau, who was not the brightest general ever to take the field, finally realized his opportunity. "But she is not alone! She is with me!"

"General, were my husband to go on tour, I'd be ever so grateful to wait for him here. I would feel safe, if it would not be too distracting."

His pig eyes gleamed as if we'd poured slops in a trough. "How could you help but distract? Yet a gentleman can always spare time for a woman in need. I am an important man, yes; I may have to issue orders, but perhaps we can issue orders from the veranda while Monsieur Gage sees how expertly we have fortified this city. You and I can have rum punch and compare memories of Paris."

"In the Paris of the Antilles," she said sweetly.

"Alas, if only you could have seen it at the height of its glory!"

"Your courageous stand gives grandeur to what is left."

"I have pledged my life in its defense."

"I cannot imagine more capable company for my wife," I put in, tired of this prattle. "And I don't need an escort. I can poke about on my own."

"And be shot by a startled sentry? No, I'm sure there's a colonel or major downstairs who is unoccupied." Rochambeau rifled through some papers as if reminding himself who served on his staff. "Enjoy my hospitality, make your diplomatic report, and critique our heroic defense." He looked at me. "I'm aware you have quite the reputation as a warrior, Monsieur Gage, both on France's side and against her."

I'd fought with the British at Acre, as I've said, but as an American my expediency had let me also do errands for Napoleon. Sometimes it's convenient to bounce about, though you do accumulate a great deal of misunderstanding.

"You're a neutral capable of honest and blunt opinion," Rochambeau went on. "I hope you'll lend your critique to the barricades of Cap-François, as Lafayette and my father did at Yorktown."

"I would be humbled to learn and teach. I marvel at your skill. I have an interest in writing; perhaps I can tell the world how you did it."

He cocked his head as if I'd gone too far, but then looked at my wife's chest again. "So. Let me arrange a tour while Astiza and I enjoy a view of the sea. That is the way home, madame. The sea."

CHAPTER 20

I wasn't eager to leave my wife alone with Rochambeau the lecher, but I also knew Astiza was the type to put even Bonaparte in retreat if she had to. I, meanwhile, might spy out something useful for Dessalines, finding a French weakness and trading it for legends of treasure. That in turn could help get my boy back. I might seem a traitor to my race, but Leon Martel had ensured my enmity by stealing my son and jewel. Besides, it appeared to me that the best choice for Rochambeau's forces was to leave before they all succumbed to fever. Why not hurry them along?

With my skin color, my reputation, my diplomatic papers, and my wonder of a wife, the French officers assumed my loyalty. They'd also been instructed, I suspect, to keep me busy for the afternoon while Rochambeau tried to maneuver Astiza to that purple couch. So I was given a rambunctious cavalry mount—it took a few minutes for us to come to a proper understanding, which is that I would indicate the general direction I wanted to go and the horse would get there in a manner of its own choosing—and a colonel for escort named Gabriel Aucoin. This officer looked as soldiers are supposed to look, with erect torso, calm confidence, easy command of his mount, and an exploding soufflé of blond curls that put me in mind of Alexander the Great.

"They gave you Pepper, American, but you sit him well," he congratulated.

"It might be more accurate to say he lets me sit. I'm not really a horseman. Still, I can ride when I need to."

"I'm not an engineer or a guide, but I can show you our gun batteries. And then share some Bordeaux. We'll be friends, I think. I like honest men, not braggarts."

And indeed, I liked him and felt guilty for preparing to betray him. But if I could help put an end to this damnable war, maybe Aucoin would live. A prolonged siege would likely mean he'd die. At least that's what I told myself to justify my confusion of loyalties. I was pretending to be a diplomat while playing the spy, and pretending to be a loyal white while hoping to betray the members of my race here in Cap-François. None of this would have been necessary if Martel had not kidnapped Harry, but I regretted having to drag men like Aucoin into my quarrels.

We rode to the flat eastern end of Cap-François where the primary fortifications are. The island that Columbus called Hispaniola is divided into two colonies, the Spanish Santo Domingo to the east and the French Saint-Domingue, or Haiti, to the west. The land is very mountainous, and so the French colony was strategically divided into three parts. In the north, west, and south were separate pans of plantations, each hemmed in by hills. The blacks had already conquered west and south and now were pressing on this last white stronghold in the north, having seized all but the city of Cap-François itself.

The struggle would be decided on the city's eastern boundary, between river and mountains.

It was hot as we rode, the scenery somnolent but luscious.

The island is a gorgeous mosaic of greens, with cane, orchards, and jungles almost glowing like my emerald under a brilliant blue sky. Birds flit like darting flames, and flowers are a scattering of paint. Oranges, lemons, mangoes, and plantains erupt for the picking like something out of Eden. Butterflies flutter, and insects drone.

Disturbing the green tableau today were fires on the distant horizon, but from war or agriculture I couldn't say. Haiti is a dream that hate turned into a nightmare, lush paradise as a portal to hell.

We rode along the stumps and graves of the Rue Espagnole. At midday, the lack of shade made the sun feel like it was pounding my straw hat. Past the city's outskirts were the French lines, and behind them mildewed military tents, hot as ovens, and trampled grassy fields. Artillery waited hub to hub next to neat pyramids of black cannonballs. Soldiers lounged beneath awnings. Muskets, too, were stacked in pyramids.

"We confine drill to the cooler morning," Colonel Aucoin volunteered when he saw me eyeing the inactivity. "Half my men are unwell, and all are thin from shortened rations."

Useful, but Dessalines no doubt knew this. "When do you sally to meet the enemy?"

"Not much anymore, because disease depletes our ranks. Dessalines's army swells, and ours shrinks. He grows bold, and we grow timid. He has the entire island on which to maneuver, and we have half a mile of breastworks."

"How many men do you have?"

"About five thousand. The blacks have three times as many. The French art of war is all that holds the rebels at bay. We have better discipline and with reinforcement could still reverse events. But now war with the British makes it even unlikelier that help from France will arrive."

"What are you hoping for, then?"

"Officially, that Dessalines breaks his army on our fortifications, letting our cannon do their bloody work. Then we pursue the remnants with our dogs."

So I should not recommend a frontal attack. "And unofficially?"

"That we are given a chance to reach an honorable settlement before they murder us all."

We passed a kennel of the man-eating mastiffs that Rochambeau had purchased from the Cubans. These were monsters almost the size of small ponies, great slobbering things that raced, barked, and lunged as we clopped past. Our horses shied and whinnied, instinctively increasing their pace. The dogs weighed about a hundred and fifty pounds, I guessed, and hurled themselves against the bars of their cages with anxious woofing and snarling. Their excitement bent the wood, which sprung them back like bows.

They reminded me of a brute of a canine owned by my old antagonist, Aurora Somerset, and I shuddered at the memory. That one had torn throats to gristle. "How do you control them?"

"Sometimes we don't. They've turned on our men several times, and we've had to shoot some. But the blacks fear them more than a cavalry charge. Besides, our horses are wearing out."

"Can the dogs turn the tide?"

"The rebels know how to shoot dogs, too."

"And if Dessalines doesn't conveniently destroy his army by throwing it against your cannon?"

"Then it will all have been for nothing." His voice was resigned. Defeat starts weeks or months before an actual surrender.

"It seems a desperate strategy."

"For desperate times." He reined up, looking at me squarely. "I am happy to show you about, monsieur, but telling the truth is depressing, and I think we won't tarry into the evening because you should return to your wife. Our general has a taste for other men's women."

"I trust Astiza."

"Which could be exactly the problem. Her loyalty could make you an inconvenience in Rochambeau's eyes. My orders are to keep you safe, but don't count on that forever. You do not want to make her a convenient widow."

"What do you mean?"

"Rochambeau and Admiral La Touche recently gave a dance aboard the admiral's flagship, the deck turned into a garden. There were plants and flowers on the bulwarks and vines suspended from the rigging. It was lovely escape, letting one pretend war didn't exist. But a young beauty not entirely in love with her husband came in a Parisian dress so scandalous she was almost naked. This Clara danced the night away with our commander, and the next day her husband was assigned to a column sent to smoke out the blacks. It was ambushed, and he never returned."

"And Clara?"

"Seduced, and then packed off to Paris."

"Astiza is entirely in love with me." Even as I said it, I wasn't sure. Her words echoed: *What if it was a mistake to marry?*

"Then you're a lucky man." His tone said he wasn't sure, either. "But anyone can be tempted. What does she most desire? Rochambeau will find that out and then offer it to her."

My son, I thought. "I'm not to volunteer for a sally, then."

"And not to take for granted the fidelity of your wife or the word of our esteemed general. No disrespect for her. It's just friendly advice, monsieur, for a treacherous island. Fear makes people do strange things."

"No offense taken, Colonel Aucoin. General Rochambeau gives fair warning by his manner, doesn't he? Is he simply greedy?"

"Afraid, I think, a man who doesn't know what to do. That's why he slaughters and tortures the Negroes, out of fear they'll do the same to him. It will only make it worse in the end, which he knows, and yet he can't help himself. I think he ruts so much simply to postpone his nightmares. Servants have heard him screaming in the night."

I liked this man's realism. But rarely are the most sensible in charge.

"You must keep this conversation secret, of course," Aucoin went on. "I am a soldier and will do what I am told, but I try to tell the truth to protect the innocent."

I hadn't been called *that* in some time.

"By the same token, you must not tell the truth about me to him," the colonel added.

"But of course. I appreciate your trust."

He shrugged. "I'm afraid, too. It puts me in the mood to confess."

While the city's eastern boundaries were flat and seemed to invite invasion, the French had used the terrain as best they could. At a low rise just to the right of the major trunk road, Rochambeau had ordered the construction of a sturdy fort of stone, earth, and logs that had just enough altitude to command the approaches. It was anchored to a much steeper mountain so precipitous that no sizable body of men could flank it from that direction. This fort, I judged, would be the key.

Aucoin led me up a causeway to the top of the bastion.

No enemy could be seen. The flat plantation country beyond seemed deserted, and with the loan of his spyglass I could make out the blackened shells of destroyed houses and sugar mills. Abandoned cane waved in the wind, a sea of ten-foot-high stalks hiding whatever was out there. Once-harvested fields had grown back wild, and smoke hazed the horizon.

"Where's Dessalines?"

"Watching us as we watch him, and hoping disease finishes his campaign for him. He's tried some assaults on our redoubts, and we've taught his men that voodoo doesn't protect them from bullets. They charge fanatically, even the women, and it only adds to the carnage. You can smell the dead."

Yes, there was a hint of the sickly sweet rot of abandoned corpses out there in the grass, apparently too close to French guns to be retrieved.

"So now he waits, licking his wounds. I'd like to go after him, but the general doesn't believe we have the strength to retain any ground we capture."

"So it's stalemate."

"Yes. He cannot conquer us, and we cannot capture him. Without siege artillery and the expertise to dig the proper approach trenches, I don't see how he can take our fort here at Vertiers. He must wait for us to sicken or starve."

I nodded. The French had splendid fields of fire, several batteries of cannon, and magazines crammed with powder. It might still be a long war. "I admire your engineers."

"You were at Acre, so we respect your opinion."

My expertise was exaggerated, but I'd developed an artilleryman's eye in the Holy Land. I saw a crease in the terrain that could be seen from up high but was probably invisible to Dessalines. The ravine was a negligible ditch snaking into the cane, but it pointed at the French walls like a siege trench, and it was hard to see its bottom. It might provide cover in darkness. Well, that was something. "Do you have enough artillery to cover every approach?"

"Not if surprised. The key is that we learn what the blacks are going to do before they decide themselves. We can see them coming when they move; the sugarcane shakes to betray their march."

"Kleber and Napoleon used the movement of wheat to their advantage in the Holy Land at the battle of Mount Tabor," I said. "What about flanking you?"

"The mountains are too treacherous for more than a small patrol. A regiment would bog in mud and snakebite. Things will be decided here, in the open, on flat, firm ground. If a French naval squadron arrives, we might still hold out."

I looked at the mountains, most so steep that attackers would fall at the French as much as charge them. Organization goes to pieces in terrain like that.

But I also saw a stream that sprang from a jungle canyon in

those same mountains, emptying into a little pond right behind the French batteries. "You have a water supply, too."

"Yes. Wells are brackish here, and while we can haul barrels from Cap-François, it's laborious. Our engineers diverted that creek closer to our lines. On a hot day, that rivulet is a real asset. There's no water on the rebel side, except the brackish river, which keeps them from camping too close."

I saw a track in the ruddy soil led along the stream into the jungle. "Is there a vantage point up there?"

"It provides a view like a map. Come. We'll have a swig of wine."

We left our horses and climbed up along the stream, sweating in the heat. A brow of hill several hundred feet above the French lines finally gave me a clear vista. Here up high, the stream leveled briefly in a hollow, hills cupping either side of the rivulet before it disappeared into jungle. The waterway ran over the lip where we stood and down to the French camp below. I could see the snake of the defensive lines, the ominously quiet sugarcane fields, the sprawl of Cap-François, and tangled mountain ranges.

"What will you tell your government, Gage?" Aucoin wanted reassurance, even though my opinion was no better than his.

"It depends on the size and expertise of the opposing army, I suppose," I said neutrally. "Perhaps I'll tell them that either side can still win."

"I called you honest. Now I'm not so sure." He offered me a flask.

I sipped and glanced about, and an idea occurred. Perhaps I did have a scheme to offer Jubal, who in turn could take me to Dessalines, his *mambo* priestess, and legends of Montezuma's treasure.

"Your engineers have expertise," I went on. That was true enough. "It's possible you could hold out forever with enough food and powder." So an idea had tickled my brain, an idea inspired by my son Harry. I looked uphill. "You've used geography to great advantage. In America, we call terrain this steep 'land that stands on end.'"

He smiled. "An apt description."

"I think I'll congratulate your general on your position. I'm just as happy being on this side of your guns, not charging them."

The colonel smiled wryly. "I hope Dessalines shares your caution."

I strode to the stream, scooped up water, and washed my hot face, taking in the geography and trying to memorize it. "But your real enemy has always been the fevers, hasn't it?"

"Disease demoralizes everyone."

"More armies have been conquered by plague than artillery."

"The *mal de Siam* lingers because our men are weak."

"And your doctors are baffled?"

"Our doctors are dead."

I thought of slavery. "Do you see God's hand in all this carnage?"

"When fortune is against you, you see the devil."

I nodded. "I'm a card player, you know. I ponder luck."

"All of life is a throw of the dice, Monsieur Gage."

"Yes. God. Satan. Fate. Fortune. My wife ponders the imponderable."

"Your wife, sir, is in as much danger from fever as from General Rochambeau. Come. I'll show you a hospital for what the British call the yellow jack. It will hurry you on your way back to your marriage, and your home."

CHAPTER 21

As expected, Astiza returned to me with virtue intact.

"I told him I was shy and feared the return of my husband," she related, "but that perhaps we could explore his quarters when you were distracted during the ball. That was enough to reassure him of his own charm and get him to postpone advances. Of his army, he told me nothing. Of treasure, I'm fairly certain he knows nothing, or he'd be seeking it. I also asked about lone children in this city, and he said there are too many orphans to count. It clearly wasn't what he's interested in."

"This city is a death trap, Astiza. I saw men dissolving from yellow fever. If Harry is here, I fear for him. If he isn't, it's almost a blessing."

"He is. It's a mother's instinct."

"But wouldn't a man like Martel draw comment with a lad at his side? He's hardly the fatherly type. Surely we'd hear of it."

"If Horus *is* at his side. What if he's hidden away somewhere? Locked in a cellar, or sold to some monster?"

"Not sold. Martel took Harry to keep control of us. He's waiting for me to find the treasure, discover the secret of flight, give him the key to conquering England, and then swap for my boy."

She grimaced. "We hope. Or he's so tired of waiting that he kills."

"He's too calculating."

"Just be sure you don't care about treasure more than your son." It was a mean statement, said in haste as partners sometimes do. But it was also revealing, and it stung. I'd gotten us free from the Barbary pirates, but she gave me no credit, and losing Harry while hocking the emerald would always rankle. If children can bond couples together, their loss can strain them irreversibly apart.

"I care about the treasure *because* of my son."

She nodded glumly, knowing I loved our boy, but also knowing how I wanted ordinary success. She'd be content in a nun's cell, while I dreamed of mansions. But I wanted both boy *and* jewel, each linked to the other and tied up in Aztec ransom. I also wanted to best male rivals like Leon Martel and the Vicomte Rochambeau, and to impress strategists like Napoleon and Smith. Yes, I wasn't as single-minded as her, but wasn't that a good thing?

"The way to Harry might be through Dessalines."

She remained reluctant. "But if we leave Cap-François, we can't get back in."

"We can if the city falls, and I think I know how to take it."

"You'll provoke a massacre with our son in the middle of it."

"It's riskier to linger here, hoping Rochambeau will let something slip as you flirt. They know the agreement on Louisiana is completed. Why then do we stay? If they learn our diplomatic papers are a forgery, or that we really came from Antigua, we'll be hanged, shot, or guillotined."

Astiza went to a window to regard the mountains beyond. "Do you really think the blacks know about this mythical treasure?"

"I've no idea, but I've met one chap I like, a great big one named Jubal. He thinks a priestess might help." This mention of a priestess was calculated to get her intrigued by the other side. "And I don't like the idea of that lecher having another go at you."

"I can handle Rochambeau."

"If he promises you your son in return for favors, what would you do?" Now I was the one being mean in the heat and tension of this besieged place, and my jealousy was silly. Yet people *will* do extraordinary things to get what they want. Astiza seemed desperate, Rochambeau seemed reckless, Cap-François felt doomed, and my instinct was to get us out and seek alliance with the rebels.

"I'd hold the point of a knife to whatever part of his body he holds most dear to get Harry back," she retorted. "I'm not leaving Cap-François until I'm certain that either our child isn't here, or I have him to take with me."

I sighed, hardly surprised. "All right. How about this? We attend this ball. You flirt with Rochambeau and learn what you can. If you discover where Harry is held, we free him, somehow. If there's no word, we go to Dessalines. After the blacks take the city we turn it upside down for evidence of our son."

"If you give me enough time."

"I lingered in Paris, and now you want to linger in Cap-François."

"But for better reason."

"The blacks have spies, you know. They might be more use than trying to pry information out of Rochambeau."

She considered this point, and offered a concession to patch over our differences on strategy. "The blacks have their holy spirits; their women have been instructing me. When we go to Dessalines, I'll call on the gods of Haiti to help us. I hear them whispering from the jungle beyond the walls."

Astiza believed in the supernatural as firmly as I believe in money and luck, and as I've said she was rather inclusive of which gods she'd call on. My wife thought all religions were a manifestation of the same central idea, and this world a mere dream of a more tangible realm somewhere beyond. I knew better than to call her wrong. We'd seen strange things together in the Great Pyramid and the City of Ghosts.

"My escort today said their gods give the blacks extraordinary courage," I said, agreeing to patch our testiness. "They put their arms in cannon muzzles."

"All political change requires belief."

"Unfortunately, their arms are then blown off."

Now she smiled, knowing the habitual skepticism that was a gift from Benjamin Franklin. "And yet the French are losing," she said. "I've been learning more about the history here. This war started, I'm told, in a gathering of African religion called voodoo held in a sacred wood. Their gods told them to rise. They have a supreme god, Mawu, but then personal spirits. There is Damballah, the serpent god; Legba, who brings change; Ogu of fire and war; Baron Samedi from the Land of Death; and Ezeli, the goddess of beauty."

"Jubal suggested I consult the latter."

"You most certainly will not. Your gods should be Sogbo, god of lightning, and Agau, the god of storms and earthquakes. You've called down the lightning before, my American electrician."

Indeed I had, and I'd no desire to repeat the experience. It was terrifying. "If gods really worked," I reasoned, "the slaves would have triumphed a decade ago."

"And if they didn't, the French would have triumphed a decade ago."

When you marry a smart woman, she'll answer all your best arguments with her own. I was filled with desire for my clever wife, and not just for her mind. Rochambeau's slobbering reinforced my own husbandly lust; we all want most whatever someone else covets. But I also never tired of her face, the lilt of her fingers as they moved, the nape of her neck, the swell of her bosom, and glory of her rump, the narrowness of her waist, the . . .

"Ethan, every race believes the spirit helps the flesh."

"And the flesh is fortified by spirits." I poured us a measure of punch. "It's getting dark, and I think religion is best discussed in bed."

"Or is bed your religion?"

"I daresay such a religion would be more practical, or at least more comfortable, than the more conventional ones. I'll also suggest that if people napped more, the world would be a calmer place. One problem with Napoleon is that he never gets enough sleep. I'll bet Rochambeau and Dessalines have the same problem. A colonel told me the general has nightmares."

"I'm not surprised."

"So are the Haitian *loa* like the Catholic saints?"

"To a degree. But I think Ezeli is the black Isis, the equivalent of Mary, Venus, Aphrodite, or Freya." Astiza moved to where we slept and lay down as if posing for a painting, bare shoulder in candlelight and the rest undulating like a serpent, making me think of anything but religion. I not only wanted to find my boy, I wanted to make another one. Or girl. Get back the emerald, retire in peace, and protect them all.

"And I think Ezeli is you."

The Government House was transformed for Rochambeau's ball.

Gone were the slovenly belongings of tired officers, replaced with pungent cascades of tropical flowers and garlands of oleander, a plant imported from Africa that I'd smelled in the ravines of the Holy Land. The marble was mopped bright, and the hardwood floors gleamed from fresh oiling. The reception hall, where the dancing would take place, dazzled from what seemed a thousand candles. Crystal and armor caught the light. Battle standards reminded us of martial glory. Rochambeau clearly put more energy into festivity than war.

The guests were equally radiant. The officers were in full dress uniform, swords clinking as they turned so the sheaths bumped and rattled like discordant chimes. Their uniforms were blue, their sashes red, their frogging silver or gold, their breeches white, and their boots polished to almost shave by. Civilian gentlemen wore fashionable tailed jackets, and servants sweated in embroidered French waistcoats, their woolly hair powdered white under tricorn hats.

The women outshone all. There are lovely ladies everywhere, but that night in Cap-François embedded pulchritude in memory, if only because the beauty seemed ephemeral and the gaiety forced, given the desperate military situation. Impending fever, the bayonet, and rape were the unspoken, uninvited guests to our party, and gave the ball poignancy.

The women's gowns were as sumptuous as they were daring, décolletage picked out by brilliant necklaces. Necks were highlighted by hair piled high. Skin tones ranged from the carefully protected alabaster of ladies recently arrived from Europe to the tan of the creoles to the dusk of the mulattos; no truly black women were in attendance except servants. Such were the color castes of Saint-Domingue. The mixed-race damsels had special beauty, I thought, as if the gods rewarded the sin of master and slave with heavenly grace. Their complexions were flawless, lips full, and their eyes offered the dark depths and promises of a houri. Astiza was still special, but here she had true competition. The swirl of fabric, skin, perfume, and dazzling smiles put all of us men in something of a fever. We were hot and constricted in our uniforms and suit coats, while the women seemed as bright and light as woodland nymphs.

Astiza and I began to circulate, and I saw Rochambeau in the center, greeting each couple and assessing each woman as boldly as if he were in a whorehouse. I was amazed some husband hadn't already shot him, but of course murder would mean a firing squad.

I also remembered something Franklin had written in his

books of aphorisms. *He that displays too often his wife and his wallet is in danger of having them both borrowed.* Once again, I feared he was speaking of me.

Astiza saw me scowling and squeezed my forearm, radiating her own smile like a beam of light. "Remember, we're here to learn about Harry," she whispered. "You're a diplomat, in control of every expression."

"Just don't be alone with the general. Soldiers shield him from answering for his appetites."

"Then stay with me."

But I couldn't, entirely. There was a regimental orchestra, and as the music started there was a roulette of changing partners as we danced. Three officers in turn twirled Astiza on the floor, and then Rochambeau swooped to grasp her arm, quickstepping with surprising grace for such a squat posture. He got firm hold of her in the waltz, that dance the older generation views as scandalous. His right hand drifted down to the swell of her hip and buttocks and gripped for purchase, and his nose aimed at her bosom. Grinning like a conquistador with Inca loot, he danced past with skill I couldn't match. The bastard was probably a good fencer, too, so I disliked him even more, deciding his stature was distinctly toadlike.

"And you are the American, monsieur?"

It was a planter's wife, with beauty and figure that would normally enchant me. I bowed and extended my arms, but as we made a great wheel on the parquet floor I kept looking past my partner to Astiza, determined not to lose her as I'd lost Harry. Rochambeau had lowered his paw halfway to her thigh, and she was whispering some confidence into his ear that had him leering. I longed to pour rum down his breeches and set it on fire.

"Excuse me." I broke off to have some punch. I wasn't used to this business of having a wife other men desired, and it put me in a foul mood. I felt half guilty for planning to go over to Dessalines, betraying every couple around me, but half vengeful, too.

Rochambeau had grasped my wife as France and the other European powers had grasped the islands of the Caribbean and the labor of Africa. I understood the wrath of the rebels.

Were we close to Harry and the stone at all?

I was brooding about my dilemmas and unjust fate when Astiza suddenly appeared from the dance floor, face flush, neck shiny, tendrils of hair escaping to stick to her temples. She pushed me hard back into the shadows. "He's here!"

"Who?" I'd almost spilled my drink. She had fire in her eye.

"Leon Martel. He slipped up to me after the music stopped and said the general was inviting me to a private audience upstairs."

"The devil he did!"

"The policeman is Rochambeau's pimp."

"Good God. Smith said he played that role as criminal. So where's Harry?"

"I couldn't ask him, Ethan. I don't think he recognized me from Nitot's jewelry store; everything happened there too quickly. He just does the general's propositioning for him. He *did* have the arrogance to introduce himself; I almost swooned before giving a false name. He'll learn soon enough who I am from Rochambeau. And he *would* recognize you, since you were caught and tortured. You have to stay out of sight."

"Out of sight? I have to skewer the bastard!"

"Not yet. We've got to learn where Horus is."

"It's a trap. The only reason to get you upstairs is to rape or capture you."

"They don't know who I am, I tell you. Rochambeau simply hopes for sex. Martel panders. I've got to learn what I can."

"No, it's too dangerous. . . ."

"He's coming." She glanced over her shoulder, and indeed, I saw Martel threading through the crowd toward my wife, swarthy as a storm cloud, feral as a fox. He had the smug bearing of a favored courtier, of a man who delighted in hobnobbing with his betters. I have the same vanity.

"Promise me you'll not risk ascending the staircase."

"Wait inside the library and let me learn what I can," she replied. "Then we'll decide what to do about Rochambeau's invitation." Another shove, and I backed reluctantly through the doorway.

I fumbled at my waist, frustrated. I'd deliberately come to Saint-Domingue without a weapon to dissuade suspicion. Now I longed for one to kill Leon Martel.

When he spoke to my wife, the kidnapper had an unpleasant rasp to his voice that I recognized over the music, even though I'd no idea what was being said. Was he really a procurer for the French commander? How had the renegade ingratiated himself into the garrison here? What if I called him out at this moment, sword to sword? Maybe Colonel Aucoin and the other officers would join me against this upstart and demand that he produce Harry!

As I stewed, a black servant annoyingly tugged my sleeve. "Monsieur, a messenger for you in the kitchen."

"I'm busy."

"Pardon, but he says he's ready to carry again." The Negro looked at me intently.

At first I didn't understand, but then I did.

Jubal. Of all the worst times!

"Can it wait?"

"Please. It's safe, but urgent."

Things were happening too fast. Heart hammering, hating the idea of leaving my wife to lechers, I reluctantly followed the slave. Surely she'd not go upstairs to Rochambeau . . . except she was entirely too self-sufficient, which is why I loved her.

"Here, monsieur." To my surprise, a shelf of books rotated and I stepped into a passageway. It wasn't secret, but rather a hidden corridor to bring refreshments to private meetings in the library. In twenty paces another door led us into the pantry, with the clatter of the kitchen beyond. Black cooks were singing as they worked, while butlers shouted orders and curses. Hams and fowl hung from the pantry ceiling, jars of pickled preserves lined the shelves, and barrels of flour and meat crowded the floor. It was a hoard of food in the midst of a siege. A few miles away a vast dark army loomed, waiting to liberate all the servants working here. What must the blacks think of nights like this?

Emerging from the dark of a pantry corner was the large form I knew well.

"Jubal, you risk coming *here*?"

"I risk what my commander orders," he said. "Dessalines has sent a patrol for you. It's the best time to escape, with army officers preoccupied. While they drink and eat, we'll climb the mountains, wading up a stream to throw off any dogs."

"I can't go tonight. We're honored guests, ambassadors, and my wife has urgent business with Rochambeau."

"There's no choice if you wish to meet Dessalines. It must be on his schedule, not yours, lest he fear that you set a trap. We go in one hour."

"An hour! What about our belongings?"

"Leave them. Take them back when we take the city."

"My wife will not agree."

"Leave her if you wish. Then, if you want her back, you'll join us in storming the walls."

By that time she'd be Rochambeau's forced concubine, or worse. What wretched timing! "Things can't happen that fast. I'm looking for my boy."

"If you don't come in an hour, you'll never meet Dessalines, unless it is to hang from the gibbet with the other whites when he conquers Cap-François."

Damnation. Yet I also knew Jubal was right: the ball was a perfect time to creep away from Cap-François. Could I persuade Astiza? "I have to ask my wife."

"Command her. Then meet me in the park just beyond here in one hour. Don't let yourself be followed."

He melted into the shadows. For a moment I hesitated, frustrated, and then I realized that Jubal's deadline was a partial solution to my problems. It meant Astiza and I must flee before her flirtation with the general went too far. I had an excuse to get her away! She had a mother's instinct to stay close to her son, but the strategic thing to do—the fatherly calculation—was to throw in with L'Ouverture's successor.

Wasn't it?

I hurried back toward the celebration. The level of noise had risen as guests plumbed the punch. Dancers twirled faster but more tipsily. Laughter was a shriek. In the corners behind the pillars, couples were kissing. Officers without women stumbled drunkenly together, telling crude jokes.

I didn't see Astiza.

Nor Rochambeau.

Nor Martel.

By the beard of Odin, was I too late?

I spied Aucoin, my earlier escort, and risked pushing through the crowd to him, betting Martel had left the ballroom. "Colonel!" I greeted.

"Ah, Monsieur Gage. So we fiddle while Rome burns."

"Have you met my wife?"

"I wish to. I saw the two of you together earlier. She's beautiful, Ethan."

"Yes, but now I'm looking for her. It's rather urgent we leave."

"You may have to wait. I believe she ascended the stairs with an aide to our general named Leon Martel. Rather formidable in personality, and forbidding in appearance. He arrived a few months ago and has cast a spell on our commander."

"Have you seen Martel with a young boy?"

"There are rumors of several boys, but they are just rumors."

My jaw ached from its clenching. "I need to get a message to her."

He put his hand on my shoulder. "Best not to disturb Rocham-beau. It hurts, but politics comes first, no?"

"Fidelity first, Colonel. And honor."

"Of course. But he has many soldiers; she is there, and you are here. Have a drink and wait as other husbands have waited."

"The hell I will."

"Or risk being ordered to a doomed patrol."

CHAPTER 22

No one takes my advice, including my wife. This may be because of my tendency to fall into political tangles, military brawls, debt, and ill-considered romantic affairs, but still—did Astiza have *any* inclination to honor and obey my admonition not to go upstairs in her desperation to gain information about our son? Apparently not. Posted on the balcony that fronted Rochambeau's office and bedchamber were sentries with muskets and bayonets. Somewhere beyond those closed doors were Astiza, two men I despised, and a grandfather clock imported from Breguet that was ticking remorselessly toward my rendezvous with Jubal.

I'd make no progress on finding Montezuma's hoard without fleeing to Dessalines and the rebels, and no progress toward regaining my son and the confidence of my wife without keeping close to Martel and Rochambeau.

But what if I could retrieve my bride from General Rochambeau, castrating the bastard in the process? What if I could capture

Leon Martel and take him with us into the mountains? No doubt he'd be a worthy prize to bring to the Negro general. Maybe I'd have the pleasure of trying to mock-drown the renegade police-man just as he'd drowned me in Paris. A warm-up before black rebels invented even more hideous tortures? I was weaponless in a house with a hundred French officers, but doesn't fortune reward the bold?

Yes, I'd capture Martel, retrieve Astiza, castrate Rochambeau, flee to Dessalines, find the treasure, get the emerald, and some-where along the way rescue my son.

I hurried back to the library, swung the bookcase open once more, and made my way down the private passageway to the pan-try. The same servant as before intercepted me.

"Monsieur? It's not yet time for Jubal."

"I need to get upstairs first, but the main way is guarded."

"Strictly forbidden during celebrations. General Rochambeau entertains in private."

"My wife is up there."

He looked sympathetic. "The general can be very seductive."

"No, she's captive against her will." I doubted this was entirely true, but I needed his help. "A husband has rights."

"And Rochambeau has sentries, does he not? It is impossible."

"I need you to get me up a secret way behind the guards. There must be a servants' stair."

"Also guarded." He hesitated, however. He knew an alterna-tive.

"Then we flee with Jubal to help liberate Haiti," I promised. "No one will know your role until victory, when you'll be a hero."

He frowned. "If they suspect, they'll feed me to their dogs."

"If we succeed, there soon will be no more dogs, and no more French. No more whips, and no more manacles."

He swallowed, taking courage. "We've a hoist to bring food above. The idea came from your own president, Jefferson. A sea cap-tain brought drawings from Virginia. Perhaps you can fit inside."

I clapped his shoulder. "Good man. Rochambeau is probably drunk, and his men half-asleep. I'll find her without a peep, and we'll slip away as silently as deer." Or bury some steel in the general's head, but why alarm my new confederate?

As the slave turned to lead me, I slipped a kitchen cleaver into my breeches beneath the back of my coat. I realized how naked I felt unarmed, which had been my state since escaping the pirates of Tripoli. I must commission another rifle, but no time for that now.

The contraption the slave proposed to hoist me in was like a cupboard, and it took some grunting and flexing to fold myself in. Lord, it's a nuisance getting older, and my mid-thirties is a stiff march from my teens. It didn't help that I had the cleaver blade to be wary of. I took care not to cut a slice out of myself.

"When the hoist stops, climb out," the slave instructed. "If they find you in the dumbwaiter, they'll stick you like a pig with bayonets so as not to disturb the party with gunshots."

"Saves powder, too." I saluted from where I lay curled. "Don't worry, I don't intend to disturb the festivities a whit. I'll slink about like a ghost."

"Just don't become one, monsieur."

A door closed, and I was in darkness. Then with a lurch I felt myself ascending, helpless as a goose folded into an oven. I just prayed that Astiza wasn't gaily descending the stairs, looking for me, as I rose to look for her.

The dumbwaiter stopped, and I pushed to get out. The cabinet door, I realized too late, was latched from the other side. I was locked in. No doubt my fellow conspirator hadn't remembered that. Or had he, and I'd squeezed myself into a trap?

I considered signaling to go down again, but I had no way to do so. With no better course I wedged my feet against the hoist and pushed against the door. Wood groaned but didn't give.

It was hot, and short of air.

So I shrank into myself as much as I could, planted my boots, and launched against the door. The latch snapped with a crack, splinters flew, and my momentum carried me out onto a wood-plank hallway. I landed with a whoof and a clump.

So much for creeping.

"*C'est quoi?*" One of the sentries, not as sleepy as I'd hoped, was trotting my way. I rolled to one side and, when he rounded the corner, tripped him and sprang. He fell, musket clattering, and I jumped on top of him and brought the handle of the cleaver down on his temple. He stilled. I'd no desire to murder, just to get my wife away from the lecher in chief. Unfortunately, the other guard likely heard the noise. Time to hurry!

I sprang up, got my bearings from our earlier visit to Rocham-beau's office, and trotted to what I guessed was the bedroom door, gripping the cleaver while realizing I should have grabbed the musket. The speed of events was confusing me, and it didn't help I was lubricated with rum punch. Ah, well. The kitchen uten-sil was a bit like my familiar tomahawk. Why hadn't I ordered a new one of those, too?

Well, because I was married and a father, quietly retired, a squire of sleepy scholarship and prudent investment.

Rochambeau's chamber was unlocked. I slipped inside and looked for my wife. I'd only seconds before the next sentry followed me. The bedroom was dim, a single candle, tropical moonlight fall-ing through open French doors. And there on a bed behind gauze mosquito curtains, a woman rode our Casanova commander. Her back was arched, breasts high, hair tumbling to her splayed but-tocks, the man beneath her grunting as she made soft cries.

Astiza! It was as if a lance went in.

I knew she was desperate to get news of Harry. But to be be-trayed so soon in our marriage, and humiliated so completely, a gaping cuckold, cut me to the quick. I mentally cursed the awful dilemma Martel's scheme had put me in, and the desperation my wife had been driven to. Rochambeau must suffer!

So I lifted the cleaver and charged. With a savage tug I ripped the bed curtain down and reached for Astiza's dark hair to heave her off the commander. She screamed.

Rochambeau looked at me in amazement. The cleaver gleamed.

And then I realized I was not yanking on Astiza at all.

It was one of the bastard's other seductions, her chest flushed, mouth open in confusion and fear, twisting her neck to relieve my grasp on her hair.

Where was my wife?

Behind me the door of the chamber crashed open and a sentry burst in. "Stop right there! Who are you?" His musket came up, the bayonet aimed at our frozen ménage à trois.

"Don't shoot me, you idiot!" General Rochambeau cried.

I released the tart and shoved her down at the general, who was reaching for a pistol on a nightstand. Damnation, where was my wife? I sprang for the French doors and the balcony before there was a bang, and a musket ball hummed by my neck. I was in it now!

"It's the American!" Rochambeau cried. "He's an assassin!"

Well, I had failed in that role since I'd entirely forgotten to cleave the bastard's head. I whirled around and hurled the weapon at him, the blade spinning as the couple ducked and the woman shrieked. The cleaver embedded itself in a bedpost. Then I vaulted the stone railing of the balcony outside, above the garden. As I did, Rochambeau's pistol fired, and this time something hot grazed my ear, stinging like fire.

I fell into darkness, my body crashing into shrubbery and damp soil, deliberately rolling so I didn't break a leg. Then I bounced up, gasping. My ear had been cut by the ball but, other than bleeding, it seemed intact. I was scratched, dirty, and bewildered. If his paramour wasn't Astiza, where the devil had she gone?

And where was Leon Martel?

What a stew. I listened to the chorus of cries as the ball erupted into panic at the gunshots. There were shouts, oaths, and the rasp of drawn swords.

I'd turned a cotillion into a hornet's nest.

CHAPTER 23

I glanced up. Two men appeared on the balcony, presumably the sentry and a naked Rochambeau. Their guns were empty, having missed. I regretted not having my own. I was curious about the size of the bastard's nutmegs, but it was too dim to judge. With no way to strike back I limped away, nursing a turned ankle. Sensing a presence, they shouted, but I carried on, melting into the gardens.

What now? No wife, no son, and no distracting festivity to give me cover as I crept to join Dessalines. Instead, I'd roused the garrison. I suppose I should have thought things through more clearly, and charged less impetuously, but the fear that my wife was in the arms of another had obsessed me. Love, lust, and jealousy can addle the mind like English gin.

I'd also been seized by the idea of using the cleaver, and not necessarily on the top of the general's anatomy. If I was caught, he might use it on me.

I could demand a trial, but I suspect my husbandly outrage would hardly mollify a French military tribunal, particularly when I'd thrown a chopping blade at their commander while he was entirely preoccupied with someone else's wife. I could hear soldiers spilling from Government House and the rattle of drums from the barracks against the mountains. I also heard the barking of dogs and wondered if they sensed a new dinner. I was probably whiter meat than they were used to, but I was fairly certain their palates wouldn't mind.

"Monsieur Gage!" It was a hiss. Jubal reached out a paw of a hand and jerked me deeper into garden foliage. "What is happening? I heard shots."

"I tried to rescue my wife."

"Where is she?"

"I didn't find her at all." It sounded foolish even to me. "It turned out Rochambeau was rogering some other spouse. Now the garrison is aroused and the general wants to kill me as much as I wanted to kill him."

"I thought we were going to quietly steal away?"

"That was the plan, but I'm afraid I became a little reckless when my wife vanished. I'm not used to being married. "

"Women make you stupid?"

"Apparently so."

"Now it is very dangerous. We must flee to the mountains, but they will be watching. Monsieur, I am a little disappointed. We were told by the British that you were a man of cunning."

"Retirement is simply more work than I imagined. I'm afraid I've grown rusty."

"*Merde*. All right, hurry, I hear their hounds!"

He turned to run, but I stopped him. "Jubal, I'm sorry, but we can't go without my wife. We spied a dangerous man who tortured me back in France, and I'm worried he has Astiza. Did you see a woman emerge from Government House, quite beautiful, mustee in coloring, hurrying on some kind of mission?"

"No woman alone. But I did see a woman more pushed than escorted, a man's hand on one arm and a child in his other."

"A child! A boy?"

"Perhaps. It wasn't evident if he was forcing her somewhere or she was demanding they leave. She glanced back, several times. They were heading for the harbor."

Bollocks. Martel had promised her reunion with Harry if they fled before I confronted him, and she'd chosen my son over me, trusting her resourcefulness over mine. Now I'd lost them both. "If it's Astiza, a bastard of a Frenchman is taking her there."

"My sympathies, Monsieur Gage, but we must go *now*, to Dessalines, or risk being hanged or eaten. It may already be too late."

"No, it's I who am sorry, Jubal, because we must go to the harbor instead, to rescue my wife. And you can call me Ethan. From now on we'll be equals."

He groaned, not at all impressed by my offer of friendship. We heard cries of command in French. A bugle in the middle of the night. A rising chorus of baying hounds. "This is a very poor idea. Our rebels are the opposite way."

"We must, my new friend. I misplace my family like an old man his spectacles, and I want to prove I can hold on. Can't you lead us to the harbor on a winding, twisting way in which we won't be seen?"

"There is no such path. The street grid was laid with the compass. A musket ball can carry down a street from one end of Cap-François to the other. They'll cut us down like rabbits. And if we do get to the sea, we're trapped between dogs and water."

"We'll steal a boat."

"I don't even think we can *reach* the sea. You've roused entire regiments." He obviously thought me mad as well as stupid. But no, I was just faithful.

I glanced about. A cluster of officers was in a cone of light spilling from Government House main doors, their sabers pointing as they tried to sort what the alarm was about. Rochambeau had disappeared, probably to put some clothes on. The barking was closer, and near the barracks I thought I could see lupine, leaping forms, their wolfish teeth white in the night. Down the Rue Dauphin toward the Caribbean a squad of infantry was assembling. In short order the dogs would sniff us out in the shadows and we'd join the men swinging on the gibbets, our odor adding to the city's scent of corruption. Unless . . .

"We can escape in that." I pointed to a wagon stacked with barrels in a dark court adjacent to the park, the yard just off the main street to the sea. Each hogshead, I guessed, contained sugar, a remnant of wartime plantation production that had been too late for a ship with room for sweets. All departing vessels were crammed with fleeing aristocrats and refugee heirlooms.

"We have no horses or oxen, monsieur."

"It's a long, gentle slope to the Caribbean. We aim, push, and ride."

Now we could hear the clatter of hooves in the dark as men mounted. The barking of the dogs was getting closer. "You've left us no choice," he admitted, looking dubiously at the heavy vehicle.

"It will fly like a chaise." I wished it would fly like Cayley's glider, but it was several tons in the wrong direction. I released the lever brake. Alone, I couldn't have maneuvered the ponderous wagon, but Jubal took up its tongue and dragged it out into the street with the brute strength of a bear. I kept his spirits up by pushing a little from behind. We aimed down the street like a boulder tumbling down a mountain. Lest the vehicle drag, I unlimbered the tongue by freeing an iron pin, and then used that pin to jam the front axle so it couldn't turn. Then I threw the heavy tongue up onto the cargo of casks. "Now, push, push, push! Point her like an arrow!"

Our chariot, weighing several tons, began to move.

Slowly.

As we ponderously accelerated, we came into faint light thrown by a house window.

There were shouts as we were finally spotted, and the excited chorus of slavering dogs. The animals came on in a streak, eyes glowing in the night's torch and lantern light. Men were running after them, holding glinting sabers.

The wagon rolled faster.

"Did you bring a gun?"

"Too dangerous," Jubal said. "I'd be flayed if caught. Of course, also dangerous not to, now."

"Hindsight is always sharpest." I eyed the dogs. "We'll use the wagon tongue. Pole like a boat."

Jubal swung the heavy timber down against the street, and we shoved. Our cargo gained more speed.

Guns flashed in the night, and bullets made a familiar hot wasp sound. My ear had stopped bleeding, but still throbbed. I thought I saw Rochambeau by his officers, gesturing while he clasped a woman's silk dressing robe around his body. A major—the wronged husband?—was shaking his fist at the general.

We were now trundling rapidly downhill, aimed at the sea like a ball at pins, but the mastiffs grew out of the gloom with astonishing speed, sprinting for our wheels and snapping. A huge dog sprang to gain purchase on our cargo, but Jubal swung the wagon tongue in a huge arc as easily as a baton. It cudgeled the beast, knocking him sideways into a building, where he bounced and fell among his fellows. They paused to snap at him, and the distraction gave us precious seconds.

Now we were rumbling with the terrifying momentum of Cayley's flying machine, buildings blurring past, the Caribbean ahead aglitter under the moon, wind warm in our faces.

"How do we slow?" Jubal asked.

"The brake lever."

"It will work at this speed?"

"Possibly. I'll give it a pull."

There was a screech and the wood snapped, stinging my hands. We jerked and went faster.

"Or possibly not. Drag the tongue!"

He tried. The wooden beam bounced, threw up a fountain of dirt and mud, caught on something, and yanked away, almost pulling Jubal off the wagon with it. Now we were racing faster than any horse could run.

The dogs and pursuing soldiers faded in dark behind.

I heard a shouted command and turned to where we were rolling. Ahead, a file of French soldiers had formed to block the road. One had a glowing match he held above a five-pound fieldpiece. "Halt!" he called.

We couldn't. Jubal yanked me down. "They're going to shoot!"

The cannon barked. There was a terrific impact, almost bouncing us clear, and our speed momentarily slackened. A barrel of sugar exploded into a cloud of sparkling white—it had been refined to the costly color, and so no wonder they hoarded it, I thought absently—and then we gained speed again. We struck the cannon and smashed it aside, wheels flying and its spinning barrel scattering the yelling infantry. I think we thumped over one or two men, all of us covered in crystals like snowmen. A few had the wits to shoot, the bullets plunking into the casks. Spouts of sugar laid lines on the street like trails of white gunpowder.

Where were Astiza and Harry?

"More French!" my companion warned.

I looked at the fast-approaching sea. There was a cluster of soldiers on the quay, and a longboat was pulling out from the stone steps and into the harbor. Sailors were pulling on oars, and I saw a woman facing backward at us and a man in the stern pointing something—a pistol?—at her. She lifted her arm to point and the man—Martel, it must be—turned to look at us. And then I saw she was holding a child.

"We're going over!" Jubal warned.

We hit the stone balustrade that marked the edge of the quay, and everything shattered, stone and sugar hogsheads flying like Britain's new fragmentation bombs. I'd read in the newspapers about their invention by a Lieutenant Henry Shrapnel, a name I'd never heard before. We flew, too, launched in a corona of sugar. There was a radiating cloud of white, and then I plunged into the dark Caribbean, the pieces of our vehicle splashing into the water all around us.

Fearing gunfire, I swam away as long as I could hold my breath before surfacing. When my head broke water, I looked wildly about, catching a glimpse of the two people I most wanted to see in the world.

"Astiza! Harry!"

"Ethan!" She shouted from a great distance. "Swim away!"

Little spouts erupted as Martel's scattered henchmen fired at my voice. Then they paused to reload. I considered which way to swim, blessing the tedious nature of ramming down cartridges.

Something seized me, and I almost panicked before realizing it was my black companion. He was dragging me away from the longboat as he swam with his other arm. "This way," he hissed. "Your foolishness has ruined everything, but maybe there's still a chance."

"I need to catch my wife!"

"You're going to outswim a launch? And then give them a chance to slit your throat as you try to climb aboard?"

I let him drag me. "This isn't going well."

"Our only chance is to escape to Dessalines, which I told you in the beginning."

"You're not married, are you?"

He stopped a moment, pulling me near, angry and impatient. "You think I never was? That because I'm black or an ex-slave I don't know what you're feeling right now? I killed the master who raped and murdered the woman I gave my heart to. But I haven't survived the last fifteen years by blundering and boasting. I've used my wits. Perhaps it's time you recovered yours."

That sobered me. I wasn't used to being dressed down by an ex-slave, but I deserved it. Instead of cleverly trailing Martel, which Astiza had no doubt assumed I'd do, I'd charged about with a meat cleaver and aroused an entire city. *What begins in anger ends in shame*, Ben Franklin had warned me.

Maybe I'd let Jubal lead for a while.

We stroked east while staying a hundred yards out to sea, paralleling the quay of Cap-François toward the mouth of the river I'd seen earlier. Unfortunately, my wife and son were headed in the opposite direction. "She's going to board a ship and I'll lose her again," I complained.

"She's away from the siege and the plague. Maybe it's a blessing. Now you must seek black help to find her again."

"You mean Dessalines?"

"Yes. And maybe me." It was said grudgingly, but the offer was sincere.

I was frustrated by my own confusion. Perhaps Astiza had tried to signal me before going off with Martel, but I had rushed upstairs. Why hadn't she called for help to the French officers? They'd have sympathized with a mother and abhorred a kidnapper.

I could see men running along the quay, shouting and pointing, but their shots went wild. Apparently we weren't easy to pinpoint in the dark, with only our heads above water. Dogs were racing up and down the stone bulkhead, too, barking wildly, but all they could smell was the Caribbean.

"I'm tiring," I confessed.

"Kick off your coat and boots and rest on your back. Here, I'll hold you for a moment." And he did, gently, as we both realized we had more in common than expected: tragedy.

"A planter really took your wife?"

"My love. To punish me. He saw promise when I was young and taught me to read and write, despite the fact my size made me a good field hand. But I used the knowledge to communicate with blacks conspiring toward revolution, and when he discovered I'd betrayed him with education, he decided to hurt me in a way deeper than any whipping. We'd become close, like father and son, and he'd promised eventual freedom. In punishment he raped her and threatened to sell her, to remind me of my station. So I killed him, to remind him I was human."

"But he killed her?"

"I surprised him with her as you tried to surprise Rochambeau. She died in the struggle, all of us screaming. Emotions are complex on a plantation."

I began paddling again, slowly. "Emotions are complex everywhere."

"Never more so than with men who have power over you. It was like killing my own father. This entire uprising has been like the killing of fathers, the destruction of a monstrous, incestuous family. Slavery is not just cruel, Ethan. It's intimate, in the worst possible way."

Apparently I wasn't the only one with problems. And now I had dragged this poor soul into the sea.

"I'm sorry, Jubal."

"You don't have to be sorry for my history. You barely know me."

"I'm sorry for the entire bollocks of a world."

"Ah, that makes sense."

We stroked more steadily. "You're a strong swimmer," I said.

"I grew up near the shore and pray to Agwe, the *loa* of the sea."

"I sensed your education. That's why Dessalines uses you as a spy, isn't it?"

"I can do many things. And I have sorrow. Revolutionaries feed on hatreds."

"Sometimes there are happy endings."

"The ending, Ethan, is always death." This statement wasn't bitter, just matter-of-fact.

We finally reached a spit at the mouth of the river that was across from Cap-François and out of easy musket or rifle shot. The two of us panted a moment while lying in the sandy shallows, looking at the city we'd fled.

"Should we run inland?"

"There's a swamp beyond," Jubal said. "Snakes. We need a boat."

"Maybe that's one." I pointed at what appeared to be a log. Disconcertingly, it moved.

"Caiman." His tone was more exasperated than terrified.

"What?"

"Alligator." The beast, of scaly mail and reptilian guile, shook off its lethargy with a rippled of muscle, slid into the water, and came toward us, tail curling like calligraphy. "It smells us when the dogs cannot, and wants a meal."

CHAPTER 24

What do we do?" The speed with which the monster swam was unnerving. It made straight at us as if we were reeling it on a string.

"Stand and shout," Jubal instructed.

"But the French!"

"Exactly."

We sprang up in the shallows, water only to our calves. "Does this scare caimans off?"

"It draws fire! Here! Over here!" He waved.

The beast's body was flexing like the arms of a blacksmith and reminding me of extremely unhappy experiences with a Nile crocodile. But when we stood the moonlight silhouetted us. A great shout went up and muskets fired, bullets peppering the water. A small cannon banged. With a scream a five-pound ball struck the water and skipped like a stone before bounding up the beach.

"This is your strategy?"

"Look." Jubal pointed. The startled alligator had turned and was retreating for the swamp. "Now run, on the sand!"

I glanced a last time at the harbor. The longboat was still clearly visible, pulling for a ship, and I thought—or did I imagine?—Astiza half standing, trying to discern what the soldiers were shooting at in the night. Then we were dashing away upriver, my feet bare, the sand hard-packed, men following on the opposite bank and shooting from two hundred yards away. We were dim shadows against the jungle swamp. I squeezed in on myself as lead sizzled by us.

"There, a fisherman's boat," Jubal pointed. A dugout canoe, again looking like a log, was pulled into marsh grass.

"How do you tell boat from beast in this cursed country?"

"If it bites." He dragged the canoe and we jumped aboard, craft rocking, and seized the paddles. "Like those." Suddenly other "logs" slid into the water. The river was thick with alligators, roused from sleep by our sound and sweat. I heard them plop, and then a snap of exercising jaws.

"Paddle fast," Jubal said.

I needed no encouragement, making a fair imitation of Fulton's suggested steamboats. The caimans followed, each sending out an ominous delta of intersecting waves. It was like being escorted to a dinner, with us the main course.

We stroked upriver, still hard to pick out against the jungle. One musket ball thunked into the wood of our canoe, but otherwise the balls buzzed by like pesky hornets. A tide had turned the sluggish current in our direction. Dark reptilian shapes followed like escorting frigates, their prehistoric eyes gauging our pace and their primitive brains calculating what we might taste like when we spilled. On the opposite shore, horses galloped and dogs loped.

The city gave way to the avenue of shorn palms and then the French camps and outposts. Orders were shouted, torches lit, soldiers roused. Rochambeau was not going to let me slip by if he would help it.

"This was a foolish way to escape, but after a mile the river bends away from their lines," Jubal said.

"Thank goodness. I did some canoeing in Canada but haven't stayed in shape. I didn't think it necessary for retirement."

"You should exercise, because trouble seems to follow you, friend. My plan was to walk quietly out of town, but with your plan, we have to fight through their entire army. This is your pattern, is it not?"

"I wouldn't call it a plan, exactly. More like an unfortunate tendency. I'm just in love."

"Then keep a better hold on your wife than you do."

I began to believe we were past the worst of it. Guns flashed, but the aim was almost random. Cavalry jingled but had no way to get to us. Dogs howled, but it was the howl of frustration. The alligators almost began to seem like a benign train, and a few slipped away as if bored.

Then we neared a bright cluster of flames on the army's riverbank, and my confidence faltered again. Artillerymen were building bonfires to cast light on the river, and an entire battery of field guns had been drawn up, pointing across the water. We had to paddle right past them.

"Should we flee into the swamp?"

"We'd be gator meat and snake chew."

"The French will blow us to kindling."

"Yes. So when I say, flip the canoe."

"Into the reptiles?"

"We have no choice, lover Ethan. Come up under our vessel to breathe. The tide will help. Kick with your feet, and if you feel caiman teeth, try to hit them on the nose. But speed first, fast as we can."

We bent to it in our canoe, setting up a little bow wave and a respectable bubbling wake, me gasping from exertion. Yet we were simply hurrying into firelight. We could hear shouted commands and count the ominous row of cannon muzzles: seven, each one aimed at my right ear. The cavalry had pulled up to watch our extinction. So had the anxious dogs. They growled and whined. With that kind of audience we seemed to crawl across their field of fire.

"Look to your guns!" The words floated across the water.

Firelight danced on the water. Alligators formed a little school.

"Aim . . ."

I felt as picked out as a fly on a wedding cake.

"Now," said Jubal. "Keep your paddle." He jerked sideways, I followed suit, and with a splash we flipped over. As we went in I heard the final word.

"Fire!"

The water was pitch, and only by keeping my hand on the rim of the canoe did I remain oriented. I shoved my head up into its overturned wooden hull. As Jubal had promised, there was a pocket of air there. I couldn't see him in the dark, but I could hear him blowing and breathing as he kicked.

Something scaly bumped my leg, and I jerked.

Then the world erupted. A projectile clipped our dugout, and it boomed like a drum. Other cannonballs plowed into the river all around us, smacking like beaver tails. I couldn't see the splashes, but I could feel their concussion. There was the muffled screech of balls sailing by where we'd been sitting seconds before and thudding into the muddy riverbank beyond.

"That will keep Monsieur Caiman away, I hope," Jubal said.

And indeed, the alligators had the good sense to flee.

I heard cheering through the wooden hull. Did the French think their barrage had overturned us? It must look so, and that we'd drowned or been eaten, since we didn't reappear. The canoe would be very low in the dark. Jubal was swimming awkwardly, holding his paddle and the boat. I did my best to assist, as we slowly drifted east past the bonfires.

"I think we're running out of air," I said.

"Wait, like patient mice."

"What if the caimans come back?"

"Then we feed them you so we don't feed them me."

"*Merci*, Jubal."

"You're the one who wanted to go to the harbor."

What followed was a little eternity of darkness, gasps in the stuffy air of the overturned canoe, occasional shots that I hoped were blind, and the queasy feeling of waiting for teeth to test my leg. I'd no idea if we were even going in the right direction, and the certainty that I'd once more lost wife and son made me almost not care. What a bloody fiasco.

I was wheezing. "Jubal, I need to go out for a breath."

"A minute more."

Then there was the drumlike thud of something striking our overturned canoe. We stopped abruptly. Had the French launched boats to pursue us? I could swim for the swamps to be shot or eaten, or surrender to be hung or burned.

Too tired to flee anymore, I decided.

"Surface," Jubal said.

"To give up?"

"To be saved."

I came up next to our craft. There was a great bright gouge in its top where a ball had hit, but otherwise it was remarkably intact; the hollowed log must be iron-hard. I blinked away water, seeing the white cross bands of uniforms in the dark, and opened my mouth, coughing, readying an apology for throwing a cleaver at the French commander.

But then I realized the faces looking down were all dark, and arms were reaching for us from a plank fishing boat.

"You're rebels?"

Strong hands seized me. "Liberators."

"It's about time," Jubal said.

"Maybe it's you who are late," the soldier replied. "Or maybe General Jean-Jacques Dessalines is angry that you went the opposite way of what he ordered."

I sighed. "I'm afraid our route was my idea."

"My companion is an idiot, Antoine," Jubal said from the water beside me. "But perhaps a useful idiot."

They hauled me aboard. "He don't look useful," a man with sergeant stripes said. "He looks drowned." They laughed. Jubal flopped in next to me. The French bonfires had receded, the night protective.

"I have an urgent message for General Dessalines," I said.

Antoine leaned close. "Then you can deliver it while he decides whether to kill you or cook you, white man."

They laughed again, and I silently prayed the hilarity wouldn't draw gunfire.

CHAPTER 25

Jubal and I staggered exhausted from the rebel boat and collapsed to sleep on the bank of the river. We were hidden from view by mangrove trees and wakened at midmorning by heat and insects. Then we shared a breakfast of pork and plantain as we watched land crabs scuttle and caimans yawn. Our escort of a dozen blacks was as armed as a platoon of pirates with pistol, musket, and bayonet. Cane knives and machetes took the place of swords. A boy of ten perched in a tree, still as a cat, watching for French patrols.

"You like to cause trouble, white man," said Antoine, a former field hand risen to full colonel. "Never have I heard so much shooting at one soggy head."

"Two, if you count Jubal."

"I think it was you they were aiming at, no?"

I conceded the point. "I am plagued by misunderstandings."

"He acts with his heart instead of his head," Jubal interpreted.

"You mean a woman," Antoine guessed. "Cock instead of caution." They laughed.

"Even worse," said Jubal. "A wife."

"Care instead of carefree!"

"I'm actually quite a careful planner, and my wife even more so," I told them. "It's just that the French in Cap-François are excitable."

"So now you try the other side."

"You do seem more relaxed."

"That's because we are winning."

I was marched under rebel escort into the abandoned sugar-cane fields, still limping from my sprain, my ear aching, my feet bare. The ground, thankfully, was the red soil of soft farmland. It was a relief to have lost my coat; I wondered why I'd worn it in the Caribbean as long as I had. The Negroes gave me another straw hat and a smear of ashes for my nose and ears, to protect against the sun.

Dirt lanes connecting the plantations led this way and that, but instead of grand colonial homes there were only hollow monuments to twelve years of slaughter. The land was humid and initially seemed deserted, but then we'd pass a clearing hacked in the cane and there'd be a platoon of black soldiers camped, dressed in a hodgepodge of captured French military dress, stolen planter fineries, and rags leftover from slavery. The men were lean, tough, and confident. One might puff a pipe, another sharpen a blade. They'd stop chatting and stare at me with suspicion as I trudged past, the lone white amid a squad of blacks. Was I prisoner or mercenary?

But studying them, I was now certain that Napoleon would never reinstate slavery on this island. The inhabitants had become independent not just in deed but in mind. It's like trying to force a boy or girl coming of age back into childhood; it cannot be done.

"I can see why the French hesitate to fight you," I said to Jubal.

"Some of these men have been at war all their adult lives," he told me. "Most have lost brothers, mothers, wives. When we liberate a plantation, we share what is seized, but any money goes to buy arms from Yankee gunrunners. We have men with American rifles who can pick off French officers before they know they are being aimed at."

"I once had a long rifle. I'm rather a good shot, actually."

"We have all the shooters we need. Dessalines seeks thinkers."

"You think, don't you, Jubal?"

"Books became bread. It was a mistake by my master. I realized there were alternatives."

"You're the kind of man who reads and ponders, and thinks before he speaks. Most men in Paris and London can't do that, you know."

"Right now, I'm thinking how to make a case for you."

Several miles from Cap-François we began to pass villages with huts of liberated black women and children. They'd already converted small sections of cane field to vegetable patches and animal pens. Chickens clucked, pigs grunted, and naked toddlers wandered, the latter reminding me of my missing son. How much would a three-year-old remember me after all these months? I could only pray he'd found succor with the return of his mother, and that she'd tell him good things about Papa.

How interesting if females ruled, instead of men with their dreams of martial glory! Less sorrow and more dullness, I guessed. More contentment and less inspiration. Not better or worse, necessarily, but different. An easier environment to sustain retirement.

A tropical wood topped the cane fields on a low hill too rocky and poor for agriculture. Within its shade was the main rebel camp. Instead of the closed tents of the French army, the blacks had stretched canvas awnings between the trees to create a network of pavilions that let through the breeze. The elevation put the headquarters at a deliberate distance from stagnant water, keeping mosquitoes at bay. Looted plantation tables and chairs provided outdoor furniture, and hammocks were strung for sleep. A haze of campfire smoke hung in the branches. I could smell roast pig and baking bread, and after our march I was as hungry as when I met Napoleon.

I didn't get any food before this meeting, either.

The rebel army was not entirely the color of coal. Some were mulattos, and others white deserters. Poles who'd hoped service with France would spread revolution to their homeland instead found themselves hirelings in the sultry Caribbean. Most died immediately of yellow fever, but some survived to flee to the rebel army. Several had become drillmasters because the illiterate field hands responded almost automatically to white command, a habit ingrained since birth. I saw a company marching back and forth to a profane, shouted pidgin of French, African, and Polish.

I also saw children and grandmothers, fancy girls and cripples, craftsmen and cooks. There were dogs, cats, pet parrots, and braying donkeys. In one corner men were clustered around fighting cocks, cheering the birds on.

Dessalines's headquarters was in the middle of this conglomeration of several thousand men and women, his pavilion roofed by what looked to be a liberated mainsail. Oriental carpets were spread on the ground. Huge black bodyguards ringed what seemed to be an open-air throne room, and the general presided on a red velvet settee that reminded me of the purple one in the office of Rochambeau. He glanced up from papers as I approached, frowning. I was pale, limping, unarmed, soiled, and barefoot. I didn't look like much of a hero, or of much use, for that matter.

Jean-Jacques Dessalines, in contrast, exuded power and menace.

He was handsomer than L'Ouverture, a Negro of forty-five years, with high cheekbones, a firm chin, powerful torso, and the erect carriage of the French army officer he'd been. His sideburns extended into muttonchops, kinked hair cut close to his skull: in the heat, skin glistening, he looked as chiseled from black marble as a Roman statue of a Nubian lord. His gaze was predatory as an eagle. The general had set aside on the sofa a bicorn hat with ostrich plume, and wore an unbuttoned full military dress jacket with epaulettes and braiding. He was African chieftain crossed with military marshal, but his look of fierce intelligence exceeded either. Dessalines was reputed to be cruel, quick, and brilliantly determined.

Jubal had told me the general was made overseer as a young man because of his obvious cleverness, had been purchased by a free black named Dessalines, and had taken his Negro master's name. When the slave uprising began in 1791, the opportunistic slave joined the revolt. Through courage, ruthlessness, and strength of personality, he became a key lieutenant to L'Ouverture. He followed Toussaint through a complex web of alliances and rifts with Spanish, British, French, and rival black armies, each side betraying the other again and again as the island's tangle of ethnicities jockeyed for power. Dessalines was L'Ouverture's fist, taking no prisoners and burning enemy homes to the ground. Just the year before, he'd heroically defended a fort against eighteen thousand French attackers, retreating only after an epic twenty-day siege. He then succeeded Toussaint when that general was betrayed in June of 1802. Now, in November of 1803, this general had squeezed the last whites into Cap-François. He met every atrocity the French could invent with cruelty of his own, and hanged, shot, burned, drowned, and tortured.

It was to this man that I'd fled for mercy and aid.

"We fished the American," Antoine announced. "He decided to swim instead of walk. Jubal was good enough not to leave him for the caimans."

"The reptiles spat him out," my black friend said.

Dessalines studied me skeptically. "Is he useful?"

"He is famous," said Jubal.

"That's not the same thing."

"And handsome!" called a black woman back in the crowd,

leaning lazily against a tree. More people laughed, which I hoped was a good sign. I straightened, trying to look the part of resolute savant instead of desperate refugee. Maybe I could interest them in electricity, share some of Franklin's aphorisms, or teach them a game of cards.

"Silence." Dessalines held up his hand, and the laughter snuffed like an extinguished candle. He turned to me. "So you've come to the winning side." His voice was low and sonorous.

"I believe we have common interests," I replied with more confidence than I felt. "The United States wishes to see you victorious so that Napoleon will complete the transfer of Louisiana to my country. The British hope you will deprive their archenemy of Saint-Domingue, France's richest colony. And the French are in pursuit of a legend they think will help them conquer the English. You've become not just the most important man in the land you call Haiti, General Dessalines, but one of the most important men in the world."

I'd rehearsed this bit of flattery because I wasn't certain how I'd be welcomed. Around me was Africa in all its dark power, and somehow I had to enlist help. His officers looked as skeptical and opportunistic as medieval earls. One whom I'd learn was named Cristophe was an imposing seven feet tall, while another named Capois tensed like a coiled spring. Even when resting, he seemed poised for attack. They were shrewd-looking, hard-muscled, swaggering men, with pistols in their sashes and tattoos on arms and faces. Some were as gaudily clothed as Dessalines, but one slim giant wore epaulettes on a cord slung around his neck so that his torso was bare in the heat. He displayed scars of an old whipping on his back.

They were still men like me, I reminded myself. *Savages we call them because their manners differ from ours*, old Ben Franklin had once observed.

"Indeed," Dessalines replied to my speech. "The whole world knows the importance of Jean-Jacques Dessalines. And men come to me now that I have power for only one reason, the hope that *I* can help *them*." He looked at me narrowly. "Is this not true?"

It would do no good to deny the obvious. "It's true of me."

"Hmph." He let his eyes roam the assembly, keeping attention on his performance with the skill of an actor. "I'm told you were the last to speak to Toussaint L'Ouverture."

"I tried to rescue him, but he was shot in prison."

"Yet he told you something."

"A secret to my wife."

"He was the first of the blacks, but now he presides over his fallen brothers in Guinea. It is I, Dessalines, who is first of the blacks now."

"Which is why I've come to you, General."

"But I only help *those* who can help *me*."

"You and I can help each other."

"The French have stolen his wife and son," Jubal spoke up. "He has reason to join us, *Commandant*."

"Indeed?" The general took up a French snuffbox, a pretty thing of silver and pearl, took a pinch of tobacco, and sneezed.

"Revenge," Jubal said.

"Hmph." The black leader pointed to a red and blue banner hanging from a tree. In the middle was a coat of arms. "Do you know what that is, Monsieur Gage?"

"A battle standard?"

"It's the new flag of Haiti. Do you see what it is missing?"

I glanced, but shook my head. "I'm poor with riddles."

"It's sewn from the French tricolor, but I had the white removed."

"Ah."

"I hate whites, white man. I hate mulattos, the arrogant *gens de couleur* who fought us and pretended they are our betters because of the lightness of their skin." His eyes darted at some of the followers he had just insulted. "I hate the French, I hate the

Spanish, I hate the British, and I hate the Americans. I and my slave brothers have been whipped and hanged by white-skins for two hundred years. I have flayed and burned and stabbed and strangled a thousand in return, with my very own hands. What do you think of that?"

This wasn't going well. Despite my battles, everyone seems more belligerent than me. I cleared my throat. "I do not want to be number one thousand and one."

There was dead silence, and I feared I'd said the wrong thing, immediately hoping for a quick shooting over a slow roasting. Then Dessalines abruptly barked a laugh, Jubal guffawed in relief, and the other rebel officers joined, too. Laughter rippled around the encampment as my joke was repeated, women shrieking with the men. I smiled hesitantly.

It's always flattering to be the center of attention.

Dessalines put his hand up, and everyone instantly went silent again. "Then you will earn your keep, as every other soldier does in my army. Are you my soldier now, Ethan Gage?"

When drafted, it's wisest to make the best of things. "I certainly hope so. I want to liberate Cap-François." I tried to make my nervous smile broader, straighten my shoulders, raise my chin, and otherwise mimic martial traits. "I support blacks, and admire what you've accomplished."

"And maybe I'll let a white man help us finish, should he prove useful."

Here was my chance. "I can help you defeat the French fortifications."

He raised his brow. "How?"

"But if I do that, there's something you must do for me as well." My experience with tyrants is that they admire a bit of cheek, so I mustered what courage I had. Bonaparte responded to my cockiness, and Sidney Smith, too.

"You dare bargain with *me*?" Dessalines glowered like a thunderhead. The whites of his eyes had a faint yellowish cast, and the pale underside of his fingers tapped the hilt of his sword with the rattle of drumsticks. But my bet was that he was acting, too.

"I'm in pursuit of an ancient secret," I proclaimed, forcing my voice louder. "It's possible that your people, and only your people, can help me. If I find it, we can share it, and it's so fabulous you can build your new nation with it. I'm the key. You'll be greater than Spartacus, greater than Washington, greater than Bonaparte."

"I want to be an emperor."

"And I can help make you one." I could do no such thing, of course, but what happened after we found the treasure of Montezuma was immaterial to me. I needed to find the loot to bargain for Astiza and Harry, and this brilliant megalomaniac was the path to it. "However, this isn't a secret to share with an entire army, and not something your military officers need know." I glanced about me at his entourage of killers. "I'll help with the attack on Cap-François; I have a plan to breach their defense. But before I do so, I need to meet those *hungars* and *mambos*, priests and priestesses, who know the most about your gods and legends. I need to learn what they know." Astiza had taught me the titles, and I missed her desperately. She gets a better reception than I do among strangers, and notices details I miss.

"Be careful of our voodoo, white man. It has power that even we can't control."

"I don't need power. Just legends. Then *I* can help *you*."

"He bargains with nothing," muttered the tall black, Cristophe. Dessalines glanced at him with respect.

In any card game, there's a time to throw all in. "I need to meet with Cecile Fatiman," I declared.

"Cecile?" asked Dessalines. "How do you know that name?"

"She's a famous priestess, Jubal tells me."

"A *mambo*, yes."

"A *mambo* from the very beginning of the revolt in Boukman Wood."

"She's our wisest, said to be more than one hundred years old."

"That's who I need. She foresaw my coming. And my wife learned that Cecile is led by the voodoo spirit Ezili Danto." There was a murmur in the crowd at mention of these names. "I need to meet with Mambo Cecile, tap her witchcraft, and solve your problems and mine at the same time."

"But what of the French defenses?"

"After I meet Cecile I'll be ready to help you surprise them."

CHAPTER 26

Dessalines said he'd consult with his officers about my request and, encouragingly, ordered Jubal and me to have something to eat. My big companion was even hungrier than me. We were led to an elegantly carved table, chipped and stained since it had been dragged from some mansion into the encampment in the wood. There we were fed pig, goat, yams, and fried plantain, our water purified with liberated rum. I've seldom eaten a meal more delicious, but then Franklin said hunger makes the best dish.

We were served by a striking young black woman whom Jubal called *cherie* and slapped on the bottom with cheerful familiarity. When I looked questioning, he introduced her.

"This is Juliet, my newest wife."

"Wife!"

She shoved him. "I no wife to you! You get a priest or a *hangar* if you want a wife! You get me some money, or a home."

"Common-law wife." He winked. "When we win, we make a home."

"And the love you told me about?" I asked.

"Long time ago." He threw down a rib bone and picked up another. "This American is famous, girl. He knows about lightning."

"Pah." She looked me up and down. "He wouldn't last half a day cutting cane."

"No white man can."

"What is he good for, then?"

"He's going to find us all treasure, and then I can buy you that house."

"Pah. You just proud to have a white man. He be dead of the fevers by Christmas." She gave me a spoonful of mashed yam. "Be careful, Jubal. He keep you in trouble."

I relaxed on the theory that they wouldn't waste food on a man they were about to hang. Then I realized they *might* fatten a man they were about to eat, and glanced about anxiously for a big boiling pot or roasting spit. I didn't really believe rumors that the rebels were cannibals, but who knew what their relatives had done in Africa? Fanciful books were popular about that continent, because the less authors know about a place the more they can invent. Everything I'd read about blacks had been written by whites, and it was the most lurid and sensational pamphlets that sold smartest in Paris.

I'd expected the slave army to be a ragged group of bandits and cutthroats, but that wasn't at all what I found. Many of the men were in captured European uniforms and, at various points in the war, had benefited from European military drill. Many had the gazellelike grace I envied, an easy athleticism, but they also exhibited discipline. They were organized into quite competent regiments, with stern officers and regular practice. They had dozens of pieces of artillery captured or bought, and most had possession of a good musket, bayonet, and cane knife. There was a cavalry bivouac nearby with a thousand good horses, and the total size of the rebel force, Jubal confided, exceeded fifteen thousand. The blacks had been fighting the French longer than Washington fought the British during our Revolutionary War, and perseverance is the secret of success. They had the confidence that comes from many victories, and the cunning that comes from springing clever traps.

More than just disease was defeating the French.

As I sipped fermented juices and calculated my own plans, I realized that if I were to get any credit for their victory I'd have to scramble to get ahead of these natural warriors. They'd win anyway, but I had to convince them that some of it was due to me, so they'd help me fetch the treasure. That is, if it even existed at all.

Finally full, I leaned back against a tree as the shadows lengthened and brooded, my thoughts turning to Astiza. I knew it had been a mistake to allow my wife to be a spy, but then she hadn't given me a whole lot of choice in the matter. She was independent as the devil. Yet why had she gone off with Leon Martel? Had he recognized her after all? Could she not resist asking about Harry? Had she struck a devil's bargain, choosing expedient alliance with Martel and sure reunion with Horus over dubious partnership with me? And what was the Frenchman's game? Was he tired of taking care of a little boy, or was he upping the ante? How could I make his greed a partner in my own cause? My head ached, my muscles were sore, my skin bitten, and soon I was asleep.

I was jostled awake near midnight. The camp slept, but some officers and sergeants wound through on various missions, sentries stood, and lanterns shone where Dessalines's throne was. Perhaps the generals were still awake; Napoleon's habit of sleeplessness might be universal among the bloodthirsty. It was Antoine who'd shaken me. When Jubal came awake, too, he laid a hand on my comrade. "Not you. The American. Alone."

I got up clumsily in the dark, disoriented. "What is it?" I still feared execution as a white man.

"What you asked for. Be quiet, and follow." He led me through the rebel camp and sleeping soldiers without a misstep, even though I could hardly see a thing. He murmured words to the men standing guard, and we came out of the woods and hiked into the cane fields. There was starlight enough to follow the dirt lanes, but I noticed the moon was waning. November would soon have dark nights, an optimum time for a surprise attack. Occasionally I'd hear a distant gunshot, that habitual popping from armies close to each other.

We walked south and east, farther from Cap-François, the ground sloping downward and getting muddier against my bare feet. More trees, and then the humid, rotting, overhanging architecture of a swamp. It was utterly dark, but I could smell stagnant water and guessed we were somewhere near the river again. Mist curled, moss hung like ragged curtains from the limbs, and my guide, who'd not spoken another word, took a lantern down from a tree and lit it. The ground had become treacherous, and this time our circuitous route threaded from island to island, with occasional wades through short stretches of black swamp water. I kept an eye out for caimans and water snakes, and started at the sight of several logs and limbs. Antoine smiled when I did so, his teeth a flash in the night.

There was the familiar chorus of frogs and night insects, but it began to falter before another sound. Through the darkness came faint drumming in time with my own heart. Thump, thump, thump. It kept pace with the tempo of our walk, an echo to the mystery of life itself. Was this the way to Cecile Fatiman? We walked in the drums' direction, the sound getting deeper, felt as much as heard. The rhythm was ominous.

"Where are we going?"

Animal eyes gleamed from the jungle, watching us slip past.

On and on, deeper and deeper. The sound of the drums grew. I shivered, despite the warm humid air clamped like a blanket.

Abruptly, my guide stopped. "Here." He handed me the horn lantern. "Go on yourself now."

"What? Wait!" I glanced to where he gestured. Darkness. Was this a trap?

I turned to ask Antoine to stay. He'd disappeared.

Frogs played their noisy chorus. Insects whined in my ears. Overlain on this music was the rumbling of drums. The solitude was daunting.

Except I wasn't alone. There was a figure ahead in the mist, I now realized, waiting for me.

I raised the lantern. This new companion looked slight, poised more than planted, meaning more likely a woman than a man. Cecile? Her figure seemed too young, so maybe just a guide. I stepped off toward this new apparition.

She waited until I came near and then without a word led me deeper into the swamp, elusive before I could make out her features. The water we threaded past was opaque, still as a well. Roots climbed out of mud like frozen snakes. The dank smell was as heavy as the blood of birth.

Yes, it was a woman, her grace over uneven ground uncanny and her speed outstripping mine. Her hood topped a loose shift of pale cotton, and while it initially made her shapeless I now saw the swing of shoulder and hip. There was something about the flow of her, natural like mist, water, clouds, the curl of a wave, that convinced me she must not just be beautiful, but beautiful in some ethereal, unworldly, impossibly perfect way. I hurried to catch up to confirm this magic, and yet she seemed to float effortlessly ahead of me, receding like a rainbow. I knew that if she left me, I'd be utterly lost.

She pulled me like filings to a magnet.

Now I was sure I was hearing the pounding of drums from deep within the swamp. I was going, I guessed, to some kind of religious or political ceremony, similar perhaps to the one in Boukman Wood that had initiated this revolution. Lightly this woodland sprite led me toward the noise, slowing if I needed to catch up, floating out of reach if I came too near. I was sweating with excitement and apprehension. Who was she?

What you seek, suddenly echoed in my brain.

We came to a clearing, a small barren island of damp ground in a swampy wilderness. In the middle was a small hut of thatch and sticks from which a single candle glowed. My guide stopped at the far edge of this isle. She pointed at the dim hut. Clearly I was to enter. Would she follow? But no, she dissolved into shadow, and I felt intense disappointment. I was left to enter on my own.

Hesitantly I stepped forward, set aside my lantern, and stooped, poking my head into the hut as nervously as if putting it under the guillotine blade.

The structure was as primitive as my mental picture of Africa, its dome a weave of fronds and rushes. The floor was dirt. The candle burned on a small altar just one foot high, covered with a red-checkered cloth so I couldn't see whether it was made of wood or rock. A goblet in the middle of this tabernacle held what appeared to be clear water, and four smooth river stones held down the cloth at the corners. On one side of the goblet was a human skull, and on the other a scattering of flowers. There was also a little heap of seashells.

Well, it was exotic, but there was actually nothing more ominous about this collection than the display in a Masonic Lodge. Certainly I didn't feel the kind of religious menace I'd experienced with the Egyptian Rite.

"The symbol for Ezili Danto is the red-checkered heart."

I looked into the hut's shadows. Against the opposite wall floated the illuminated face of an aged crone, her skin leather-colored in the candlelight. Her age was not evident in the creasing of her face—in fact, her countenance seemed remarkably smooth, if mottled—but her long years were betrayed in the wispiness of her gray hair and eyes sunk like stones in dough, their depths holding wisdom that comes only from time and hard experience. Her parted lips showed the tip of her tongue, as if testing the air for scent like a serpent. This, I guessed, was Cecile Fatiman, the famed *mambo* of revolution.

"I'm something of a student of religious symbolism. My wife more so. And the flowers?"

"Ezili's. She is flower herself."

"The water?"

"Purity of life. The stones anchor the four directions." Cecile's voice signified approval; she liked my curiosity.

"And the shells?"

"Cast to divine the future. To see your coming, Ethan Gage."

I crouched in the entrance, not certain what I was supposed to do.

"You didn't bring your sorceress wife with you," she continued in her husky French. It was half reprimand and half question. "The shells talked of her as well."

"She was taken from me by an evil Frenchman."

"And now you come to us, the white who needs the blacks."

"Yes. I'm seeking information to win back my son as well. The same information can help you."

"You mean my people."

"The revolutionaries of Haiti. You are Cecile, yes?"

"But of course. Sit." She gestured to a spot near the entry. The hut was no bigger than a small tent. I crowded in and crossed my legs. Sitting, my head almost brushed the rush dome. The candle was red as blood, the wax melting down the edges of the altar like rivulets of lava.

"Can you help me?" I asked.

"Perhaps the *loa* can help you. You know what *loa* are?"

"Gods, or spirits."

"They speak to believers."

"Then I will try to believe. I'm not as good at it as my wife."

"The *loa* speak through the power that animates all true religions. Do you know what that power is, seeker?"

"Faith?"

"Love."

The hardest thing to earn, and give. I was silent.

"Only love has the power to ward off evil. Without it, we are damned. Now. Drink this." She handed me a wooden bowl filled with cool liquid that smelled rancid. "It will help you listen and see."

"What is it?"

"Wisdom, white man. Drink."

I sipped, confirming its bitterness. I hesitated.

"Do you think wisdom should be sweet?" she asked.

What you seek. I shrugged and downed it all, almost gagging. What choice did I have? There was no point in poisoning me; they could kill me in a thousand simpler ways. They might drug me, but for what? So I swallowed, gasping, its taste of bitter vines, cobwebs, and grave liners.

I grimaced and handed the bowl back.

She laughed softly. Half her teeth were gone.

"Are you really more than a hundred years old?" I asked, fighting back bile.

"A slave has no name of her own, a slave has no birth of her own. A slave just is. So I count my age from what I remember the French say went on in the world as I grew. Yes, I see more and remember more than anyone. I go back a century, maybe more." She laughed softly again.

My stomach lurched, and settled. I began to feel drunk, but in a very odd way. My body tingled, not unpleasantly but unnaturally, and the candlelight oscillated. Yes, drugs. I would see *loa*, all right. Was that the intention?

"I'm looking for stories about a treasure you may know about, but only to share after using it to win my family back." I had to work to sustain my concentration. "If you help me, your people can keep the loot before the British or French get it. You can build your country. And I will help you take Cap-François from Rochambeau."

"What treasure?"

"Montezuma's."

She smiled. "If I knew of treasure, wouldn't I have it by now?" She cackled at her own joke. Her face seemed to melt and reform in the candlelight. I saw now that she was a round woman, well fed, swathed neck to ankle in a patterned dress, colors muted in the dark. Her nose was flat and wide, and her nails long on fingers as gnarled as driftwood.

"I don't know." I felt confused. "L'Ouverture told my wife a secret. The British believe your people may know more. I only hope."

"You saw Toussaint alive?"

"I saw him killed. I was trying to rescue him. He was very sick."

"Napoleon killed him." She turned and spat into the dirt, a dark glob that suddenly seemed as menacing as serpent venom. "A man like Napoleon, he accumulates many curses."

"Great men attract great enemies."

She drank from the bowl herself, slurping, gave a sigh, and put it down, dragging her hand across her mouth. "And what did L'Ouverture tell you, Ethan Gage? The *loa* said you would come to us from across the sea with word of our hero Toussaint."

My tongue was thickening from the drink. "That the emeralds were in the diamond."

She frowned, disappointed. "I do not know what that means."

My own spirits dropped. "I was sure you would! You're the wisest *mambo*."

"There are stories. The escaped slaves who hid in the jungle are called Maroons, and there were always tales that some of them had found a great treasure and hid it, for reasons unknown.

But no one remembers where it was stowed. And no one has ever mentioned a diamond. No treasure has appeared."

"L'Ouverture was sick. Could he have been raving?"

She considered, then shrugged. "But the *loa*, the spirits, they know. You want to understand what L'Ouverture told your wife, American?"

"Of course."

"Then come. You must dance with Ezili Danto, the dark seductress of wood and water."

CHAPTER 27

I backed out of the hut, and Cecile ponderously followed. She picked up my lantern and waddled toward the sound of the drums. Once more, I followed. She was as sure as my other guides in twisting through the maze of land and water, but much slower, and she stopped sometimes to wheeze, insects droning in time to her breaths. I waited uneasily, feeling I'd been brought on a test, not an invitation.

The wood throbbed with sound.

"I feel things watching us," I said.

"Just *baka*," she dismissed. "Small monster."

"Small *what*?"

"They watch in the night. *Diab*, too. Devils. Don't let them take you."

"And how am I to do that?"

"Stay on the right path. You are in Haiti now."

What you seek. I followed so close her skirt brushed my ankles. The forest seemed malevolent, as if I'd stepped through a portal into an underworld. I'd sense something watching or creeping and whirl around, but there was never anything I could see.

Cecile cackled softly.

I finally spied firelight through the leaves, and I knew we were coming to the source of the drumming. Our damp trail broadened to a beaten lane bordered by two rows of poles like lampposts. I glanced up at what I first thought were flowers or ribbons decorating the posts' tops. But no, black roosters dangled upside down, the throats of each one neatly cut and drained.

"The poor will eat tomorrow," Cecile said.

We entered an open-air church, the swamp trees a cathedral wall, the ceiling a cone-shaped thatch roof. At this peristyle's center, jutting toward the roof's peak, was a stout phallic pole fifteen feet high. At least a hundred people lined the periphery of this temple, focused on the pole the way a Philadelphia congregation would be focused on an altar. A fire pit illuminated dark faces. The celebrants swayed to a mesmerizing drumbeat. The music came from four male drummers opposite our entry, their instruments flared at the top, narrow at the bottom, and made of hide stretched over jungle wood. Other musicians had flattened bells, bamboo flutes, and wooden triangles. The rhythm pumped like a heart.

"Now you see voodoo," said Cecile. "This is the oldest religion. It comes from when man was born." She took a gourd shaped like a rattle and shook it, and I could hear seeds inside. "This is an *ason*. I must consecrate this place for Ezili."

She moved around the perimeter of the peristyle, acknowledging the greetings of robed worshippers by shaking her instrument while they bowed. They set a beat with their feet, the ceremony as electric as if charged by the generator I'd once built at Acre. The air itself seemed to prickle. My own senses were heightened, as if I could hear distant whispers and see in the dark.

Cecile accepted a pitcher of what I assumed was holy water. This was offered to the four compass points, and then poured three times: once at the post, once at the peristyle's entrance, and once, oddly, at my feet. Was I some sort of sacrifice? Cecile spoke in slave Creole, the crowd answering, and I followed only a few words. Sometimes I thought I heard a name of one of the voodoo gods that Astiza had mentioned to me, memories of old Africa scrambled with stories of the Catholic saints: Mawu, Bosu, Damballah, Simbi, Sogbo, Ogu. The old woman stooped stiffly and began sketching patterns on the dirt floor. If Communion is designed to bring Christ into the souls of its participants, I guessed these drawings were designed to bring voodoo gods into the assembly.

Just what I was doing here I still didn't know, but the drums were slowly accelerating, the swaying of the celebrants becoming more pronounced. Finally they began to dance and chant, moving in a circle in serpentlike undulation. They sipped from bowls as I had, and responded in chorus to Creole calls from Cecile. The dances were stately and intricate, not savage or erotic, and choreographed as carefully as the cotillion I'd just seen in the Government House of Rochambeau.

Black hands tugged at me, and I hesitantly joined the circulation, not dancing exactly but swaying as best I could, feeling clumsy and conspicuous. My companions, however, smiled at my attempt. Another bowl was offered, and I drank the bitter broth, just to be polite. I found the taste not quite as acrid this time, but my mouth was growing numb. I was thirsty, and drank more.

Time ceased, or rather my perception of it. I'd no sense how long we danced except that it seemed both a moment and an eternity, and the melody permeated so deeply that I felt myself *becoming* music. The noise was a bridge between our realm and the supernatural, and did indeed invite spirits from another world.

The crowd suddenly parted, as if pushed by an invisible force, and a new figure stepped onto the stamped floor of the temple. I stumbled and gaped. It was my earlier hooded guide, the elusive woman of the swamps, except that now the hood was down and her luxuriant dark hair cascaded to her waist. She stepped toward the central post with the grace of a doe, eyes large and dark, lips sensuous, neck high, gaze transfixing. There was something animal about her, human but wild, uninhibited, skittish.

"Ezili," the crowd murmured.

She could not really be a goddess; it was a young woman playing the part. Except that in my inebriated condition she did seem to float instead of walk, and glow with translucence instead of blocking the light. When she reached out to touch the central pillar, a spark seemed to flash between flesh and wood, and I jumped. I was transfixed, hypnotized, reason gone and emotion roaring.

Women, as Jubal had observed, make me stupid.

This creature put her back to the post and rotated her head to smile at all of us, but especially me. At least I thought her attention was focused on me. I gaped, trying to remember dignity. Astiza was beautiful, but this woman was beyond beauty; she was luminous as a Madonna, polished as a marble saint, delicate as Venetian glass. Her complexion was mulatto but with a golden tint, reminding me of amber, or celestial honey, its flow somehow explaining the languid precision of her movements. All her features were perfect, in an almost unnatural way, which attracted and repelled at the same time. Ezili seemed like an idol forbidden to human touch. Her smile was dazzling, and when she lifted her arms above her head and planted one foot on the post to lean back, the pose lifted her breasts, arched her back, and emphasized her unworldly sublimity. Where had they found this damsel? But perhaps she really wasn't a girl at all but truly Ezili in the flesh! Or, at least Ezili as I might imagine her after three bowls of Cecile's broth. I couldn't look away. Now her shift seemed artfully draped by an erotic sculptor, toga folds as light and fine as spider silk.

The drums grew louder.

"Damballah!"

The crowd gave a shout that was almost a sigh, and I startled to see a snake slither into our gathering. No one jumped away. The serpent was thick as my arm and longer than my body, but undulated across the dirt toward Ezili as if trained like a pet. Her eyes gleamed welcome, and its tongue flicked in and out. I glanced at Cecile. The tip of the *mambo*'s tongue was between her lips.

"Damballah blesses us with his visit!" she shouted.

The snake seemed to have no more fear of people than they had fear of it, and came on toward the woman at the post as if to squeeze or devour her. I was transfixed, horrified, fascinated. Would no one rescue the beauty?

But no, Ezili stooped, held out an arm, and the snake slithered up as if climbing a tree limb, the congregants moaning in appreciation. Woman and animal entwined, the snake curling around her shoulders. Its diamond-shaped head dipped as if to explore her torso, a tableau both revolting and erotic.

"Damballah says it is time," Ezili told her audience in a clear, commanding voice. Men stepped forward, took the serpent from her, and carried the snake back to the surrounding jungle with reverence befitting the Ark of the Covenant. They dropped the reptile into foliage, and it swiftly slithered away.

Now there was a squeal and a scrabble of small hooves. A black pig was dragged into this jungle church, straining against a red leather rope. The animal was scrubbed clean as a cat, its tail and ears tied with ribbons. The eyes were wide as if guessing its fate, its body heaving.

Ezili's eyes—and that's how I thought of her now, Ezili Danto the *loa*, the compelling beauty goddess of the voodoo world— shut in welcome.

The pig skidded into the designs Cecile had drawn to call down the gods, and the old woman waddled forward with a bright steel knife. She called to the congregants; their chorus chanted in reply. Call and chant, call and chant. It was a sacrificial song. Now the goddess-girl was holding a silver bowl—when had it been brought to her?—and when Cecile bent to expertly slit the animal's throat, the assembly roared and sang. Ezili caught the arc of blood in her metal receptacle, and when the spurt subsided and the pig lay in the dust (with the tired dignity of sacrifice, I thought), she lifted the bowl high and danced a twirl, as spritely as an Irish jig. The Haitians raised their own arms and whirled to mimic her.

Then she brought down the crimson liquid and Cecile threw in herbs, salt, and a hearty splash of rum. Ezili danced around the edge of their church with this pagan communion. Some dipped fingers in the bloody broth and sucked them dry, while others scooped up enough to paint a cross on their own foreheads.

It was blasphemy, and yet blasphemy synchronized with the life-and-death truths of our earth, like the symbol of wine at Communion.

Blood was sprinkled on the post, on the trampled designs, and on the instruments of the musicians, bright droplets flung from Ezili's fingers. She laughed as she danced.

I was the last to be served. The goddess twirled and stopped before me, hair and dress settling as she posed. She gave me a seductive smile, eyes probing. What was I supposed to do? But I knew what, and as she and everyone else in the assembly watched I dipped my fingers and sucked the blood as the others had done. It was salty, fiery with rum, and the herbs made my vision waver even more. The congregation roared, the drumming grew even louder, and then I was dancing round and round the periphery with Ezili, not touching her but somehow turning with her, as if the drums of Africa themselves had instructed me in the dance. I was hopelessly drunk by her beauty and wondering if I'd just become damned.

Cecile suddenly gripped my shoulders, her old claws strong as talons. "The answers come from her, monsieur," she whispered fiercely.

"I want her. I'm terrified of her."

"You must follow her to learn what you want to know."

What you seek. Without conscious decision I trailed Ezili out of the peristyle and into the jungle, moving as if in a dream. Once more she floated ahead but never so far that I couldn't keep up my pursuit. She led me from swamp into low jungle hills, farther and farther from the drums, up along ridge crests and down into small ravines, her gown aglow like fairy light.

As I followed I sensed another presence as well, predatory and looming. This wasn't the devils I'd sensed with Cecile before, but something huge, dark, ill intended; it was stalking me, its breath hot. Except when I furtively looked around, I couldn't see its eyes or anything else, only feel it in my imagination. It was not an animal that tracked me but a man, a sorcerer, a *loa*, unshakable as a shadow or the guilt of a horrible secret. I whirled about, again and again, but nothing was there. At least, nothing that I could see. The forest shut out the sky; I had no sense of stars, moon, or direction. I hurried after Ezili, panting now. Her dress had become almost transparent, accentuating every curve of her body. I dimly remembered I was married and that I was here for my wife, but could no more stop following this apparition than I could stop breathing.

What was I thinking? Nothing at all.

The drumming of the ceremony had grown so faint that it was overtaken by a new sound, pouring water. Ferns six feet high were a door that Ezili pushed through. I followed into a grotto of cliffs, a phosphorescent waterfall dropping thirty feet down a fern-fuzzed cliff into a pool of dark water. Now I could see stars, thousands of them, reflected in the water's mirror. It was cooler here, the air moist, and she stopped at the edge of the pool and turned to me.

"This is our sacred spring. What do you want to know, Ethan Gage?" Her voice was like music.

Mine was a croak. It was difficult even to remember my question. "What is the diamond?" I finally managed. Did it even matter?

I could feel the man-beast behind me, crouched in the shadows.

"Come, and I will tell you." Her clothes slid off her body without a touch. She was, of course, perfect, but so flawless as to seem eerie, forbidden. Her form was regal, her skin what we lost in Eden, and her breasts, belly, thighs, and dark triangle all hopelessly seductive. She was sex incarnate. I groaned with lust and longing. Ezili waded into the water, the ripples seeming to reflect her flowing form, her posture as graceful as a swan's neck. I stumbled forward like the fool I am, all sense gone, my mind as engorged as my erect member.

The dark thing loomed high and dark behind and over me, but if I could only reach and fuse with Ezili, it would leave us alone, wouldn't it? She was a goddess! A *loa*! Every dream, every fantasy. The enchanted water was midway up her thighs, accentuating the nudity of what was still visible.

"Wait," I gasped.

I reached to strip off my clothes. She smiled the smile of a seductress.

And then I lurched to a stop, blinking.

Astiza. The name exploded into my muddled consciousness like a shattering of glass.

I staggered. My God, I was married, and not just married but melded to the mother of my son, the most wonderful woman in the world, an epic beauty in her own right. I had taken vows! I had grown up!

Suddenly I felt sick. It was as if a blow hit my stomach, and I groaned, leaned, and heaved, vomiting up the noxious stuff I'd tasted so that it splattered all over the water. It smelled vile.

Ezili watched me despoil her pool with disdain. I stepped back, emptied, ashamed, confused, my body shaking with illness and humiliation.

Her seductive smile vanished, and with it her luminescence. The pool had gone dark, the reflected stars winking out. She'd become a silhouette. The waterfall was merely a line of gray in the dark. Had I offended the supernatural?

"What's the matter?" she asked across the water, watching me with a cool objectivity.

She was still achingly beautiful, but something had fundamentally changed. I could not betray my captive wife. And with my resolve, a spell had been broken. "I'm married."

"And?"

"I'm trying to save my wife. I can't do this."

"It is your choice, to seek and resist me."

"I'm sorry."

"For what?"

"I just wanted an answer to L'Ouverture's riddle."

Her head rose slightly, and she looked at me squarely. "The diamond is in Martinique."

"What?"

"The diamond," she repeated slowly, "is in Martinique."

"How will I find one diamond in an entire French island?"

"It will be right in front of you, Ethan."

My mind was whirling. The dark shadow arched like a cloud, ready to pounce, but furious at being suspended. Ezili receding. Had I made an irrevocable mistake? Or saved us all?

"But how could emeralds be inside?"

"They carry the curse of Montezuma." Her voice was distant now. "They've carried death for nearly three hundred years. Are you ready to risk?"

"For Astiza. For my son."

She was becoming insubstantial. "But will you save her?"

Something evil, potent with malevolence, reaching for me. "Wait! Please . . ."

She was fading like dreams at dawn. "Strength, Ethan. But if you choose wrong, what you most love will be gone forever."

"Wait . . ."

A frozen coldness brushed my cheek, a touch clammy as death, but it didn't seize hold. It was like the scale of a caiman, the slither of Damballah, the cold steel of the French guillotine . . . and then gone, retreated.

I staggered to the bank a drunken man, looking into the most profound darkness I'd ever seen.

What wrong choice could she mean?

Then I fainted.

CHAPTER **28**

I came to with what I thought was wind in my ears, the blades of the great mills of Antigua churning fragments of nightmare. Then I realized I was hearing water and feeling sunlight. I winced, squinting up.

There was a dome of sky above the pool where I'd followed the goddess Ezili. Trees all around, a bright green well. Bright birds sang and flew in paint-box colors. Flowers curled like little gold trumpets. Ripples radiated out from the falls in bands of silver. An enchanted place, with no enchantress.

Groaning, I sat up. The beautiful woman was gone, leaving behind a sense of gaping relief and irretrievable loss—of temptation I'd never be offered again. I felt hollowed. I'd also, I believed, passed a test, and in passing it somehow saved myself. That dark presence waiting to devour me had gone.

My head ached, instead of swam.

But wait, someone *was* present. Stiffly, I turned on the muddy bank. Sitting on a stone was Cecile Fatiman, old, rotund, and serene.

"You drugged me." My mouth was cotton, my cheeks still numb.

"I showed you the opening." She smiled, the gaps in her teeth making her seem more matronly in daytime, and less devious.

"I hallucinated. I thought I was following a woman here."

"You followed Ezili. She does not lead just anyone. She liked you, white man."

"A *loa*? She is not, could not, be real."

Cecile said nothing.

"She was too perfect to be real."

Cecile still said nothing.

Groggily, I took stock. My clothes were damp and dirty, my face covered with stubble. My stomach was too queasy to feel hunger. I did feel fiercely thirsty so drank some from the clear pool.

Cecile kept watching me.

"What are *you* doing here?" I finally asked.

"Deciding if you are a zombi," she said matter-of-factly.

The word had a feeling of wickedness about it, and for just a moment the jungle seemed to darken. I remembered that hideous spirit. "What's a zombi?"

"People risen from the dead, or rather, never dead at all."

I was puzzled. "Like Lazarus?"

"No. You don't want to meet the zombi. They are cursed slaves of their masters, the magic priests known as *boko*. The *boko* give a potion to their enemies that make the enemy lie as if dead. The enemy is buried. Then the *boko* dig out the grave and revive the enemy, but only as the zombi, the living dead who must serve their master. Instead of returning to Guinea for re-unification with their ancestors, the zombi is an eternal slave, trapped in Haiti. No revolt will ever free them. It is a curse far worse than death."

"Your drink was a zombi potion?" I was appalled, and more than a little offended.

"No, and apparently you did not take what *was* offered. A *boko* followed you and Ezili. Did you lie with her?"

"No, of course not. I'm married. Faithful. The newly reformed Ethan Gage. She disappeared."

Cecile regarded me with dubious surprise. "Ezili is not accustomed to being rejected."

"I'm not accustomed to turning a woman like that down."

"Maybe there's more strength to you than I suspected, white man. I think your loyalty warded off the *boko*. Ezili wouldn't let him touch you, because you didn't touch her. The *loa*, she protect you, saving you for something else. But she's a jealous spirit, and there is always a price."

"Then I'm not a zombi?"

"Still foolish, perhaps, but not stupid like the zombi. They have slack mouths, vacant stares, and clumsy walks. They are ugly and smell of the grave. You not that bad."

I take compliments where I can.

"It means the *loa* have greater uses for you, which will surprise Dessalines. You did not impress him. But now, perhaps, he will take you into his army. Did Ezili solve the riddle for you?"

"I'm begging you to clarify. That woman was not *really* Ezili, was she?"

Cecile said nothing, regarding me with mild impatience.

"She was? I mean, how could that be?"

"You did not answer *my* question."

"She told me to go to Martinique. That I would find the diamond that holds the emeralds there. I don't even know what that means. And even if I figure it out, it means going to a French-controlled island and trying to wrest a treasure from under their noses while rescuing Astiza and Harry. I don't know if I can do that without help."

"Then you must ask for help, from Dessalines."

"Will he care about my mission?"

"If you care about his."

•   •   •

I still didn't have a comprehensible answer to the riddle of the jewels that the dying L'Ouverture had given my wife, but I at least had a new destination and, I hoped, new allies. My thought was to persuade Jubal to come with me to Martinique, but to get his loan from the rebel army I needed to make partnership with Dessalines. So I returned to the black general's camp, explained in private the treasure all sides were after, and asked for men to help find it. This black king had given me opportunity by sending me to Cecile Fatiman. Now I had to make best use of it.

"This is a very colorful tale you tell," Dessalines said, eyeing me shrewdly. "Aztec emperors, lost jewels, and flying machines."

"Some of it must be true. I'm not that imaginative."

"I do not believe it true, but I don't believe it untrue, either. I don't have much confidence in your courage, Ethan Gage, but I sense an instinct for survival that sets some men apart. I can only spare you soldiers after I take Cap-François and force out the French. I've received word a British squadron is approaching to blockade Rochambeau, and an attack on land could decide the issue. To which side are you actually allied?"

That was the question, wasn't it? "To whichever side helps me get wife, son, and emerald. Which is your side now, and I must succeed before British and French catch up to me."

He nodded. Ambitious men understand expediency. "You promised an idea of how to surprise the French lines, and you must first help me win my battle before I help get back your wife or son. Otherwise, it's easier to impale you on a pole and plant you, alive and screaming for your mother, in front of the French fortifications. This will demonstrate what will happen to white men when we finally win. Your shrieks would dampen their morale, I think."

He suggested this alternative rather matter-of-factly. In thinking back to forbidding acquaintances such as the Egyptian Rite's Alessandro Silano, Djezzar the Butcher, the warrior chief Red Jacket, or Pasha Yussef Karamanli, the one thing that unites them is an appalling indifference to my health. There seems to be a discouraging correlation between power and ruthlessness. My instinct for sympathy probably disqualifies me for high command; I couldn't bring myself to execute as many innocents as seems to be required.

I am, however, a clever adviser, with no desire to be left on a stake. "I will win your battle, or help win it, at least, with a scheme that will crack the French lines and bring an end to this war. But I *am* a white man, so you must promise you'll let the defeated French flee, once they give up."

"They don't deserve to escape."

"What they deserve is irrelevant. If cornered, they will fight even harder."

He considered, then nodded. "I might let them go if it saves the blood of my people. But how do you propose to win the siege when my entire army cannot?"

"With an idea from my three-year-old son." And I explained in detail what I intended to do.

CHAPTER 29

Two storms gathered before the morning of November 18, 1803. One was the tower of rain cloud building on the horizon, a roiling interplay of sun and impending shower. The other was the final approach of the black rebel army toward French lines.

It was a human tide that couldn't be disguised. Cane fields were trampled as regiment after regiment moved into position, cannon were hauled, temporary breastworks built, shot stockpiled, and bivouacs pitched. The French were equally busy, and through a glass lent to me by a Negro officer I could see the bustle of a defense readying against attack. Bugles called. Earthen redoubts were heaped a little higher in hopes that a last spade full of dirt might stop a fatal bullet. More tricolors were raised to snap in the tropical wind, to convince those charging that they faced impossible odds. Cavalry rode importantly about on both sides to advertise menace with the thunder of their hooves. French artillery fired ranging shots to reinforce their point. Dessalines's cannons barked in reply. This pawing and snorting reminded me of stags in the dust and heat, which know that the key to any fight is not just to rip the throat, but to open the gut of churning fear on the other side. War is bluff, shock, surprise, desperation, and scarcely contained panic.

Precipitating *more* panic was my job.

While the armies postured, I prepared to lead a night march in the hours before the final attack. Jubal, Antoine, and a dozen handpicked comrades would follow me to the left of the rebel lines toward the mountains that anchored the French flank.

We deliberately kept this party small. A large black force could be spotted and ambushed as it slowly climbed the tangle of jungle that matted the hills around Cap-François. But my doughty group would trot in bare feet without a firearm among us so that no gun would accidentally discharge and give us away. Instead, we were equipped with captured cutlasses and plantation cane knives. Dessalines had decreed me a captain and offered a pair of blood-spattered epaulettes that I declined, but as their leader I was armed with a spear. It was an African weapon the rebels had forged, with a tear-shaped spearhead as long as my forearm that was attached to an ironwood shaft.

"Our forefathers used this against the lion," Dessalines told me.

"Had to get rather close, didn't they?"

"They smelled its hot breath."

"I prefer to use my brain."

In fact, I was inclined to leave this prehistoric baggage behind. But Jubal persuaded me that it was foolish to go into battle unarmed, and that the spear made a rather convenient standard, walking stick, tent pole, and mark of authority. The spear seemed entirely savage, but once my hand closed on the polished wood I did feel rather fierce. This was the first real weapon I'd possessed since losing my rifle in Tripoli, and it fortified my confidence the way a primitive might have felt when going up against one of Jefferson's woolly mammoths. The former slaves seemed to regard it as a badge of rank, signifying the trust Dessalines had placed in me, and followed my lead without complaint. I was so unaccustomed to this (most of the time, no one listens to me at all) that I was rather excited. There's definitely a thrill in being warlord.

So we waited until the dusk before the battle, then set off.

Even with sunset my squad was soon panting and sweating. We each had a thirty-pound black powder keg strapped to our backs (another reason not to risk firearms, lest one set off a barrel of gunpowder and turn us into a chain of eruptions) and when game trails turned the wrong direction, we had to hack at foliage to get through the jungle.

For refreshment we had calabash gourds carrying water cut with mobby, that bitter brew fermented from sweet potatoes. The drink eventually made some of the men want to hum, and Jubal had to hush them, since it's a danger to be too jolly when sneaking about. I'd also brought a flask of rum, a swallow of which I shared with each man to keep up morale.

Jubal was our guide once we reached the mountains. He knew the trails like a puma, leading us up a twisting ravine where a tropical creek cut through the ferns with a steady murmur that masked our footfalls. It was so dark under the trees that I could barely make out my guide's broad back, so I stopped us, had a volunteer tear his ragged white shirt to shreds, and tied one on each gunpowder barrel so we'd keep the man ahead in sight. Jubal retained the lead, Antoine the rear, and I marched in the middle.

We slipped, scrambled, and stumbled. Admirably, any curses in English, French, Creole, and African were kept under our breaths.

Higher and higher we went. The trees dripped and steamed from earlier showers, and I could hear wild pigs grunting and moving out of our way. I thought again of lurking devils, but the superstition seemed silly when I was sober of voodoo drugs and banded with a group of soldiers. We stopped periodically to listen for French patrols or to spy the light of a sentry's pipe, but we seemed to have this world to ourselves.

None of my men was allowed to light a cob, lest we blow ourselves up or give ourselves away. So I just watched the whites of
their eyes as they tilted their heads back to enjoy their mobby,
while they said I glowed like a ghost.

The hike seemed to be taking forever. "I want to climb above
the French lines, not crest the Alps," I complained to Jubal, wip-
ing at my sweat.

"Mountains are steep in Haiti, yes?"

"And muddy. Infested with vermin, feral livestock, and sharp
thorns."

"We'll crest a ridge soon and come down where we need to be.
Don't worry, Monsieur Ethan, Jubal knows the mountains. Dessalines preaches that a drop of sweat can save a drop of blood."

"I'm sure that's true. But we're doing the sweating, and saving
him the blood."

My companion laughed. "I'd rather have our sweat than his
worries."

Finally our route leveled at a crest, and a welcome breeze blew
off the Caribbean. We were above the French stronghold, the
dark sea beyond. As I'd planned, there was no moon, and only a
few lights shone in distant Cap-François. I could also see the low
campfires of the French line to its east. If my calculations were
correct, we were above the dell where I'd climbed with Colonel
Aucoin to see his redoubts and water supply.

Now I was going to use this geography to help end the war.

The night was already half gone, and we didn't have much
time to implement my scheme. "We'd best hurry. Your army will
attack at dawn."

"Yes, but we're already atop the French like an ax poised atop
a block," Jubal said with satisfaction. "And these boys are hard
workers, aren't you, my uglies?"

They grinned, a dozen crescent moons in the dark.

"Good," I replied. "Otherwise, we're all dead."

Descending was easier on the lungs though harder on the legs, and we quickly heard the murmur of another stream and broke out of jungle. We'd come to the small mountain pool in that cup of hills on the heights before the stream dropped to water the French. We crept along the creek like panthers. Then the smallest and quietest of us, a former slave named Cyprus, volunteered to scout ahead. We waited silently for ten minutes, trying to ignore the mosquitoes, until he slithered back to report.

"Six soldiers, four asleep and two on guard, at the lip of the stream."

Half a dozen cane knives came out from sheaths.

"No sound," Jubal reminded. "From them or you."

I swallowed. This was war, at its closest and most horrible.

The assassins crawled ahead, with us bringing up the rear for a reinforcing rush if needed. I feared gunfire, shouts, and struggle. Instead, the silence was profound. We slunk along the pool until we were at the lip overlooking the French fortifications. I'd heard nothing, seen nothing. But six severed French heads were lined up next to the stream outlet like a row of melons. Their eyes were shut as if relieved it was over.

Where the bodies went, I never learned.

"Very fine," Jubal complimented.

I tried not to identify with the pale skin, taking a shaky breath. "Now, like beavers, we must dam the creek as vigorously as my son did in France."

"What's a beaver?"

I was at a loss for its African equivalent. "Like an elephant," I finally said. Those beasts built things, too, and Harry had watched one work in Tripoli.

"What's an elephant?" These former slaves had apparently never seen one of those creatures, either, in Haiti or in Africa. What zoology did we have in common?

"A beaver is a hairy, very hardworking mule," I described. "Come, let's drag this wood." And we set to work as industriously as my boy.

CHAPTER 30

Sunrise came from behind Dessalines's army, shining in the face of the French. Given our height above the impending battlefield, it was in our view before anyone else's. I watched the Battle of Vertiers unfold as if studying the diagram of a military textbook, columns of soldiers moving like arrows on a map. Some black, some white.

The purpose of my dam was twofold. One was to cut off the flow of water to the garrison below. Indeed, at first light there were shouts of surprise when the soldiers' watering pond began to drop. A company of infantry was roused and began climbing laboriously up toward us to investigate why the stream had suddenly gone dry. We had to finish before they got in musket range, or we'd all be killed.

Our second objective was to create a timely diversion. We'd turned the lazy stream pool into a substantial reservoir at our altitude by dragging logs and rocks, cutting saplings, and hurling mud. Now we took the kegs of powder and strung them along the dam's base, each with a jutting fuse. We had to surprise the French lines below at the precise moment when Dessalines's best regiments were prepared to storm the defending redoubt. My plan was to send a flash flood into the enemy rear just the way Harry and I had broken our own dam at Nîmes, enjoying the havoc it created by swirling away leaves, sticks, and insects. Astiza had shaken her head at our excitement.

I watched the reservoir fill, enjoying my own cleverness with the satisfaction of a child. The blacks lay on the crest of the dam, watching the French climb toward us. Between each was a severed head. My men had arranged them like trophies, recalling the worst days of the Terror back in Paris.

"I suppose we should prepare to light the fuses," I told my band. I was so slathered in mud by this time that we looked identical, a dozen grubby, grinning beavers, or mules. The reservoir would soon top our dam and threaten to wet the powder kegs. I felt in my vest pocket for a tin I'd brought with some coals, and brought it out with some tinder I'd carried from camp.

I frowned. The tinder was soggy. The tin was cold.

In my enthusiasm for dam construction, I'd failed to remember I was getting quite wet. Water and mud had penetrated the ventilation holes of a coal tin I'd neglected to nurse, thanks to enough swigs of mobby and rum. I opened the container. My little bit of fire had gone out. I looked at it stupidly. Well, hell.

I was a three-year-old, indeed.

I cleared my throat. "Now, who brought flint and steel?"

Jubal and his companions looked at me blankly. "Lots of steel, Ethan," he said. "No flint."

"A pistol, then." We could use the flash of its pan.

"You ordered us to leave all the guns back at camp."

"I suppose I did." I was thinking furiously. "The weapons of the French sentries?"

"You told us to throw them in the water to avoid any discharge."

"That is entirely correct. I have been very careful to keep us quiet as mice." I realized I hadn't thought the contingencies of my plan entirely through, which is a habit of mine. Perhaps I should start writing things down.

Then I thought of a trick Fulton had told me. "Phosphorus, anyone?"

"Who they?" one of my doughty dam builders inquired.

I'd experimented in Paris with a phosphorus bottle. One uncorks the airtight container, inserts a splinter, and the chemical ignites when lifted into the air. Quite magical.

"Ethan, there's no phosphorus in the black army," Jubal said.

"You are correct. A pity."

"Some of the men can make fire with sticks."

"Splendid!"

"It takes about an hour," Antoine amended.

Hell's bells. At one time I'd helped find a gigantic ancient metal mirror capable of setting whole ships on fire, and now I'd dragged a magazine's worth of powder up a mountainside with no means of setting it off. We did have steel, but we were on a slope of wet clay. I sent men scurrying to find a stone capable of striking sparks, but the clinking and scraping was futile. I had as much chance of striking fire in this mudhole as finding dry kindling in a downpour.

I wished my genius had more consistency.

Down below, the company of infantry climbing toward us had stopped to take a breath, wary at the odd noises coming from above. They shouted for their sentries, but of course there was no reply. We watched them take their muskets off their shoulders. Then their officer snapped a command, and they came on again, wary but determined.

Meanwhile, Dessalines's column was almost at the end of the ravine, ready to attack. If the sun climbed high enough to light their position, a single cannon loaded with grapeshot could sweep the defile like a hurricane, halting the rebels before they got started.

Unless we provided a distraction.

Think, Ethan, think! What would Ben Franklin do?

By failing to prepare, you are preparing to fail, he used to lecture me with his annoying homilies. He claimed I'd inspired at least half of them. This couldn't be true, but it got his point across about my dubious character.

What else, what else?

Hide not your talents. They were made for use. What's a sundial in the shade?

Sundials. Sun. The sun! Of course! I had more than one venerable philosopher to draw from. Archimedes had built a gigantic mirror to harness the sun in a terrifying way, and perhaps I could use the same idea to set off my kegs of black powder. The tropic dawn had cleared the mountains to the east, rays striking brilliantly where we stood. Fortunately, I still had the magnifying glass I'd bought to confirm the emerald that I would inevitably retrieve from Martel once I had my hands around his throat. Sometimes it helps to be prudently greedy.

In our scramble for spark-inducing rocks, Jubal had hunted up some dry firewood from the underside of forest logs. Now I directed him to put it where I could use my glass to focus the dawn's new rays. "The convexity of the aperture may focus the radiative effect," I told them importantly, not certain what I was saying myself. When playing the part of a savant, it's best to be as incomprehensible as possible.

They looked impressed while I fumbled. Meanwhile, I could hear the advancing infantry shouting to one another below as they climbed toward us. We had nothing to slow them down. They were just a hundred yards away, in the trees.

I took the glass, oriented it to the tropical sun, and concentrated its light, tense with impatience. It's not true that time is constant; depending on one's circumstances, it crawls like misery or spurts like passion. It races through a spring day and drags through a sick, rainy one. Now it seemed almost to stand still as I waited for the duff to smolder, me groaning that the sun wasn't already higher and hotter, and wondering if this would work at all.

Clouds were climbing, too, building on the eastern horizon. What if they blotted my light source? The wind was rising.

Hurry, hurry!

"Wrap my spearhead with dry fronds like a torch," I ordered with a mutter as we waited. "Douse it with the rest of the rum. If this works, we'll use it to ignite the fuses."

The blacks nodded. They actually thought I knew what I was doing.

An eternity passed, as we heard the clank and slap of equipment as fifty Frenchmen labored up the hillside toward us.

"They draw closer, Ethan." My companions lay while the water of the creek crept steadily toward spilling, lapping their bodies. When, when, when? How could I have forgotten something so elementary as nursing fire after sweating for hours with a barrel on my back? First I'd lost a son, then a wife, and now, apparently, common sense.

It had been a hectic week.

But I'd not entirely lost my ingenuity. The tinder began to smoke.

"Damballah, do not forsake us," Jubal prayed.

And finally, a snake's tongue of flame. "Get off the dam," I warned.

The French saw movement, and a shot rang out from below. I could imagine heads turning on the redoubts from where regiments waited for Dessalines, puzzled by this disturbance in their rear. Perhaps it would alert the French to surprise from their front. The whole assault was about to be put in jeopardy by my stupidity.

"Your torch, white man."

They handed me the spear, its head wrapped with fronds and wet with fiery rum. I dipped it into my tiny fire, and it flared.

"They're lining up to shoot!" one of the rebels called.

I turned to our dam. The water was at the brim, kegs poised below, fuses poking like wheat stalks, and down the slope more than two score men gave a great shout at the sight of me standing up with my torch. They knelt, pointing their muskets up the mountain. It was suicide to leap down in from of them to light the gunpowder, but this was all my idea, wasn't it? I looked at my companions. No slaves anymore to do the dirty work. Only me and the need for rash courage.

So I jumped and swung my makeshift torch, its smoke leaving a trail in the air as it swooped to touch the first barrel. With a flash and hiss, the fuse ignited.

Gunshots cracked.

I sprang to the next keg and it lit.

More shots, and now I could hear bullets whapping against the mud of our dam, a sound that had become disturbingly familiar in recent days. Thank goodness they had inaccurate muskets instead of precision long rifles. Water began to dribble down the dam face, running toward the explosives.

"Hurry, Ethan!" Jubal called.

What the devil did he think I was doing?

Three kegs, then four, five, a rattle of musketry, a bloom of smoke from the French volley rising prettily into the dawn light, fuses burning merrily and sending up their own plumes, me bright as a coin in the sun, shouts now up and down the main French line far below. I was scrambling like a target in a shooting gallery across the face of our dam, lighting each gunpowder keg. Madness.

"Ethan, the first be burning down!" Jubal warned.

Men were charging toward me now, bayonets fixed as they struggled up the steep slope, an anxious lieutenant waving his sword in my direction. They were shouting warnings about the powder kegs and clearly meant to put them out.

We'd no weapons to fire back.

So I turned and hurled the spear, a fiery meteor, giving a grunt like an African warrior. The young officer was only yards from me, face red with exertion. His eyes went wide at my missile. What did he think in his last moment, thousands of miles from France, half his companions dead from yellow fever, his commander a cruel lecher, and a black army pounding on his garrison doors? And now a flaming spear thrown by a mud-smeared lunatic, a line of smoldering powder kegs, and the heads of six sentries on the crest of the dam gaping sightless in his direction?

The spear struck, and the man gave a cry, his sword arcing harmlessly across the air, spinning like a windmill blade. Then he somersaulted back toward his comrades, my primitive weapon in his breast.

I scrambled to one side of our construction and noticed that the day had abruptly dimmed; the clouds I'd seen earlier were continuing to mount. The sun was already winking out. It was sheer luck I'd had light for my glass.

The first keg erupted.

The others went off in a chain like fireworks, a rippling explosion from one end of the dam base to the other, mud and sticks blowing out toward the advancing infantry in a great, gaping gout of woody splinters. Then the rest of the structure and its severed heads collapsed and thundered down on the attacking infantry like an avalanche, skulls bouncing, and after it came a wall of water.

The blacks were whooping while the water roared and became a chaotic slurry of mud, trees, and foam. The tide caught the slowest victims and snatched them with it as livelier soldiers sprang out of the way. On the redoubt between the cane field ravine and the camp reservoir, gunners turned and gaped. The unleashed waters poured down the mountain and crashed into the encampment, sweeping up tents, scattering screaming horses, and roaring across to dash against the backside of the earth-and-log redoubt like a breaker. Artillery was abandoned as soldiers ran in both directions to escape the punch of the cascade.

The flash flood didn't break the redoubt but briefly topped it, and then left a tongue of wreckage from the base of the mountain to the French front line. Everything was in chaos.

Then came the charge.

The coiled serpent of blacks that had been creeping forward in the ravine gave a tremendous shout that echoed across the battle-field and punched toward the confused gap in the defenses. It was a column of steel, bayonets gleaming, and then a ripple of brighter light as they shot a volley. There was a bloom of smoke. The answering fire was fierce, and both black men and women fell like scythed sugarcane. The attackers simply charged faster, surging up against the French. Their leader François Capois, that keg of energy I'd seen at Dessalines's headquarters, led them through a hail of bullets while waving a sword. His horse went down, and Capois sprang up. Another bullet took his hat off. When a Haitian banner fell, he scooped it up, waving it high to rally his men and women.

Hundreds of rebels swept the French lines, and I could hear the great shout of their valor from my high perch on the mountain. They came on so recklessly that some of the astounded French actually applauded.

There was still chivalry in 1803.

Then the former slaves surged over the battlements in a great dark wave, lifting high those red-and-blue battle flags with the white cut ominously from the middle. They butchered with bayonets and cane knives, seizing cannon and turning them on their foes. Their column spread out along the French line to flank it. Musket and artillery fire rose to a crescendo. Gaps were blasted in the attacking ranks. In return, whole lines of blue-coated Napoleonic infantry were cut down.

I'd made a temporary diversion, and the rebels had taken full advantage.

The overwhelmed French were ebbing toward Cap-François and the interior emergency lines they'd dug there, but I knew we'd checkmated their last great garrison. The fort at Vertiers had the height to command the eastern approach to the city, and the rebel guns would soon breach the final French line. The fighting was desperate—my view was soon obscured by huge rising thunder-heads of gun smoke—but the ultimate outcome was no longer in doubt.

Rochambeau was finished.

I saw Dessalines, surveying his assault with the calm of a Bonaparte, seated on a rock and taking snuff as columns of cheering troops trotted past him. Real clouds were joining the plume of powder, and as if an answer to the clamor, lightning flashed and thunder growled. I felt like a god on Olympus.

"Ethan, get back!"

Jubal jerked my arm, and a bullet whizzed past. The French company climbing toward us had been decimated and disrupted, but the bravest were still shooting, determined on revenge.

I took one last look at the chaos we'd caused. Everywhere the rebels were sweeping forward, tricolors falling and Haitian banners lifting up.

Then the skies opened and rain sluiced down, flashes of electricity announcing a change in the world as white fled from black. In a moment, we were drenched, our view of the chaos lost as if a curtain had been drawn.

We retreated into the jungle.

CHAPTER 31

Our flight was brief. The French infantry surged over the lip of land where the dam had been, halted to shoot a volley into the jungle, and waited for return fire that might show where we were. When we declined to oblige, they prudently retreated. Their army was pulling back, and they didn't want to be cut off.

We watched them from the ferns.

"Your *loa* Ezili protects you," Jubal congratulated, "even though you're a madman." Word of my strange sojourn with Cecile Fatiman had spread like a contagion. "What did you do to her for such favor?"

"Nothing," I said. "I followed her, but then I remembered my wife, and the *loa* vanished, although Cecile suggested she saved me from becoming a zombi. As usual, I don't understand a thing that has gone on."

"Man is not fated to understand anything important, especially about women," my companion philosophized.

"They're as mysterious as the wanderings of the stars. But you are lucky."

"Perhaps," I said. "We're going to win, my friend, which means I can follow the clue that Ezili gave me. Will you come to Martinique with me to rescue my wife and son and hunt for treasure?"

"If you have the *loa*'s favor, yes. You're foolish enough to be interesting."

I was heartened. Jubal was the best ally I could imagine, as sensible as I was sly. I feared what Martel was doing to my wife and son and needed all the help I could get.

"Our companions believe in you, too," he added.

I'd need them all to win through on a French-governed island.

By the time we cautiously crept back to the overlook, we were behind the lines of Dessalines's triumphant army. Thousands of rebels were digging new precautionary trenches in front of the inner line of French defenses, while hundreds were turning captured cannons around and bringing up field guns of their own. The blacks had the high ground, and Rochambeau's strategic position had become hopeless.

I looked out to sea and realized it was filled with new ships. Since I'd fled the city with Jubal, a fleet had arrived. If the vessels were French, my enemies (my ability to stumble from side to side surprises even me) might hold for a time. If English, it was over.

"Let's get down to Dessalines," I said. "I need a spyglass."

We descended to the usual butchery of a battlefield, blood staining the mud puddles left by the downpour. Wounded crawled and groaned. Spouses and partners who followed the army and came to look for loved ones discovered and wept. Soldiers deafened by muzzle blasts bled from their ears. It's corruption I've grown familiar with, made tolerable only by victory.

We skirted the French dead. One, I saw with sadness, was Colonel Gabriel Aucoin, shot through the breast and trampled in the charge. His last expression was sardonic. My betrayals had not saved him.

Corpses from both sides were being dragged for quick mass burial before becoming bloated in the heat. Operations for the badly wounded were performed by bloody machete in the same brutal way as Lovington's sugar mill: a swift chop that was perhaps, in its speed, more merciful than the surgeon's saw. However, some crawled off to die rather than face the steel.

Despite our diversion, the charging blacks had suffered several hundred dead and wounded. The heap of chopped-off arms and legs was a more powerful testament to their courage than the later medals would be, the dark flesh stacked like a cord of wood.

I watched Rochambeau's man-hunting dogs being executed in their cages, the rebels firing muskets into the yelping animals with glee. Then the doors were opened so wild pigs could gnaw at the remains.

Dessalines himself was at the highest point of captured Vertières, dressed in martial splendor. He was soaked from the tropical shower, but with his bicorn hat with black plume, gold-braided uniform, and French cavalry boots, he looked as magnificent and ruthless as the Mameluke warriors I recalled from Egypt. He gave crisp orders to a legion honed by a dozen years of war. I was about to witness a historical first, the complete triumph of a slave revolt. L'Ouverture was being avenged. Spartacus would be envious.

I waited for a moment between messengers, and then pushed my way. "Congratulations, *Commandant*."

"Monsieur Gage," he said. "You waited until the very last moment to spring your surprise, and I confess I feared you'd deserted us. But finally the flood came, as the Christian God promised Noah."

"We had to wait for God to get the sun high enough to light our tinder. He took his own sweet time, I'm afraid."

"We almost had no sun at all."

"Providence gave us just enough." I decided to omit my lack of more reliable ignition methods, but he guessed my character anyway.

"You gamble, monsieur."

"I improvise. It's a fault I'm working on."

"Well, victory is ours. British ships are offshore. Rochambeau is as trapped as Cornwallis was at Yorktown. My new nation will be born much as yours was. We'll pay back the French. They have centuries of crime to answer for."

I'd expected this response. The problem with being mean, as the French overseers had been, is that sooner or later your victims learn that same meanness and give turnabout. What terrified the French was that they were about to experience all the tortures they'd invented first. Our Savior hoped forgiveness would prove contagious, but so far I've seen little sign of it. People return the worst, not the best, and the habit makes me gloomy. The likelihood that I'd helped enable a massacre didn't appeal to me, either.

"Maybe you can let bygones be bygones," I tried.

The general looked scornful. "When did they ever offer that to us?"

"Yellow fever has taken all the collar out of them, you know that. It's not like the French army hasn't suffered. Cornwallis was allowed to surrender with honor."

"If all white men are as meek as you, it's no wonder they are losing. Perhaps I will not stop with Haiti. Maybe I'll take my army and conquer the world."

"You wouldn't like most of it. Europe is cold and drafty. America, too. L'Ouverture could tell you, if he was still around."

He scowled, and I decided the sooner I left Haiti, the better, given the color of my skin. "If those are British ships, let the English do your work for you," I argued. "You can no doubt take Cap-François, but if thousands of whites are faced with extinction, they'll fight to the death and take many of your soldiers with them. If they're allowed to flee to English ships, you've won your cause without more bloodshed. Saint-Domingue becomes free without stain on its honor. Foreign nations will recognize your nation more quickly."

He considered. *Vengeance is so tempting.*

"You become not just a liberator, but merciful," I continued. "A hero in the salons of Paris, an example to the English Parliament, a partner to the United States. Dessalines the Just! Men will salute you. Women admire you."

"I suppose temperance is the mark of great men." He said it with considerable doubt.

"Benjamin Franklin thought so. He was my mentor, you know. Something of a nag, but sharp as a razor."

"But this negotiation must be my idea, not yours."

"Of course."

"It must resound to me, not you."

"I am utterly obscure."

"It must be negotiated by someone the whites would trust and yet is entirely expendable, since I don't trust Rochambeau not to seize any messenger and disembowel him in full view of my army. He is rash, venomous, and wicked."

Villains recognize each other the way dogs do a scent. "I don't care for the fellow, either."

"Yes." He'd come to a decision. "The man to negotiate the French evacuation, Monsieur Gage, is you."

The trouble with offering advice is that there's a danger people will actually accept it. So I found myself in the broiling noontime sun, planter's hat off, marching with white flag between two embittered armies. I estimated that at least ten thousand muskets were aimed in my direction from all points of the compass. I thought the disemboweling idea was a real possibility, since the last time I'd seen General Rochambeau I'd interrupted him in mid-coitus, throwing a meat cleaver at his head while he fired a ball at me. Best to keep to myself that the diversionary flood was my idea. And that I'd been tangled up in voodoo, Haitian goddesses, and the severing of French heads for display on a makeshift dam. Diplomacy, like romance, is simpler when the other side doesn't know everything that is going on.

I hoped that the last few days of excitement might have caused the French general even to forget who I was, but he recognized me with that baleful expression typically reserved for tax collectors, naval press gangs, or mothers-in-law. I gave back as good as I got, still smarting from being a potential cuckold even if Rochambeau hadn't, apparently, actually lain with my wife. He'd certainly wanted to, and had misplaced her in the process.

We met at the base of his last redoubts. Our conversation was blunt.

"The traitor and assassin Ethan Gage dares return?" he began.

"To save your lecherous hide."

"How could you desert to the blacks and participate in their butchery?"

"How could you stalk my wife and pack her off to a ship with your pimp Leon Martel?" I gave back. "Having failed to rape her, are you prostituting her instead?"

"How *dare* you insult my honor, monsieur!"

"And how dare *you*, General." I realized this kind of acrimony could go on for some time, so I tried to move things along. "It's plain enough to all your soldiers how God has rewarded your crimes. And if you don't listen to me, they, as well as you, will pay horrifyingly."

A cluster of colonels drew nearer at these words.

Rochambeau looked volcanic, but he was also trapped and knew it. If Ethan Gage was his only chance of escape, it wouldn't do to spit me on his sword. He swallowed rage with difficulty and stood taller. "Is Dessalines asking for terms?"

"His guns command the city. His troops are poised to initiate a massacre, not only against your men but against the city's women and children, with all the cruelties you've taught him. Black Africa is at the gates, General, waiting to take revenge." I let this work a moment on his officers' imaginations.

"Why are you here then?" Rochambeau asked grudgingly.

"To prevent further bloodshed, Dessalines is offering you the opportunity to evacuate by British ship if you promise that France will leave Saint-Domingue forever."

"We are at war with Britain as well!"

"But I am not. As an American, I'm the only negotiator fit to shuttle between the three sides. You may despise me as much as I despise you, but if you confirm the location of my wife and son, I'll talk the British into taking you all off and saving your miserable life. Better captivity with the English than revenge from Dessalines, am I not correct?"

There was an audible rustle and sigh from the officers around us. They heard reprieve and looked at their general with expectation.

Rochambeau squinted at the sea. If he acquiesced to sailing with the British, he'd almost certainly become a prisoner of war. But he could save ten thousand lives by doing so, the first decent thing he'd done in some time. He still hesitated, as if weighing which was the better path to honor.

Finally he scowled. "Very well."

"Very well what? Where are Astiza and Horus, a tiny child that your monster of a criminal has kidnapped?"

Now there were some gasps from the assembled officers, who knew nothing of this. Rochambeau's face darkened with fresh embarrassment, but he also decided to try to turn it to advantage.

"Fort-de-France in Martinique," he said shortly, an admission that he did know about my wife's abduction. "Sent there for their own safety, you imbecile. To protect your wife from her sorry excuse of a husband." He turned to his men. "This idiot wanted to drag her into the jungle with the blacks, and we all know what the result would have been. I, however, saw she wore a medal of trust from Bonaparte and was determined to save her. French chivalry protected her from American recklessness."

Now they all looked with rebuke at me. The truth was, I *had* rather fumbled the governing of my family. I decided we'd both said enough and returned a contemptuous silence, which was enough to make the assembly wonder which version of events was correct.

When I didn't reply, Rochambeau plunged on. "Yes, you can thank me for safeguarding your family. Meanwhile, we'll row you out to the British to end this bloodshed. Bonaparte will hear of your treacheries, and I will go down in history as the savior of the good people of Cap-François." He turned to his officers. "I will be recorded as a hero, you'll see."

I nodded. "Agreed. And I want a letter of introduction to the governor of Martinique."

CHAPTER 32

I'll admit that once I was a few yards offshore I had an overwhelming desire to cut and run, finding passage to Martinique with the British and leaving Dessalines and Rochambeau to their own devices. I desperately missed Astiza and Harry. Saint-Domingue would have a troubled future after the apocalyptic war, and I knew the final evacuation would be chaotic and heartbreaking. The French Creoles who'd been born on the island and invested their lives in Saint-Domingue would finally have to give up on what would become Haiti, exiles from all they'd known. I'd be delayed waiting for the surrender and transition to play out.

But I also knew that as a go-between I might save a few lives. Besides, if I earned Dessalines's satisfaction (I don't think I could ever count on his approval or friendship; he hated my race too much), I'd have the help of Jubal and his men in fetching my family, and give a little payback to Martel. So I boarded the British flagship and informed its commander that without firing a shot, he could offer refugees the transit that would finally rob France of what had once been its richest colony.

"The French have lost to the slaves?" He seemed dumbfounded.

"Not just lost, but are in peril of their lives."

Accordingly, a combination of British warships and French merchantmen closed with the harbor to take on the defeated. The evacuation began in good order, demonstrating only the absurdity of what people try to save. They came to the quay lugging oil portraits of ugly ancestors, tarnished tureens, a pet goat, a trunk of theatrical costumes, cases of spirits, antique dueling pistols, hat boxes, silverware, fresh-baked loaves more than two feet long, voodoo carvings, silver crucifixes, and an ornamental saddle. Little ones clutched dolls and toy soldiers. Mothers peered into their own cleavage to double-check the safety of jewelry temporarily deposited there, and men patted jackets to confirm the presence of coin or currency. Rochambeau's officers and English ensigns organized them into lines, weeding out the most ridiculous heirlooms (one family trundled a harpsichord down to water's edge) and for a while the mood was of shared hardship and goodwill.

But as dusk fell and wine cellars were liberated, both French troops and civilians got drunk, and looting began in abandoned corners of the city. As the waiting rebel army saw disorder, black soldiers began filtering into Cap-François to join the pillage. Fires started and ignited panic. A queue quickly became a mob, some longboats swamped and had to be righted, and the last crammed French ship set sail so anxiously that it hit a reef and began to sink. Its occupants had to be offloaded to another English vessel.

I was amazed there was not more rape and murder, given the conflict's history. At my advice, Dessalines kept a stern rein on his men to avoid a retaliatory bombardment from European ships. On board the vessels was chaos, as an escaping throng squeezed between guns, pushed into sail lockers, and tucked under longboats. Even madmen were evacuated from the city's asylum and chained to a gunwale, raving in the confusion. Mothers sobbed, children wailed, dogs barked, and army officers climbed aboard with pet monkeys, macaws, and parrots. The vessels were so jammed that some of the baggage was heaved overboard by impatient sailors.

A few blacks fled as well as whites, some servants refusing to abandon their masters. And some whites and mulattos chose the risk of staying ashore. But the overwhelming effect of the surrender was a final division of the races. The ships, their decks crammed with pale faces, visibly settled in the water. Some quarterdecks were so crowded that the helmsman could scarcely turn the wheel. The vessels did not so much sail as lumber out of the crowded harbor.

On shore, the Paris of the Antilles, newly renamed Cap-Haïtien, smoldered.

As night fell, the victors rejoiced and danced in the streets with that rhythmic energy I'd seen in the jungle. Burning homes threw lurid light on the celebration. There was a pungent smell of smoke, gunpowder from shots fired aloft in victory, rot from broken larders, and roast pig, goat, and chicken cooked in street bonfires. I saw a few white and mulatto faces, but they were rare and subdued, watching the slave army from the shadows with apprehension.

Impatient as I was, I knew better than to approach Dessalines at the height of his triumph; he was preoccupied with organizing a nation. I applied for an appointment at his convenience and remained at my inn, since there was no one left to collect rent. The general didn't even enter the conquered city until November 30, 1803. I finally got to see him the following afternoon, where he reigned in the ballroom of Rochambeau's Government House, looking weary but grimly powerful, the western half of Hispaniola finally his. He had a steady stream of visitors seeking promotion, trade, or redress of grievances. On a long table to one side of his desk, aides kept tally of what had been captured and lost.

Officers bustled in and out on assignments to put Cap-François in order again, and newly appointed ministers began forming a permanent government. I realized I was witnessing something akin to the start of my own nation thirty years before. I should have taken notes, had I pen and paper. But no, I was impatient to find my family, not play historian.

"I congratulate the new Spartacus," I greeted, after waiting more than an hour past my appointed time.

"I have exceeded L'Ouverture and shall crown myself emperor," the general pronounced. "Napoleon himself could not stand before me."

Napoleon was five thousand miles away, and Rochambeau had been no Caesar, but I knew better than to amend this self-assessment. I changed the subject. "I did what you asked to help win our victory, and now I can do even more for Haiti," I said. "All governments need gold. Maybe I can find some."

"Those legends you spoke of."

"Lend me Jubal, Antoine, and a few companions, and I'll search for the treasure of Montezuma. I'll split with your regime and finally retire from public life."

"You want my help to search for your wife and son."

"Of course."

"Then Haiti has given you sense, perhaps. Family is worth more than baubles." This was a pronouncement, spoken loudly enough so that all in the hall could hear it. "Loyalty worth more than fear."

I understood the need to express such sentiment. He was a new Moses for a new kind of country, but a bloody-handed Moses with a dozen years worth of enemies waiting for him to fall. Somehow he had to establish an ethic, and I didn't envy his power or his responsibility. "Then I can have your men to go look for my loved ones and the relics that Maroons are rumored to have hidden away?"

"If my men will come back. You'll look where?"

"Martinique, the *loa* told me. My enemy Leon Martel has gone there."

"Perhaps we blacks will rise in Martinique next."

"Let me have a look around first."

He waved me away, our interview over. "You should be sailing already. Next!"

Part Three

CHAPTER 33

The ruler of France and his wife both came from island colonies. Bonaparte is Corsican, the real spelling of his name Italian, and his heritage is of Roman generals and Renaissance plotters. Martinique, the island of Joséphine's birth, childhood, and the place where I hoped to bargain for my wife and son, is languid paradise under the slow match of a volcano.

The island rears out of the Caribbean like an emerald dream, its northern half summiting in smoking Pelee. The isle is more dramatic upon approach than Antigua, Atlantic breakers crashing on its eastern coast and turquoise Caribbean shallows lapping its western beaches. Plantation homes climb lush slopes to make a checkerboard of white and green, and French ships huddle for protection from the British under the guns of lava-stoned Fort-de-France, on the island's principle bay. After the horror of Haiti the island looked entirely serene from the sea, but I knew my little company of Negro warriors couldn't simply spring ashore and ask for the address of Leon Martel. They'd freed themselves, and thus were the worst nightmare of the ruling whites on this island.

My black platoon included the cheerfully practical Jubal, the logical Antoine, and six other Negroes hungry for more adventure and a glimpse of Aztec gold. Excitement is addictive. We sailed from Cap-François with a Dutch trader looking for a hire that would keep him a safe distance from British forces assaulting his own nation's islands. The Caribbean sugar isles changed flags as frequently as a courtesan changes clothes as rival fleets swept in and out on the trades, guns thundering and marines sweeping ashore.

Our vessel was the coastal lugger *Nijmegen*, with two masts, a small cabin that the captain, mate, and I slept in as segregated whites, and an open deck where Jubal's comrades—once they got over seasickness—made a comfortable home under an awning rigged from a damaged sail. Captain Hans Van Luven was dubious about having a Negro cargo not in chains, but he soon discovered that my adventurers, who paid in advance with Dessalines's captured coins, were better company than cranky Europeans. They were also willing to help tack, reef, and anchor.

"It's as if they're as human as the rest of us," he marveled.

We were two weeks scudding down the Leeward Islands to Martinique at the northern end of the Windwards, anchoring each night in a different bay on a different island and avoiding any sail we spotted.

Now we were at an isle where French power was still intact.

Our plan was to round Cap Salomon south of Fort-de-France Bay and put ashore at one of the coves on Martinique's southern coast. On the charts, a valley led from the village of Trois Rivières north toward the main settlements, and I could skulk along this for more information before presenting myself to Governor Michel Lambeau with Rochambeau's papers. Finding my wife shouldn't be impossible. Astiza is the kind of woman who's noticed, and unless she'd been entirely hidden away, gossip of her would filter into all corners of the island.

Then fortune provided even more clarity.

As we tacked southeast toward our goal, I noticed a peaked volcanic rock two miles offshore of Martinique. It was shaggy with shrub and reared almost six hundred feet out of the sea. Its summit came to a point, and its entire architecture was quite imposing, the monolith visible for miles. It overlooked the sea-lanes toward the island of Saint-Lucia to the south. We kept well clear in case there were fringing reefs.

"The Gibraltar of the Caribbean," I commented idly.

"Or the prick of Agwe, the god of the sea," Jubal said.

"If so, he must be looking at Ezili," Antoine joined in.

"More like a diamond, Yankee," our bearded captain replied. "Look at it sparkle in the sun."

For a minute I let that comment pass by, and then suddenly it jarred my slow brain. "Diamond?" I sat straighter, looking at the rock.

"From the facets of the cliffs. *Le Diamant*, that's what the French call it. It can look like one in bright light, after a rain."

"That rock is called the Diamond?"

"Didn't I just say so?"

I felt a chill. Ezili had prophesized that the diamond would be right in front of me. "Are you sure?"

"Read the chart, American."

My luck had turned. "Are there caves in that rock?"

"Wouldn't be surprised. But I don't know anyone who goes there, unless they want cactus and gull guano. No water, and no worth. Now Martinique, in contrast, has a resource. Most beautiful women in the world. One of them captured Bonaparte, I understand."

"Joséphine, his wife."

"Yes, the crafty Creole. Must have been a prize."

"Actually, he was poor, and she was desperate," I said with the authority of knowing them both. "Her first husband had just been guillotined. Social climbers the pair, and they calculate like an abacus. Made for each other, I suppose. Joséphine is six years older but understood Paris society. She *is* pretty, or perhaps I should say charismatic, though her teeth are bad."

"It must not be her teeth he was interested in."

"She was the more worldly of the two, at least in the beginning. She netted his ambition like a fish."

"And now she sits on top of the world. You can't tell me, Gage, that the whole stinking mess of life isn't chance piled on circumstance, multiplied by calculation, and divided by luck. There're a thousand women ashore lovelier than Joséphine, I'll wager, but what does it matter when God rolls his dice?"

"I'm looking for just one woman. My own wife, stolen by another man."

"*Ja*, now there's trouble. Ran away from you, eh? And you're asking for more trouble to land with these blacks. Slaves from Haiti? Your reception will be torches and pitchforks."

I'd been pondering that. "We need to camp quietly, not parade into port. How much do you want for your longboat there and some fishing line?" For expenses, Dessalines had given me some money looted from Cap-François.

Being a Dutchman, Captain Van Luven named a price double the craft's real worth. You can be fleeced in New York or shaven in Amsterdam.

"Done," I said, since it wasn't my coin. "And food?"

That was triple.

"Done again. Work in close at dusk, and then we'll launch your longboat. The blacks will put me ashore."

"And what about us, Ethan?" Jubal asked.

"I anoint you free fishermen, plying your trade around Diamond Rock. That may be where Toussaint L'Ouverture, the Black Spartacus himself, told us to go."

•   •   •

I landed on Martinique armed, but not with something as conspicuous and primitive as a spear. My work at negotiating the
evacuation of Cap-François resulted in the rebels awarding me a
pistol, powder, ball, officer's sword, a dagger sheathed under my
coat in the small of my back, and a tiny gambling pistol tucked
up one sleeve. If I discovered a blunderbuss on this new island, I'd
buy that, too. I expected I might have to shoot my way to success.

My little company came ashore by moonlight on a beach of
sand as fine and white as sugar. It glowed, the lapping water phosphorescent. We slept by the sigh of the sea as the Dutch vessel
tacked for Cartagena. The next morning I directed Jubal and his
team to make a secret camp and discreetly scout Diamond Rock,
fishing to supplement the provisions we'd purchased from the
sharp-fingered Dutchman.

Meanwhile, a two-hour hike down the shoreline took me to a
plantation, its lane, and then a road, and I soon hailed a passing
cane wagon and begged a ride. The slave teamster had no objec-
tion to my company. When we came to the first village, I paid
two francs to switch to a swifter and more respectable carriage,
explaining I was a French-speaking American dropped rather
abruptly by a Dutch vessel fleeing a British frigate. I said I was
making my way to Fort-de-France to discuss business opportuni-
ties that had arisen with renewed European war, and showed my
papers from Rochambeau.

Since the United States made good money selling to belligerents
on all sides, this explanation was readily accepted. By day's end I
was in the island's capital, a place immeasurably gayer, more pros-
perous, and crowded than Cap-François. Some Haitian refugees
had come here, and inns were crowded. Nonetheless, I bought my
way into the best hotel, had a bath and the finest meal since I'd left
Paris, and sent word to the island's Government House that I was

an American trade representative with French papers requesting to see Governor Michel Lambeau. There I would inquire about beautiful but distressed Greek Egyptian females accompanied by a disreputable roach of a man who thieved other men's belongings and kept small children in bondage. If Martel was a criminal, why not get French help in tracking him down?

I'd settle accounts, and then search Diamond Rock.

A letter came directing me to call on the governor at half-past ten, and I brushed out my coat and trousers as best I could. But when I came onto the dazzling street, palms waving in the breeze, I was quickly accosted by a tall, thick, ruggedly built European with tropic tan whose eyes darted as watchfully as a reptile's. He was dressed in dour black, was poorly shaven, and had teeth the color of rancid butter. His smell made me instinctively pull away.

He gripped my wrist and hand with both of his own, a fierce familiarity I didn't expect, his smile broad but not friendly. "It's Ethan Gage, is it not?"

"Do I know you, monsieur?"

"We met in Paris."

I looked him warily up and down.

"In Nitot's jewelry shop. You knocked me over and broke the nose of my employer."

That got my pulse up. My other hand went to the butt of a pistol. "And you missed me with your shot, if I recall. I've found it works well to practice; otherwise, the target survives to possibly shoot back."

The rascal leaned close. "Perhaps we'll test that someday."

"I warn you, I've the protection of the governors of Saint-Domingue and Martinique."

"Rochambeau has capitulated."

"But not Lambeau, here."

He shrugged. "I'm not here to harm you, but involving officialdom would complicate our cooperation at this stage. My employer wishes to extend an earlier invitation." He'd not dropped my hand. "There's no need to draw your weapon, and even less choice since I have friends who at this very moment are aiming at your head. They'd shoot you down before you cocked a hammer."

I resisted the temptation to glance about, trying to look calm even though I was sweating. "Your employer is the scoundrel Martel?"

"The French patriot, Leon Martel."

"A sharp, a rogue, and a ruffian."

"Ambitious, expedient, and bright. He's been waiting for you, and invites you to dine with him at his château in Trois-Îlets."

"That gutter thief has a château?"

"Friends in high places, including Lambeau. And he has a woman and child he thinks you'd like to meet. So much simpler than audiences with governors that raise awkward questions."

So I didn't have to find Satan, but merely wait on him at tea. "He's imprisoned my wife and son?"

"*Au contraire*, he's their host. While they're grateful for his hospitality, they're also quite impatient for your arrival. Everyone needs you to start."

"Start what?"

"Find what we're all seeking together. So we can all take what we need." He finally dropped my arm. "One thing we can agree on. You're as greedy as us."

CHAPTER 34

We walked with two of his companions past the massive basalt walls of Fort-de-France and down to a dock with ferry. Once aboard, brawny black oarsmen rowed us across the wide harbor to the village of Trois-Îlets, which looks northeast to the rest of Martinique. My escort, who introduced himself as the Raven—spies, apparently, get to adopt dramatic nicknames—said that Joséphine had grown up in this suburb and that some of the island's finest families lived there. "They've been urging their native daughter to explain to her husband the necessity of sustaining slavery, and believe she's had some success."

"Yes, Bonaparte believes her. Which has meant slaughter in Saint-Domingue."

Like Martel, this rogue favored black for his fashion, as did his poorly washed companions. The costume is damnably hot in the tropics, but looks appropriately intimidating. Raven seemed ridiculously pretentious to me, so I thought of him as Crow, and his escorts as Vulture and Buzzard. All three could use a preening.

"Martinique will never be allowed to become Haiti," Crow said as we rowed. It was said with more hope than certitude. "Revolutionary fervor does not apply to the black man here."

"Martinique's slaves will decide that."

"We make freedom more costly than servitude."

"With torture and execution?"

"Violence, monsieur, is the price of prosperity."

There was a carriage waiting. Crow gave me a little history of this island as we clopped into the lush vegetation of fig and gumbo trees, the road like a green tunnel that glowed with light. Martinique had developed in much the same way as Antigua, but with a French flavor. The abundant mountains and rainfall meant waterpower took the place of windmills here. Slaves, sugar, fever, and caste.

"Up that lane is where Joséphine was raised." He pointed.

"She's quite the social climber, as able as Nelson's Emma Hamilton."

"Bred, born, and trained to it. There are no politics more cutthroat than island politics. I'm not surprised that a Creole and a Corsican rule Revolutionary France. Islanders are survivors."

We went two miles beyond and came to a gracious château in the French style, not as imposing as Lord Lovington's mansion on Antigua but with more grace. Artfully planted trees created a cascade of flowers on the periphery of lawns, and the place had the heady scent of hibiscus, orchids, and oleander. Cedars soared in back of eucalyptus and chestnut trees, everything swollen by the humid climate to gigantic size. Banana leaves were as wide as windmill paddles. Vines hung like cables on an opera stage. Bright as a convention of cardinals were the flame trees, a riot of red against the cream of the house. This was Astiza's prison? It looked just like the place I'd dreamed of retiring to.

We dismounted and walked up a gravel drive. Then Crow

stopped short, gesturing for me to wait, and a little figure ran out from the gardens. He spied us, stopped, considered, and hesitated like a fawn.

My heart lurched, and I fell to my knees to put us nearer in height. "Harry!" He looked skeptical, recognizing me and yet trying to file me with proper memories. "It's Papa!" I was wounded to have to remind him.

"It's all right, Horus," Astiza called.

I looked past my son. She stood by a red anthurium, pretty as a flower in a white French dress. Her safety, and her beauty and poise, was a relief that was also startling. I'd expected my family to be manacled to a dungeon wall, but they looked turned out for an Italian holiday. Had they negotiated some weird parole? Harry finally came cautiously over to me, looking serious as only a three-year-old can look when something of uncertain gravity is going on. He studied me for any changes.

"I missed you, Harry. Are you all right?" Clearly he was, which was selfishly disappointing. I'd expected a blazing rescue of distraught prisoners.

"Mama said we had to wait for you. I want to go home."

My God, how the heart can careen in one's chest, crashing from rib to rib with longing and remorse. "I want to go home, too." Wherever that was.

"Will you play with me? It's boring here."

"Of course I'll play with you." My voice caught as I spoke. "Can you show me your favorite place?"

"There's a pond, with fishies."

"Then let's catch one." I stood.

"One minute, Gage." Two more of Martel's ruffians appeared, and a gang surrounded me. I was humiliatingly relieved of pistols, sword, and knife while my son watched. Then they stepped back. "A few minutes, to demonstrate our goodwill," Crow said. "But hurry. Martel is waiting."

"*I've* been waiting for six months."

"Don't begin our partnership with a poor attitude."

"Partnership!"

"Everything is different now."

Different as twins, by my eye. This bunch were evil as the *diab* of the woods of Haiti, and uglier than zombis risen from the grave. The henchmen watched sourly as my family reunited. Astiza kissed me quickly and whispered, "I'm sorry, but I had to go to him," while Harry pulled my leg with impatience. "I'll explain more later," she said.

The fish were skittish, so we made some boats out of leaves and set the flotilla sailing above the carp. Then Crow said, "Time," and Astiza's hand slipped from my fingers as if I were hot. "Make a bargain," she murmured.

"Why didn't you wait for me at the ball?"

"He promised me Horus. We knew you'd come. There were old stories from Martinique, so he told me it must end here."

Then they led her away.

I stepped inside the mansion looking for a weapon to slay Leon Martel. But there was nothing, of course, and I was hopelessly outnumbered. I was ushered into a room by half a dozen bandits, and two women who I assumed must be the pimp's whores were shown a back door. Had he raped my wife?

There sat Martel, smug as a cat with cream, his nose satisfyingly bent but the firm set of his features giving him an aura of command. This kidnapper of my wife and child smiled as if we were old friends, which was doubly annoying. I certainly didn't trust him, and he was a fool if he trusted me.

Martel gestured to a chair. "Monsieur Gage, at last. It's been far too long. Sit, sit, after your long journey. I confess I doubted your pugnacious reputation, and yet here you are, bright as a button and taut as a bow after the battle of Vertières and the sack of Cap-François. Please, relax. You deserve it! Word is that you helped negotiate the city's surrender, saving countless lives. It must be splendid being a hero."

"A feeling you'll never know."

"Your manners." He winced. "I had correspondence from our defeated army and was told you're not shy about calling people unkind names. Even General Rochambeau, in front of his officers! It's a wonder you haven't been killed in a duel or shot by a firing squad."

"Men have tried."

"It's much easier to be polite."

"I only say what is true. If honesty offends you, you'll be upset all day."

Martel sadly shook his head. "We started poorly in Paris. I should have believed you were the ignorant half-wit you claimed instead of continuing to try to drown you, but my nose hurt very much."

"From the size of it, I shouldn't wonder."

"Despite that, I took splendid care of your son."

"Care? As his jailer?"

"Am I? A better father to Horus than you, I contend. I've spent more time with him than you have his entire life, and kept him closer and safer. Your wife, whom I've also treated with propriety, tells me you didn't even know you'd spawned him, left him alone in a ship of Barbary pirates, and dawdled in Paris to play diplomat instead of giving him the security he deserves. Bastards get better treatment than your boy. You're in my debt."

A better father! How I longed to kill him. "Easier to be polite, Martel." My voice had low menace.

He leaned back in his chair in a show of easy superiority, happy to turn his monstrosities around. "His mother elected to accompany me, rather than you, so there's intelligence on *that* side of the family. We relaxed while waiting, researching history. Martinique is in the legends, you know. Now, here you are, no doubt with information that will leave everybody happy. You'll get your family, I the treasure, and France the ancient aviation secrets of the Aztecs."

He had the cheek that came from having me outnumbered a dozen to one, and I was half tempted to start my own war right there. But that would gain me nothing. I'd endure him until I didn't have to. "How can I trust you?"

He spread his arms expansively, a gesture of generosity. "How can you not, when I've yet to kill you?"

"Let's start with my emerald."

"But of course." He'd expected this, and the devil hauled it out with the aplomb of Catherine the Great, tossing it at my feet like a worthless pebble. "I'm not a thief, Monsieur Gage."

"The hell you aren't."

"I only borrowed it to encourage our partnership."

"Then return it like a borrower, if you want manners."

At that we stared like rival lions. It's amazing what the eyes can convey: contempt from Martel and hatred from me. Hatred and a stubborn determination that our "partnership" needed to be modified in the extreme. Starting now, or by God I'd throttle him then and there and punch in his throat, before his bullyboys could get me off him.

Satisfyingly, I finally saw the scoundrel drop his eyes and nod.

Crow reluctantly came forward, picked up the emerald, and handed it to me with more grace. Without a word, I reached inside my shirt and hauled out the same magnifying glass I'd used to ignite the powder kegs at Vertières. Taking my time, I studied the gem, remembering its beauties as vividly as the charms of my wife.

"So untrusting," Martel said.

It was the same stone. I pocketed the jewel. "Finally, a start."

"You know where the remainder of Montezuma's treasure is?" he asked.

"I know where it may be."

He smiled. "Then let's go look. France and America, united."

"Just as soon as I have my family back, and your agreement to a third, not all, of whatever we find." I actually had no intention of giving him any of the booty, except maybe an Aztec jade dagger to his heart, but I needed this manipulator just a little while longer. If I could bundle Astiza and Harry to Jubal and his men, we'd shuck these French criminals and the British entirely, restore some of whatever we found to Dessalines, and keep a generous share for ourselves. I'd retire a gentleman after all.

This was assuming the hoard existed.

"Your family will be reunited, monsieur, when we have the treasure."

"You will have the treasure, monsieur, when I am reunited."

"Then I'm afraid we're at an impasse, except that I already have your family while you, as yet, have nothing." He looked at me coolly. "I've returned your gem as a gesture of goodwill. I've presented your wife and child, unharmed. You must extend courtesy to me. Tell me what you know, and I'll release them."

"Napoleon, sir, would hold you in contempt for such blackmail."

He shook his head. "No man is more practical and ruthless than Bonaparte, if we're being honest here."

I considered. If I shared what I guessed about Diamond Rock, there was nothing to prevent Martel from shooting me, keeping my wife, and selling my child, actions I was certain he was perfectly capable of. Yet he was right, I didn't have anything to exchange for them. Yet.

"Since you want a pirate pact, I'll comply," I said. "Loot for family. But I'm going to test what I know with my own companions, not yours. If I find something, I'm going to trade part of it—not all of it—for my family."

"I want the flying machines."

"If you harm my wife and son, you get nothing. If you try to betray me, you get nothing. If you bungle a discovery that could cost Napoleon the chance to cross the English Channel and conquer England, Bonaparte will have you shot. Be very careful, Leon Martel."

This was the kind of thieves' bargaining he understood. "And if you find nothing, you do not get your family," he countered. "If you don't share with me the secret technology of the Aztecs, I will kill you myself. If you take your secrets to the English, Bonaparte will make you a hunted man no matter where in the world you flee. Be very careful, Ethan Gage."

We stared, again.

"And with that, monsieur, I believe we have established an excellent relationship," he finished.

"I'd like a word with my wife."

"Not possible. She's a very clever woman, and quite impatient by now. I'm relying on her to interpret what clues you find, or what the treasures mean. Let your desire to talk to her spur you on. The sooner we have the Aztec treasure, the sooner you reunite."

"If you touch her, I'll destroy you."

"I don't need your woman. I have many of my own." He sighed, as if exhausted by my distrust.

"I want another kiss from her, then," I said stubbornly. "And a hug from my son." I wanted, but could not admit it, to be reassured. I wanted love. She'd left me in Cap-François to go with this monster.

"I'm afraid not. *Au revoir*, Monsieur Gage. Poke about as you wish with what you know, and come back when you're ready to consummate our alliance. Treasure has a way of bringing people together."

CHAPTER 35

Diamond Rock, *Le Diamant*, looked lonely and somber when Jubal and his men ferried me out to its imposing bulk. Scrub and cactus clung to cliffs spattered with salt and guano. The Caribbean heaved uneasily against the rock's base, the sea making a sigh like a giant. Sun and cloud wrestled for control of the sky.

"Looks as impregnable as the pyramids," I said.

Jubal looked at the sheer cliffs. "Empty like the desert."

We had the place to ourselves. Submerged volcanic reefs surrounded the monolith so ships steered clear. Seabirds wheeled around this Gibraltar as if playing sentry. Undersea gardens of seaweed undulated in the shallows. Time had carved caves into its flanks, but there was no easy landing place.

"We can anchor in the lee and swim ashore," Jubal said. "The boys here will remain in the longboat and pretend we're fishing."

"Wear some shoes. Those cliffs look rugged."

"Shoes are for the white man. I grip with my feet."

So I plunged in with boots and Jubal did not. The sea was a delight, soothing as a bath, and I wondered again at doctors' abhorrence of it. I bobbed a moment, feeling buoyant of care. Then I remembered what I was here for, and we swam. I timed a swell, let it pitch me toward a shelf of basalt, and clung while it receded. Then I heaved myself up, Jubal following. I balanced in my boots on narrow ledges, while he wrapped his feet as adhesive as a limpet.

"A rather awkward place to secrete a treasure," I said.

"Yes, and it sticks up like a flag," my companion observed. "Not secret at all. Maybe Ezili meant something else?"

Was I mistaken? "No, she knew this would draw me."

We clambered about, looking unsuccessfully for hiding places, and then slowly worked our way to the top, clutching rubbery vines and resting on outcroppings. There were several small caves in the monolith, shallow and weather-beaten, but none gave sign of occupation. The recesses were barely deep enough to provide shade, let alone hide the riches of Montezuma.

The top of Diamond Rock was roomier than it appeared from the sea, with a craterlike depression that held a pool of rainwater. A shelf gave just enough room to camp. But there was no sign of excavation, hidden hatchways, or secret doors.

The view was magnificent. Martinique soared into tropic clouds in hazed green glory, surf prancing on its headlands. Parts of the Caribbean glittered where shafts of light from the broken overcast turned patches of sea silver. At six hundred feet elevation, we counted several sails that had been over the horizon at sea level; the rock gave command of the southern approaches to Fort-de-France like an eagle's nest. One vessel, a warship by the look of her, was trimmed as if to go into Fort-de-France, and I had a boy's delight in looking down at her like an eagle.

"When Harry's bigger, I'll bring him up here."

"You have to get him back first. And persuade his mother he won't fall."

Straight down, the deep blue of ocean turned to sapphire and turquoise, mingled with the shadow of submerged rock. Our little longboat bobbed like a toy. Yet the monolith seemed as impregnable as the Great Pyramid had been, which I'd penetrated only with Astiza's help. There we'd found an underground lake, a sluiceway, and . . .

"Jubal, what about an underwater entrance?"

"A cave, American?"

"A submerged sea cave. Leading, perhaps, to a grotto inside. That would make sense as a hiding place, wouldn't it?"

"Only if you can get in, and get back out."

"We've both proven we can swim, with caimans and cannon fire."

He smiled. "I prefer not to jump from here."

"No. Let's pick our way down and spy underwater."

We used the longboat to circuit the rock, looking for likely spots, but nothing was obvious. We finally anchored again on the southeast side, in an area I'd judged promising from above. It was spotted with submerged outcrops, and the sea seemed to undercut the rock's base.

"I'll try first."

I dove, opening my eyes in the salt water and being startled by the clarity. It was like looking through bottle glass. My first three dives yielded nothing, just a maze of underwater rocks and ravines with clean sand on the bottom. But on the fourth I spied triangular-shaped darkness, and as I neared a current swept me forward as if toward a drain. I caught the face of rock at the opening, hesitating. Huge sea fans waved in the surge. Total blackness beyond.

The emerald is in the diamond.

That promise didn't prevent me from being wary.

I kicked for the silvery surface.

"I found a cave, but I've no idea where it goes. The current wants to suck you inside."

"Let me try," said Jubal. "I can hold my breath a long time."

"You might not be able to get out."

"He outwrestled a caiman, once," put in Antoine. "We weren't sure who was drowning whom."

"Then tie a rope. When you need to come back, give a tug, and we'll haul you to the surface."

Jubal nodded, knotted a line, inhaled several deep breaths to fill his lungs as deeply as he could, and went over with a great splash. We played out the hemp, our boat rocking gently on the surface.

I counted. Two minutes went by.

Then three.

I began to worry. Surely Jubal couldn't hold his breath this long. Was he dead? I waited for a tug, but none came.

Four minutes. Impossible.

"Maybe we should pull him in," I muttered.

A rebel named Philippe put his hand on my arm. "Not yet, monsieur. That Jubal, he know what he is doing."

So we waited, me fearing my new friend was drowned.

Finally there was a tug, urgent and insistent. I hauled as frantically as a fisherman whose net is full. Jubal burst the surface to blow like a whale, grasping the gunwale a moment to rest. Water beaded his head like diamonds.

"*Mon Dieu*, where did you go?"

"The current captured me. Whoosh, poor Jubal was carried like a leaf. So I felt frantically upward, and finally there was air. I came up, all breath gone, and was in some kind of cavity with a crevice giving dim light. It's small, no treasure. But the water still goes somewhere. Too far for Jubal! So finally I had enough breath to dive again, but now I can't swim against the current. So I tugged, and you pulled."

It sounded like a death trap, but also the kind of place you might hide something not easily refound.

"By Poseidon's lungs, how the devil can we follow the cave to its end?" We needed Robert Fulton's plunging boat, the *Nautilus*.

But of course I'd managed to help sink *that* submarine in Tripoli harbor. It's hard to plan for all contingencies.

"We need a way to take our breath with us," my black friend said.

And then it came to me, a solution as simple as Jubal's canoe. Just as Harry had made me think of dams and destruction, my companion made me realize we could make do with a much cruder submarine.

"I think I know a way to get in, my friends. I don't know about getting out."

"Ah. It sounds like an Ethan Gage plan."

My doughty platoon looked at me as if I really was a savant, and I congratulated myself for a moment on my cleverness. Then a geyser shot up not a hundred yards from our anchored longboat, and following close was the crack of its cannon, echoing across the water. We whirled in alarm. That warship that we'd spied from the summit wasn't making for Fort-de-France, it was bearing down on Diamond Rock, flying not the French tricolor but the Union Jack of the Royal Navy. What the devil? The British had nothing better to do than shoot at a rowboat of Negro fishermen?

"Who are they?" Antoine asked.

"The enemy," I said. "Except when they're friends. Which I suppose they are, except when they aren't. Don't worry, European politics confuses even me."

Could they suspect that the treasure was here? But that was impossible, wasn't it? I was the only one with Ezili's clue. "Let's raise anchor, lads, and row for shore before they send another cannonball our way as encouragement. I'm going to lie down on the boards here so that all they spy are harmless black fishermen."

"Yes, we play the fool."

We pulled as fast as we could. Apparently the cannon shot had been only a warning to stay clear; the frigate hove to a half mile from the monolith and lowered its own longboat. The English seemed to have no interest in pursuing us.

"I think they're going to explore the rock," Jubal said. I peeked up. There was a great bustle on board the warship and a crowd of redcoats. Of all the times to take an interest in this jutting phallus of thorn and bird nests, the English chose now?

I have very strange luck.

And our task had just gotten much harder.

CHAPTER 36

I'm afraid I need your help."

Few sentences have been harder to spit out. Leon Martel looked as triumphant as a Caesar viewing a barbarian chieftain in chains. He had my wife, he had my son, and now he thought he had me. The British arrival at Diamond Rock was going to make us allies of convenience. I'd seen his kind of smile a thousand times when gambling; it was the smile of a man who has seen the other's cards and knows he has a winning hand.

"Bonaparte would be pleased," he said.

"Napoleon sent me to negotiate for Louisiana, not to hunt for Aztec flying machines. If he knew what we're trying to do, he'd throw us in the asylum with de Sade."

"Don't be so sure." We were sitting on the terrace of Martel's opulent headquarters, which I still didn't understand how he could afford. The jungle was a throbbing wall of green, birds and frogs sending up chorus enough to mask any conversation from eavesdroppers. He took a sip of wine, sighing in appreciation at

the vintage. Having me as a supplicant gave him even more pleasure. "And you need my help because?"

"The British navy has claimed Diamond Rock."

"The British?" Now he sat erect.

"I'm afraid they're making a fort of it." It was typical Albion
cheek. The limeys had sailed in as smart as you pleased, scaled
the Caribbean Gibraltar like a bunch of goats, and winched artillery to the summit. Now they could bang away with impunity
at any French vessel that ventured near. The cannon fire would
force ships approaching from the south to make a long detour to
safety to the west, which in turn required them to beat against
wind and current to get into Fort-de-France. Many trading vessels
wouldn't bother, crippling Martinique's economy. To add insult
to injury, the English flew their flag from their perch. They'd even
christened the monolith HMS *Diamond Rock*, but it was a ship
that couldn't be sunk. It was rudeness that bordered on the inspi-
rational, and I couldn't help admire the wicked genius of it. Yet
the jack tars were squatting over what might be the world's most
fabulous treasure like an ignorant goose, atop an egg it doesn't
realize is golden.

"England!" Martel exclaimed again, with the same venom
I'd heard from Napoleon. "They're gobbling everything because
their superior navy allows it."

"I believe it's called war."

"We have a cowardly fleet."

"No, a leaderless one. Your best naval officers fled or were executed during the Revolution. It takes decades of experience to
command a ship of the line, and your nation called such experience royalism. You chased it away."

Martel scowled. "Someday France will have its revenge, but
for now we're on the defensive. The English have been pirates and
barbarians since the retreat of the Roman Empire. No one knows
that better than America. You and France are natural allies, Gage.
I tried to tell you that in Paris."

"By drowning me in a tub of water?"

"I am sometimes impatient. But bad introductions can lead to good friendships. Now we're partners, in search of a treasure that will have great importance strategically, historically, and scientifically. England will finally be conquered, and the world will find itself at peace under the visionary direction of Napoleon Bonaparte. You will be rich, I will be powerful, and we'll dine with the first consul and bring Joséphine gossip of her home village of Trois-Îlets."

He certainly had imagination. Since I've the same fault, I was anything but encouraged; too much vision tends to obscure reality. Yet my Negroes and I needed technical help and a way to distract the British. So here I was plotting with a renegade policeman with my wife's reluctant blessing.

When I'd returned to Martel's château after scouting the rock, I insisted upon meeting Astiza before striking a bargain. Since my enemy sensed that my truculence had softened, he'd allowed us to meet alone in the plantation library.

It was a passionate reunion. I'd earlier watched a land crab on the beach stalk and pounce on a mate buried in the sand with the single-mindedness of a landlord on rent day. I'd done much the same with my beloved, striding across the room like a frenzied youth to seize and kiss her, my hand roaming from her waist to bottom while another clutched a breast. It had been a long separation! While I groped I was secretly alert for any sign of hesitation that might hint at infidelity or violation. But no, she kissed me back with ardor of her own, gasping when we broke for air, and melted against me in a way that made me want to take her on the carpet. Damnation that Crow and his guards were right outside the door.

"Did he assault you?" I asked.

"If he'd tried, one of us would be dead."

"Why didn't you wait for me in Saint-Domingue?"

She kissed me again and leaned against my shoulder. "He said that he had Horus and that the ultimate goal was likely Martinique. If I wanted my son, we must take temporary leave from my dangerous husband. Meanwhile, he tempted me with his own research into the legends. Ethan, I didn't want to go into the jungle with Dessalines when my son was in Cap-François in the hands of a madman. So I went with Martel in hopes of safeguarding our boy until you found us. And I couldn't explain. You'd disappeared from the library, and there was no time to find you."

I'd folded myself into a dumbwaiter. "I thought you'd been taken to Rochambeau. I almost killed the general."

"So impulsive! And so unnecessary. Why would I be tempted by a lizard like Rochambeau when I already had Adonis as my husband?"

Well, I liked that. Truth be told, I'm a handsome rascal. "When we retire, they'll want the two of us at the best parties. We're very stylish."

She's also learned when to ignore me. "Martel knew the city was about to fall. He wanted out and knew you'd follow. I didn't choose Horus or Leon over you. I simply made the only choice I could."

"I'm going to kill Martel, you know."

"He knows, too, so he'll be prepared when you try. It's what men do, isn't it? All I want is a chance to get away from him as a family. I don't care about this treasure or war. Can we please do that, Ethan? Simply get away?"

"Absolutely. But I don't think we'll have an opportunity until he's distracted by treasure. We find it, bargain, fight, and flee."

"And this treasure is . . . ?"

"Under a rock as massive as the Great Pyramid. Maybe. We've found an underwater cave but need a means to get through it, and now the British are sitting on top. That's where Martel comes in."

"The treasure is cursed, Ethan. The Aztecs put a spell on it. I saw troubling things in the little temple I made in the *Hecate* when we crossed the Atlantic, and read more here. You mustn't be tempted. Let the French have it; they'll regret their discovery. We just need to get away."

"What did you read?"

"Martel discovered reports of a pirate ship in these waters manned by black Maroons, two centuries before. They circuited Martinique as if looking for a hiding place, perhaps this rock you've found. Since they didn't prey on merchant ships, the speculation was that they were burying treasure instead of seizing it. Planters have dug Martinique's shores ever since, without success. But that isn't the odd thing. I found more documents Martel doesn't know about."

"Records of what?"

"Weeks later, their pirate vessel was found drifting at sea."

"And?"

"No one was aboard. All the Maroons had vanished. No bodies, no combat, no clue."

I felt a chill. "They went ashore and the ship broke anchor, perhaps."

"Perhaps." She looked at me steadily. "But here's my question, Ethan. If they came from Saint-Domingue, did these blacks come here to hide a treasure? Or get rid of it? Were they determined to return for it? Or bury it so deep that no one ever found it again?"

"You think *they* were cursed."

"Think of all the trouble a single emerald has caused, both to Yussef Karamanli in Tripoli and now us."

I shook my head. "First of all, I believe in luck but not in curses. Second, I already have the emerald back, and it's still going to finance our retirement. Third, it's foolish not to take a king's ransom, should we find it. So let Martel be cursed. Or let Jubal and the blacks take it and strike a deal between their gods and the Aztec ones. We just need a chance to escape together, but won't have one until we're all as rich as Montezuma." Frankly, I also wanted a peek.

"Your family for the gold. Don't forget, and don't be greedy."

"Agreed. But to win, we must have a plan of revenge. So here's what we'll do."

Lacking a Robert Fulton or a working submarine, the scheme I'd come up with was inspired by Jubal's overturned canoe. We'd use a diving bell, a device dating back to ancient Greece.

The idea is simple. Invert a cauldron and drop it in the water so that it traps air, just as the canoe did. You can test the idea by putting a bucket upside down in water. Dive, surface within the container, and breathe in the space of the upended vessel. If possible, refresh the pocket of air with a hose.

A diving bell the size normally used to salvage ships, with barges and air pumps, would be unwieldy in the cave under Diamond Rock. Such an apparatus would also attract the attention of the English.

My scheme was less complicated. We'd sheathe a rum barrel with lead to give it the necessary weight and tightness to remain underwater while trapping air. A small window would be fit on its side to look out through, and to navigate by. Foxfire, the phosphorescent luminescence sometimes found in rotting bark, would shed a little light. Without a hose and pumps, we'd refresh our atmosphere from leather bags filled with air. I'd wear this keg on my shoulders with a harness. My torso would be in the Caribbean, but my head would have something to breathe.

We'd attach a rope, as we had to Jubal.

It was cleverness worthy of a savant, except it wasn't original with me. In fact, we looked at diagrams in a book in Martel's rented library to help puzzle the thing out. Other tomes showed plans for the kind of warship we'd need.

"If the cave goes nowhere, I give a tug and am hauled back out," I reassured Astiza when we met with Martel and Jubal in the library. To hold a council of war with a woman and a Negro was extraordinary, but these are modern times. "If there's treasure, then I ferry out an armful at a time."

"And the English?"

"We'll distract them with a naval attack on the side of the rock opposite from where we're working," Martel said.

"All in trust." Her tone was skeptical.

"Of course not, madame. Business partners use contracts and lawyers, not trust. We'll have you, and your husband will have the hoard. But there's honor among thieves, is there not, Monsieur Gage? A friendly exchange, and your family free to go. To the United States, I suppose."

"As far as we can get from you."

"A third goes to Haiti," Jubal insisted.

Martel frowned. "I am not accustomed to bargaining with blacks."

"And a free Haitian is not accustomed to consorting with men who are allied with slave masters," my massive friend said. "So we do as a slave does."

"What's that?"

"Partner with whom we must, and spit afterward."

Martel laughed. "You'd make a fine criminal in the Paris underworld."

"And you a fine field hand with a cane bill and straw hat."

The Frenchman regarded his gigantic new ally uncertainly. "In two weeks we'll have the dark of the moon," he finally said. "Best to work when it's hard for the British to see."

"And then we'll be done with each other once and for all," I said.

CHAPTER 37

As we made preparations I belatedly realized we'd slipped into a new year, 1804, and that I'd entirely missed Christmas. Martel did give three chances to play with my son, the two of us under guard. So Harry and I dug a cave, crept through the shrubbery, and threw rocks at the pond. But I was mostly kept busy in boatyard and workshop. Astiza oversaw the sewing of leather air bags.

As the moon waned, Martinique's dazzling sunshine also darkened, giving way to sultry haze. Jubal watched the sky for omens. "It's bad weather coming, more like September than January," he muttered. "We must hurry."

"A squall could give us cover," I reasoned.

"This kind of storm is no cover," Jubal warned. "It upends the sea. We want to dive before it begins, and be done before it climaxes."

"A little rain to blind the British. Pray for that."

"And I'll pray for the success of your plan to checkmate the French."

Our scheme was necessarily complicated. We needed daylight to dive. But with England atop the rock, we could approach only under cover of darkness.

Our strategy, then, had three steps. Jubal, Martel, and I would be the treasure divers, and we'd approach Diamond Rock at night. Antoine and the rest of Jubal's men would join Crow, Vulture, Buzzard, and the rest of Martel's men on a bomb ketch, a sailing ship designed to fire at the summit of the rock by using a high, arching mortar mounted in the bow. The ketch had two masts astern of the huge gun, with both square-rigged and fore-and-aft sails, and would be skippered by a few seasoned sailors on loan from the governor of Martinique. My wife and son would sail as hostages.

A French bombardment of the captured rock would commence the next day, and we'd use the distraction to begin our dive. Any treasure would be found, removed, and stored on the sea bottom. Then the ketch would return under cover of darkness, and we'd retrieve the loot from the bottom sand before escaping.

In other words, everything had to happen perfectly.

Leon Martel came readily with Jubal and me—he had arrogant courage, so long as my family was pawn—and the three of us rowed toward *Le Diamant* on a moonless night, taking a bearing because the course was ink except for the dazzle of phosphorescence in our wake. I worried that the English might see our sparkle, but then decided our longboat was so small that the danger was remote. We pulled in silence, nothing in the universe except our tail of blue fire. The wind was warm, my mood anxious. There was swell, the kind that heralds a distant storm.

In the middle of our longboat were the converted rum barrel and air skins.

An hour at the oars brought us to within sound of waves slapping against Diamond Rock. Looking up, I could see the glow of British lanterns at the summit. We coasted to a small indention on the cliff that faced Martinique and pulled into a "cove" that was little more than a crevice the width of our longboat. An overhang shielded us from easy view by the garrison. We tied off, arranged the diving bell for quick deployment, and settled down to wait for dawn.

Sleep was elusive.

"So, Ethan, what will you do as a rich man?" Jubal finally asked.

I shifted, uncomfortable and nervous. "As little as possible."

Martel snorted. "No one would bore more quickly than you, Monsieur Gage. You don't know your own character."

"So what would you do, Leon? Whores and horses?"

"Money is power, and power is rule. I want men answering to me instead of my answering to them."

"Another reason to keep my distance. And you, Jubal?"

"I want to rebuild my homeland. Haiti was the most beautiful country in the world before the war. It could be again."

"Doesn't that sound nobler than our motives, Martel?"

"So noble that I want to buy your black friend and put him to work. His race can restore our plantations."

"No longer, Frenchman."

"Mark my words, your damned revolution will prove a mistake."

"It was your own revolution that gave us the idea. Freedom and equality, France preached! And now planters on every island lay awake in the dark of the night, waiting for their throats to be cut for liberty." He gave our temporary ally a ghostly grin.

"Are you going to cut mine?"

"No, because I'm already a free man and we're partners, as you say. This is much better than having a slave, is it not, for both you and me? That's what your race must understand."

Martel rolled to one side to doze. "All right, then. Ethan, be bored. Jubal, throw your money away on a country that will never appreciate it. I'll buy status and position in France and rule like a lord."

"At least you're candid," I allowed.

"I'm honest. Everyone is corrupt, but only I admit it."

The sun came over Martinique, flooding our little crack but also shining into the eyes of any English sentries who happened to look in our direction. Unless they climbed down on some improbable mission, I felt us reasonably invisible. As light came, Jubal quietly slipped over the side with a wooden buoy holding an anchor and line. He swam to a spot directly in front of the submerged cave, dove down to set the anchor, and adjusted the length of the line so that the marker was just underwater. Then he led a rope from the buoy back to our boat. When the time came, we could swiftly pull ourselves to the anchored buoy to deploy the diving bell.

The sun climbed higher, the sea turning from black to blue, and then to aquamarine. I watched Martel lazily watching me. He was waiting for me to try to kill him, while thinking of any number of ways to betray me. Corrupt indeed. Jubal lounged between us like a referee before a prizefight.

Finally we heard shouts from above, and even a trumpet.

"The tide has turned, and they've spied your wife's present," Martel whispered. "By afternoon, we can act."

As much as I hated to admit it, Martel and I had things in common. We were both instinctual opportunists and clever improvisers. It wasn't easy assaulting the English on their rock because their new gun battery was higher than the masthead of any ship, Accordingly, the renegade policeman had used my papers from Rochambeau to enlist the governor of Martinique in an elaborate diversion. We refit an eighty-foot vessel into a bomb ketch christened *Pelee*, copying the habit of naming such weapons after volcanoes. Workers removed its foremast, reinforced the deck with timber cribbing, and installed a massive mortar. The gun was so heavy that the new ketch listed slightly at the bow. In theory, the mortar could lob shells high enough to reach the summit, but *Pelee* was a clumsy sailor, its canvas set too far back to properly balance. Distraction was its real mission.

We told the governor nothing about treasure but assured him that one lucky hit on a British magazine could blow their entire garrison to hell. "We're using the expertise of the doughty mercenary and sage savant Ethan Gage, hero of the Pyramids," Martel said, Governor Lambeau entirely missing his ironic sarcasm. The chance of success was enough to persuade the loan of a fortress mortar that weighed more than a ton; victory over this British "ship" on a French rock could lead the governor to promotion back in France.

Lambeau, too, wanted to escape home before taken by fever.

That manipulation by my criminal ally was clever enough.

Even better was Astiza's suggestion of a preliminary ruse, so calculated that I wished I'd thought of it myself. The same night we rowed to the rock, the ketch drifted between *Le Diamant* and Martinique to drop several half-filled kegs into the sea. By dawn they were bobbing past the rock opposite our hiding place. We heard excited cries when the garrison scrambled to salvage this flotsam. Everybody loves to beachcomb.

Even better, the kegs were half full of rum.

"Obviously you've studied the English navy," I told Astiza.

"I'm a student of human nature and know how lonely and stupefyingly boring it must be to be stationed on that rock. Those half-full kegs will be a quarter full by the time they're hoisted to where the commander can inspect them, and British aim will be degraded accordingly. Nor will their lookouts be as alert. The first goal in any battle is to help the enemy destroy itself."

"You sound like Napoleon, my lovely."

"I've studied with you, my devious electrician."

So how could I get Martel to help destroy *himself*, when the time came?

It was hot and boring while we bobbed, waiting for the gunnery duel to begin. Orbiting birds, clearly annoyed by this human interest in their castle, occasionally spattered our boat with retaliatory guano. The sky turned grayer. As rum was sneaked, voices from the top of the rock increased in volume. Laughter, songs, angry commands, heated lectures . . . yes, the liquor had gone to work. Then more shouts when the bomb ketch was spotted bearing down on the rock opposite us, the mortar on its deck a gaping mouth.

Maybe this insanity would really work.

What if the treasure wasn't here?

Then either Martel or I would never emerge from the cave alive, I guessed.

At two o'clock we heard the bang of the mortar and then a crash as a bomb erupted somewhere above. Fragments of stone and shell flew wide and pattered the sea around like a rain of gravel. Martel smiled. "It has begun. All eyes will be on the ketch."

There was another thud, answering the first, and another, and another, as English guns replied. An artillery duel was soon fully under way. We expected that even drunken English gunnery would eventually drive away our ship, and I worried a lucky shot might hit my wife and son. We had to be quick.

Casting off from Diamond Rock, we swiftly pulled ourselves out to where Jubal had set the buoy and readied our makeshift diving bell. "The guess that we're in the right place is mine, so the risk is, too," I said manfully. I'm not really that brave, but I wanted as much control over our situation as I could manage.

So I slipped over the side holding our longboat by one hand and a sack of musket balls in the other. The leaded rum barrel was upended over my head, its leather harness keeping me in position when I let go the side of our boat. My head and shoulders were above water, my body immersed, and my only view was through the small glass we'd fashioned. The weight of lead and musket balls sank me like a sack of grain, and I plunged about fifteen feet before my feet landed on an underwater rock. I looked out at the sea. I was in a bubble of breathable air inside the diving bell. I swayed and steadied. A line led from our contraption to the buoy, through a ring, and on to the stern of our longboat.

The leather air bags were tied behind me. My companions would pull themselves back out of sight while I explored, but in a quarter hour would haul back on the keg, whether I was attached or not.

If things were going well, I was to tack a white handkerchief, like the white cloths we'd tied onto the powder barrels on Saint-Domingue. It would be a sign I'd found the treasure. Then Martel could decide whether to follow me inside the Diamond.

I gave myself half odds, so I made Martel swear a promise. "If I drown, you must release my wife and son."

"Agreed. They'll then be of no use. See? I am a gentleman."

"You're a schemer."

"Yes. We're brothers, you and I."

Now I took stock at the bottom of the sea. I could see, barely, the triangular opening of the cave and the glorious sea fans at its entrance that undulated as if waving encouragement. *Ethan, in here!* Was it Ezili speaking, or some other siren luring me to my death?

The thud of artillery carried through the water.

I spilled some of the musket balls to give myself more buoyancy. Trimming the diving bell was like operating the altitude of a balloon, and I hovered a few feet off the rock I'd initially landed on.

Then the current caught me, and I was pulled toward the dark opening. The barrel scraped a side, caromed toward the other, bounced again, and slid into blackness. It was like falling into a hole, with no way to climb back out.

But what was inside might change the world.

CHAPTER 38

I was briefly in utter blackness. There was a quick blue glow, as if a crevice was letting in light from above—was that where Jubal had taken breath?—and then darkness again, as forbidding as a sewer. On I swirled, bobbing in my barrel. I'd gambled that the rock was only a few hundred yards wide and that the cave couldn't go far, but what if the ocean descended to the very bowels of the earth?

Only the need to bargain for my family kept me from panicking and signaling to be pulled back out.

Suddenly I yanked to a stop, and at first I thought my companions *were* trying to reverse me. I looked out my porthole for a landmark, but all was dark outside the little window. I had a faint glow inside my contraption from the bottle of fox fire, but it illuminated little but my own hands. Then I realized the trailing line must have snagged. I loosened my harness, plunged my head down into the sea, and reached outside the barrel with my arm to jerk. The line finally freed, and the barrel floated forward once more.

I hurriedly rose back into its air space and continued like a leaf in a drain, blind and stuffy. Then I slammed rock and could feel, with my feet, a cliff face. I was at a dead end, pinned by current. Darkness like pitch, my breath going stale.

I refreshed my air first, hauling in one of Astiza's leather bags and bringing its stopper into my little air space inside the diving bell. I released the plug and felt my head clear.

And now, time to explore.

I released myself from the harness, took a breath, and swam out and upward, feeling for the cave ceiling.

Instead, I broke clear of the surface. I was in a grotto.

I sucked in air. I could breathe! The cliff where the diving bell had grounded was wet, rough, and silent. There was no sound of guns or sea. I felt until I found a ledge above water. I dared go no farther lest I lose the position of the diving bell, so I calculated the few feet I'd come, carefully worked my way that distance back, and felt the barrel with my feet. I reached inside my shirt for the white cloth, dove, and pushed its tack into the barrel's soft lead. This would signal it was safe to enter the cave. Just as I did so the bell jerked as if with a life of its own and began to be hauled in by my companions. The quarter hour was up.

I swam to the ledge and hauled myself out. Let there be light.

Having learned my lesson at the battle of Vertières, I unwrapped an oilskin parcel with flint, steel, tinder, candle, and a phosphor bottle. I carefully uncorked the latter invention and withdrew a splinter. It flared just enough to light my fuzz of oiled cotton and wood shavings. Then I lit the candlewick, and shadows retreated even more. I put the wax taper in a crevice, seeming bright as a chandelier after utter blackness. The pool I'd emerged from glittered.

Finally I looked about.

I was sitting below a rock dome that peaked fifteen feet above the surface of the sea. There was a crevice above, an old volcanic vent that must be providing distant air. Everywhere but where I sat the dome plunged sheer into the sea. But behind . . .

I turned and jumped. An alligator crouched, giving me a toothy grin as if it had been waiting patiently for dinner to crawl out of the sea. Its teeth gleamed.

But this monster was golden, I realized, its eyes great emeralds and its rows of teeth quartz crystals. It was long as my arm. Behind, receding into the shadows, was a reef of gold and silver. I'd found a dragon's hoard of necklaces and crowns, great silver wheels with mysterious writing, and sculpted animals studded with gems. On some the turquoise and jade was bright as the sunny Caribbean, and the workmanship as exquisite as anything in Nitot's jewelry shop. There were also little hillocks of loose emeralds, green as a model of Ireland.

I'd found Montezuma's lost treasure, or at least what was left of it. This remnant equaled the wealth of a thousand kings. Whole armadas could be financed, I calculated. Palaces erected, armies recruited, cathedrals built. How had the salvagers been persuaded to leave it here?

As if in answer, I realized there were adjacent piles of white, and I looked more closely. Bones, lots of them. Skeletons clustered around the hoard like soldiers at a campfire. Their skulls looked at the treasure as if in reproach, flesh and clothing long rotted away.

The Maroons had apparently never reemerged. Killed to keep a secret? Trapped by the current? Or sacrificing themselves to bury a discovery too dangerous to harness, as Astiza suggested?

Superstition.

All I knew is I didn't want to join them.

I crawled to the booty for inspection. There were hideously beautiful metal masks, jade-tipped swords, and golden necklaces as heavy as slave collars. Golden toys rolled on tiny wheels, and simple cast bars of precious metal were stacked like bricks. I suspected the conquistadors had melted some of the Aztec art down for transit.

Finally there were curious triangular objects I didn't recognize at all: sausage-shaped machines with delta wings and helmeted riders. They were contraptions different than anything I'd ever seen, except that they reminded me of the reckless canvas goose at Fort de Joux that madman George Cayley had launched into the air.

They were, in short, flying machines, or at least representations of one.

Maybe Martel was more than just a lunatic. Was there really enough detail to allow French savants to devise something to fly the English Channel?

I knelt as if before saints, overcome by the fabulousness of the find and bewilderment at its meaning. How and why had escaped slaves salvaged this from some storm-washed reef and carried it here for hiding? They'd avoided the temptation of spiriting it away and spending. Why? Had they no greed? Or had the treasure tricked and trapped them here?

There was a splash behind, and I jumped again. But it was only Martel, surfacing from the diving bell as lithe as a seal. He hauled himself up beside me, shook water from his thick hair like a dog (me quickly shielding the candle from this idiocy), and then gaped at the wealth of an empire. For a moment, even he was at a loss for words.

Eventually he crawled to one of the peculiar birdlike toys, gingerly holding it as if it were magic and might fly away on its own. He had an almost boyish look of wonder and triumph.

"I told you so, Gage."

CHAPTER 39

I realized why no one had ever retrieved the treasure of Montezuma when I attempted to exit with a handful. The seawater didn't dead-end in the cavern; it found another underwater crack and continued, possibly all the way through Diamond Rock. This meant there was a constant tide running into this cave, and none out. Without help, it was a tunnel of no return. No wonder it contained bones of the dead!

I plunged into the pool, strapped inside the diving bell, and jerked the rope for Jubal to pull me out, and that's the only way I emerged alive. Escape was like trying to breast a river while encased in a sausage. My black friend had returned the longboat to its hiding place and swum to a perch above the cave entrance to handle the towline, but even with that platform he had to haul like a longshoreman.

His reward was when I unstrapped myself, surfaced, and held up a golden necklace heavy enough to make its wearer stoop from the weight.

"It's really there, Jubal!"

"By Damballah's scales, that collar alone is enough to start rebuilding my country."

"Ezili favors us, I think."

"Ezili favors herself, as our French partner favors himself. Everyone has their own dreams."

Yes. Once we got the treasure out we'd have more temptation than schoolboys at a brothel. In the meantime, we all had to work on trust.

"I'll swim this underwater to the buoy anchor, drop it on the bottom, and go get more."

He pointed toward the sky. "Hurry. The weather's getting worse."

I looked. The sea was grayer, waves higher. I could still hear the artillery duel, but it was beginning to be muted by the drum pound of surf. I hoped our bomb ketch would pull away soon, before my family got hurt. "Maybe that will make it easier to sneak under the noses of the British."

"Agwe, the sea *loa*, is restless. Something's wrong, Ethan."

"Jubal, if you saw the wonders of that cave, you'd realize that everything is finally very right."

His nod conveyed doubt. "Why did the Maroons bring and hide it here? Why did they never come back for it?"

"They left their bones. We won't."

"Maybe we should just leave Martel now, and go, with the necklace and the longboat."

"No, his men have my family. And there's an entire treasury down there. This is payback for all you've suffered, Jubal: years of war, the loss of your lover."

"I don't think life balances its ledger." He sighed. "How many trips to carry it all out?"

"Dozens."

"I can't pull that long." The black glanced upward. There were flashes like thunder against the clouds, the crash of British artillery. "It's too hard to pull you or Monsieur Martel through the tunnel so many times. You send him out next to help me. Then you fill a sack, tie it to the barrel, and we just pull that. We empty the treasure, you pull back this line, and together we transfer all the gold and jewels to the anchor. The last time you come out with the diving bell."

"Agreed. I trust you. But you shouldn't trust Martel."

"Ethan, I was a slave. I don't trust nobody."

So we set to work, and work it was. I strapped myself back into the barrel and drifted into the cavern to inform Martel of our plan. I was amazed at how much shorter the distance seemed now that I had traversed it before.

Martel was at first as skeptical at leaving me alone with the treasure as I was of leaving him with Jubal. I explained that, first, I had nowhere to go without his help, and second, as we transferred I would be leaving *him* with the growing heap of gold. "But not the toy birds, or whatever you want to call them."

"Flying machines."

"Those stay until I come. And if you try to betray me or kill Jubal, you lose them. And remember, my blacks are aboard your ketch."

"As is your wife and child. And my inspectors and sailors."

"The only way this will succeed is if we all work together."

"I've tried to explain that to you from the beginning, Monsieur Gage. It's good to have partners, no?" And with a Gallic snort he plunged into the diving bell and jerked on the line to be pulled out, the water helping neutralize the golden alligator that weighed at least a hundred pounds and that he cradled in his arms.

I set to work before my candle burned down completely.

We set up an efficient system. Jubal and Martel traded tasks, one swimming gunnysacks of gold and precious stones out to our anchor depository, the other tugging on lines to haul out the treasure or to signal me to pull the empty bell back. With each relay I loaded a gunnysack with loot, hung it on the floating barrel, and watched it jerk away before returning empty ten minutes later. Slowly the Aztec hoard diminished, my labor as mechanical as if I were shifting coal. The hoard was only half depleted when I swam down to attach a sack and found a crude note that Jubal or Martel had tacked inside the air chamber before I pulled it back.

"Storm coming. Finish now."

I didn't argue. Yes, I left a dragon's nest of gold behind, but we had enough treasure to buy Napoleon's palace at Saint-Cloud three times over. The candle was guttering. So I took the flying models, tucked them in my shirt, filled the gunnysack with some last precious idols, strapped myself into the leaded rum barrel, and gave a tug.

I still braced for betrayal. If the line went slack from being cut, I was determined to grab the rough sides of the tunnel and try to kick my own way up and out.

But no, my journey went smoothly. Hands grabbed. I came to the surface with the last of the treasure, blinking away water. Light was rapidly failing. I heard no more gunfire.

"Did the British hit our vessel?"

"No, we would have heard cheers."

The twilight was an odd, ominous green, and the swells were growing higher. It was so hazy I couldn't see the top of the rock. I bobbed uneasily up and down in the waves, and I could hear our longboat scraping where it was hidden in the cleft. The air felt very heavy.

"Yes, no time for more gold," I said. "When will the ship come back?"

"Midnight," Martel said. "You brought the flying machines?"

"If that's what they really are, yes. You'll win my consternation if you make them into something that actually flies."

"Your challenge is accepted, monsieur. French science leads the world."

"You have the lunacy of a true savant, Martel."

"And you the nerve of a good grave robber."

Compliments exchanged, we swam to the tiny cove where the longboat was moored, hauled ourselves aboard, donned more clothes—I had a vest—and gobbled cheese and wine. Our bread, alas, had gone soggy, and I missed a spoon of sugar, too. Jubal eyed the storm while Martel tried to puzzle out the triangular objects, and I watched Martel. The first priority was to safeguard Astiza and Harry, waiting on the ketch. And then?

If all else failed, I still had the emerald.

I've learned to be cautious around my enemies so I'd swallowed it, in case Martel tried to take it back from me. To time its emergence correctly, I shouldn't eat much anyway. So I dropped my share of the spoiled bread overboard and watched fish come to gobble.

"So can you fly to London?" I idly asked Martel.

"Look, here are the wings. And here a man sitting between to steer. This is sculpted from something the Aztecs had seen, I'm certain of it. But did the wings flap? This will require much study."

"I've been on a glider that crashed. It would be a brave man who first mounts a contraption based on a toy."

"I will be that man."

Night came, and we lost all sight of Martinique. It was as if we were marooned, no stars overhead, the wind continuing its alarming rise. Surf was beginning to boom against stone. The longboat bucked uneasily up and down. Anchoring the ketch to scoop up the treasure wouldn't be easy.

Time dragged. Were the French not coming? I'd row to shore before dawn rather than risk another day here.

Then there was a scrape above and bits of grit and pebbles rained. A hundred feet above a horn lantern swayed in the wind. "Look, a glim," I whispered to the others, pointing to the light.

Men were working down the cliff. Had they seen us?

One if by land, two if by sea, the British were coming.

CHAPTER 40

Life is never simple. My captured family and I were now within imminent gunshot range of English, French, and Haitian rivals; the weather was deteriorating toward a real storm; and fish had gotten all our rolls. I was sticky with salt, windburned, thirsty, and weary. Any man who tells you adventuring is a lark is a liar.

"Maybe the English won't see us if we row out to the buoy," Jubal whispered back.

"In these seas? We'll splash like a duck," I said.

"They'll see no more if we meet them with steel," Martel suggested. He drew a stiletto as wicked as a warlock's wand, and it gleamed in the night like a shard of ice. The bastard looked as anticipatory about sliding it between a man's ribs as I do about stroking a woman. Our renegade policeman was a dog needing to be put down, but we could use his bite now.

"You've certainly more pluck than I can muster," I said to encourage him. "Could you show us how to stalk, please? Jubal and

I will guard the rear until *Pelee* heaves to. We'll keep your flying machines safe as well."

He looked at the lantern bobbing above. "I prefer that we cut English throats together, Gage. Just to continue our partnership."

"I rather like the Albions, despite our differences at Lexington and Concord. They're terribly earnest but have a dry sense of humor. Slitting English throats seems more of a French than an American task, don't you think? Not that my hopes and prayers don't go with you."

"You'll strand me on the rock."

Excellent idea. "Not if you're quick," I lied.

But before Martel could demonstrate his assassination skills or, even more conveniently, be killed, more pebbles rained down and a shout came from above. "There's a boat down here!"

"Too late," the Frenchman muttered. He tucked his stiletto away, unwrapped an oilcloth, uncovered a brace of pistols, and tossed one each to Jubal and me. He took up a third, stood in our bouncing craft, aimed, and fired. There was a cry and the lantern tumbled, bouncing into the air like a meteor and then plunging in the sea, leaving us in darkness again. *"Vive Napoleon!"*

"Frogs!" the British sailors exclaimed. Muskets flashed above, and balls pinged and whined about our heads.

"Couldn't we have discussed our strategy before you cried out like a charging regiment?" I grumbled.

"French élan, and a commendable shot in these conditions," Martel replied. "*Pelee* will be here soon. Make them hesitate, Gage."

So Jubal and I fired, too. British pistols banged back, I heard the richest variety of curses this side of a Portsmouth alehouse, and then we were all busy reloading. More lights appeared at the top of the rock, and a general alarm was raised. A trumpet sounded, and drums rattled. We'd spent the entire day slipping out treasure from under the British noses, and now, in the dead of night, we'd raised the entire garrison. Was Martel trying to get us killed?

"We can't fight the whole bloody fort," I said. "Let's row for Martinique and you lads can come back for the treasure later. I'll take Astiza and Harry and be on my way." Leaving an emperor's ransom hurt, of course, but I had my emerald on deposit.

"They'll wonder what we were here for, dive, and find it," Martel replied. "We need that treasure, Gage. No man should understand the importance of money better than a drifting pauper like yourself."

Alas, he had a point. We work all our lives for filthy lucre in hopes of not working at all. It makes no sense, but then neither does love, fashion, or the American Congress.

A cannon boomed from atop Diamond Rock. They couldn't depress the barrel enough to hit us, the shot flying overhead. But the spout of water it raised out to sea reminded us that retreat had its own perils. Then more musket shots rose from above, one ricocheting off rock and thunking into the wood of our longboat. Too close! While the overhang gave us protection, we ultimately were fish in a barrel in our little cleft of a cove.

I looked up. More lanterns, ropes slithering in descent as they uncoiled. I'd no doubt sailors and marines would soon be swinging down them like angry apes. I could see musket muzzles poking out from crevices above, pivoting to look for us like the antenna of insects. I envied Jubal his dark skin, figuring it made him more invisible.

"There they are!" the cry echoed down. "In that tight cove! Ready . . ."

Muskets swung to aim at us. I winced, wondering if I was about to expel my emerald long before I'd planned to.

And then a boom of a different cannon, this time from the other direction, and with a crash a cannon ball hit the cliff above and rock splinters flew in all directions. Men howled.

It was *Pelee*, leaning hard in the wind as she scudded out of the night, smoke drifting off the muzzle of a deck gun. Then another of her cannon fired, the flash like lightning. Martel whooped at the arrival of our allies and lit our own lantern in the longboat, uncovering the side that faced the water to signal where we were.

The ketch banged again and again, shot bouncing off the flank of Diamond Rock like a castle wall. The British sailors were in full retreat, scrambling upward even faster than they'd swung down. Their own artillery crashed in reply, water geysers shooting up. The French mortar on the ketch barked, and a shell screamed up toward the clouds to burst. In the flashes of illumination, we joined the tumult by shooting our pistols again.

Martel untied the longboat. "We salvage under their gun muzzles," he said. "Prepare to dive where bullets can't reach us."

I didn't have a better plan. Jubal and I pushed off toward *Pelee* and the buoy we'd set. Musket fire peppered the water, cannons crashed, but the French ketch had turned into the wind so close to Diamond Rock that the British couldn't help but overshoot her. She dropped her mizzen and anchored, continuing to lob with her mortar while spraying the side of the rock with swivel guns. Her captain, a man named Augustus Brienne, was showing élan of his own.

"Come on, comrades!" I heard Antoine call.

I studied the crowd on board. Yes, there was Astiza, waving to me over the gunwale. *Stay down, darling.* Harry must be somewhere below. I also saw other Negro heads besides Antoine, assuring me that the French hadn't betrayed Jubal's men yet. There was still a chance.

Once we got to our submerged buoy we dove over the side of our longboat, eager to evacuate before British fire found it. The sea was inky below, its heave pulling and pushing below the surface. At night I could imagine a thousand hideous things coming at me from deep. But the surest way to get out of this mess was to retrieve what we'd come for, so I followed the buoy line to the bottom, groped by the longboat anchor, and seized slick metal.

Aztec gold!

I swam up, narrowly missing knocking my own head on the

tethered launch. Then I kicked over to the ketch and hollered for a ladder. A rope-and-peg one uncurled down the side. The little ship was bouncing up and down in the seas like a coach on a potholed American road, the weather both screening us and making salvage difficult. I had to time my grab to avoid the scrape of barnacles that girded the vessel's waterline. At last I climbed partway up and slapped what I'd grabbed—it was one of the gold necklaces, I saw—on deck. The French gaped.

"Get it in a strongbox," I ordered. "There's *much* more to come."

Martel squeezed up beside me, crying for help to lift the golden alligator. "Yes, and don't cut anchor until we're all aboard," he added. "Send the blacks to help."

We dropped back into the sea, bullets whapping into the ketch's hull and plunking into the water. Jubal swam by, hoisted his own piece of the hoard on deck, and shouted to his comrades. "Dive, freemen! The faster we fetch, the faster we leave!"

Men leaped from the ship and swam with us back to the buoy. Even Crow and Buzzard jumped in to help. Down we ducked like otters, groping for gold, and then swam gasping to *Pelee*'s far side. The ship's coughing mortar gave fits of illumination. British cannonballs kept arcing over us to fall harmlessly into the sea beyond, and their gunners swore like the sailors they were, frustrated they couldn't depress their cannon barrels far enough and no doubt wondering what the devil we were doing down there.

Finally they tried just pitching a cannonball by hand. This, to a certain extent, worked: the sphere fell three hundred feet, hit an outcrop, and bounced outward toward our salvage operation. There was no good aim, but the ball made a disturbing impact when it splashed into the sea a few yards from where we swam.

Madness! But gold, too. I dove again.

With our team of bandits, the treasure was transferred quickly. We thrashed blindly—one poor lad got a handful of urchin spines—and it gradually became harder to find whatever was left.

I could hear the plonk of ricocheting cannonballs as they struck the water, and finally thought we'd done a good night's work. I'd decided to suggest this to Martel when there was another splash, different this time, and something bobbed on the dim surface. I dove and felt a last time for treasure.

Suddenly there was a thud, kick, and agony in my ears. I was punched sideways, and the surface of the sea erupted. Then a confusion of sounds and things hitting the water. I swam up, dazed. Other heads poked up around me, all of us rising and falling on the waves that pounded and thundered against Diamond Rock. Several ears bled. One man floated facedown and still.

Our longboat and buoy had disappeared.

Martel shouted something. My ears were ringing.

"What?"

He swam closer, looked at one ear, and then turned me to shout in the other. "Powder keg!"

Ah, the English had dropped a fused one with enough air to let it float, and the mine had gone off next to our precious longboat. Our buoy rope marking the treasure had slithered to the bottom.

"Time to leave!" Jubal shouted.

We didn't have to be persuaded. Another barrel came down, and we swam for our lives. It erupted with fury and a huge fountain of spray as we scrambled up the side of *Pelee* like squirrels. One black took a splinter and fell with a cry back into the sea; we fished him out, blood running.

Something thumped our side. It was the diving bell, kicked out of our boat by the explosion. With more sentiment than sense, I insisted we haul it aboard. The leaded rum barrel thumped down, its little glass porthole intact.

Then I collapsed on deck, dripping and exhausted. An ax swung, the anchor cable parted, and a jib unreeled to catch the wind. The ketch's bow swung as sharply as a wayward compass needle, cannonballs still crashing, and then we were off, flying from Diamond Rock.

A shout went up from the British side as they saw us sail through the range of their guns, but by now rain was beginning to fall, obscuring us further. Their cannon boomed, and a lucky shot might still have sunk us, but we had only a couple balls scream harmlessly through our rigging. We'd snatched one of the most fabulous treasures in history out from under English noses, and chances were they didn't even know what we'd taken. When the storm abated, they'd probably clamber down and scratch their heads, evidence of our expedition churned away by the storm's surf.

They might signal an English frigate, however, to hunt us down. So we hoisted more canvas, the overload pushing a rail into the sea, and were off like a racehorse, men scrabbling to catch treasure sliding on deck and carry it to storage below. I'd no doubt more than a few trinkets disappeared into trousers or shoes, but we had no time for inspection. The ship raced, bucking and pitching in the building waves with the sickening swoops of Cayley's glider. *Pelee* was badly balanced with the mortar and rolled more than was normal.

Still, we'd recovered what the conquistadors had lost. The Sad Night of Cortés had been reversed.

I wearily sat against a mast and looked for Astiza. There she was in the stern as planned, exactly as I'd told her to be. I waved again, our smiles a flash in the night. The signal confirmed that Harry was tucked safe in a sail locker.

And that payback could soon begin.

CHAPTER 41

We sailed from the artificial thunder-and-lightning storm coming from the British output on Diamond Rock, a blind bombardment of artillery like bolts from Olympus. The monolith was finally lost behind us in rain and mist, spray flying from wave tops, stars hidden. The nearby mountains of Martinique were invisible. Now the only sign of the isle was the white glow of warning surf.

Had Martinique been a lee shore, wind blowing toward it, we'd have been hard-pressed to keep off its reefs. But the wind was boiling out of the southeast, pushing us northwestward into the open Caribbean.

"Hurricane coming!" Jubal shouted in my ear.

"Not this season," I protested.

"This one is from Agwe. Or perhaps the god of Montezuma?"

"God should favor us. We're putting treasure to liberty's use." The wind snatched my words away like leaves in a tempest.

"Only if we win." My friend was looking at Martel.

The renegade policeman was snapping orders like an admiral. Sailors ran to the lines, looking apprehensively up at our rigging.

"My God," I said, "he's going to try to jibe in this wind. He'll risk snapping the boom."

"He wants to sail into Fort-de-France."

We'd expected as much. Once under French guns, any chance of our keeping some treasure would be gone, regardless of the promises Martel made. My family would still be at his mercy. My black companions would be reenslaved. The scoundrel would return to Paris, triumphant with triangular toys. I rose from the mast and put my hand on a sailor's arm. "No." The man hesitated, his muscle jumping under my palm. "For your own safety, get to the rail."

But then a sword point pricked the back of my shoulder. "It's time for you to go below out of the weather, Monsieur Gage." Martel had put on a greatcoat over wet clothes, its hem stuttering in the wind. "We'll make you warm in the dungeons of Fort-de-France."

"I thought we were partners, Leon."

"Indeed, we were. But all partnerships must end."

It was the betrayal we'd been waiting for, counting on. Martel's squad of scoundrels had pistols out pointing at Jubal's men, and swords in case guns didn't fire in the tropic rain. They meant to take it all, not just the flying toys but every necklace, every idol, every golden alligator. Even the emerald again, if he held me captive long enough for my body to expel it. Or he'd slit me from arse to throat to get at it, if he knew where I'd put the jewel.

"Jibe in this wind, and you'll risk the mainmast," I warned.

"It's our only chance to make Martinique. And I don't believe you're a sailor, Gage. Leave it to experts who are."

I glanced at Captain Brienne at the helm, eyeing the booms and yards of the sails as nervously as a groom his approaching bride. "To Haiti, Martel, downwind," I tried. "For a fair division as promised."

He smiled. "Come, Gage. You knew it had to be this way from the beginning. We're all pirates here. It was either me imprisoned in Haiti, or you imprisoned in Martinique. And I'm not a man to share. So . . . down the hatch. You can say good-bye to your son a final time while we run for the harbor. Your wife and boy can hire as domestics, or she can work as a whore; she'd make good money at it. You'll win delivery back to France in chains to answer to Napoleon. It's an honor, to merit such trouble."

"I'm Napoleon's agent, you idiot."

"Are you really that naive? Maybe they'll give you L'Ouverture's old cell, which I'm told was very large. I'm not a cruel man. Just . . . determined."

"And arrogant."

"Only around my inferiors." He motioned with the sword tip. "Go, go. I don't want to stab you in front of your wife. I hate the sobs of women."

Which was as good a cue as any. I looked beyond him to the stern of our ship. "Astiza?"

"Ready, Ethan." There was a squeal of metal, and she pivoted a swivel gun on the stern rail and aimed its muzzle down the deck. Captain Brienne's eyes went wide, and he ducked down.

"Packed with musket balls and waiting for hours," I told Martel.

He considered my wife. The calm captive of Martinique had disappeared. Now Astiza looked the avenging banshee, her dress and coat shuddering in the howl of wind, wet hair loose and flying like a flag. A glowing match was sheltered in her hand.

"You must be joking," Martel tried. "She's a woman. A mother. Tell her to get away from that gun before she hurts herself."

"She *is* a mother, and you took her cub," I warned. "I advise you put your sword down. Partners, you said. It's still not too late."

"She's bluffing," he called to his men. "Use Gage as a shield!"

They shoved Jubal's blacks, whom they'd surprised, toward

me, everyone swaying and stumbling to the ungodly roll of the ship, bunching into a target.

We had just an instant before ropes clasped around us, but Antoine had drilled the men ashore. Training and timing is everything.

"Now," I said.

Jubal and his blacks joined me in dropping flat to the deck.

"No!" Martel roared.

Astiza fired.

The swivel gun banged, and there was a sizzle as a cone of lead balls swept the deck like a wicked broom. French ruffians cried and toppled as bullets tore flesh. Balls pinged off the mortar on the foredeck, whining away or whapping into wood. Martel staggered from an impact, and I tripped him and leaped atop, hurling his sword overboard and holding his own knife to his throat. Jubal's men were doing the same to the others. In an instant, the situation was reversed.

The sailors at the rigging had frozen, including the one I'd warned. Astiza had stepped from the stern to Captain Brienne at the wheel to hold a pistol to his body. "Stay your course, or you'll have no backbone."

Martel was gasping with pain. One ball had torn his belly, another his arm. "No woman would do that," he complained. I could feel the stickiness of his blood.

"My woman would, to a man who stole her child."

"Damn you." He coughed wetly. "I watched everyone but her."

"You've damned yourself."

"Listen to the wind, Gage." His voice was a bubbling wheeze. "It's rising toward a hurricane. If we don't make port now, we never will. Jibe for Fort-de-France, and I'll parley with the governor and split fairly with you, I promise. If we don't make port, we're doomed."

"Split what? You just lost your share of the treasure, including your foolish flying machines. That's what comes of breaking an agreement."

"Those models are the property of the French government!"

"I think they're the property of the Haitian government, now. Or perhaps I'll take them to London. You can explain your mistakes in a letter to Bonaparte."

"Bonaparte will hunt you to the ends of the earth if you flee with this treasure. He's expecting ancient secrets to help him conquer Britain. This isn't about money: it's about power. You've understood nothing from the beginning."

"If Napoleon were here, he'd have less mercy on you than I will. The first consul is my patron. He'd be appalled that renegade French policemen have tortured, kidnapped, and betrayed."

Martel groaned. "Fool."

"You're the fool, for assaulting my family."

"Gage, do you think I have license to accost you in Paris, dally with Rochambeau, and be set up like a prince in Martinique?"

"You've a talent for roguery, I give you that."

"It's all been at the orders of Bonaparte. The theft of the emerald, the kidnapping of your son, the hunt for the legend. Napoleon's not your patron. He's your foe. He didn't keep you in Paris for Louisiana, which was near bargained already. He flattered you to follow this treasure, manipulating you with the theft of your family. You've been his plaything from the beginning."

"*What?*"

"Nitot told Joséphine about the emerald, who told Napoleon, who told Fouché, who told me. You've been our puppet since Saint-Cloud. I'm merely an employee. It wasn't I who stole your son and wife. It was Bonaparte, who knew you'd never volunteer to look for Aztec technology on your own. But he knew you might be tricked into it with the right incentive, such as a kidnapping, and that you have a knack for learning clues that elude ordinary men. Whether you explored for Dessalines, the British, or France hardly mattered. You'd come after your family, and when you did, Napoleon would get his due."

"You're lying."

"The Corsican wants those flying machines and is perfectly willing to sacrifice a family to get them. He'll sacrifice a million families for a chance at England. Your only hope, Gage, is to return to Fort-de-France and throw yourself on French mercy. Napoleon will forgive but never forget."

"*Napoleon* forgive? For betraying my family?"

"That's what the great do, to remain great. And the lesser accept their calculations for a moment's favor. That's all we can hope for. I'm amazed how naive you remain after all the treacheries you've endured."

It's true. I am by instinct good-natured and want to believe the best of people, except when I have to shoot or stab them. It's a fault, I suppose. So now my mind reeled like the heave of the ship. Martel had been working for the same first consul who'd supposedly deputized me to work on the sale of Louisiana? And that master considered me entirely disposable? Of course Napoleon felt himself impregnable, in his own grand palaces.

"I don't believe you." But my tone betrayed me.

"You think an unemployed policeman can order a bomb ketch? Lambeau converted this ship on Napoleon's orders, not mine."

"Why didn't Bonaparte hire me directly?"

"Because you kept insisting you'd quit."

I felt dazed. A wash of seawater ran from side to side of the deck, mixed with blood from dead and wounded men. Now I had a choice of surrender to Martel's government or a ride in a hurricane with a wounded crew at one another's throats. "I only wanted to retire," I said hollowly.

"You can only retire when the powerful say you can retire."

"And you, Martel, wounded, wet, five thousand miles from home?"

"I'm a policeman. A soldier. I accept my fate."

I glanced about, considering. Astiza still stood behind the helm and our captain as the ship surged on, surfing down growling swells. Brienne looked frightened at our course, but clung fatalistically to the wheel. Martel's look was mocking, pitying, disdainful, proud, pained, as if he were the moral superior. So I had to jolt him into place. "Perhaps what you say is true. We'll let Dessalines finish your interrogation to make sure."

Finally he paled. "Monsieur, that is monstrous . . ."

"He has his own ideas of justice for slavery-loving Frenchmen." I dragged the bleeding bastard to the hatch leading to the hold. "You've a gift for conversation. I'm sure you can persuade him."

"You're a traitor to your race if you give me up to Dessalines!"

"Don't talk to me about treachery."

"I warn you, Gage, I'll never go! I'll kill myself first!"

"You're too much the villain to dare." I dragged him down the ladder, bumping, and found that chains had been prepared for our own capture. So I snapped them in place around him and the other scoundrels and took the ring of keys. I almost let Martel bleed to death, but at the last moment wrapped rags around his wounds so we could save him for later torture.

I can be ruthless, too.

In a sail locker I found Harry, rolled into a ball and terrified by the gyrations of the ship. I crawled in and hugged him. "Harry, it's Papa! Are you all right?"

He was crying. "Where's Mama?"

"Guiding our ship." I reached out to touch him, and he shrank. His fear was wounding. "I'll take you to her. You'll stay in the captain's cabin." I bundled him in my arms. "It's almost over, son."

"I want to go home."

"The cabin is like a home."

I carried him up to Astiza. "I'll guard Brienne!" I shouted against the wind. "You keep Harry in the captain's quarters!" I handed her one of Martel's flying models. "He's betrayed us from the beginning, but this is what he came for."

She looked. "This is what the Aztecs saw, not what they made," she guessed. "They're too crude. The Indians were copying something extraordinary."

"Agreed, but I'll show one to Fulton anyway. Keep Harry warm."

She retreated to the compartment in the stern.

I turned to Captain Brienne, who looked more frightened of the sea than my pistol. "Can we hold this course?"

"It's too late to jibe; the masts would break. So we run downwind. But feel for yourself."

I was shocked at the pull of the wheel and feared the rudder would snap. The ship was trembling as we surfed down the seas. We needed to take down more sail; trying to manage the clumsy bomb ketch was like holding a halter on a drunken cow.

"It would be better now without the mortar, monsieur," the captain said.

I looked at the gun. The ketch rolled as if an anvil was tied round its neck. "Agreed."

"But it's impossible in these seas," he went on. "If we try to cast it overboard, the gun will break loose, go through the gunwale, and take half the hull with it. So we must make port instead."

"Any bay we choose has to be downwind on an island that isn't French."

"We may not have that choice."

"It's not a choice to be recaptured, either. Jubal, you help reef sail, and I'll fetch a chart. We just need to ride this out." I said it with more confidence than I felt, remembering Astiza's foreboding.

"I'll get my men to help the sailors," the black said.

"And pray to Agwe, Mary, Neptune, or Benjamin Franklin."

His nod was grim. "Soon that's all we'll have strength for. I've never been so tired, Ethan. Not even in the cane fields. Pray to Ezili, too."

CHAPTER 42

A ship under control is in balance between the push of the wind and the resistance of the sea, a rudder squirting it forward. But if overcanvassed and badly balanced, vessels can veer dangerously out of control. At Brienne's direction, we lashed a rope to the wheel to ease the strain of holding it, got down our remaining shreds of canvas, and rode bare poles before the wind, but still had to steer carefully. The storm kept shifting in a great gyre of cyclonic fury, cranking to push us more and more to the north. For hour after hour in the night all I could see was the dirty gray of sea foam as breaking waves rushed past our stern quarter, a boil that bore all the malevolence of whatever gods we'd offended. Despite the latitude, I was numb with cold and dull with exhaustion. Astiza emerged from Brienne's cabin and kept me alive with rum and sausage.

"Harry's gone to sleep," she told me. "So has Martel."

"I envy them."

"I think the Frenchman might die of his wounds."

"Better for him than meeting Dessalines."

Our bow was invisible in the dark, but I could hear seas breaking there, as if against a rock. Then a surge of water down the length of the deck that poured back off. The diving bell had been lashed to the mainmast, its window looking back at us like a Cyclops eye. The ship lifted itself from each swell as if old and weary. French sailors and black freemen got the sails off except for two that had ripped to shreds and flailed in the wind, and then hunched and clung like crustaceans, everyone praying to their favorite saint. The storm shrieked as I'd never heard anything before; it strummed the spars till they whistled and drummed, a moan that ate at me. I waited for the entire shaking ship finally to come apart, to dissolve into woody spray and be flung by the wind in a sleet of sawdust, until nothing marked where we'd ever been.

Yet the bomb ketch, while clumsy, was also stout. The ship wallowed like a sturdy toy, staggering up from every swell, and with each rise hope flickered. Maybe we could ride it out. We'd dive into a trough, water would pour across, and then we'd surface, a weary whale.

Without any clear announcement of dawn our surroundings eventually grew lighter, visibility slowly extending to the tip of the bowsprit and then beyond. Lead seas raced beside, and we staggered up slopes of great watery hills for a view of salt mist before sliding into darker valleys. I'd grabbed a chart, but there was no possibility of telling where we were. My vague plan was to return to Cap-François, deliver the treasure and prisoners, and then simply get away. No lingering in Paris, no playing the diplomat. I was done with great affairs and needed a thousand years to make up for the trauma I'd inflicted on my family.

I'd still find us a place where nothing ever happened.

"Will Harry come through?" I asked Astiza when I visited.

"He's sick, but his stomach has emptied." She looked as exhausted as me. "He doesn't even know who he is, Ethan. Captivity, separation, war."

"What a life I've given him. I'm sorry, Astiza."

She looked doomed, seeing something I couldn't. "We can't take the treasure to Saint-Domingue."

"I promised the blacks."

She shook her head. "The treasure is cursed. Look at this storm. It will do them more harm than good. It was buried in that rock for a reason."

"You say every treasure is cursed."

"Hasn't it been?"

"We're not cursed to be poor. I don't believe that."

"What if the Maroons weren't storing the treasure but getting rid of it? What if they'd found it wicked? What if they went into that cave knowing they couldn't get out, simply to save their own people?"

"No. They were trapped by the current."

"The treasure should go to Mexico."

"Mexico! There are no more Aztecs, just Spanish overlords, crueler and greedier than French and British combined. It's too late."

"We've made a devil's bargain. Ezili is a trickster, Ethan." It was one woman's suspicion of another.

"We'll get to port, and it will feel so right." I tried to sound more confident than I felt. "We've been through worse, remember?"

"Not with a child." She bit her lip.

"This storm will have to pass sometime."

And miraculously, it did.

First there was a gap in the clouds and light flooded down, pushing back the boundaries of how far we could see.

We'd been sailing through an atmosphere in which the border between sea and air was indistinct, a fog of whipped spray and spume. We breathed mist. We tasted salt, heavy as we staggered up watery slopes and weightless as we plunged down. Our universe was the heaving ocean.

But as the light broadened and brightened, the wind began to drop precipitously. The change was eerie. The howl of the rigging subsided as if a discordant orchestra had taken an intermission. *Pelee* still lurched and dipped on chaotic seas, but now the sound was the slap of slack lines against wood, the creak of mortar against tackle, the groan of the hull, and the gush of sloppy water.

Blue sky appeared overhead.

The blacks and French sailors shakily stood and looked up in wonder. We'd been reprieved! In all directions was a dunescape of cresting seas, water streaked white. There was so much salt that even as wet wood gleamed, the ship looked dusty. Little streams ran up and down gunnels, and the air still smelled thick. Yet in minutes the tempest had turned into a weird calm.

Was this divine intervention? Had God answered the Catholics? Had Astiza found the correct prayer? Was Ezili present and helping?

Jubal rotated, looking around. No land was in sight, just a wall of clouds a few miles distant in every direction, rearing into the sky. "This is very odd."

"It's like being in a well." Astiza looked thousands of feet up to that blue dome of sky.

"It's salvation," I tried. "The treasure isn't cursed, it's blessed. If ever there was a sign from God, this is it, don't you think?"

Our ketch swayed like a crazed cradle, confused seas pitching it this way and that. Men crossed themselves.

"I've heard of this," Brienne said fatalistically. "A false lull."

"A miracle," I insisted, with more spirit than I felt. "We need to answer this mercy with our own. When the waves subside, we'll start a fire in the ship's oven and make something hot for everyone, even Martel's survivors. Jubal, divide the crew into three shifts and let some sleep. When the storm settles completely, the French sailors can take some sights and we'll set a proper course. The stars tonight will be brilliant after such a wind; we can navigate. Let's tie down what is loose, heave the dead overboard, and get ready to hoist a steadying sail again. Astiza, food into Harry."

People began to do as I suggested. Four of Martel's ruffians were dead, from wounds and exposure. These were rolled without ceremony into the sea, sinking in our wake.

I checked below. My archenemy was still breathing, and he opened his eyes to give me a weary, baleful stare. Crow and his companions had a gimlet eye as well.

"What happened to the wind?" Martel asked.

"It's dropping."

"What does that mean?"

"You lost, Martel."

His head lolled, fatalistically. "Water."

I gave him some, and the need for the kindness made me doubt my own instinct for revenge. Should I really give him to Dessalines? But he'd planned to send me a prisoner to France, hadn't he?

I returned above, debating.

The ship had become even more ungainly without the stiff wind, so I asked Brienne which sail to risk. Canvas would steady our roll and begin to give us a feeling of command.

He glanced around. "None, monsieur."

"Surely a staysail would help, would it not?"

He pointed. The clouds to our stern had drawn much closer, while those at our bow were drawing away. "It's what I feared. We were simply in the storm's eye." The well of light was moving away from us, our ship drifting from one side of it to the other. The sky dimmed as if the Almighty were drawing a curtain. "It was not a miracle, monsieur, but cruelty. We're not through the storm. We're in its middle."

And then, with doubled violence, the storm struck again.

CHAPTER 43

Now the wind rose above comprehension, and visibility vanished with hope. Rain and spray combined into a kind of soup you could almost drown in, and the seas were cresting mountains. They broke with thunder that competed with the ceaseless trumpeting of the sky, and green water smashed down on *Pelee* as if to drive us to the bottom. The ship staggered, the mast tips cutting great arcs, and the weight of the mortar held the bow under for agonizingly long submergences. Then we'd slowly stagger to the surface again, water pouring off, each watery pummel stripping away parts of our vessel like a remorseless rasp. Boats, barrels, lines, and guns broke and disappeared. I feared the bomb supply below would break loose and roll like marbles until a strike and spark set them off, blowing us to pieces. I waited for ropes to snap, chains to break, anchors to carry away. We raced across the Caribbean with only sheds of flapping canvas, steering down swells like a sled before a force that was terrifyingly implacable.

I clutched the wheel with Captain Brienne and Jubal. "I thought the worst was over."

"The hurricanes make a great wheel, and we've simply gone from one rim to another. Now it will get worse." He pointed. "We're too sluggish."

I looked at the mortar. Its muzzle had become a pot, seawater slopping out. *Pelee* was dangerously unbalanced. The huge gun yanked against the deck every time we rolled, planks bulging and seams working. The ship wouldn't point as intended, or ride as designed.

"What can we do?"

"Everything's a risk. Wait, I think."

So except for us at the wheel, everyone else retreated below. We lurched for an hour in the gloom, timbers groaning as the waves grew higher.

Then the decision was made for us. Jubal pointed. "Surf!"

I squinted. The compass was spinning so wildly as we bucked and plunged that I had no idea of our true heading, or what land we might be near. But through the miasma I could see a menacing line of white on some lee shore, marking a reef, cliff, or beach. We had to steer around it or we'd wreck, but the hurricane was pushing us remorselessly toward disaster.

I turned to Brienne. "Can we claw off the land by sailing into the wind?"

"A jib might do it, but only if we aren't so bow heavy. We can't sail as close to the wind as we need. The mortar is a millstone."

"I thought you said it too dangerous to get rid of."

"And too unwieldy not to, now. We need to chop or saw."

"I'll get the men!" Jubal had to shout it inches from my ear. Such was the fury of the storm.

"There's a carpenter's locker in my cabin," Brienne instructed.

Jubal dropped to the main deck below. I staggered into the captain's cabin and explained to Astiza why I was breaking out axes and saws. "We're going to get rid of the mortar."

She nodded, clutching a listless Harry with one arm and holding on to a ship's rib with the other. She was seated with legs
askance on the deck to brace herself as the vessel gyrated, my wife
and son both physically ill. The floor was littered with smashed
ceramics, flung captain's hats, and a tin pot that rattled like a toy
as it tumbled from one side to the other. Sheets of water obscured
the stern windows. The roar of the waves in here was like the
boom of surf in a sea cave.

"Throw away the treasure, Ethan. That will lighten us more
than the mortar."

"We can't survive on superstition." I wasn't giving the loot up,
not after what we'd all endured. I looked at my son, half unconscious. "We're just having an elephant ride, Harry!"

He pressed his face to his mother's breast in response.

Pushing aside the fear we were all doomed, I grabbed an armful of tools and went below. The hold was almost black, lit by one
wildly swinging lamp. Water leaked from above and churned from
the bilges below, with an ungodly stench of sewage and vomit.
The noise was less catastrophic, but the blind motion was terrifying; the deck would drop as if were levitating and then lurch to
slam like a bucking bull. I had to slap some of Jubal's men to get
them out of catatonic panic.

"We're going to get rid of the mortar!" Stiffly, tentatively,
holding on to the deck beams overhead, men began to rise.

I turned to a sailor. "Who's the ship's carpenter?"

He pointed to an older man crouched in the gloom.

"Stir yourself! Show us where to use these axes and saws, or
we're all going to drown."

"That's a big gun to move even in dry dock," the carpenter
muttered.

"If we chop out the pins, we can lever it overboard while timing the roll."

"A sweet trick if you can manage it, and disaster if you can't. If
it gets away, it will crush the ship like a boot on a wedding cake."

"And if it stays in place, it will take us down like an anchor on a balloon."

We divided into two crews. Those in one group began hacking at the foundation of the mortar from the bottom, wielding their tools overhead as best they could. Others crawled to chop and saw at the gun base from the exposed deck above, tying themselves to a line that we stretched from mainmast to bowsprit to keep the men aboard as waves washed the deck.

"Hurry, hurry!" I shouted to them as they climbed up the ladder to the outside. "We're nearing a reef! But time the final release to a wave when we can safely roll the monster."

"Monsieur Gage, what about us?"

It was Martel, sitting in the hold in chains where the former slaves had locked him. He seemed more alert now and pointed to his fellows.

"Just stay out of our way."

He grimaced from the pain of his wounds. "It will go faster with more help, and four of my men are still fit enough to labor. Chain me like a dog if you must, but for heaven's sake use stout backs to save your wife and son."

I hesitated. I trusted Leon Martel about as much as an arthritic earl should trust the flexible filly of a wife he bought with ill-gotten inheritance, but time was of the essence. Every second we saved getting iron off our bow gave us a better chance to steer away from that lee shore. I had a pistol and a knife, and he and his scoundrels did not.

"Don't leave us here to drown, American!" one of his men added.

Well, some of the bastards were dead, others wounded, and the starch had been beaten out of everyone.

So I unlocked the four healthiest ones, including Crow. They wept with gratitude. "You have chosen as a saint would," Crow assured.

"Then work to save your life and ours. Rocks are near."

The hammering and rasping had become more frantic. I turned to join the others on deck.

But I'd promised Martel a fatal meeting with Dessalines, hadn't I? The last thing that bastard wanted was a successful conclusion to our voyage. And the only way his henchmen would get freedom and the treasure was by dooming the rest of us, they figured. All this I realized later. They'd plotted with the desperation of the condemned.

So I was clubbed from behind.

I fell and skidded, dazed, the shackle key ring leaving my fingers. Someone snatched it up, and I heard the rattle of more chains unlocking. I rolled and tried shooting, but my pistol was soaked and snapped uselessly. A wounded ruffian staggered at me, and an ax fell toward my head. I jerked to one side just in time. The weapon thunked into the deck, sticking, which gave me time to heave up and shove a knife into the bastard's ribs. He was Buzzard, I think. He gasped, stiffened, and fell.

Everything was in awkward slow motion from the sickening heave of the deck. The other gang members were ignoring me, crawling forward to frantically knock open strongboxes and stuff their pockets with treasure.

Where was Martel? I yanked out the ax from the floorboards, the bloody knife in my other hand.

The Frenchman was crawling the opposite way, making for the stern. A length of chain was still hooked to one ankle and dragging like a lizard tail. Was he trying to hide?

No, he'd seized a hatchet. With horror, I realized what he meant to do.

"Leon, stop!"

He turned, eyes haunted, lips a crooked sneer. "Mercy is always stupid."

"If you don't work the ship, we'll die!"

"And if I do, I'll still die, but slowly and in a great deal of pain for the long, cruel pleasures of the Haitian rebels. Good-bye, Ethan Gage. I'll take my chances with the sea."

He wriggled into the compartment where the wheel's cables led down to pulleys and the straining rudder.

"No!" I cried. "There's a shoal . . ." I scrabbled desperately after him.

Perhaps his plan, if he had one, was to throw the vessel into such chaos that his own men could retake the ship.

More likely, he simply wanted to take us down with him.

"I won't let you kill my family!"

"You killed them by defying me," he called. "You killed them by letting your wife shoot me. Me, Martel, your only hope."

I threw the knife, but he was too far away and wedged tightly amid the wheel ropes. The blade bounced harmlessly off a timber. I charged with the ax, but couldn't reach him in time. He swung his hatchet, grunting against the pain, and chopped one of the rudder cables. "For Bonaparte!"

The rope was already tight as a harpsichord wire, strained against the relentless push of the ocean. Now it snapped like a whip, lashing him as it did so. He was flung like a toy, ribs audibly cracking, and smacked against the slack cables of the suddenly useless rudder, evil satisfied. Martel glanced up toward the deck where my wife and son waited.

Instantly we lost steerage. The ship spun and everyone tumbled, screaming as they realized we were lost.

If our orientation to the waves couldn't be controlled, a loose mortar could be catastrophic.

"I'll see you in hell, Gage!"

I grabbed the ladder to ascend to the quarterdeck to shout warning. The storm was catastrophic as we yawed. I dimly saw Jubal and his fellows in front of me, clinging for purchase, each wave that cascaded down the deck's length washing wood chips with it. The mortar was rocking violently, its foundation loose. But instead of tipping it carefully, we'd created a one-ton peril.

Now the ship was turning broadside, entirely out of control. Captain Brienne clung to the wheel, looking at me with horror.

"What have you done?"

"It was Martel." And then, calling ahead, "Jubal! Don't loosen the mortar! Get back!"

My friend heard his name. He pulled himself by line toward the mast, one ear cupped.

The entire ketch began to tilt. We were broaching, sideways to the seas. A monster comber rose, a cathedral of water, and because we were at the far edge of the storm now, a watery sun thrust beams of light on the chaotic sea. For just a moment, the crest of the wave glowed green as an emerald.

Then it broke, an explosion of foam, and rushed down like a mountain avalanche. Jubal grabbed the mast just in time. I braced myself in the hatchway.

The breaker hit.

We rolled completely sideways, masts parallel to the sea, and light vanished. We were underwater, or rather smothered in a mattress of foam, tons and tons of seawater slamming as if to drive our vessel to the bottom.

Even submerged I heard a snap as the mortar, its pins half chopped through, broke loose. It tore out of the deck and smashed overboard, plunging for the bottom like a stone. A ragged mouth in the deck marked where it had been.

Water surged through the sudden gap and poured into the hull. The gun had also broken the stays holding up the foremast so it went over, lines jerking like dancing snakes.

The ship's rigging was broken, and all hope of controlling the vessel was gone.

Several of Jubal's companions and French sailors vanished into the sea with the gun, pulled underwater by the rope they had tied to.

Miraculously, *Pelee*'s ballast worked its leverage and we rolled upright again, staggering. Then another crack, like a tree falling in a forest, and the mainmast went over. A broadside wave, and the mast and my black friend were washed away like driftwood.

I looked back at the wheel. It had disappeared, too. So had Brienne.

With water pouring in, the loss of the mortar had the opposite effect we'd intended. The ship settled at the bow even more sluggishly than before, and pitched in the seas as aimlessly as a piece of driftwood. The angle of the deck was steepening as the vessel began to sink.

I crawled toward the captain's cabin, fighting through surf.

All was lost, and there was only one thing left to accomplish now.

I had to save Astiza and Harry.

CHAPTER 44

It was an uphill climb to the cabin of the *Pelee*. We were at the complete mercy of the sea, being driven toward a reef, every man left now to God and glory. The strongboxes were broken, the glorious artifacts of Tenochtitlán clutched desperately like talismans by drowning men, or rattling loose like seashells in the surf. My own mind fogged with fury. That Napoleon Bonaparte himself had set this disaster in motion, as Martel claimed—that he'd used my family and me as puppets—was beyond ordinary political calculation. I'd spent nearly a year plummeting toward this disaster, in pursuit of ancient trinkets that were no more likely to produce real flying machines than scribbles at an asylum. My son had been kidnapped and his mind likely scarred. All to further lunatic aims of invading Britain?

Madness!

What I could do now was what I'd been trying from the beginning, to save my family.

The cabin's latch had broken and its door flapped and banged.

I hoisted past it to the chaotic cave the cabin had become, awash in water and broken furniture. The tier of stern windows was half smashed in, shards of glass sliding in seawater. It was dim to see. "Astiza!"

"Holding Harry! What happened? Everything upended!"

I saw her by Brienne's bunk, her face cut. "You're hurt."

"Afraid. Are we going down?"

"Martel cut the rudder cable. We're nothing more than a driftwood wreck."

"I love you, Ethan." She called it, yards out of reach. "You did what you thought best."

I clung to that thought like I did to a bulkhead, but had more urgent things that needed saying, or so I thought. The confirmation of my love for her could come later.

So do we miscalculate.

The dim light was growing even darker, and I could see a mountain of water rising astern, a wave higher and higher, green and glassy, streaked with foam, the largest wave, in fact, that I'd ever seen. It filled the view from the windows. Then it filled the sky.

"The masts are gone. We need to get out. Maybe we can find a hatch cover or grate to float off. There's a reef nearby, which likely means land—"

The cabin exploded.

The rogue wave blew in the last of the windows to shove out the air and kick me against the boards. The cabin filled with the sea, foam boiling against its ceiling beams. Then the ocean sucked out as I tried to grip, hauling at my weary fingers. I gasped for air, neck-deep in swirling water. Where were my wife and son?

"Astiza!"

The storm answered me.

Pelee was upending, the decks becoming walls, and I climbed its floor like a ladder, leaping for the windows in the wreckage of the stern. Mullions hung like ragged ribbons. Beyond was the wilderness of water that had sucked out my wife and son.

I didn't hesitate. I crawled through, stood on the stern, and watched the useless rudder come out of the sea to flap like a broken whale fluke. Then I dove as far as I could. I managed to thrash to the backside of a comber trying to bury the ship, which meant that instead of being pulled under by the vessel's sinking, I successfully struggled a few yards away, kicking against the suck of the disappearing ketch. Even with my head above water it was hard to breathe; the boundary between sea and air was indistinct. I looked wildly about. Where was my family?

Something bumped me, and I frantically grasped. It was the ship's wheel, a modest float but wood enough to help keep me from drowning. I clung like a kit raccoon to its mother—my ship, my treasure, my friends, and my family all gone. The weight, power, and chill of the churning seawater seemed unbelievable.

I thought *Pelee* was gone, too, but no; at the edge of visibility she rose again like an emerging iceberg, picked up by a wave curling toward that wicked line of white that marked a reef or a beach. Was Martel still aboard? Her broken stern climbed toward the sky, the rest still under, and the entire mass of the vessel was hurled forward in the wave as if shot from a sling. Then the comber broke with a roar, and there was a larger crash as thousands of tons of wood hit something solid, splinters of oak and coral tossed up in the air like an exploding grenade.

The vessel had disintegrated after colliding with a reef. Fragments were whipped away by the wind.

"Ethan!"

I whirled in the water. Astiza! She rose in view to the top of the swell, clutching what must be Harry, and then sank out of sight in the trough on the other side.

Kicking while holding the broken wheel, I began swimming to where I guessed she must be, faster than I thought possible.

For a long minute I thought I'd lost her again in the chaos, and then rain parted and I saw her hair like a tendril of seaweed, playing on the water as she struggled to float.

I thrashed toward her. She'd disappear under the waves, then rise again in tired struggle. I kept fearing she'd sink for good before I could get to the pair of them.

But no, I made it! I grabbed her hair and hauled her to me. As she hacked and coughed I roughly took Harry. I feared the boy dead, but he blinked at my squeeze and spat out seawater. He was in shock.

Incongruously, on Astiza's neck was the golden pendant Napoleon had granted us, that N surrounded by a laurel leaf. Maybe that was the curse! I yanked it off her and let it drop in the sea.

Around my own neck was still the magnifying glass for the emerald I had swallowed.

The three of us clung to the wheel fragment, but now our weight was almost doubled. The wood sank, and we sank with it, the sea closing over our heads.

Astiza released her grip and we floated up again, Harry and I carried by the wheel and my wife thrashing.

"We need more wood!" I cried. "There! Salvation!" One of the ship's masts rolled in the tempest like a log.

She gasped and paddled to me again, exhausted. As she grabbed we sank again, so I decided to let go. But when I tried she insistently pushed Harry and the wheel against me and let go herself.

We surfaced.

"Ethan, you're stronger. Hold on."

"You take it, too!"

"It won't float the three of us." She coughed. "My strength is almost gone. Hold Harry, and we'll both swim for the mast."

"Then you take the wheel!"

She shook her head. "Harry needs it. I can't carry him anymore, Ethan. I'm fading." She was drifting out of my reach. "Keep the wood and our son."

"Come here! I'll help you swim!"

"Don't you dare let him sink." Her eyes were glazed, but her tone still urgent. "You mustn't let him go, Ethan. He's your responsibility now." She made swimming motions, but they were feeble. She almost lolled in the waves, trying to take a breath. In my exhaustion, she was a thousand miles away.

"This way!" I don't think she heard me because I sobbed the words and didn't have the strength myself to chase both her and the mast. Harry was wheezing, half full of water, and the wheel seemed pitifully inadequate. I glanced back. The breakers on the reef were close, furious, crashing down to throw off huge clouds of spume. Would any of us survive crossing those shallows? We needed the mast! A wave closed over Harry and me, pushing us down, and so I kicked until finally the wheel fragment helped bring us up.

The mast rolled closer.

Where was Astiza?

There, on a swell.

I saw the wave lift her up as if she'd floated free of our miseries, her beautiful black hair framed against green water like a sea fan. As her head slipped below the surface the wave kept lifting her up, up, up, so that I saw her entire body for a moment, suspended as if captured in glass, backlit by a watery sun, a silhouette that left me aching with longing, regret, and shame. Her legs, her dress, suspended in green amber.

There was something else in the wave, too, a dark blob just below the surface. It was our diving bell, I realized, like a waterlogged cork. When the mainmast went over, it must have floated free.

Then Astiza slid onto the swell's backside and was gone.

"Astiza!" It was a croak, not a cry. Harry and I went under again, about to follow his mother. I had energy for one last rise, breaking clear, the wheel beginning to loosen.

The wood, our last hope, slipped away.

So we sank a final time. We, too, were doomed.

And then something gripped and hauled, as strong as the arm of Poseidon.

We erupted out of the water and were thrown onto the mast. I retched, trying to get air. "Hold, white man!" It was Jubal. He'd been clinging to the timber and snagged us. I tucked my arm inside a rope, and as Harry threatened to slip free, the Negro grabbed him and pulled my boy to his own chest, his other arm locked on the mast as if welded. No, he was *tied*; he'd lashed himself to the wood.

"Astiza?" It was merely confusion. I was about done.

"Hold!" And then it was our turn to be lifted skyward, higher and higher, impossibly high, rising on the crest of a breaker as if the mainmast of *Pelee* had become a flying machine itself. We were hurled forward, impossibly fast toward whatever was beyond that line of white, and then fell as it broke. We plummeted down like going over a waterfall.

Thunder as the wave hit and broke on the coral, the whole mast underwater. We bumped and skidded on the reef. I clung from instinct, not sensibility, while we rolled.

Then somehow we were beyond, tumbled upright into the air for another agonized breath, and skimmed toward a beach where sand was almost black. The log grounded, started to suck back out, and then another wave struck and we lurched even farther in. Water hammered, sand filled every orifice, and I had no sense of where I was or what I was doing.

"Let go!" Jubal was waist-deep, yanking to free me from the rope. I came clear, body battered. Harry hung from Jubal's arm as if dead. The sight of my son was the only thing that kept me going, so I stood, staggering in the swirling surf, and then we awkwardly plunged toward land. The mast pursued, as if to knock us flat after saving us.

I fell and it struck, but it just knocked me farther ashore. I crawled in foam while the wooden spar rolled away from me.

A final wave carried me far enough to get clear of the sea. I wiggled upward like a turtle.

I was on terra firma.

I looked back at the fury we'd survived. The reef was a leaping boil of crashing waves, and the water between it and shore a soup of foam. Beyond was a tormented sea, some swells picked out by the sun and glowing green and blue, and others shaded by dark cloud and gray as iron. My body ached as if beaten by a club. I was half blind from salt, reddened from cuts and scratches, and emptied of will.

I was also alive, and horrified by that fact.

Because it meant that I was still conscious enough to recognize that Astiza, who'd seen our fate as she peered into the future, was gone.

CHAPTER 45

I shuddered as I'd never shuddered in my life, from cold, exhaustion, anxiety, sorrow. Harry! I couldn't stop shaking.

I looked dimly about. There lay a great still form, almost as dark and massive as a sea lion. It was Jubal, lying on his side on the beach.

Blowing sand made a horizontal hail that stung like insects. I couldn't stand, or even properly crawl on hands and knees; the strength required was beyond me. So I bellied toward him, pitted by grit, dreading the vacancy I might find on his other side.

But no, there was little Horus, coughing and shivering as the great black hero kneaded his chest and served as human wind-break. Jubal's staring eyes bulged from exhaustion, like stones of quartz and obsidian. He was enfeebled as I was, but he gave a weary grin. "Alive."

The Negro had saved my son. And me.

I dragged myself around so we formed shelter on both sides of

Harry. The beach was dark volcanic sand. Just yards behind us mountainous surf was crashing, but I couldn't bear to look at it. I dreaded that it might give up the corpse of my wife.

So the three of us fell unconscious.

When I woke, it was late day. The sun was lost behind black cloud to the west, where I presumed the hurricane had gone, but the sky to the east was clearing. The sea was pitching chaos, and I was stiff with cold in this tropic clime. We were pimpled with blown sand, and surf had thrown so many great white drifts of foam upon our strand that it looked as if it had snowed. Palms had been stripped of most of their fronds. No bird dared fly yet. The world had been scoured.

Groaning, I sat up. I felt completely hollowed: of strength, of emotion, of purpose. I'd presided over catastrophe. I'd failed in what I now realized was the only important task in my life, to love and be loved, and to preserve that love by all means possible and necessary.

Love, the *mambo* had said, that was the basis of faith.

My wife was gone for jewels and glory, the vanity of my being important, the nudging of world affairs. She'd suspected her fate when we first crossed the Atlantic. We'd tried to steer destiny a different direction. Futility.

And yet she'd gone with me onto *Pelee* in the end, never breathing a word of fear. Somehow she thought it would save Harry. Somehow she still loved me, she'd said. I clung to those words with wonder.

It took a while to steel myself to squint up and down the beach. Yes, there were bodies there.

None looked like that of a woman.

Jubal was stirring, too.

"Can you take the boy up into the scrub while I check for survivors?"

He followed my gaze; we both knew there wouldn't be any. Why expose Harry to a line of corpses?

"*Oui*. I'll look for uncontaminated water and meet you at that shattered palm." He pointed, and I nodded. My mouth was cotton, too.

I stood, bent as an old man, and staggered down to where the drowned rolled at the edge of the surf. Out beyond the waves still boomed on the reef, and a thousand fragments of wood had been cast ashore from *Pelee*. Enough to build a warm fire, if I could figure out a way to light it.

I fingered my chest. The magnifying glass was still around my neck.

Maybe tomorrow, if the sun came out.

Astonishing how quickly we begin to think of the future, even when defeated by the past. We close ranks like a Roman legion stepping over its own dead.

The beach was a quarter mile long between headlands. I found five corpses. Two blacks, three whites.

One had his mouth set in a rictus of a snarl. It was Martel.

Napoleon's agent seemed smaller and deflated in death, his clothes shredded by coral, his shoes missing, his feet wrinkled and white. Our nemesis would have only one aerial flight, it seemed, a glide down to hell. His eyes were open and staring with horror as if he'd seen that descent.

Yet was he really a tool of the first consul? Could his last act have been to lie about Napoleon simply to torment me, to mislead me that the political Prometheus I'd been tied to for years, the great Bonaparte, had betrayed me and my family for a miniature model of what might or might not be a flying machine? I still had one of the toys in my pocket and reached to finger it.

With horror I felt a chain as well. Astiza's pendant, with Napoleon's cursed *N*, had not sunk in the ocean. It had perversely fallen back into my vest like a curse I couldn't get rid of.

Was Martel laughing from Hades right now, amused to think he'd left me trusting nothing?

I nudged with my foot to roll over his body. As I did so an arm flopped free, its sleeve disintegrated. The skin was so laced with coral cuts that for a second I didn't even spy the design on the inside of his bicep. Then it startled me. I leaned closer.

It was a tattoo.

Burned into his skin was a N, surrounded by a laurel wreath, the mark of Bonaparte that the villain could tuck privately against his body. Leon Martel hadn't lied. He had not been a renegade policeman, a refugee from the criminal underworld, or at least not *just* that. He'd truly been Napoleon's agent.

As if on God's cue I doubled over then, my gut wrenched, and I scampered up the beach to answer nature's urgent call at the edge of the scrub. A gush of waste and seawater came out of me, the filthy torrent leaving me shaking. And there it was, spattered with shit, the stone I'd arguably sacrificed my wife and happiness for: the wretched emerald.

Cursed indeed.

I looked out to sea. Somewhere on that reef was the treasure of an ancient empire, and I'd leave it to Jubal whether to lead Haitians back someday to dive if they dared. Salvage when the sea was smooth sapphire and angry gods were remote. I couldn't bear it anymore.

And my own stone? I was sorely tempted to kick it away or bury it in the sand. Its beauty was bitter reproach. But then I thought of my boy, motherless now, and his father with no trade but gambling and adventure. What kind of upbringing could I give him?

Life doesn't stop, and he had all of his ahead. If Astiza was truly gone, I was his sole parent now and would have to decide what to do next. Maybe Philadelphia, and Quakers, to help put sense into him that I didn't have. Maybe he'd absorb Franklin's wisdom when I had not. I owed him time, and hope.

Or maybe a school in London, where I'd be closer to my enemies.

So, grimacing, I wiped the damnable stone off and pocketed it, too, determined to sell it as a trust for my son.

I must remain destitute myself to remind me of the dross of dreams. I must commit to something larger than my own retirement.

I had to find grim meaning out of disaster.

So I limped to make reunion with Jubal and Harry.

"Papa!" No cry gladdened my heart more, that at last he seemed to recognize and need me. He clung like a little monkey, sobbing for reasons he didn't fully understand himself. Finally he asked, which he must, "Where's Mama?"

There was no corpse. I'd seen the diving bell, and other jetsam. Yet there could be no reasonable hope, either. "Swimming, Horus." I hadn't the heart to tell him what must be true.

"She's not coming?"

I sighed. "I hope she's saved herself somewhere else. We'll pray for that, you and me, because she'd like that."

"I'm cold, and scared of the ocean."

"We're safe for now, and tomorrow we'll find help."

"I miss Mama."

"Me, too, more than I believed possible." And so we wept, united by tragedy. "I've missed *you*, more than you know."

We slept as best we could, the wind slowly dying in the night, and by the next morning the sun was bright and birds were flying above a ravaged forest. The sea had settled a great deal, and thankfully sucked the bodies back out of sight. Of Jubal's remaining comrades, including Antoine, we saw no sign.

So I'd killed them, too.

I still trembled lest the sea give up Astiza. So long as it didn't, there was the cruelest kind of hope. I knew she must be dead, so why did my heart deny it? Because there was something magical about her I'd sensed when digging her out from that first cannon-shattered room in Alexandria. I couldn't imagine the world without her light. I'd watched her drown, yet didn't have the instinctual sense of loss I would have expected. We'd ended, but I didn't feel it. I needed a body and didn't have one.

"Where are we?" Jubal asked.

I looked inland. A huge mountain rose in the haze, its top smoking. "Perhaps Montserrat. I think we should walk the coast, looking for a settlement or a boat. Antigua is not far, and from there we can get passage home."

"I found some plantain and coconut. You hungry, boy?"

Harry's gaze was a million miles away, but not his appetite. "Yes."

So that was it. I'd been married and apparently widowed in less than a year, and as stripped to my core as it was possible to be. My survival was the worst punishment I could imagine. I would see her, suspended in that last green swell, the rest of my life. And yet her spirit still inhabited us.

Why did I feel nagging hope?

I looked down at Harry. How, what, when would I tell him?

Yet I was surprised by his expression. He looked more determined than devastated. "Let's look for Mama while we walk." Did he share my instinct?

I swallowed. "Yes." And not find her lifeless body, I prayed.

We started trudging down the beach. I told Jubal how he could decide whether to come back for the treasure. "Astiza said it was cursed, but maybe only for some of us."

"I'll ask Cecile Fatiman. She'll decide what to do."

"Be careful. I think Ezili misled me."

"She's a jealous goddess."

"What will you do next, Jubal?"

"Try to rebuild my country. And you, Ethan?"

I was silent, looking east at the watery horizon as we hiked. "Martel said he was sent to betray me by the leader of the French. I was an errand boy manipulated into a fatal quest."

"So you must flee to America?"

"I thought that, at first. But Britain, I think, to establish my boy in a good school. I need to make him a future. It's the one country that has the resources to stand up to the French. The English have flooded the Continent with gold and spies to undermine Bonaparte's dictatorship. Which suggests, Jubal, my real task."

"Which is?"

"Revenge. It's the only meaning I can think of. I'm going back to France."

"Harry needs a father, Ethan."

"He'll have one. But first there's one task I owe the world."

"You must forget the world."

"No. I'm going to hunt down and kill Napoleon Bonaparte."

HISTORICAL NOTE

As with other Ethan Gage novels, the primary historical events in this novel are true. Haiti's expulsion of the French in 1803 concluded the first successful slave revolt in world history, and (although France did not recognize the country's independence until 1825) represented creation of the world's first black republic. The revolt's success haunted slave-owning aristocracies for decades, including the South before the American Civil War.

The war that Gage experiences was but a chapter in a long series of Haitian invasions, revolutions, coups, foreign interventions, embargoes, and economic upheavals that, combined with natural disasters such as earthquakes and hurricanes, have conspired to keep Haiti the poorest country in the Western Hemisphere. France demanded 90 million gold francs in compensation for lost property in return for recognizing Haitian independence, saddling the young nation with crippling loans it did not finish paying until 1947. While the American and French revolutions left the infrastructure of those nations relatively intact, Haiti was burdened by utter devastation at a time the Caribbean sugar economy was already in decline. Jean-Jacques Dessalines declared himself emperor in 1804, oversaw the massacre of more than three thousand surviving whites, and then was assassinated himself by black rivals in 1806. The nation temporarily split, rejoined, and has struggled to establish a stable political and economic system for much of its subsequent history. While a place of beauty and promise, it remains burdened with overpopulation, erosion, and disease.

The revolution's culminating battle of Vertières outside what was then Cap-François, and today is known as Cap-Haïtien, took place generally as described. Ethan's hydraulic diversion is fiction, however. The actual black assault was so valiant that French soldiers at one point actually did stop fighting to applaud their enemy's courage, a very Gallic thing to do. The French still lost, and evacuated.

Toussaint L'Ouverture, the "Black Spartacus" or "Haiti's George Washington," preceded Dessalines as the revolt's primary general. After negotiating with the French and retiring to his plantation, he was betrayed, seized in May of 1802, and imprisoned in the alpine Fortress de Joux near the French-Swiss border, a bleak and beautiful place visited by tourists today. There's no record of an escape attempt engineered by a renegade American and his Greek Egyptian wife, aided by an early glider flight, so we'll have to take Ethan's word for that. Conventional history records that L'Ouverture died of illness on April 7, 1803.

Yellow fever played a decisive role in the slave war, and not only helped free Haiti but was instrumental in doubling the size of the United States. The havoc that mosquitoes wrought on Napoleon's armies in Saint-Domingue left him with no troops to hold New Orleans and its vast Louisiana Territory, thus giving him the incentive to sell property extending from the Mississippi to the Rocky Mountains.

Many of the characters in this novel were real people, including aeronaut George Cayley, the spy Charles Frotté, Sir Sidney Smith, Antigua's Lord Lovington, the French commander Rochambeau, General Dessalines, and *mambo* Cecile Fatiman. Many of the opinions ascribed to Napoleon are taken from statements recorded in history. The pessimistic appraisal of the Haitian revolution written by doomed General Charles Leclerc is quoted as he wrote it. The Palace of Saint-Cloud was as described, but was destroyed in 1870 during the Franco-Prussian war. Its site is now a park.

The treasure of Montezuma is a real legend, and treasure hunters have sought the lost wealth of Tenochtitlán for generations. Some speculate the Aztec hoard was lost at sea, while others contend it was carried north by refugee Indians and hidden in what is today the American Southwest. Among surviving Aztec relics are objects oddly resembling airplanes, with pilots, explaining the aerial passion of Leon Martel and inspiring modern speculation about what such figurines represented, or copied. Ancient astronauts? Or a delta design that has nothing to do with flying at all?

Certainly when Napoleon threatened invasion of Britain the English imagined attack by all kinds of weird contraptions, including an armada of balloons and a tunnel dug under the English Channel.

Diamond Rock, or *Le Diamant*, is real and has an underwater cave popular with experienced scuba divers. None have reported finding emeralds inside. The volcanic monolith was seized by the British early in 1804 and christened HMS *Diamond Rock*, shooting cannon at passing French ships and infuriating Napoleon. The British held out against numerous French counterattacks until June 3, 1805. Floating rum kegs were indeed used to "soften" the garrison.

Voodoo is a serious religious mix of African and Christian beliefs—not just witchcraft—and I have attempted some accuracy when recounting its spirits and ceremonies. The zombi belief is real.

A midwinter hurricane of the kind I describe would be seasonally unusual but not impossible: hurricanes have been recorded in every month in the Caribbean.

The bomb ketch was a common kind of warship; the "bombs bursting in air" of the American national anthem refers to mortars fired from British ships in the War of 1812. The "rockets red glare" refers to Congreve rockets that will play a role in an upcoming Ethan Gage adventure.

ACKNOWLEDGMENTS

For the commissioning of this book I must thank former HarperCollins editor Rakesh Satyal. This book's perceptive editors are Maya Ziv and publisher Jonathan Burnham. Agent Andrew Stuart has nurtured the birth and continuation of this entire series; this is the fifth Ethan Gage adventure. As always, my appreciation to the entire hardworking Harper team, including publicist Heather Drucker, production editor David Koral, and foreign rights marketer Carolyn Bodkin. Once again my wife, Holly, served as muse, travel companion, and first reader for wayward Ethan. She's still trying to straighten him, and me, out.

ABOUT THE AUTHOR

William Dietrich is the author of eleven novels, including four previous Ethan Gage titles—*Napoleon's Pyramids, The Rosetta Key, The Dakota Cipher,* and *The Barbary Pirates.* Dietrich is also a Pulitzer Prize–winning journalist, historian, and naturalist. A winner of the PNBA Award for Nonfiction, he lives in Washington State.